A ROUT
BECOMES A PLANE
OF TERROR!

Fear gripped the passengers of the hostaged airliner. Mack Bolan sat among them and watched, helpless but unafraid, confident that he had known every kind of enemy... until he heard the chilling voice of the hijackers' leader.

"I am the Raven."

"Anyone who stands against the civilized forces of truth and justice will sooner or later have to face the piercing blue eyes and cold Beretta steel of Mack Bolan... civilization's avenging angel."

—*San Francisco Examiner*

DON PENDLETON's
MACK BOLAN

FLIGHT 741

A GOLD EAGLE BOOK FROM
W☉RLDWIDE

TORONTO · NEW YORK · LONDON · PARIS
AMSTERDAM · STOCKHOLM · HAMBURG
ATHENS · MILAN · TOKYO · SYDNEY

First edition May 1986

ISBN 0-373-61405-5

Special thanks and acknowledgment to
Mike Newton for his contributions to this work.

Printed in Canada

Terrorists are the shock troops in a war to the death against the values and institutions of a society and of the people who embody it.

—Jeane J. Kirkpatrick,
former U.S. representative
to the United Nations

I see terrorists for what they really are, cold-blooded killers and thugs, and as such no different from the Mafia. Therefore my duty is to escalate, expand my war.

—Mack Bolan

To the victims of terrorism everywhere.

Prologue

The great bird sat and baked beneath a broiling desert sun. Her silver wings appeared to droop, signaling defeat. The sightless cockpit-eyes stared vacantly across a vast expanse of sand. Once proud, she seemed to crouch, humiliated in the heat, waiting for the end.

Her living cargo had departed hours earlier, the transit buses rattling on their way to Tripoli. There, negotiations would drag on for weeks or months, depending on the stamina of all concerned. But it would matter little to the silver bird. Whatever happened at the conference tables, she was all alone with her despoilers now. And she was doomed.

The demolition team was disembarking, piling gear and rolls of wire into the jeeps provided by Khaddafi, putting ground between themselves and the disabled carcass of the bird. The dark man watched as they drew nearer, trailing plumes of dust, but now his mind was racing on beyond the patch of desert that had been his home for eighteen endless days.

The dark man had a war to fight, and he was being wasted here.

The demolition crew were scrambling from their dusty jeeps, all smiles and wringing handshakes now, producing clouds of dust from filthy tunics as they slapped each other on the back. Their mood of jubila-

tion did not touch the dark man, and his eyes were fixed
on something far away, invisible to those around him.

At Amal's approach, he broke the spell and turned to
face the leader of his mop-up crew.

"Ready?"

Amal was beaming at him as he nodded, passing on
the radio-remote control. The dark man looked at the
little detonating device. It was the best available, but
then again, Khaddafi could afford the best.

"A triumph," said Amal.

"A start."

He fingered the remote control, his gaze riveted upon
the steaming carcass of the silver bird. She was a marvel of technology, a wonder to behold—and for the
price of one such aircraft, he could feed the people of
his village for a hundred years.

An ancient anger stirred inside him, the pulse inside
his temples taking on an independent life. The silver
bird, this 747, was a symbol of the life that he and all his
people were eternally denied. The decadence of Western culture sat before him, sleek and fat, its mere existence mocking his despair.

Enough!

Morality and all the rest of it belonged to others, the
negotiators, waiting on the sidelines of his war. He was
a soldier, first and last, his essence pledged to the er-
adication of his enemies.

He had accomplished much in very little time...but
there was so much still to do.

Beginning now.

"A start," he said again to no one in particular, and
keyed the small device. A silent signal flashed downrange, and triggered a spark inside the belly of the bird.

An oily ball of flame erupted from amidships, shattering the fuselage and shearing off one wing. The forward section of the aircraft shuddered, fell away, at once consumed by greedy flames. A string of secondary blasts blossomed as the fuel tanks blew, and now the tail was totally involved, its silver siding peeling back and melting into nothingness, the blazing skeleton revealed.

He would remain until the 747 was reduced to ashes. He would remain and watch the flames, hoping to find an answer there. Today, the past three weeks, had been a start, but nothing more. His war had just begun.

The worst—and best—of it were yet to come.

But he could wait until the silver bird consigned itself to desert sand. There would be others waiting for him on the Continent. Increased security would not dissuade him from his mission now. The scent of victory was in his nostrils; there was no turning back. If he should fall, there were others like him to continue in his place.

The man's black eyes reflected tiny, twin flickers of the conflagration in the distance, which provided a febrile intensity and gave the swarthy face a devilish appearance.

He continued to stare at the burning plane and the heat seemed to reach out and touch him, warming him inside and lighting hungry sparks behind his eyes. It was a start, and he could afford to wait, to watch and plan.

And that was good enough for now.

Tomorrow was tomorrow, and he would be ready for another chance to strike against his enemies. To teach them fear.

It was a lesson that the dark man had been well equipped to share.

Chapter One

The weapons came aboard in Munich with the cleanup crew. Although security precautions in the terminal were stiff, no one detected their presence before they reached the plane. And for the personnel involved with terminal security, the members of the cleanup crew did not exist.

The scrubbers went about their jobs unnoticed, unsupervised. Their uniforms and ID cards rendered them invisible, except in an emergency. If some unfortunate lost his breakfast on the concourse, or if the toilets overflowed, an urgent summons brought the men and women up "from maintenance," a kind of limbo somewhere out of sight and out of mind. But in the absence of a crisis, they were faceless and forgotten, worker ants who scoured the terminal and picked the grounded aircraft clean. If these cleaners had private lives and secret dreams, nobody paused to give the matter any thought.

Karl Geiger was a man of private dreams and secret visions. In recent years his dreams had crystallized around the Baader-Meinhof Gang's Red Army Faction, and he pledged himself to serve the cause in any manner possible, no matter what the risk. He was prepared to die, if necessary, and so achieve the glory that had managed to elude him all his life.

This day his task involved sequestering a cache of weapons in the cabin of a 747 bound for Frankfurt and beyond, for the United States. He understood it was a contract mission, undertaken by the Baader-Meinhofs on behalf of other parties, but it was all the same. If the Baader-Meinhofs thought the matter was significant, Karl Geiger thought so, too, and he would do his best to carry out his mission.

Still it might be too much for a single man, and Geiger's fellow reds had made arrangements for a backup. One of his associates, a regular in maintenance, had suffered an untimely accident the night before, and his emergency replacement was a veteran shooter for the Baader-Meinhof Gang. The union had been pacified with cash, conditioned by a history of dealings with the underworld and petty revolutionaries. If it occurred to Karl that his backup was in fact his supervisor, he did not allow the thought to prey on his mind.

Karl Geiger didn't have to ask himself what kind of show the "other parties" had in mind. A blind man could have seen it coming, and the airport janitor was far from blind. He read the news, was conscious of the sudden rise in airline hijack incidents over the past few months. The last one, outside of Tripoli, in Libya, had been a beauty, with the destruction of a 747 on its desert runway once the passengers were bused away. Negotiations for their mass release had been completed less than two weeks earlier, with the Israelis backing down again, their jails disgorging yet another troop of *fedayeen*.

The revolutionaries liked this airline. Karl knew that much, and he recognized the reasoning behind their preference. The airline was America incarnate, symbol of the jet-set running dogs who held the masses down. It represented money, world exposure, a direct connection to the mighty American media. The airline's jumbo jets were easy marks in every airport on the Continent, indeed, in North Africa and the Middle East.

Karl loved to argue revolution, but plotting strategy produced a throbbing pain behind his eyes. He felt it coming now, and made his mind a blank until he felt the pulsing ache recede. He had a job to do, and if the Baader-Meinhof Gang had wanted policy decisions, well, they would surely have called on someone else.

The container drum of Geiger's vacuum cleaner held four Ingram MAC-10 submachine guns, plus extra magazines. The canvas bag he wore across one shoulder held six RGD-5 antipersonnel grenades. The egg-shaped Russian hand grenades possessed an average killing radius of twenty yards, and they would wreak a bloody havoc in the confines of a 747's cabin.

If it came down to that, Karl thought.

Concealing weapons on the plane had never been a problem. It was in the terminal, where passengers and baggage were subject to demeaning searches, that the problems could arise. Enlistment of the cleanup crew had virtually eliminated first-phase risks. The danger came in flight, when the shooters retrieved the weapons and ordered the aircraft to its new, unscheduled destination. Then, there were many risks, but none of them would prey on Geiger now.

The antipersonnel grenades were stowed in a compartment just above the starboard emergency exit, overlooking the wing. Originally used to store the aircraft's life rafts, the compartment was ignored now that new rafts were installed inside the exit doors themselves. Karl knew from long experience that no one checked the holding bins before the aircraft taxied off.

He stashed the lethal Ingrams and their extra magazines inside a crawl space set above the lavatories, in the rear. It was another wasted space, Karl thought, but he knew the submachine guns and their ammunition would be safe up there. The average airline passenger would be too busy thinking of his forthcoming vacation or business trip to even contemplate rummaging to find secret compartments. In any case Karl pushed the thought away, determined that his fledgling mission should succeed.

It was two long years since Karl Geiger had joined the Baader-Meinhof Gang, and in that time, his service had been limited to passing on bits of information to others like himself. If Air Force One was scheduled for a touchdown, if there was a fluctuation in security around the terminal, if someone in the union raised the specter of a strike, he passed the word along. He had begun to think it was his lot in life to carry bits and pieces of the revolution, but now he had been chosen for a greater task. He had been called to serve.

While Geiger worked, his backup was secreting other weapons on the plane: three Makarov 9 mm pistols, with their surplus magazines, above the port-side exit hatch; a folding-stock Kalashnikov inside the closet normally reserved for duty-free items purchased in flight.

His task completed, Karl grudgingly began to clean the deck. In seven years of servicing the jumbo jets, it was the first time he could remember not cursing all the fates for placing him in such a menial position. Karl had always known that he would never be a wealthy man— such honors were reserved for bigger, "better" men than he—but he would make his mark this day, albeit hidden by a cloak of anonymity. Today, the cleanup man had made it possible for bolder men to clean up part of what was wrong with modern-day society. Instead of passing on an idle bit of gossip from the crew, he passed along the tools of revolution into other, willing hands.

As Geiger pushed his vacuum sweeper down the 747's aisle, he was consumed with pride at having carved himself a place in history.

STEVE KORNING NEVER PAID ATTENTION to the cleanup crew. As flight attendant on a 747, working international, he had sufficient problems of his own without borrowing more from the maintenance team. Flight crew and passengers would be boarding soon, and in the interim, he spent a moment gazing through a rain-streaked window at the Frankfurt terminal.

Security was tight all over Europe now, but he had never seen the lid come down as tightly as it had in Frankfurt. Men in uniform, with submachine guns slung across their shoulders, stalked the tarmac, heedless of the rain. There would be others like them in the terminal itself, prepared to move on signal if the need arose. And tucked away behind a hangar, almost out of sight, an armored tank stood ready to defend the terminal or block the runway as the circumstances might demand.

The flight attendant shook his head, unable to suppress a smile. The Germans took their business seriously, and there was nothing quite like overkill to make a point. If any terrorists had thoughts of bringing down a plane at Frankfurt, they would only have to glance around the field before they changed their minds.

Steve Korning didn't like the state-of-siege mentality inspired by recent skyjacks on the Continent. He knew the risks as well as anyone, had listened to the briefings that explained why psycho gunmen chose his airline over all the others, three to one. Sometimes he felt as if he was sitting on a powder keg . . . but still, there had to be some kind of happy medium.

He thought about the incident two weeks before, when he had tried to bag an empty jump seat on a Frankfurt outbound 727. He was out of uniform, but pinned to his lapel was the standard-issue ID badge of an employee. Even so, he found himself spread-eagled on the asphalt with the muzzle of a submachine gun pressed between his shoulder blades, while snarling soldiers shook him down and rifled through the contents of his bag. They held him long enough to make him miss his flight, and then released him, minus any hint of an apology, still watching him as he scooped up his toiletries and jockey shorts from the sodden runway.

The need for strict security had never escaped Korning, but there was something in the German attitude that seemed to relish giving orders, taking liberties, demeaning others in the name of law and order.

Now, as he moved away from the window, he vowed to seek a transfer back to the domestic schedule. No point in putting off the move this time. He would begin the paperwork the moment they touched down at Kennedy.

But first he had a job to do, and passengers were boarding. Still forty minutes left to flight time, but it took that long to settle in the mothers with infants in their arms, the children traveling alone, the seniors with their walkers, wheelchairs or what-have-you. All of them were allowed on first, before the regulars began to embark by rows, and part of Korning's job—together with the other nine attendants on the flight—would be to get them settled before the crush began in earnest.

Boarding was a hectic time. Everybody milled about in the aisles, obstructing traffic while they stowed their coats or bags in overhead compartments, wrestling with seat belts that had slithered down between the cushions of their seats. This one required a blanket and a pillow, that one couldn't see the movie screen, the next one had requested smoking and expected satisfaction before the plane took off. Predictably, a handful homed directly on the rest rooms, cheated of their dignity by shaky bowels and bladders. Others checked the pocket of the seat in front, relaxing only when they spied the airsick bag there.

You didn't have a lot of time to scope on passengers, but Korning spotted several interesting faces, filing them away for future reference. There was the prisoner, for instance, denim-clad and wearing chains that jangled when he walked. He was American, and Korning vaguely recognized the face from television news reports. Some kind of payroll robbery, he thought, with several people killed and other gunmen still at large. The name would come in time.

And there were others. Near the galley modules, a vivacious blonde, whose sweater hugged her like a second skin. He would have marked her as a first-class ride, and thanked his lucky stars that she had gone for coach instead. A tall man sat midway back along the aisle; he was athletic, muscular, with blue-steel eyes that didn't fit his dark complexion. There was a clutch of somber Arab types, four scrawny men in all, who made a beeline for the last row, huddled up against the lavatories in the rear.

So many faces, Korning thought, and he could never hope to mark them all. Perhaps 350 riding coach, another 66 up front, divided by a curtain into first class and ambassador. With crew, they numbered some 430 souls, and Korning never ceased to wonder at the marvel that would keep them airborne, hurtling through clouds above the Atlantic, toward their destination in the States.

It might have been miraculous...except that it was just a job.

The passengers were in their seats at last, securely belted down, and Korning watched as the selected flight attendants gave their spiel about the life rafts and flotation vests, the oxygen and exits that would theoretically permit survival if the plane went down. In theory, yes, but in reality, he knew that rafts and life preservers wouldn't mean a damn if they went plummeting nose-down from thirty thousand feet. The water might as well be concrete.

He pushed the morbid thoughts away and turned his smile back on full force. Steve Korning didn't fear his job, had never worried long or hard about the possibility of cracking up. It happened, sure...but always to the other guy, the other airline. Most of the disasters came on takeoff or on landing, anyway. You never heard about a jumbo dropping from the sky.

Well, almost never.

Anyway, the biggest risk around these days was humanoid, the terrorists and skyjack bandits, flashing back to private dreamworlds from the early seventies. Their art form was passé, except they didn't seem to know it yet, and lately they had focused their attention squarely on the airline Korning served.

It used to be El Al, but the Israelis took reprisals with ferocious energy and left their adversaries reeling, beaten to their knees. Once Castro closed his sanctuary and started sending outlaws back to face the music in the States, the skyjack industry had gone to seed.

Till now.

Four months, three planes, so far with only one fatality among the passengers and crew. Steve Korning didn't see it as a renaissance of terror, but rather as a desperate asshole bid to reap publicity, to hog a stolen moment in the sun. In time the phase would pass, the perpetrators hunted down or driven underground, and it would all be status quo again.

Melodic chimes alerted crew and passengers that it was time for takeoff. Korning made it to his jump seat, buckled in and searched the nearest rows until he found the chesty blonde. Well, if we're going down, he thought, let's try to find a nice deserted island, big enough for two.

Not bad.

Not bad at all.

They lifted off, and Korning felt himself compressed against his seat. It would be now or never, if they lost it, but he wasn't really worried in the least. This made almost a thousand separate flights without mishap, and he was looking forward to a thousand more.

En route, there would be opportunities to start a conversation with the blonde, to feel her out about an evening on the town once they were safely grounded in the States. He would be looking forward to it.

The plane was banking sharply over Frankfurt, climbing steeply toward its cruising altitude. Steve Korning settled back in concert with the pull of gravity and, smiling, closed his eyes.

Chapter Two

Flight 741, from Munich to New York, had never been a favorite run for Julie Drake. The transatlantic haul consumed nine hours minimum, and while the outbound flight to Europe was a longer run, it held the promise of adventure and excitement—even romance—at the other end. Returning home, conversely, was the end of an adventure, a resumption of the tried-and-true routine.

The passengers in coach would be worn-out, dejected by the swift evaporation of their holidays, and she could count on half a dozen minor crises every hour they were in the air. Between the meals and beverage runs, she would have her hands full keeping up with the requests for blankets, pillows, aspirin, magazines and airsick bags.

She could already spot the children who would make a nuisance of themselves by running in the aisles, the parents who were too burned out or too damned negligent to care. The passenger in chains was something else again, but with a guard in tow, he promised to be more sedate than many of the tourists in her charge.

She had been flying international for eighteen months, which made her practically the novice of the crew. Seniority on international resulted in a higher average age among the flight attendants, not to mention the cockpit crew. At twenty-six, she was the youngest staffer on the flight, though two attendants had been working international for shorter lengths of time. To some extent they looked to her for pointers and advice, but there was still a trace of condescension in their attitudes.

She had been glad when Steve Korning drew Flight 741. He wasn't Julie's type—she tended more toward continental flavors—but he had a ready wit, a sexy smile, and best of all, he didn't treat her like the new kid on the block. Her senior by a year or two, he clearly still remembered how it felt to be the tenderfoot, the butt of jokes and snide remarks from older veterans. He took a measure of the burden off her shoulders, buoyed her spirits when they hit a rocky stretch of turbulence. He was her friend, and then again . . .

They had come close in Frankfurt, just the week before. Equipment failure laid them over for an extra night. They had no plans, and it had seemed natural to pass the time with Steve. But Julie hadn't counted on the schnapps, the sudden rush when he had slipped his arms around her outside the door of her hotel room, kissed her with a passion that was missing from her latest string of one- and two-night stands. She had been taken by surprise, and she had needed every ounce of strength to break the clench and push him forcefully away.

He wasn't Julie's type, and yet . . .

At least he didn't hold a grudge. So many others would have worn their wounded egos like a Purple Heart, but Steve had taken the rebuff in stride. There were some awkward moments—awkward on her part, that is—but he had not alluded to the incident in any way these past nine days. Ironically, she found herself concerned that he might not recall the kiss, the flash of chemistry between them . . . but she saw where that was leading, and she put the thought away. Not out of reach, perhaps, but safely out of mind. For the moment.

They would be over France by now, the patchwork countryside concealed beneath a solid floor of clouds, and she had drinks to serve, immediately followed by the in-flight meal. She hoped Steve would be working the other cart along the starboard aisle, but still she felt afraid that her hands might tremble and betray her when she looked into his eyes.

Julie caught a jerky movement to her right, and turned in time to see a passenger invade the galley module. Slender, swarthy, hair slicked back, she recognized him as a member of the ragtag Middle East contingent seated by the lavatories in the rear. He had been smiling when he boarded, smiling almost idiotically through takeoff while they climbed to cruising altitude . . . but Julie noted that he wasn't smiling now.

Before she had a chance to ask if she could help him, the intruder raised one foot and kicked her squarely in the chest. The impact took her breath away, propelled her backward, shoulders slamming hard against the beverage cart before she lost her footing and toppled to the floor. A flush of anger brought the color to her cheeks, immediately tempered by the fear that something had gone hideously wrong.

She struggled to her feet, but now a second Middle Eastern type was blocking off the other exit to the galley module, glaring at her with a kind of crazy hunger in his eyes. Another flight attendant—Mary Fletcher—stood beside him, facing Julie, staring at her blankly, on the verge of shock. The Arab had one arm around her waist; his free hand clutched a stubby automatic weapon, muzzle pressed against the trembling woman's ribs.

"My God."

And Julie Drake could think of nothing else to say. She turned to face the Arab who had kicked her, found his stupid grin in place once more.

"You take us to captain now," he told her in his broken English. "Follow orders, and you don't be hurt."

"MY PLEASURE, MA'AM."

Steve Korning summoned up his most ingratiating smile and held it as he turned to leave the blue-haired dragon to her magazines. It was the third time she had called for an attendant since departure, and the act was getting old.

A slender figure jostled Korning, muttering apologies, dark eyes averted with embarrassment. Korning's smile was glued in place now as he followed the retreating figure with his eyes. An Arab, one of four who had been seated in the rear, and Korning wondered what he wanted at the galley module.

He saw the second Arab even as the thought began to form itself, unbidden, in a murky corner of his mind. Already homing in on the galley, number two was walking briskly, with a jerky, nervous kind of stride that set Steve Korning's teeth on edge and started small alarm bells sounding in his head.

A sidelong glance informed him that the other Middle Eastern types were on their feet as well, still hanging back and loitering beside the lavatories. Korning tried to tell himself that they were used to open spaces, walking. They would need to stretch from time to time.

It didn't work.

For starters, they were too damned small to feel confined in normal airline seats, and never mind that seats were smaller, more congested, here in coach. And even granting that the four of them would all decide to stretch their legs in unison, it didn't answer why the lavatory flankers both had hands stuffed inside their matching knee-length coats.

Beside the galley module, numbers one and two were similarly dressed in raincoats. It had not seemed odd in Frankfurt, with the omnipresent German drizzle, but the other passengers had stowed their coats, umbrellas, scarves, relaxing in anticipation of the transatlantic flight. The Arabs were alone in clinging to their rain gear after boarding, and it didn't help at all to tell himself that they were simply strangers to the climate.

A sick sensation in his stomach told him that they wore the raincoats for a reason, sure. And it was not because they were afraid of sudden squalls inside the cabin.

The blue-haired dowager was tugging at his sleeve.

"Young man—"

He shook her free. "Not now."

"I beg your pardon?"

Korning didn't hear her injured tone. He was already moving toward the galley module, trying desperately to keep it casual, praying that he might be wrong.

Ahead of him, the slender Arab seemed to be in conversation with a member of the crew. Korning recognized the profile—Mary Fletcher—but the sudden, stunned expression on her face was something new. The Arab had an arm around her now, his free hand out of sight. Across the intervening rows of seats, Korning watched the second Arab step inside the galley proper, vanishing from sight.

Oh God, oh Jesus Christ, it's happening!
And not to someone else, some other airline.
Here and now.
To him.
Flight 741.
He might be wrong, of course. There could be countless reasons why a pair of Middle Easterners would check in at the galley. Special menus for their Muslim palates? No, the specials were requested in advance. A lump formed in Korning's throat and he could not come up with any other reasons.

When he was touching close, Korning tapped the Arab on the shoulder.

"Can I help—"

The wiry man exploded, dragging Mary Fletcher with him in an awkward pirouette as he pivoted to face Korning. Surprised, perhaps embarrassed that he had been taken unaware, the Arab snarled at Korning, lashed out with the stubby automatic weapon.

There wasn't time to raise his hands, and Korning took the slashing blow across one cheek, the Ingram's foresight opening a ragged gash below his eye. He staggered, fell to one knee, stopped himself from sprawling with a superhuman will. Behind him several passengers had seen what happened. Three or four rows back a woman screamed.

Hot anger flared behind the bloody fog inside his skull, but Korning fought it down. He was aware of several passengers standing, and now the Arab flankers were approaching from the rear, their automatic weapons surfacing from under raincoats as they shouted for attention, desperate to be heard above the general din.

"Sit down! Silence!"

Within a moment, something close to order was restored. From his position on the floor, Korning spotted
two more swarthy passengers, erect and scrambling toward the starboard exit hatch. For just an instant he was
terrified that they had panicked and now meant to blow
the hatch, creating an explosive decompression in the
cabin, but they rifled through the empty life-raft stor-
age bin instead. He saw them coming out with automatic pistols, with what looked like hand grenades, and
knew that they were not attempting to escape. What he
had taken for anxiety on their faces was revealed as dark
excitement now.

The nearest gunner had released his hold on Mary
Fletcher, shoving her aside. He stooped and slid a hand
around Korning's arm, revealing an unexpected
strength to get the flight attendant on his feet once
more. The muzzle of his Ingram nudged at Korning's
ribs.

"We see captain now!" he snapped, propelling
Korning in the direction of the cockpit with a straight-
arm thrust between the shoulder blades.

Steve recalled the briefings they had received for such
emergencies, and there had been frequent updates in the
techniques of handling madmen, terrorists, potential
suicides. The first and foremost rule that came to mind
now was to protect the cockpit crew, deny a gunman
access to the all-important flight deck. It was fine, in
theory, but with six guns ready to unleash a bloody
holocaust on some 350 passengers, Steve Korning
couldn't think of any way to carry out the plan.

He could attempt to grapple with the Arab gunner,
but he was dazed by the blow he had received, and any
sluggish move to seize the terrorist's machine gun would
most likely set him off. If the bastard began to fire, the

others might react by kicking off a massacre—and any single round might smash a window, drill the fuselage, and thereby drill them all.

As he moved toward the cockpit now, Steve clenched his fists in frustration. If only he could string the lousy fucks along, then there was a chance of coming out alive. The other recent skyjacks had been harrowing, but there had only been a single death among the passengers and crew. From past experience, it stood to reason that the gunners would request an audience, concessions, even cash, before they started freeing hostages. But somewhere down the line, the hostages *would be* exchanged. If Steve tried to grandstand now, they might be killed before the sleazy assholes had a chance to bargain for their moment in the sun.

A startled gasp came from someone on his left as Korning and his escort reached ambassador, disturbing beverage service with their unexpected entrance. Midway along the aisle, in the direction of the galley module, Korning saw a virile jock type rising to his feet.

"Sit down!" Korning's captor shrilled. "No danger if you keep your seats and do as you are told."

The golden boy glanced back and forth between the Ingram's muzzle and his busty girlfriend, finally deciding that survival was the better part of heroism. He tossed a last defiant grimace at the Arab, then took his seat.

Their voices would have carried, and the first-class flight attendants had already interrupted beverage service, moving on a cautious interception course when Korning and his captor threw the curtain back, emerging into view. The Arab saw them coming, and seized a fistful of the flight attendant's jacket. Using Korning as

a shield, the gunman braced the Ingram across his captive's shoulder, muzzle against his cheek.

"Stand back, or I will fire!" he shouted, laboring
with unaccustomed English. "We will see captain now."

Steve Korning knew that meant a hike upstairs, and
no one on the flight deck was expecting them. There had
been no opportunity for any warnings or alarms. If he
couldn't think of a diversion on the way, these bastards
had another 747 on their hands.

Except, he realized, the bastards had it—had them
all—right now. Their mission was accomplished from
the moment the guns came out, and there was nothing
he could do to turn the thing around. He could prolong the agony, provoke a bloody melee here among the
first-class passengers...or he could play along, and try
to save them all.

Disgusted with himself and with his circumstances, he
began to climb the spiral stairs.

IN COACH, the passenger named Michael Blanski calmy
weighed out odds of life and death. The nearest gunner
stood some fifteen feet away, covering a quarter of the
passengers as best he could. From time to time he swiveled toward the galley, keeping visual contact with his
cohorts farther up the plane.

It would be simple.

Seated on the starboard aisle, Blanski had only to
wait until their captor made his momentary pivot,
turning toward the nose. A silent rush, an arm across
the Arab's windpipe, shutting off his oxygen, a twist to
snap his weasel neck before he knew that he was dying
on his feet. Once Blanski had the Ingram, he could—

What?

Take out the gunners by the galley module? Risk a stray round rupturing the fuselage? Destroy them all?

Of six commandos who had seized the 747, only three were still in sight: the one in coach, and his cronies stationed at the galley to command a view of sections fore and aft. The other three—providing there were only three—had been dispersed to cover first-class and ambassador, together with the flight deck crew.

And Blanski knew that he could never hope to take them all.

Assuming that he took the nearest gunner, that he tagged the galley flankers perfectly, without a stray round out of place on either side . . . his gunfire would alert the others instantly, and bring them rushing back to find out what the hell was going on. They would be nervous, frightened, ready to unload on anything that moved. And he could never hope to stop those three before they opened fire—into the passengers, the bulkhead, anywhere at all.

It would take only one round to bring about explosive decompression. And oxygen, human flesh or anything that wasn't bolted down would be sucked out through a pin-size bullet hole. Some passengers would probably survive, provided that they were belted in or that decompression forced the aircraft down to altitudes where they could breathe. Provided that no one on the flight deck panicked, or was wasted by an edgy terrorist before they got the 747 stabilized.

Mike Blanski weighed the odds . . . and kept his seat.

He had no decent chance at all, no right to gamble with the lives of some four hundred human beings. Later, possibly, when they were on the ground . . .

It rankled him to watch the gunners in their trench coats, hovering above the frightened passengers. Under other circumstances, Blanski would have treated them to sudden death, but the odds were all against him now. He swallowed anger, unaccustomed impotence. And waited.

Skyjacks played according to a formula. The early moments were the worst, surprise and sudden terror working at the nerves on either side. If there was trouble, violence, it would happen soon. Statistically, he knew that airline pirates were less likely to dispose of captives after several hours, even several days. Once their plane was on the ground, negotiation could offer focus for the minds of captors and their hostages alike. The terrorists and terrorized would come to share a common goal: release.

Mike Blanski settled back into his cushioned seat, relaxing with an effort of will. When they were down, when a facsimile of calm had been restored, there would be ample opportunity to make his move.

When they were safe…at least, as safe as they would ever be beneath the gun.

The passenger named Blanski took a breath and held it, willed his pulse to stabilize at normal levels. He could feel the tension melting, giving way to something like the old, accustomed calm.

He visualized the nearest gunner dead, the other stretched beside him in the narrow aisle like hunting trophies, knew it could be done.

In time.

But first they had to find the earth again.

The upper lounge had not attracted many visitors so far. Emerging from the spiral staircase with the Ingram's muzzle pressed against his spine, Steve Korning scanned the room and almost overlooked a solitary figure standing to the rear, beside the lavatories. It took a second glance to reassure him that his eyes had not deceived him, that he wasn't in the middle of some hallucination.

No. He wasn't seeing things.

The man beside the lavatories looked like Richard Nixon.

It was a mask, of course, he saw that now. The kind that covers face and head and all, available from any one of several thousand magazines or party shops. The likeness was incredible, particularly at a distance, but up close, the latex Nixon smile was inflexible.

Steve's captor never flinched at their encounter with the Nixon look-alike. The Arab was expecting someone, obviously, and the mask told Korning he was in the presence of the skyjack's mastermind. The only one of seven gunners with the sense—or the desire—to preserve his anonymity.

A chilling thought intruded on the flight attendant's consciousness. Suppose the others didn't hide their faces from the passengers and crew because they had no hope of coming out of this alive? Suppose they were some kind of ape-shit suicide brigade, intent on taking out the 747 in a fiery final gesture to their adversaries of the moment?

If they planned to crash the aircraft or to instigate some kind of massacre, why would the leader hide his face? It didn't play, and Korning drew some solace from the fact that one of them, at least, had plans for living past the present confrontation. If the bastards planned that far ahead, there might be hope for everyone aboard.

His captor jabbered briefly in some singsong dialect, then hauled out a pistol from beneath his coat, passing it to the masked man with a flourish. San Clemente's finest nodded briefly, jiggling the tip of his exaggerated latex nose, and led them in the direction of the flight deck.

Korning's thoughts were racing. He could try to stop them now, but it would certainly be a suicidal exercise. There was no hope of wrestling a gun from one of them before the other intervened. Still, he could provoke them into shooting him, and thus alert the flight deck crew.

To what advantage?

They'd lock the door—would have it locked already, more than likely—but the damned door wasn't bulletproof. If the leader and his sidekick had to shoot their way inside, they stood a chance of knocking out controls and slaughtering the only persons qualified to keep the plane aloft.

It was a frigging no-win situation, Korning thought, but the lesser of two evil choices still kept everyone alive. In theory, anyhow.

They reached the cockpit access door, the gunners flanking Korning, prodding him with weapons from behind.

"Go on," the Nixon face instructed him. And then, incongruously, "Please."

The sound of rubber Nixon's pistol being cocked beside his ear made up the flight attendant's mind. His knuckles drummed the cockpit door. Jay Stevens opened it without inquiring who or what might lie beyond.

"My man, what's happening?"

Confronted by the guns, by the Nixon face, by Korning's battered countenance, the flight engineer lost his usual smile.

"What the hell?"

Korning lowered his eyes.

"Take your seat," the leader commanded, his weapon jabbing at Stevens for emphasis. Crowding past Korning, he entered the cockpit. "Remain as you are. I am taking control of this aircraft."

"Like hell."

Captain Murphy was glowering at the intruders, examining the situation and weighing the odds. To his right, Marty Reese, the first officer, seemed to be racking his brain for a prayer.

"You are the prisoners of the Islamic Jihad," pseudo-Nixon informed them. "From this moment on you will do as I say."

"And supposing we don't?"

Korning's escort was trembling now, knuckles white as he clutched the machine gun. Steve sensed the terrorist was losing it, nearing the edge.

"They've got five more below, Captain. Armed. I think they could blow."

Pseudo-Nixon was watching him, keeping his gun trained on Murphy. His eyes glittered darkly through slits in the mask.

"Your servant speaks truly," he said. "We are seven, committed to justice for Lebanon."

"Sweet heaven."

"You will please bring the aircraft around to this heading," he ordered, producing a note card from one of his pockets and handing it over to Murphy.

"Now, listen—"

"No more!" The sudden shriek made Korning jump, and Captain Murphy flinched as the masked leader thrust the pistol toward his face. "You will obey, or watch your passengers and crew begin to die."

"Goddamn it!"

But the captain had his hands on the control yoke now, prepared to take the 747 off its scheduled course. He rattled out the new coordinates, provoking startled looks from Reese and Stevens as they went to work.

No navigator, Korning knew enough of latitude and longitude to recognize that they were shooting for a clean 180 here. Their destination lay behind them, slightly to the south, but what the hell?

And suddenly, he had the answer. As if the grinning Nixon face had spoken it aloud.

Beirut.

MIKE BLANSKI RIFFLED through the pages of the in-flight magazine, pretending to examine each in turn. He had already weighed the possibility of rolling up the magazine, converting it into a lethal weapon. Tightly rolled, it could be thrust against an unprotected throat or abdomen with force enough to traumatize internal organs, bring about a hemorrhage, death....

Blanski stowed the magazine inside the pocket of his seat. He could accomplish equal damage with his own bare hands, but he would stick with his resolve to make no moves while they were airborne. There was risk enough to all the innocents around him, without compounding danger through some reckless action of his own.

He scrutinized the gunners, listened to them muttering among themselves. The ones he'd seen had all been Arabs, certainly. He could not understand their dialect, nor place it geographically with any more precision than the Middle East, but it reminded him of something he had heard before.

Algeria, perhaps? Or Lebanon?

The latter seemed more likely, if he played the odds. The recent spate of skyjacks had been perpetrated by a hard-core Shiite Muslim cadre, seeking sympathy, publicity—whatever—for their internecine war in Lebanon. They had already turned Beirut into a slaughterhouse, with some assistance from the "Christian" opposition, and there seemed to be no end in sight. Demoralized by months and years of stalemate, fighting house to house, they had of late begun a cruel, selective exportation of their war.

The battlefield was everywhere these days. The target: any innocents who crossed their twisted path.

The skyjacks were a calculated risk with the potential for disastrous backlash on the terrorists, but their anachronistic ploy had worked so far. The great democracies were talking tough and taking certain steps to back their words with action, but the President of the United States could ill afford to blithely sacrifice his people by the hundreds.

The aroma from a wholesale massacre would linger through election year, and if appeasement was the price of several hundred lives, if half a dozen terrorists must be released to bring the captives safely home, it was a price the Oval Office was prepared to pay.

The gunners would be Shiites, certainly. Blanski felt it as a hunter feels his prey beyond the thicket. He had hunted others like them in the past, and he could recognize the smell.

But he was not the hunter now. If anything he was the game, trussed up and ready for the kill if something should spark a shooting frenzy in the cabin. They could only kill so many, and he stood a better chance of hanging on to life than others in the seats around him, calling on the training that had kept him more or less intact so far.

But it would not be worth the risk.

Not now.

Not while they were in flight.

He was aware that they had doubled back some time ago, and now he tried to puzzle out their destination, checking off the possibles. Three recent skyjacks, and he couldn't even play the odds; there had been no pattern. One flight was hijacked on the ground in Rome by overanxious gunners who could not contain themselves. The plane had never taken off, and everyone had been released unharmed once amnesty was granted to the terrorists.

A second hostage flight had landed in Beirut, where government negotiators feigned surprise and acted out their roles as intermediaries for the West. They had secured the release of prisoners in fits and starts, encouraging the terrorists to ask for more concessions as they went along, and there had been a death among the passengers before the situation was at last resolved.

The third flight went to ground in Libya, the terrorists protected by Khaddafi's warped regime, and they had settled for publicity, together with some cash to fill their coffers back in Lebanon. The aircraft was demolished by explosives once the hostages were clear.

And Blanski put his money on Beirut. It made good sense in terms of distance, flight time, past success. The Western threats to boycott Beirut airport had been empty until now; with the exception of Israeli strikes, no serious reprisals had been undertaken toward the Lebanese nongovernment. Another skyjack, more or less, would make no difference in the long run.

It made the kind of sense that terrorists would readily appreciate. They had a haven in Beirut, and once their various demands were met, it was a short drive from the airport to the urban killing grounds, to pick up where they had left off.

Except that they might be faced with some surprises this time out. The President might not accede to their demands. There might be some effective counteraction for a change. Perhaps a small surprise or two on board the plane itself.

Perhaps one *large* surprise.

Once they were on the ground.

He could afford to wait, unless they forced his hand.

He had the time, and none of them were going anywhere, for now.

BOBBY MAXWELL RECOGNIZED a golden opportunity when it arrived, and he knew that he was looking at one now. If he played his cards right, he could ride it all the way to freedom.

The goddamn cuffs and shackles wouldn't hurt him any when he made his move. He knew about these freaked-out bastards and their hang-ups on the penal system. Every time you turned around, they were demanding freedom for some asshole, breaking someone out of jail in Germany or Israel, even down in South America.

The victims of oppression.

The way he saw it, Bobby fit the bill precisely. He had felt oppressed for days now, since the goddamn German cops had stopped him on a traffic beef, discovering the guns and other shit he carried in his bags. It hadn't taken long to run a make through Interpol, the FBI—whatever—and the feds were on his back before he had a chance to turn around.

They wanted him in Massachusetts, on that beef about the armored car. Two cops had bought the farm on that one, and a third was hanging on the edge with worse than fifty-fifty odds. The murder charge was nothing; Massachusetts had an execution statute on the books, but they had never used it. He had also been in for life before—in California—and had walked in seven years, with good-behavior time deducted from his term.

It wasn't Massachusetts that depressed him now, but rather Texas. They were looking for him there, although they might not know it yet. They had a fair description, but extradition out of Germany would have him on the evening news, and any one of several surviving witnesses might catch a glimpse of Bobby Maxwell's likeness on the tube.

They kept the death house busy down in Texas, for sure. He knew about the latest fad in executions, how they strapped you to a gurney, let you ride the last few yards in style, before they jammed a poison needle in your arm. It was humane, they said. So much more merciful than lethal gas, the chair, a firing squad.

But dead was dead, and Bobby had a lot of living left to do.

The hijack was a blessing in disguise, a final chance to pull it out before his fat was really in the fire. If he could make it work, ingratiate himself with one or two of these manure-minds, he might persuade them to begin their liberation of the helpless here, on board the 747.

Starting with yours truly.

His escort might have other thoughts, but Bobby knew there would be ways around him. He was armed, of course, a snubby .38 secured on his hip, but he would be reluctant to produce the piece with frigging Ingrams pointed at his face. And this guy was no hero. His escort was a civil service type, secure enough behind his badge and his authority when it was one-on-one, but looking rather shaky now.

It was the best—the only—break that Bobby could expect. He had to make it count, or run the risk of taking one last ride aboard that Texas gurney.

And it was risky. He knew that much. The gunners had a jumpy look, like convicts in the middle of a prison riot, waiting for the heat to come down hard on them. They were nervous and any sudden moves might spark a massacre, with Bobby numbered among the dead.

His plan did not include some Arab blowing off his ass at thirty thousand feet, and Bobby knew that he would have to bide his time, feeling out the wisest course of action as he went. It wouldn't do to push his luck too far, too fast . . . especially since he had so little left to push around at all.

It would be tricky, but he had a con man's skills to see him through, and his incentive was no less than life itself. The most important thing was timing.

And Bobby realized that he would have to wait until they landed somewhere, anywhere, to touch base with the press. When they were safely down, once tempers had a chance to cool a fraction, he would make his move.

Before he finished with these jerk-offs, they would volunteer to waste his escort for him. Hell, they just might make him an honorary A-rab of the month.

He knew that he could pull it off.

The shattered Beirut skyline **was** obscured by a drifting
pall of smoke, the residue of a society incinerated in a
crucible of hate. Beneath the dirty haze, commandos,
regulars and armed civilians scuttled through the ruins
of a once-great city, bent on a perpetuation of anarchy.

Mike Blanski watched the distant fires dispassion-
ately, drawing little satisfaction from the fact that he
had been correct about their destination. They were
parked outside the shaky boundaries of a charnel house,
with borderline psychotics in control of all their fates,
and anyone deriving satisfaction out of that would be a
goddamn fool.

The passengers in coach had calmed themselves to
some degree, the hours of their flight providing enough
time to make some sense of what was going on. In
whispered conversations they summoned up the recent
skyjack histories, recalling that the single innocent fatality had been a serviceman who balked at following
the orders of his captors.

Aboard Flight 741, the terrorists had grudgingly allowed their captives access to the lavatories singly, under guard. If children couldn't wait their turn, they wet
themselves and squalled until a glare or gesture from the
nearest gunner galvanized their parents into action, silencing the tiny outrage with a muzzling hand. Among

the adults, there were those who wept, and not only women. Terror was a universal constant, and the lucky ones were those who still remembered how to pray.

Mike Blanski knew the words, the motions, but a lifetime in the killing grounds had worked its metamorphosis upon his view of life and death, the deity and afterlife. He knew from grim experience that Truth and Justice didn't necessarily come out on top in any given confrontation with the other side. He recognized that men and women dead were men and women gone, no matter what their destination. And while he had already come to terms with death, Mike Blanski had no pressing wish to die.

The Shiite gunners—he was still convinced of their identity, despite the lack of an announcement from the enemy—would hesitate to kill their hostages while they had anything at all to gain. Negotiations might drag on for days—three weeks, if he recalled, had been the maximum so far—with tempers fraying as the time wore on. There might be ugly incidents, depending on the individual proclivities of those who held the weapons, but it should be possible for everyone aboard to come out on the other side alive.

Unless this team had been intent on suicide from the beginning. It was possible, of course, that they would seek a ground-side audience in lieu of blowing up the 747 over France or Germany, away from television's searching eye. They might be more inclined to tossing bodies out the door than other airline pirates in the recent past. And at the bottom line, they might have nothing left to lose.

If it came down to that, Mike Blanski knew that he would have to move. He could not play the voyeur's role while those around him were selected for death as martyrs. If it came down to executions, he would have to intervene somehow. But for the moment, he could wait.

He did not wish to call attention to himself unnecessarily. So far he was anonymous, and with a little luck he could remain that way. It would have served no useful purpose to provoke the terrorists, to stage a hopeless incident for honor's sake.

The greater part of honor, given every salient circumstance, would be survival. Avoidance of explosive contact with the enemy.

Unless the enemy himself should make it absolutely necessary.

He could afford to watch and wait. He had the time, no one was waiting for him anywhere.... Whatever happened in the next few hours or the next few days would be assimilated into Blanski's life experience, becoming part of who and what he was, for better or for worse.

And if he had to make a move against the terrorists, he wanted every small advantage on his side. The intervening hours, days, would give him opportunities to study them, to weigh their strengths and weaknesses against his own. They had the numbers and the hardware on their side, of course, and yet . . .

A single man could make his mark against the odds, with grim determination and audacity. Mike Blanski would be certain that his move did not unnecessarily endanger any innocents. He would be going in with eyes wide open, drawing off the hostile fire and striking where he could with best results.

But it might not be necessary, after all.

There was a chance that they would pass through their captivity unscathed—at least in body.

Blanski knew that there was nothing he could do about the minds.

But he would bide his time, observing everything about the enemy and waiting for the opportunity, the *need* to make his move.

And he would pray, as well as he remembered how, that there would be no need to make that move at all.

THE DEAD-END FLIGHT TO LEBANON had taken something out of Julie Drake. Her duties had been scratched for the duration, but the terrorists permitted her to move among the passengers, to comfort them as best she could. Somehow the simple act of conversation, staring into frightened eyes and panicked faces, drained the flight attendant of her normal energy reserves. It should have been so easy, but somehow Julie Drake had taken on the fears of those around her, until the burden lay across her slender shoulders as a crushing weight.

The pain in Julie's chest had gradually receded to a dull, subconscious throbbing, keeping time with the accelerated rhythm of her pulse. She would be bruised, of course; distractedly, she wondered if the gunman's footprint would be outlined on her flesh. It was impossible, she knew, and yet…the mental image of his brand came back to her repeatedly, embarrassing her, bringing angry color to her cheeks. When this was over, it would take some time before she went to bed with anyone again.

Julie stopped herself, acutely conscious of the fact that she might not survive the afternoon. A bruise between her breasts would be the least of all her problems if the terrorists decided it was time to stage a demonstration for the world outside, selecting sacrificial victims from the passengers and crew.

The mental image of a footprint on her chest was suddenly replaced by visions of a bloody, broken body lying on the runway.

Hers.

No way, she thought, and wished that she could summon up a greater certainty within herself. She knew that airline pirates rarely killed their hostages, unless there were some hostile overtures by passengers or crew. On rare occasions they selected victims as examples, but there was a common pattern, even so. The sacrificial victims were predominantly male and, in the case of Arab terrorists, predominantly Jewish.

Julie glanced around, searching for the ones who might be offered in her place . . . and she was instantly ashamed. The passengers were in her charge, she was responsible for seeing to their needs. Indeed, she was responsible for keeping them alive.

No bigot in her heart or mind, she searched the rows of faces once again, afraid that any Jewish passenger might recognize her secret guilt on sight. And for a painful instant, Julie realized how decent men and women could be terrorized, coerced, until they reached a point where they would gladly offer other victims in their place. Take anybody, please God, but pass me by!

The vast majority of passengers in coach were too consumed with private fears to notice Julie Drake. She moved among them, edging past the gunners at their posts, providing water, whispered solace, sometimes nothing more than a smile. Where frightened or angry eyes met hers, she tried to look inside the hostage's hearts, allowing them in turn to see inside her own.

The prisoner in transit offered her a smile, undressing Julie with his ferret eyes. If he was frightened by the terrorists, it didn't show. He seemed at ease.

His escort, on the other hand, was tense, perspiring freely, dark hair plastered to his forehead. Glancing back and forth between the gunners, he would slip a hand inside his jacket surreptitiously, Julie saw, as if he kept a treasure hidden there. His ramrod posture had begun to wilt slowly, once the 747's engines and its air-conditioning were shut down.

Another passenger who caught her eye was seated on the aisle and traveling alone, distinctly separate from the older married couple wedged in to his right against the window. Tall, athletic looking, he reminded Julie of a soldier, but he wore civilian clothes. A minor movie star perhaps? In coach?

His rugged face projected strength and confidence, together with a hint of something else. She could not give that something else a name, but Julie was grateful for his warm and reassuring smile. If there was worse in store, she hoped that he would be nearby.

The idea almost made her laugh, when she had the chance to think it through.

He wasn't going anywhere, of course.

None of them were, until the terrorists were satisfied that they had milked the situation for all it was worth.

It might be days before the crisis broke. Or weeks, she told herself, and quickly put the morbid thought away. For now, the problems of the moment were sufficient.

Tomorrow, with any luck at all, would be another day.

If she could just hold on and do her job until negotiations were completed for their safe release.

It was her duty—to the passengers, the other members of the crew.

It was her duty to herself.

And she was coming out of this alive, no matter what it took to see her through. Determination, perseverance, were the keys in a survival situation. She had learned that much from training courses, from the day-to-day realities of life.

She could do anything, provided that she kept her wits about her.

She would not break, disgrace herself, or let her duty fall to other hands. It was a sacred trust that she would not surrender while she lived.

And that might be the problem, after all.

"TAKE HIM BELOW," the grinning Nixon face commanded. "He has work to do."

Steve Korning felt the Ingram's muzzle jab between his shoulder blades, propelling him in the direction of the stairs. He made no effort to resist; if anything, he was relieved to put the flight deck and the smiling latex countenance behind him.

He had passed the hours of the flight in the upper lounge. Occasionally, he had been permitted access to the lavatory, but otherwise had been restricted to his seat. The slender gunman watched him like a hawk at first, but gradually came to take his presence in the lounge for granted, glancing at him only when the flight attendant shifted in his seat or raised his hand to indicate a pressing call of nature.

Korning had observed the pseudo-Nixon in his glory, treating Captain Murphy and the others like some kind of cut-rate flunky crewmen on a private charter flight.

The gunman's sneer might be invisible behind his mask, but you could read it in his voice.

The touchdown in Beirut had come as a relief to Korning, even though he recognized that they were still in danger. If it came to shooting now, no matter if a bullet tore the fuselage, they would be safe from an explosive decompression, and sudden death at thirty thousand feet. They weren't home free, but they had gained a certain safety margin once the landing gear touched down.

Throughout the flight he had been listening for any sounds of violence from below, his stomach twisted into anxious knots. He felt for Mary Fletcher, Julie Drake, the rest of them, and wished that he could be among them now. And yet he balked at calling on the terrorists for any favors, anything that might provoke their anger.

He was frightened, but Korning was surprised to find that terror had given way to something like a nagging apprehension. It was ever present, but distinctly less severe than the initial shock of facing down a loaded submachine gun in the early moments of the crisis. Smiling to himself, he wondered if he had already grown accustomed to the danger, if it was a similar reaction that enabled soldiers, cops—whoever—to perform their duties under fire.

He reached the spiral staircase and started down, the Arab gunner on his heels. The flight attendant knew that if he was going to attempt a break, he would never have a better time. His escort would be concentrating on the steps, a portion of his mind consumed with the logistics of descent. If Korning acted swiftly, throwing caution to the winds...

He would be killed.

No way on earth could he reverse his track, disarm
the terrorist and claim the submachine gun for himself.
No way at all, before the terrorist had time to stitch him
with a disemboweling burst and blow his leaking carcass down the stairs.

He let it go, and concentrated on the man upstairs.
He was alone with Captain Murphy and the others.
Three on one, with nothing but his latex Nixon-face and
automatic pistol standing in their way. They could disarm him, and make a silent getaway.

The cockpit roof on every 747 boasted five emergency escape vents: one each for the captain, his first
officer, the flight engineer—and two more in anticipation of some other crewmen being on the deck. Designed for sudden exit if the cockpit access door was
blocked by wreckage or flames, every vent was fitted
with its own inertia reel, a coiled rappeling line that
granted access to the ground. Intended to provide the
flight crew with a second chance in case of fire, the
hatches and inertia reels would serve as well to take the
captain and his personnel beyond the line of fire.

Another gunman passed them on the stairs, ignoring
Korning, nodding to his escort as he headed for the upper lounge. So much for sudden getaways, goddammit.

Tension hovered over first class like a living thing.
The privileged few were unaccustomed to receiving orders, let alone confronting terrorists with guns, and they
were not withstanding pressure well. With one exception—an inebriated dowager with bright-orange lacquered hair—each of the eleven women present had
been weeping.

A handful of the men were red around the eyes, but
most of them were staring at their hands or glaring at

their captors with affected courage. Korning knew that none of them would make a move unless the terrorists laid down their guns—and even then, the first-class swells would need some time to think it through.

The atmosphere was slightly less intense as Korning reached ambassador. Two gunners, stationed at the galley module, covered forty-four submissive passengers with submachine guns at the ready, hand grenades protruding from trouser pockets. He brushed on past the starboard gunner, with his escort bringing up the rear, and made his way direct to coach.

It was here, he knew, that trouble would most likely arise. One full-time sentry, scant attention from the other two who had their no-man's-land staked out around the galley module, and 350 passengers confined to narrow seats, eight souls across. How long before a child broke loose from its distracted parents, or an angry redneck screwed up courage to confront the terrorists? How long before the gunner grew fatigued, or sickened of the low, incessant sobbing that pervaded coach like morbid background music? Could they hold it all together, or was Korning staring in the face of a massacre impatient to erupt?

He spotted Julie Drake and said a silent prayer of thanks that she was hanging in there with the rest. He had no way of guessing at her injuries, but Korning knew that she had taken a substantial knock from one of her assailants.

Some nerve, that lady.

Korning hoped they'd have another chance to get acquainted, off the job. Another chance, please God, to walk away from 741.

No point in dwelling on the future now, he realized. There might not be one, anyway. A moment or an hour or a day from now, their captors might decide it would be fun to line up some passengers or flight attendants and test their marksmanship.

But he could hope. The bastards couldn't take that away from him. No matter what they said or did, they couldn't get inside his mind and steal his will to live.

So flight attendant Korning told himself.

He was dead wrong.

Chapter Five

Mike Blanski half imagined he could feel a rising sense of agitation in the claustrophobic cabin of the aircraft. Three long hours without air-conditioning had transformed coach into a large, communal sweatbox. But the new sensation was a separate something else. He picked up snatches of a muffled conversation from beyond the curtain barriers up front, a mounting expectation on the faces of the Shiite sentries, and he knew they were about to meet the skyjack's mastermind.

But he was not prepared when the Richard Nixon figure brushed the sliding drapes aside, emerging with an autoloading pistol in his hand.

A mask, of course, but it would do for playing to the television cameras lined along the runway. Another jab at the United States. A little Shiite humor mingled with the ever-present stench of death.

The Nixon figure spoke.

"Good afternoon, my friends." The sheer presumption of it stuck in Blanski's throat. "We very much regret the course of action forced upon us by the client-state of Israel and her master, the United States . . . but such is life. It has become imperative to dramatize our situation for the world."

The guy was educated, Blanski gave him that. The Arab accent almost seemed an afterthought, as if he had to consciously remind himself that it was necessary. Blanski marked him as one of those who didn't mind accepting U.S. hospitality, absorbing every morsel made available at this or that exclusive university, before he turned around to maul the feeding hand. A rotten hypocrite... which was no more than just another way of spelling "terrorist."

"I have transmitted our demands to the authorities," the Nixon figure said. "To guarantee your safe return, the state of Israel must release a number of political detainees from its dungeons by the hour of twelve o'clock tomorrow."

The political detainees would be terrorists, of course, convicted in the courts, and Blanski wondered how much cash had been demanded to accompany their release from the Israeli "dungeons." In his personal experience, it wasn't like a terrorist to take such risks without the possibility of some financial compensation somewhere down the line.

"Regrettably," the pseudo-Nixon told his captive audience, "I have this message from United States authorities."

He hauled a crumpled paper from his pocket, cleared his throat and started reading aloud.

"Unable to negotiate these terms. Regret the loss of hostages, but the United States cannot involve itself in an Israeli state decision."

There was angry muttering among the passengers, some fearful looks exchanged across the aisles. And suddenly, two rows in front of Blanski, an American was on his feet.

"That's bullshit," he declared in ringing tones. "You wrote that crap yourself."

A Shiite sentry rushed him from behind, the stubby Ingram crashing down upon the man's skull behind one ear. He slumped back in his seat, unconscious as he sagged into the arms of his hysterical wife.

The grinning Nixon figure held his scrap of paper high.

"This note is signed by the United States ambassador to Lebanon, on orders of the President. They have abandoned you without regard for what may happen if our very moderate demands should be ignored."

Another ripple ran around the cabin, more fear than anger audible this time. The lie was taking root already, gnawing at the personal resolve of every passenger in coach.

"We of the people's revolution can afford to wait," the voice behind the latex lips declared. "I have proposed a deadline, and we will observe those terms regardless of this...this dismissal by the great United States. We shall preserve your lives until the hour of twelve o'clock tomorrow."

"What then?"

The question came from somewhere down in front.

"If our demands have not been met, it will be necessary to select a suitable example as a token of our dedication to the cause."

"You mean to kill us?"

"Twelve o'clock," the mask replied. "Perhaps your government will find its conscience in the meantime, eh?"

A hush fell over coach, disturbed but faintly by the sounds of weeping somewhere off to port.

The Nixon figure cleared his throat again.

"Because our stay might be protracted, I must call upon you for cooperation with the soldiers of our cause.

You must remain at all times in your seat. No movement whatsoever in the cabin.''

"What about the bathroom?" someone blurted down in front. A childish voice.

The rubber Nixon smile was mocking in its joviality.

"No movement whatsoever in the cabin," he repeated, relishing the words. "Our men are few, and we were not prepared for an extended siege. If some of you experience distress...I urge you to remember whose intransigeance has placed you in this sad position."

"Who are you?" someone called from the direction of the lavatories.

"We are soldiers of Jihad."

"But who are *you*?"

The latex Nixon hesitated momentarily, and when he spoke at last, his answer chilled Mike Blanski to the bone.

"I am the Raven. It is name enough."

STEVE KORNING RECOGNIZED THE NAME, of course. You had to be some kind of hermit not to recognize the Raven, but lately there had been a lot of speculation that the bastard had retired.

So much for speculation.

From what he could remember, he knew that for years the authorities of half a dozen countries had been looking for the Raven. The guy had surfaced in the middle-seventies with some spectacular achievements—if you looked on murder, bombing and the like as achievements—carving out a footnote in modern history beside the likes of Black September and the Red Brigades. Sporadic incidents had kept him in the public eye until he seemed to drop from sight a year or eighteen months before.

But he was back, and his trigger-happy reputation didn't put the flight attendant's mind at ease. From what he'd read, the Raven was as likely to provoke a bloodbath as he was to carry out negotiations for their safe release. He didn't care how many lives were wasted on the way, so long as he could hog a headline here, extort a ransom there, and come out clean.

Korning knew the adversary now—knew of him, anyway—but that did not relieve him of his duty to the passengers, his fellow crewmen on the flight. He had to try and keep everybody calm as long as possible. No easy task, once bowels and bladders started making their demands, but they could see it through as best they could.

Unconsciously, he glanced in the direction of the nearby lavatories. The simple knowledge that he would not be allowed to go provoked an angry growl in Korning's stomach and he grimaced, thinking of the hours ahead.

They had about twenty hours in which to keep their minds off biological necessity.

But the more you tried ignoring something, the more that something would intrude upon your every thought, becoming an obsession. They would be lucky if they didn't have a diarrhea epidemic on their hands by sundown, and he didn't even want to think about the kids, the pregnant mothers or the seniors trapped on board.

His stomach growled again, or was it lower down?

He forced himself to think of something else.

Like Julie. He spotted her across the cabin, huddled on a folding jump seat by the starboard exit hatch, perhaps ten paces from the nearest Shiite guard. She looked a little pale, but otherwise she seemed no worse for wear.

He would have liked to slip his arm around her shoulders and tell her everything was going to be fine. She would have seen right through his bullshit, but it would not have hurt to try.

But Korning couldn't reach her now. Eleven passengers and one lone gunman separated them. No more than thirty feet apart, they might as well have been on different planets. He had his orders with the rest, and he could not afford to move unless the grinning Nixon face or one of his helpers changed the rules of play.

Initial terror had given way to something that resembled nagging apprehension now, but Korning realized with vivid certainty that he was not prepared to die. Not for something as mundane as a secluded place to squat. He was resigned to soil himself, secure in the knowledge that he damn sure wouldn't be alone.

Korning made his mind a blank, erasing images of urinals and toilet bowls. He set about to weave a fantasy instead, with Julie Drake in a provocative supporting role. His fantasies would serve the purpose of a fair rehearsal, just in case they had another night together, somewhere down the road.

In case they managed to survive the Raven's siege.

IT WAS A CALCULATED RISK, but Bobby Maxwell felt the time was right. He shifted slightly in his seat, the clanking of his chains enough to make the nearest gunner glance in his direction.

Maxwell wore his most ingratiating smile.

"You guys've got the right idea," he blurted, conscious of his escort shifting, reaching out to seize his wrist. "Don't give the bastards any slack."

"Shut up," his captor growled.

"Hell no, I won't shut up!" He raised his hands and shook the manacles directly in his escort's face before the deputy could wrench them down. "I said they've got the right idea, and that's exactly what I meant. I don't expect the likes of you to understand."

He felt the Arab watching them, delighted as the red-faced marshal glared at him with pure contempt.

"I said shut up, goddammit!"

"Blow it out your ass! These guys're heroes, pig! I only wish I had the chance to help 'em out."

He struggled halfway to his feet before the marshal caught him with a stunning backhand, rocking Maxwell's skull and throwing him off balance, back into his seat. He cringed and braced himself to take a second blow.

But it never landed.

Suddenly the Arab triggerman was standing beside the marshal, slamming down his little submachine gun on the deputy's skull. A spurt of blood erupted from his lacerated scalp before his eyes rolled up inside his head and he collapsed in Bobby Maxwell's lap, a crimson stain spreading through the convict's denim uniform.

Exultant, Bobby shoved the deadweight back, then began to rise.

"Hey, thanks a lot. I really mean—"

The Ingram stopped him, closed his throat around the words, its muzzle aimed directly at his face.

"Sit!"

"Okay, no problem. Don't get nervous, huh?"

His heart was hammering against his ribs, but Bobby forced another smile as he regained his seat. It might take time, but he had laid the groundwork now. The rat-eyed little bastard had responded to him, helped him out instinctively, but Bobby didn't want to push the guy

too far, too fast. He had some time—till noon tomorrow, anyway—and he would have to take it easy until he
had established a rapport with this one first.

When he was finished with the stupid bastards, they
would be convinced that he was one of them. If there
was any trouble, it would come from the one who called
himself the Raven.

Bobby didn't recognize the nickname, but he knew
the guy's type. He'd seen them on the street and in the
syndicate, around the lockups where he'd spent at least
a quarter of his life. The guy was on a power trip, and
that could make him dangerous to anyone who stole his
thunder, sure.

But there were ways around him, too.

A lifetime in the joint or on the run made Bobby
Maxwell versatile, if nothing else. He could appear to
be whatever those in power might desire. In maximum
security, he was a model prisoner, a goddamn saint.
When he was laying out a heist, supported by the local
mafiosi, he exuded competence and confidence until the
greasy bastards knew that he could pull it off.

And with the Raven, Bobby knew he could exude
humility. He'd kiss the bastard's spit-shined combat
boots if that was what it took to get the shackles off.
He'd kiss the psycho's *ass*, if it came to that. And blow
his fucking head off if he got the chance.

But for the moment, Bobby had to play it cool. He
hadn't gained acceptance from the Arabs yet, but he
could feel it coming. This time tomorrow, he would
have the bastards eating from his hand.

This time tomorrow.

Or sooner.

All it took was patience. And brains.

A NAGGING DREAD had settled over Julie Drake with the appearance of the man who called himself the Raven, and it grated at her now that violence had erupted in the cabin once again. She should have made some move to help the officer, but she was frankly terrified to face the Shiite gunner, to provoke a fresh attack against herself. From where she sat she saw the officer begin to stir, and told herself that he would be okay. He didn't need her, after all.

But she could not escape the burning shame that rode the coattails of her fear.

She had been trained for situations such as this, indoctrinated with the message that her duty to the passengers came first. It was her job to keep them safe from harm, no matter what the risk...and she had failed.

Across the cabin, Julie met Steve Korning's gaze. He forced a smile and shook his head, as if to warn her off any foolish action that might make their situation worse. She wondered briefly if he had the power to read her mind—or if her angry impotence was written on her face for all to see.

She would have liked to take his hand or to feel his arms around her now. If she could tap into his strength, reduce the naked fear to something she could live with, function with...

And suddenly she wished she had taken him to bed when she had had the chance. The mental image took her by surprise and left her feeling weak inside. Was she reduced to seeking solace from an act of casual sex...or was there something more? Had Korning touched some part of her she wasn't even sure existed anymore?

It was a startling thought—and had no place among the negative emotions that consumed her at the moment. Julie knew there would be time for them to get together, to explore their inner feelings, when the nightmare of the skyjack was behind them.

Assuming they survived.

A little chill raced up her spine, a memory of the Raven raising gooseflesh on her arms.

He had a killer's eyes; the Nixon mask had not been able to conceal the hungry gleam. He was anticipating death aboard Flight 741, and looking forward to it with the rapture of a connoisseur.

The Raven was a man in love with death, and having recognized that basic fact, she knew that no one on the flight was safe. He might as easily destroy them all as choose a single human sacrifice. The killing might become a game he was reluctant to postpone.

If she could only talk to Steven, touch his hand...but she was on her own. The sentry had sequestered Mary Fletcher near the lavatories in the rear, and several other flight attendants were corralled inside the forward galley module. But for Julie Drake, the terror was a solitary thing, contained within herself.

And she would ride it out alone.

Whatever came to pass, she would rely upon her training, on the vestiges of inner strength that still remained. She had not attended church since she was a girl, but perhaps she might remember how to pray.

If all else failed she'd think of Steve, and keep his face before her like a shining icon in the dark.

And it just might be enough to keep them both alive.

Chapter Six

Something woke Mike Blanksi an hour before dawn. He had been dozing fitfully, a portion of his mind remaining half alert to any sudden sound or movement in his vicinity...but he was certain that he had not been awakened by either. A rapid scan revealed the Shiite guards in place, the passengers securely in their seats.

Then he had it.

A feeling.

He was accustomed to relying on the hunches that forewarned him when an enemy was near, when he was moving into danger. Combat intuition had already seen him through more battles than he cared to think about right now, and Blanski knew enough to trust his instincts.

But now the enemy was all around him. Danger was a constant, like the stagnant air they breathed inside the 747's cabin.

What had shaken him awake?

Without a conscious reason, Blanski focused on the federal escort and his prisoner. The con was sleeping, or pretending to, but his companion was alert and checking out the sentries. The blood had crusted in his hair, but he ignored it now, intent on what he had to do.

Blanksi shifted in his seat, already plotting out a course of action if and when the marshal made his move. There was no way to stop him from taking on the guards. If Blanski tried to reach him, he would be cut down before the marshal knew of his approach.

But did he want to stop the lawman?

If the officer was armed, he had a chance—of sorts—against the Shiite guns. His move, whatever shape it finally took, would offer Blanski a diversion, time and opportunity to take some action of his own. With any luck, he might be able to disarm the nearest gunner; failing that, he might improve his own position, alter the logistics of the situation in his favor for a change.

If he could shift his own position forward, toward the galley modules, he would have a slender chance of moving on the Raven when the ramrod of this operation showed himself again. It would be perilous, but once he had the bastard in his clutches, there would be time to renegotiate their situation.

The Shiite gunners would not move against their leader. Blanski knew it with the kind of perfect certainty that leads a man to bet his life without a second thought. The kind of certainty, perhaps, that fortified the federal officer to make his move.

The guy was fast, you had to give him that. Although he had been watching, Blanski almost missed the sudden lurching movement that propelled the marshal from his seat. A hand was digging back inside his jacket, coming out with what appeared to be a standard-issue Smith & Wesson .38. Incredibly, the nearest gunner hadn't seen him yet, or else his own reactions had been lulled by unrelenting tedium. The marshal might have pulled it off, had his prisoner not betrayed him at the final instant.

Churning up and out of sleep, the convict lunged against his escort, knocking him off balance, ruining his aim.

"Look out! He's got a gun!"

The warning shout was all it took, and now the marshal's target was alert, swiveling his Ingram toward the lawman as the .38 exploded harmlessly, its wasted round impacting on the bulkhead. Before the marshal could correct his aim, the Shiite milked a precision burst out of his stutter gun, no more than half a dozen rounds, despite the Ingram's awesome cyclic rate of fire.

The lawman took it all. He seemed to shudder, then stumbled facedown between the rows of seats. A dozen women screamed at once, and they were followed instantly by dozens more, their keening voices filling up the cabin and igniting sympathetic terror in a few of the men.

The gunner's lips were moving, but Blanski couldn't hear his voice above the din. He watched the Ingram rise, its stubby muzzle pointed at the ceiling, and hunched his shoulders as another, longer burst exploded overhead. A second gunner aimed his pistol in the direction of the rear lavatories, squeezing off three rounds in rapid fire, for emphasis.

"You will be quiet!" they were shouting. "Quiet now!"

It took a moment for the muttering to die away, but no one dared to raise his voice above a whisper. A kind of eerie silence settled in around them, focused on the prostrate body of the marshal lying in the aisle.

His killer stooped, retrieved the .38 and tucked it in the waistband of his slacks. Attracted by the shooting, two other terrorists had suddenly appeared from their stations in ambassador and first class, and now a jerky motion of the killer's head dispatched a runner to alert their boss.

Mike Blanski cursed under his breath. The opportunity was gone. The marshal's prisoner had bitched it for them all.

He didn't have to check his watch to know the killing had begun too soon. It would be more than seven hours yet before the Raven's deadline passed...and now he had a body to explain.

It wouldn't prey upon his mind, of course. There were too many other corpses in his past for yet another death to faze him now. But Blanski recognized the smell of blood—both literal and figurative. He was worried how the odor might affect their captor, how he might react to knowledge that the killing had begun.

Perhaps he would dismiss the incident as an aberration under stress. But if he decided on reprisals, then Blanski would be forced to move without a strategy.

He took a deep breath and held it, waiting for the sudden rush of nerves to pass. No matter that he had been face-to-face with sudden death on numerous occasions, Blanski could not totally escape the nervousness, the tightness in his stomach, that preceded lethal action.

The agitation was a killer, nine times out of ten. It skewed perception, dulled reaction time, made nimble fingers clumsy at the crucial moment. He could not predict the Raven's ultimate reaction, and he saw no need to try. The situation would resolve itself—in one way or another—soon enough.

And there was nothing left to do but wait.

THE THUNDER OF HIS PULSE was making Bobby Maxwell dizzy. He only had to glance across the empty seat

beside him, catch a glimpse of what was stretched out
in the aisle, to feel another rush come boiling up inside.

He had done it.

It had been touch and go there, feigning sleep for
hours, actually drifting off from time to time until he
pinched the inside of his thighs with shackled hands and
held it. The pain had given him an edge, and it had been
enough.

Of course, his escort could have ruined everything by
sitting tight and staying cool. It was a calculated risk,
but Bobby had already tested his reactions, recognized
him as a macho type who couldn't let an insult slide. He
had reacted violently when Bobby tried to make his little speech, and had been beaten for his pains. No way
on earth could he accept the sheer humiliation of a
public beating; he did not possess the inner strength to
let it go and get his own licks in when it was safe. He
had to try a grandstand play.

It had been easy to predict what he would do, but
waiting for the jerk to play his hand was something else
again. As hours passed and Bobby huddled in a crude
facsimile of sleep, he had begun to wonder if his feeling for the marshal was correct. Suppose he was a cow-
ard underneath the bluster, and he took it lying down?
Suppose he had more smarts than Bobby gave him
credit for?

But never fear.

When he finally cracked, the sound was almost audible in its intensity. The guy had given off some heavy
vibes, his anger and embarrassment mingled with fear
and pride—the stupid macho bag. He telegraphed his
move the way a punchy fighter lets you see the right

cross coming seconds in advance…and dammit, no one had been watching!

Bobby Maxwell had to save it for them at the final moment, clumsy bastards that they were. If he had not alerted them, and spoiled the marshal's aim, the little Arab with the stutter gun would have a brand-new asshole, right between his eyes. Who knows, the marshal might have dropped a couple of them, seized their automatic weapons, even armed the other passengers before the reinforcements could arrive.

He might have ruined everything.

But Bobby had prevented that, and he was feeling pretty good about it, stretching out and taking full advantage of the empty seat on his left. He didn't bother looking at the other passengers; they would be glaring at him hatefully, imagining a hundred different ways to waste him, nice and slow, for ruining their two-bit hero's play.

Well, fuck 'em all.

They didn't have his stake in how this all turned out. Not one of them was looking forward to a life in prison, or a one-way gurney ride. They didn't have the faintest damned idea what it was like *inside*.

But maybe they were learning. And maybe they would learn some more before survival class was finally dismissed.

The runner had returned, and he was followed by the one who called himself the Raven. Silently, the hijack honcho studied Maxwell's escort, peering at the body through his Nixon eyes before he raised his head to scan the cabin proper.

"You have seen the price of foolish, impotent resistance," he declared in ringing tones. He gestured in the direction of the corpse. "This man committed suicide."

An angry murmur, quickly stifled, from the middle rows.

"I had intended to restore your privileges. Instead, you give me no alternative but to impose a strict security."

He hesitated, and beneath the Nixon mask, Maxwell could have sworn the bastard licked his lips.

"I must protect my men, myself, from any others who may carry weapons on their person." Relishing the words, he took his time. "You will remove your clothes at once, and pass them to the aisles."

There was a momentary silence as they took it in and realized the terrorist wasn't playing games. Then the outraged voices drifted back from every quarter of the cabin.

"No!"

"You can't do that!"

"I won't!"

"You can't be serious!"

Three Ingrams, cocked and leveled, cut the protest off before it had a chance to go beyond the hot-air stage. The Raven let his automatic dangle casually at his side, but when he spoke to them again his voice was taut.

"At once."

No one in the cabin missed a syllable. They couldn't cope with what had been demanded of them, women weeping silently, men attempting awkwardly to comfort them, or simply glaring at the gunner with a kind of numb hostility.

It wasn't nearly fast enough to suit the Raven, and he swiveled toward the nearest hostage, picking out a stewardess who occupied a jump seat just behind him. Reaching down, he hooked his fingers in the neckline of her blouse and gave a vicious yank. As she recoiled, her own momentum helped him do the job. A ripping sound, and he was stepping back, the tatters of her blouse and bra like pennants in the victor's hand. She raised her arms instinctively, but Bobby Maxwell caught a flash of rosy breasts before she covered herself.

The Raven had his automatic leveled at her.

"The rest," he said, and there was sudden hunger in his voice.

"You bastard!"

Maxwell swiveled toward the angry voice in time to see a flight attendant rising from his seat, advancing toward the Raven in a rush, fists clenched. The nearest gunner took him out without a second thought, his Ingram slamming into the hero's forehead, dropping him. The stutter gun was pointed at his head, the gunner's finger tight around the trigger, when the Raven called him off.

"Enough," he growled, forgetting about the woman for the moment and turning on her would-be savior. He was on the guy in half a dozen strides, and when he kicked him in the ribs, the movement was a smooth extension of his gait.

The impact literally lifted the attendant. Rebounding off some nearby passengers, he slithered to the floor. The Raven stood above him, and landed two more vicious kicks against the flight attendant's ribs.

The absence of resistance seemed to bore him, and he left the hero lying where he fell, returning to the stewardess.

"Stand up."

She did as she was told, eyes fixed on the pistol, arms hanging limply at her sides. From where he sat, the prisoner could see it all. He felt his own erection rising as the Raven ripped her uniform away in shreds and left her standing nude in front of everybody.

The Nixon eyes examined her, the disembodied voice demanding that she turn, display herself, unmindful of the tears that streaked her pallid face. When he had seen enough, the Raven turned to face the other passengers again, his automatic aimed somewhere between the ceiling and the floor.

"The rest of you. *Right now!*"

It all caught up with Bobby Maxwell then, and his erection wilted like an orchid in a heat wave. He was on his feet before he had a chance to think it through, his hands outstretched to show his chains before the Ingram muzzles homed in on his chest.

"Hold on a second, okay?" He pitched his voice to sound subservient, and settled for a slavish whine. "I can't get out of these. I'd like to go along, but you can see I have a problem here."

The Raven looked him over, glanced in the direction of the fallen marshal, and Bobby realized that the bastard understood at once. His eyes were glittering inside the Nixon face. A shackled prisoner would have no weapons, pose no threat. The honcho could decide to leave him as he was, or fish around inside the marshal's pockets for a key, permitting him to strip once all his chains had been removed.

It would be worth the brief embarrassment to get the cuffs and shackles off.

"Sit down."

Maxwell slumped back in his chair, unable to control the trembling in his limbs.

It was a victory of sorts—and never mind the burning, hate-filled stares of those around him. They were doubly angry with him now. Not only had he foiled the marshal's bid for freedom, but he sat among them fully clothed, as they themselves were forced to strip.

He would have liked to ditch the chains, but that would come in time. The Raven had decided he was harmless, and it just might prove to be the next best thing. The guards would take his cue and they would concentrate on others, finally ignoring him until he was invisible.

He liked the feeling. It was like something from a fantasy.

The invisible man, and in the middle of a frigging nudist colony.

He almost laughed aloud, but choked it off, preserving the charade of mock humility. Around him they were getting down to skin, and Maxwell settled to watch the show.

He'd missed the in-flight movie, after all; the goddamn Raven owed him one. And it was paying off right now.

THE PAIN HAD NO SPECIFIC POINT of origin. It radiated from his skull in throbbing waves. His face was swollen, aching, and his rib cage felt like broken glass. When Korning tried to move, the shock waves left him dizzy, nauseated, on the brink of consciousness.

He wasn't dying, Steve was sure of that. It wouldn't hurt this much if they had broken anything of consequence inside. He had observed the aftermath of lethal accidents, the victims hanging on despite their obviously mortal wounds, and knew that shock was nature's anesthetic for the doomed. He had been hurt but he would live—unless the bastards took it into their heads to waste him as an afterthought.

He finally realized that he was nude. The nylon carpet felt rough on his skin, and even in the muggy cabin he could feel a draft that raised the gooseflesh on his back and arms. He lifted his head, experienced a nauseating burst of pain behind his eyes before he brought them into focus.

He was staring at the naked legs of passengers, just inches from his eyes. He followed feet to ankles, calves to knees . . . and closed his eyes, embarrassed, when he found the men and women staring back at him with curiosity, shame and hot resentment mingled on their faces.

Someone must have stripped him while he was unconscious . . . but the rest? It was bizarre, a form of degradation dredged up by a twisted mind.

And yet it made a certain kind of sense.

Undressed, they were defenseless. There could be no hidden weapons passed from hand to hand, no boots or belts, no secret items tucked away in pocket books to serve in the alternative. A woman stripped of clothing in a crowd of strangers would devote her time to salvaging some vestige of her dignity as best she could. A man, no matter what his skill or training, would think twice about confronting enemies buck naked.

Korning couldn't catch a glimpse of Julie Drake from where he lay, but he hoped they hadn't hurt her any further.

He struggled to his knees, and it was as far as he got before the pain washed over him in giddy, gagging waves. The spastic pain of cracked or broken ribs reminded him to take it slow.

He had to find a seat before his captors got the urge to play some soccer with his skull. Then he had to look for Julie Drake, suppress the dread that undulated through his bowels.

He had to know the worst, and knowing that, he would decide upon a course of action, a *re*action to the enemy. There might still be a shock or two in store for Mr. Raven and his greasy backup team.

If they had injured Julie Drake. If they had . . .

Korning concentrated on his empty seat, and closed his mind against the pain, the picket fence of naked legs that formed the boundary of his narrow world.

It all came down to first things first, and Korning had to put himself together before he could be any use to someone else. He needed time, a measure of the strength that had been beaten out of him, before he got around to evening the score.

Chapter Seven

Huddled on the narrow jump seat, Julie Drake was trying desperately to make herself invisible. Eyes closed, her arms and legs all folded in upon themselves, she salvaged what she could of her tattered dignity. Humiliated, terrified, she dared not raise her head to face the scrutiny of passengers and crew.

The passengers were lucky, seated in their sardine rows and facing forward. Only those to the left and right could stare at any individual; the others—those in front, behind—were blocked by high-backed seats, their own aversion to a sudden move that might attract attention to themselves. For Julie, planted on her jump seat near the forward galley module, there would be no fortuitous escape. She was at center stage, a piece of meat displayed before 350 pairs of prying eyes.

Of course, she realized that each and every passenger aboard was frightened and humiliated, stunned by what had taken place around them in the hours prior to dawn. The federal marshal's body had been dragged away, but leaking blood had stained the carpet where he fell, and piles of rumpled clothing in the aisles did nothing to conceal the mark of sudden death.

Their captors hadn't bothered sorting through the clothes. She realized that caution, fear of hidden weapons, had been secondary to the degradation of their hostages. As gunners moved among the cast-off items, they would pause from time to time and lift a lacy undergarment or a dingy pair of boxer shorts, displaying their discovery and chattering among themselves in Arabic.

It helped that she did not understand their words, but she could read their faces well enough. The tall one in particular had hungry eyes, and he had made a point of brushing past her several times, his submachine gun dangling beside him so its muzzle brushed her ribs, her thigh.

He wanted her, the flight attendant knew that much. There might be other, more attractive women on the flight, but he had witnessed her humiliation by the Raven, something in her helpless posture touching off a spark inside. Something told her that he would love to finish what his master had begun.

Please, God, not here. Don't let it be like this.

She thought of Steven, knew he had been beaten by the terrorists for trying to protect her. She was frightened for him, worried, but she dared not face him now. Her own embarrassment eclipsed the gratitude, concern, the warmth she automatically experienced when thinking of him. It almost masked the fear of death.

Almost.

Steven might be dead, she realized. They hadn't shot him, she was sure of that, but he could have died from the beating just as easily as from a gunshot wound. He had received a savage stomping from the Raven. And suddenly, she had to know. She opened her eyes and found the hungry gunner standing just in front of her, the buckle of his belt level with her face.

"You come with me," he said, and jerked his head in the direction of the lavatories to the rear.

"I won't." Her voice was tremulous.

The Shiite raised his submachine gun, nudged the stubby muzzle toward her face. "Do what I say."

One of his comrades rattled off a warning, but the gunner sneered, dismissed him with a grunt. "You come."

"I won't!"

She didn't see the backhand coming, and it rocked her on her perch and brought a galaxy of colored stars behind her eyelids. Julie was attempting to recover when his fingers tangled in her hair and she was lifted from her seat.

Desperately she fought him, clawing at his hand, his face, unmindful of her nudity before the others now. She raked his chest, was briskly shaken in return. It felt as if he might be ripping out her hair by handfuls, and a muffled shriek escaped between clenched teeth as Julie fought.

He twisted her off balance, then struck her with a stunning forearm from behind, across the shoulder blades. It drove the wind from Julie's lungs, propelled her several feet along the aisle. Before she could recover or turn to face her captor, he stepped up and kicked her from behind, his boot heel making solid contact with her buttocks, driving her to her hands and knees.

Another jarring kick, and Julie scuttled down the aisle through heaps of cast-off clothing. Tangled slacks and shirt sleeves tried to snare her, tangling around her hands, her legs. Already blinded by the burning tears of shame, she groped her way along until a hidden sneaker turned beneath her hand and dumped her on her face.

"Get up!"

A kick rebounded off her thigh, and Julie struggled to all fours. Disoriented, she attempted to recoup her strength. Her captor, with his wounded macho pride, could not resist the target that she offered, crouching on the floor in front of him, her pelvis raised.

The boot exploded in her groin, propelling Julie forward to slither facedown among the shirts and shoes and tangled underwear. The pain was everything; she couldn't catch her breath, and now she *knew* that she was dying.

No.

It couldn't hurt this much to die.

With almost superhuman will, she pulled her body up into a fetal curl, her wounded genitalia cupped in trembling hands. Convulsively she retched, dry heaves, with nothing in her stomach to absorb the pain. Julie told herself that if she lived through this, she could survive anything.

The spasms passed, and Julie wavered on the brink of consciousness. It would be so damned easy to slip away and leave it all behind. Embrace the darkness for a while, and never know or care what happened to your aching body in the meantime.

Fingers tangled in her hair again, igniting angry brush fires in her scalp as Julie's captor started dragging her along the aisle. She had no strength to fight him now, her arms too weak to try and slow him down.

It couldn't be much farther to the lavatory now. Inside, she would at least be safe from prying eyes, until he finished with her.

And would she have to face the others, then? Would they be lining up and waiting for their turns?

They reached the lavatory, and she heard or felt her captor force the door. In sudden desperation, Julie Drake began to scream.

FROM HIS SEAT ALONG THE AISLE, Mike Blanski watched the Shiite gunner drag his female captive toward the lavatories. He had watched them scuffle, seen her kicked and beaten while the anger churned inside of him like something animate and hungry, clawing to get out. His gut demanded that he move, do something— *anything*—but he was thinking now, and sitting on the gut reaction, knowing any sudden move could spark a wholesale massacre.

A sudden movement caught his eye, and he turned in time to see the flight attendant who had drawn the Raven's wrath some hours earlier erupting from his seat. It was a foolish move, but the damn guy had an overdose of guts. He must have known he wouldn't make it, but he couldn't leave the lady on her own.

A second gunner saw him rise and moved to intercept, approaching from the rear with silent strides. The Shiite whipped his autoloader in beneath the steward's ribs, impacting on a kidney. The attendant staggered and stumbled to the floor. The pistol rose and fell mercilessly against his skull, his neck, his shoulders, until his arms and knees gave way before the onslaught.

It interested Blanski that they had not simply gunned the flight attendant down. The Raven must have issued orders after he had finished stripping down the stewardess. Another death among the passengers or crew might weaken his position when it came to bargaining on faith.

Or did he simply want the next kill for himself?

No matter. If the gunners had been ordered not to fire...

A ragged scream disrupted Blanski's train of thought, and suddenly he realized that he had let the woman and her captor slip away. They were behind him now, grappling in the narrow entrance to the lavatory. In another moment, they would be inside.

He didn't think about the movement—didn't dare to, anyway. If they were under orders not to fire, he had a chance. If he was taking too damn much for granted... well, he might be dead before he made it halfway down the aisle. But even so, the desperate scream had banished any options that he might have had.

He moved, acutely conscious of his nakedness and trying hard to put it out of mind. It was a psychological advantage for his enemies, the fear of injury enhanced by the removal of his clothing. At a conscious level, Blanski knew the risk of injury was only slightly greater, if at all—a pair of jockey shorts and jeans would not protect him from a boot heel in the groin— but he could not suppress a shudder as he closed upon his human target, cringing inwardly against anticipated pain.

First contact broke the spell. He tangled his fingers in the Shiite's hair and dragged him backward off the woman, grappling with his free hand to immobilize the shooter's weapon. His opponent back-kicked, scraping Blanski's shin before he drove the Arab's face against the doorframe. Twice. A third time. And the jamb was slick with blood now as his adversary folded, slumping in his grasp.

Somehow the bastard kept his death grip on the Ingram, and there wasn't any time to pry his fingers loose.

Blanski heard the rush of footsteps from behind and braced himself against the flying tackle, knowing that he didn't stand a chance of staying on his feet. The impact drove him through the lavatory doorway, banging face and forehead on the stainless sink, and he was lying on the prostrate woman now, one knee between her thighs, as someone pistol-whipped him from behind. He struggled, fought to rise and heard her moan beneath him as he rammed her with his knee before he shook the human burden off and tumbled clear.

The would-be rapist hit him with a looping right, his snarl obscured by blood and mucus draining from a flattened nose. The punch closed Blanski's eye and snapped his teeth together, even as a boot slammed between his shoulder blades. The two of them were on him as he toppled, sprawling, and his one clear eye beheld a third assailant pounding in to join the melee with an automatic pistol in his fist.

They battered him with fists and boots and weapons while he did his best to fend them off, prevent them from inflicting any lethal damage. Once he saw an opening and kicked out sharply, heels together, cutting one man's legs from under him and toppling him backward, but then the other two bored in with a renewed ferocity, their fists and firearms hammering his ribs, his arms, his face.

They hadn't shot him, dammit, but the vindication of his hunch was scarely any consolation now. They didn't need to shoot him, once they had him down and at their mercy. As conscious thought began to flicker, fade, Mike Blanski knew that he had lost his gamble.

He took the bitter knowledge with him into surging darkness, broken only by the sallow flares of pain.

STEVE KORNING HEARD THE SHOOTERS grunting with the animal exertion of the beating they were dishing out, but he required another hazy moment to be certain they were working over someone else. His body was a twisted tapestry of pain, and with the sudden understanding that the bastards had themselves another human football, he experienced a rush of sweet relief.

Supplanted instantly by shame.

It might be Julie, and the bitter vision brought him to all fours, the dizziness receding as a haggard fury took its place. The greasy shits would have to kill him this time. They would have to use the guns as something more than bludgeons, if they hoped to keep his fingers from their throats.

But for the moment, Korning's hands were climbing hooks, not weapons. Incredibly, he made it to his feet, a bloodied human punching bag who made the passengers avert their faces, frightened or embarrassed to observe the damage he had suffered while they played the role of captive audience. He scanned the cabin, glancing automatically in the direction of the lavatories, spotting three of Raven's men intent on stopping someone who was lying prostrate in the aisle.

"You fucking bastards!"

Korning moved to intercept them, lurching woodenly on legs that felt like fence posts, fighting for his balance as the giddy waves came back full force. Whoever they were whipping might be a memory before he reached them, and he knew he couldn't pull the attackers off in any case, but he could lock his hands around *one* throat, and he could take one rotten bastard with him when he went.

Except that he would never have the chance.

Before he took a dozen shaky strides, the curtains rattled open and the Raven jostled past him, shouldering him roughly to the side. Determined not to fall, he clutched the nearest seat and held himself erect with desperate strength. He heard the Raven shouting at his men in Arabic, berating them in angry tones, and watched him pull them off the prostrate figure of a man.

The victim was unrecognizable, his face averted, veiled with crimson—but it was a man! Steve did a double take and spotted Julie crumpled in the lavatory doorway, knees drawn up against her chest, eyes closed.

Unconscious?

Dead?

He put one foot before the other haltingly, aware that they might turn on him at any moment. It didn't matter anymore. He had to know if Julie was alive, if there was anything that he could do.

The tallest of the gunners saw him coming, turned to head him off, and Korning realized the bastard's nose was broken, flattened like a piece of pepperoni on his face.

The bloodied gunner braced himself, his feet apart, the submachine gun rising in his hands. There was a glint of madness in his eyes, and Korning knew that it was death he saw reflected in the mutilated face.

Still, Korning took another shaky step. The Ingram found a point of reference on his chest, and he could see the gunner's knuckle whiten as he took up trigger-slack.

The Raven interposed himself, facing down the gunner, shouting at him through the Nixon mask in mixed-up Arabic and English, ordering him out of coach. The gunner hesitated, felt the others watching him, knew that they would back the Raven in a showdown. Finally he retreated, with a final bloody sneer for Korning as he passed.

The Raven didn't try to stop Korning as he went to Julie, pausing long enough beside the unconscious man to see that he was still alive. The blood had flowed from ragged scalp wounds, cuts above his eyes, but if they hadn't fractured anything, he ought to come around in time.

Korning reached the lavatory entrance, knelt to run a trembling hand through Julie's hair. She flinched instinctively, then risked a glance and saw him bending over her. A sluggish recognition, backed by tears, and when he put his arms around her there was no resistance. Only bitter weeping, as her soul and battered body purged their pain.

He held her, and they rode it out together, isolated for the moment from the danger that surrounded them. A moment or an hour hence, they might be called upon to offer up their lives, but for the moment they had each other, and it helped.

Chapter Eight

He couldn't say precisely where the nightmare ended and the slow return to consciousness began, but through it all Mike Blanski was aware of pain. Before it got a toehold on his mind, he opted for diversionary hypotheticals, comparing his sensations of the moment with a host of other pains he had experienced across the years. A bullet wound. A stabbing. Tumbles from the ancient backyard oak tree, as a child. A broken heart.

No contest.

He had lived through worse, and he would live through this, provided the bastards hadn't ruptured anything inside. He tried to move and regretted it at once, but couldn't let it go. Slowly he straightened, checking his limbs and finding that he could see once crusted blood was wiped away. His ribs and back were throbbing, but there was no tightness in his abdomen, none of the bloated feeling that accompanied internal bleeding.

He would live.

His mind flashed back to grappling for the girl, her slender body crushed beneath his weight and that of his assailants. Blanski tried to look around for her, but his position on the floor precluded any serious reconnaissance. From where he lay, he could see that he was naked, bloodied—hell, he knew that anyway—and that the other passengers were staring at him with concern. Or was it simple curiosity?

No matter.

Sitting up was half the battle, and he got it on the second try, his ribs and spine protesting loudly all the way. Once up, he slumped against the armrest of the nearest seat to keep himself from falling back again.

It seemed to take forever, but finally he braced his back against the seat, securing a view along the aisle to either side. The lavatory door stood open, empty, but he smiled in satisfaction at the brownish bloodstains on the jamb. Score one for his side, sure, and if the bastard walked away, at least he would be hurting now, remembering that it could cut both ways.

It had been foolish for him to risk his life—the lives of everyone aboard—but now in retrospect he didn't mind the cost. If he had spared the stewardess a moment of her terror, it was good enough. The rest was simply gravy.

He had moved against the Shiite guards, and lived. They hadn't used their weapons, hadn't sparked a general massacre on board, and that confirmed his hunch that they were under orders not to fire except in case of bona fide emergency. The Raven would be waiting, counting down the hours to his deadline, wondering how far the Western whipping boys would go to keep a load of tourists safe and sound.

He wondered what time it was and checked his watch. Then he remembered that it had been taken from him with his clothes. But his gut was speaking to him once again, alerting him to danger as the Raven's deadline crept around. For all he knew it might have passed already, leaving them at the mercy of a madman.

Counting down the doomsday numbers in his head, Mike Blanski wondered if the Raven would make good his word. He had the reputation of hard-core homicidal maniac, responsible for murders, bombings and assassinations, but a hijack wasn't quite his usual style. If he was walking unfamiliar ground, he might tread gingerly—or he might go overboard the other way and kill them all.

Whichever way it went, the Raven deserved some credit, of a sort. He had been active twice as long as any other big-name terrorist, and the authorities had never laid a finger on him yet. They had come close, but *close* was only good enough to get a number of their men annihilated in the process. They had never boxed the Raven, never wounded him as far as anybody knew. And he had never spent a night in jail.

If he was shifting gears to airline piracy, reverting after all these years, Beirut was perfect for his comeback. There would be no prosecution here, especially with the Shiite backup team he had selected for the mission. If and when the Western powers cracked or agreed to terms, he simply had to free the hostages and walk away. There were a million places he could hide in Lebanon or Libya, once he dumped the 747 and its human cargo.

Unless he wanted something more from the experience.

It was entirely possible, of course. The Raven had been out of touch for better than a year. He might be looking for a comeback that would reassert his status in the world of slay-for-pay. Commercial terrorism was a thriving industry, with bombings and assassinations catered on demand, and no one carried out a contract better than the Raven. Except that in his absence, there were those who hinted that he couldn't cut it anymore.

Some even said he had been killed, disposed of by a sponsor who was disappointed with his services.

Wherever he had been, whatever might be in his mind, the deadline for delivery was closing fast.

From what Blanski could determine, peering past a row of huddled older women, gauging the position of the sun, it must be nearly noon.

As if in answer to his thoughts, the curtain separating coach from more exclusive seats was suddenly withdrawn, and Blanski saw the Raven in his Nixon mask, surveying his domain. He wore the Russian automatic tucked inside his belt, and he was carrying an ax. The flankers held their Ingrams up and ready, just in case.

The Raven moved to center stage, and gave the naked passengers in front a chance to squirm before he spoke.

"Your government has failed to meet my deadline," he declared, and Blanski heard an anxious groan begin to worm its way around the cabin. "They have made it necessary for me to present a sacrifice."

He raised the ax and let it rest across one shoulder.

"Volunteers?"

THE CUFFS WERE BINDING HIM, and Bobby Maxwell shifted in his seat to take the pressure off, his eyes fixed firmly on the Raven. In his gut, Bobby knew that he might never have another chance.

He tried to raise his hands, was stymied by the chain around his waist and finally struggled to his feet.

"Hold on a sec."

He felt three hundred pairs of eyes converging on him, but he concentrated on a single pair. The Nixon eyes, and the intelligence that lay behind them, thinly veiled.

The Raven faced him, moving back in Bobby's general direction with the ax still propped across his shoulder.

"Ah."

Just that, and nothing more.

"I really don't belong here," Maxwell blurted out. "I'm like those guys you're trying to spring, you know? Political."

The Raven stopped ten feet away, his own eyes boring into Maxwell's through the hollow Nixon orbs.

"What is your crime?" he asked.

"Armed robbery. It was a revolutionary act."

"I see."

Bobby Maxwell had heard enough of all that revolutionary crap inside the joint to fake it like a pro, and never mind that politics had been the farthest thing from anybody's mind when they had taken out that armored car. They'd left a note to cover all the bases, and the state police were searching high and low for militants until the goddamn FBI had turned a latent fingerprint. Not Bobby's, bet your life. He wasn't dumb enough to make that kind of mistake, but once the federals had started popping his accomplices, it wasn't long until they had his name and his record.

"You are a... revolutionary?"

Bobby didn't like the way he hesitated, rolled the word around inside his mouth as if he was testing it for traces of corruption.

"Right. We popped an armored car to raise some money for our unit." Terrorists would understand that kind of shit. "I was shopping for some weapons when they ran me down in Frankfurt."

"There are guns in the United States."

Oh, shit.

"We didn't want to risk it, okay? The undercover pigs are into everything these days. You can't get laid without . . ."

He let it trail away, sensing that he'd edged beyond some boundary, invisible though it might be. Were Arabs puritanical on sex? He knew they didn't go for pork—or, hell, was that the Jews? Whatever, he was in it now, and what a frigging time to have to cope with Third World attitudes on sex.

"We thought it would be safer overseas," he finished loosely. "Guess we screwed it up."

"You did, indeed."

"How's that?"

The Nixon face was smiling back at him insipidly.

"A revolutionary is prepared to sacrifice."

He didn't like the sound of that, but he was in too deep to turn around.

"That's right."

The Raven beamed approval at him through the latex mask. "You have a chance to serve the people's revolution now."

"That's all I ask."

The Raven swiveled toward his flankers, never lowering the ax. "He'll do."

The backup gunners sidled forward, waited while he hobbled out to meet them in the aisle. They stood on either side of him, and their free hands slid beneath his arms.

"Hey, I can walk."

The Raven turned away, and Bobby Maxwell was propelled along behind him, shackles scarcely hampering him now. The Arabs were a good deal stronger than they looked. They fairly lifted Bobby off his feet, and in an instant he was close behind the Raven, standing near the exit hatch, above the wing.

The hatch release was set on manual, and Bobby watched the Raven as he threw the lever, let the cover fall away. A blinding shaft of daylight made the convict squint, but he was not about to miss the show. A rubber slide was rolling down and out in front of him, inflating like some kind of giant life vest, ready to receive evacuees.

The Raven turned to face him once again. "Do you believe in God?"

"I never been the real religious type. Too busy with the politics."

"Ah, well."

The Nixon face was nodding, not at him but at the flankers now, and Maxwell didn't have a chance to think what that might mean before a pair of boot heels caught him in the hollows just behind each knee. His jarring impact with the deck took Bobby's breath away, and several heartbeats passed before he realized that he was kneeling in the open doorway of the 747, staring into space.

"Hey, hold on a second now—"

The Raven stood behind him now, and when he spoke his voice was distant, hideously calm.

"Perhaps your god remembers *you*."

FROM WHERE HE SAT with Julie Drake, Steve Korning watched the Raven's gunners lead their prisoner in the direction of the exit hatch. The idiot might believe that he had snowed them with his line of crap, but Korning read a different message in the Raven's attitude, his voice. His gut suspicion was confirmed once they had blown the hatch, and Raven's flankers dropped the pigeon to his knees.

"What are they doing?" Julie whispered.

"Shh. Be quiet now. Don't watch."

He used one hand to turn her face away and felt her burrow in against his shoulder. She had already seen enough, and he would spare her what was coming if he could.

Korning watched the Raven as he stood behind his sacrificial goat, the crash ax balanced on his shoulder, both hands wrapped around the curving handle. They should have hidden it away...but there had been no time. No time for anything when he had taken Raven to the cockpit. Captain Murphy and his crew had more important problems on their minds than hiding axes from a gang of men already armed with guns.

"Perhaps your god remembers you."

The words were spoken softly, but they carried in the stillness of the cabin. Off to Korning's right, a burly red-faced man anticipated what was coming, and he vomited between his naked feet.

In one electric motion, the Raven raised the ax above his head and brought it flashing down. His target panicked at the final instant, twisted to the side and took the blow across one shoulder. He grunted as the force of impact carried razor-steel through flesh and cartilage and into solid bone. The blow released a bloody geyser that left droplets clinging to the manic Nixon face.

Disgusted that his stroke had failed, the Raven tugged and twisted on the ax. Finally he resorted to kicking at his human prey until the blade wrenched free.

He struck again, and this time the dying convict took it on the skull.

Steve Korning felt his stomach turning inside out, but there was nothing left to give. He choked the spasm down and watched, frozen, as the Raven took a step back and gestured to his henchmen with the ax. They shuffled forward, bending down to roll the tattered bundle out and through the exit hatch.

And Korning realized that he was clutching Julie tightly enough to crush her now, and with an effort, he relaxed. The worst was over. Please, God, it had to be.

One of the Raven's crewmen had produced a bullhorn—yet another token from the cockpit—and he passed it over now. The Raven lifted it, the mouthpiece pressed against his latex lips.

"You see that I am serious now," he told an audience invisible from Korning's seat. "I give you six more hours . . . as a token of good faith."

He passed the bullhorn off before the laughter bubbled up behind the rubber mask, the distorted sound made even more horrible by something in the tone itself.

They were in mortal danger now. The rest of it, the beatings, the attempted rape, the reflex killing of the marshal, had been a prelude to the main event. The Raven had *enjoyed* his sacrifice, and Korning knew that he was looking forward to the second deadline's passage with a special hunger all his own.

The skyjack's architect would not be disappointed if negotiators let him down again.

He would be pleased.

It would provide him with another chance to slake his thirst, and next time out, they wouldn't have a convict standing by to volunteer. Next time would be the Raven's choice.

They had six hours left, and suddenly it didn't seem like nearly long enough.

But Korning knew that it could be a lifetime.

It could be all the lifetime any of them had.

Chapter Nine

The cabin had begun to reek by sundown. Younger children were the first to soil themselves, but after thirty hours in the aircraft, stationary in their seats, a growing number of adults were giving in to nature's call. The stench of perspiration mingled now with the wafts of feces, vomit, urine, to create a rank miasma in the cabin of the 747.

Julie Drake had drifted in and out of sleep throughout the afternoon. Still shaken, hurt, humiliated from the beating, she had sought a brief oblivion, but nightmare shapes pursued her there and drove her screaming back to wakefulness.

Each time she woke, Steve Korning had his arms around her, holding her and rocking her as if she was a child. It might have rankled Julie at another time, but now she didn't mind at all. It seemed appropriate, and she ignored the fact that they were naked, drawing warmth and solace from his flesh, his closeness.

Memory was coming back in bits and pieces, worming underneath the wall of her resistance and compelling her to face reality. She had watched the brutal execution, peering through her fingers like a youngster frightened by a horror movie, Steven's arms around her even then and helping her to keep the scream inside.

The prisoner was gone, and the exit hatch was open, though its extra ventilation did little to alleviate the captive stench inside. It registered with Julie that the slide must be in place. If she could make it to the hatch, drag Steve along behind her...

Then what?

The Raven's men would riddle them before they reached the bottom of the slide—assuming that they weren't cut down before they reached the door itself. Besides, out there she would be naked, surrounded by the cameras and the prying eyes of men in uniform. Inside the cabin she was merely nude, as all of them were nude together, and she had the shelter of Steve Korning's arms.

She knew that he had tried to help her when the Raven stripped her uniform away, and later, when the gunner with the rodent's eyes had tried to...

The terrorist scum must have beaten him unmercifully. She had no cogent memory of the event, but he was bruised and bloody now, his ribs and chest and dear, sweet face a motley canvas of black and blue and other colors in between. He seldom moved, as if afraid he might awaken her, but when he did, there was a stiffness to his movements, and the breath caught in his throat.

The tears were sudden and not unwelcome. At the moment she was not embarrassed for herself, the fact that everyone aboard had seen her stripped and beaten, mauled and nearly raped. She wept for Steven, and the selfless courage that had made him risk his life on her behalf. A feral warmth was radiating from her now, and Julie realized, astonished, that she wanted him.

It might have been the proximity of death, a sudden urge to reaffirm their life force, but she *wanted* him, and knowing there was nothing she could do about it only made the wanting worse. She would content herself with holding him, with feeling Steven's arms around her, knowing he had suffered, bled, to keep her safe. It was the best that she could do, for now. But if she ever got a second chance...

That "if" was cold and hard enough to break her train of thought and force a sharp diversion back to grim reality. They had perhaps six hours left until the Raven's second deadline passed, and he would be returning with his ax to choose another sacrificial victim. Julie began to tremble uncontrollably, and Steven drew her closer, shushing her and whispering that it would be all right. Instinctively, she held him tight and sought his warmth.

Outside, the tower and the terminal were swathed in shadow, blending into desert twilight. In the cabin it was dark already, but for scattered bulbs that cast a faint illumination on the aisles. The darkness lulled her fears; it beckoned to her, calling irresistibly. She held on tight to Steven as it carried her away.

KORNING WAITED FOR SEVERAL MOMENTS, making sure that Julie was asleep before he shifted in his seat in an attempt to restore circulation to his legs. Huddled with her for the better part of half a day, and underneath the constant throbbing pain of his assorted cuts and bruises, he was stiff, his muscles crying out at him to move, do something. He wasn't ready to complain just yet; it wouldn't have accomplished anything, and Korning knew that things could be a whole lot worse.

He might have been alone.

The nightmares plaguing Julie were a problem. Their guards were getting nervous as the time wore on, and the breathless little screams that woke her up each time had caused the gunners to regard her with suspicion. It didn't seem to matter that she obviously couldn't stand, much less attack her captors. They were spooked, and nervous men with guns could make mistakes.

So Korning tried to keep her quiet, smoothing out her tangled hair and whispering soothing words to her.

It was becoming difficult to breathe, the cabin's stench pervading everything, invading throat and nostrils even when he tried to hold his breath. The sewer reek brought tears to Korning's eyes, and he was thankful that the lady in his arms did not appear to be affected.

Or should he have been concerned?

Did Julie's sluggishness denote some injury that he was unaware of? Was she slipping into shock? Might she be dying in his arms?

He put the morbid train of thought behind him, concentrating on the prospects of survival. There were hours yet before they should expect another visit from the Raven with his crash ax. Still time for someone, anyone, to strike a bargain for their lives.

And if the Western powers wouldn't budge? What then?

They would be treated to another round of death. With better than four hundred sacrificial lambs to choose from, Korning wondered how the son of a bitch would decide on who went next. He also wondered if the Raven would propose another deadline, if it would be shorter than the last. He might decide to execute a group of hostages at once, to force his adversaries' hand.

It was a puerile line of reasoning, and Korning cut it off before it had a chance to carry him away. No point in second-guessing. They would find out soon enough, but in the meantime, the flight attendant sought to push the grinning latex mask from his mind.

No luck.

He wondered what the Raven really looked like underneath his mask. A fuzzy newsprint photo came to mind, but Steve could not remember any details of the face, the attitude. What kind of twisted brain and convoluted logic made him kidnap, maim and murder for his cause? Was it genetic? Or environmental? Had the bastard been abused when he was still a child, or had he suffered some debilitating illness? Was he impotent? A homosexual?

Who cares?

It mattered only that the rotten fuck was *here*, right now, and that he held their lives precariously balanced in his bloodstained hand. He might decide to close that hand at any time, to make a fist and snuff them out collectively... or he might play with them a while, prolong the suffering and take them individually, feeding on the terror.

Steve fervently wished that he could get his hands around the bastard's neck. It would be worth the cost. If he could take the Raven with him, he would give it up right now....

Korning shook his head sadly.

He had responsibilities, not least among them being Julie Drake. The lady was depending on him now, and he couldn't let her down. He didn't want to let her down, not after suffering so much to come this far.

And there was still a distance left to go.

They might not get there all together—some might never make it through at all—but they would have to try. It was the least that they could do, and every mother's son and daughter on that 747 had a moral duty to survive, by any means available.

Steve Korning settled back and drew the lady tightly in against him, relishing her warmth. She might be feverish for all he knew, but at the moment she was like a welcome fire, her inner heat enough to drive away his chill.

With any luck at all, they just might get each other through the night.

MIKE BLANSKI WOKE TO PAIN, and was surprised that he had slept at all. Outside, the runway lights were winking at him, beckoning to airborne traffic, luring the corporate jets and jumbo liners down. Beyond the terminal and tower he could see the streetlights of Beirut ... except that there had never been such lights, so tainted with the red and orange of wildfire, flickering along the underside of scudding clouds.

The city was in flames.

Again.

It wasn't Blanski's problem, but he couldn't quite head off the stab of sympathy, regret that it had come to this. The people of a once-proud city were turning in upon themselves and hunting one another through the streets like vermin. Killing in the name of Allah or Jehovah, never realizing how their mayhem had perverted and degraded everything that they professed to honor in their souls. So many innocents, inducted forcibly and slaughtered in a war they couldn't even hope to understand.

He turned away and left them to it now, his mind consumed with problems of his own. Survival was the top priority, of course, and he was hanging on despite the superficial evidence of wear and tear.

It had been worth his time to help the woman; he had owed it to himself, and expiation of that private debt had been worth the pain. If he had spared her anything...

Unbidden, Blanski's mind flashed back to Vietnam, another night of fire and blood, above Khe Sahn. They had pursued a team of VC sappers, tracking them as much by mutilated bodies as by jungle signs, until by chance their course had taken them into a nearly deserted village. Corpses had been scattered everywhere, their blood so fresh that he could smell the coppery odor on the wind. Their mission had precluded anything beyond a superficial recon, and his team was pulling out when Blanski found the woman.

She was still alive but sliding fast, beyond the reach of any known first aid. A lovely woman-child, she had distracted several of the sappers with her beauty, slowed them down enough that Blanski and his men would overtake them close to dawn, before they reached the safety of the DMZ, and kill them where they stood.

Her dying face had been emblazoned on a youthful soldier's brain, and he had been too late for her.

But he had been in time to even up the score.

No, some scores were never evened up. Some crimes were never adequately punished, even when the criminal was dead and in the ground. Some wounds could never heal.

Mike Blanski hoped the lady flight attendant carried no such wounds. He hoped the anger and the pain would fade with time, until the incident and everything surrounding it acquired some rational perspective in her life.

He hoped she had the time.

A certain stiffness of the sentries now, a semblance of attention, and he knew the Raven was approaching, stalking back through first class and ambassador, his lackeys bringing up the rear. It wasn't time to choose another victim, Blanski knew that much, but it was possible their captor had decided to accelerate the pace, extend the limits of the game.

The curtain whispered back and now he stood before them, looking crisp and cool, as if the temperature had been a pleasant seventy degrees instead of pushing eighty-five. Someone had sponged the convict's crusty essence from the Nixon face, and Blanski wondered if the scrub-down signaled any softening of attitude.

The Raven stood before them like a cultured orator. The ax was not in evidence, but Blanski saw the Makarov thrust down inside his belt. The Raven waited for sporadic muttering to die away before he cleared his throat, began to speak.

"Your government had managed to prevail upon the kosher pigs of Israel," he declared. Seconds passed before the import of his words sank home. "They have agreed to our demands, and are preparing for release of certain hostages imprisoned by the Zionists."

The Raven paused, allowing them to whisper now among themselves. Behind the mask, Mike Blanski half imagined he could *feel* the burning eyes, the twisted smile.

"A sum of cash will also be delivered," they were told, "to compensate the revolution for its time and energy. Delivery requires perhaps an hour. In that time, you may prepare yourselves to disembark."

A ragged cheer was raised behind him from the general direction of the tail, but Blanski's face was grim, his jaw set tight. In place of the relief he should have felt, a creeping numbness wrapped itself around his entrails, reaching out with icy feelers toward his heart.

Relax, an inner voice demanded. It's okay.

Except it wasn't.

No.

They were alive, some scrambling for their clothes already, anxious for the ordeal to become a distant memory. The worst was over now.

Or was it just beginning?

Blanski broke the spell, retrieved his clothing from the aisle, began to dress, unmindful of the others all around him now. They were survivors, dammit...but it still felt wrong, somehow.

A chunky man in jockey shorts and nothing else was poking at his elbow.

"Hey, it's great, you know? We made it! Ain't it great?"

"You bet," the soldier answered, turning stony eyes in the direction of the fires that ate Beirut. "Just great."

Chapter Ten

The uniform felt strange when Korning put it on again. It didn't seem to fit the way it had before, almost as if the man inside had shrunk slightly. He checked the name plate just in case there had been some mistake.

The uniform was his.

He was suffering from shock, no doubt. Between his hunger and the beatings, more than thirty hours in the septic chamber of the 747's cabin, he was lucky still to be alive. And damn it all, he had done nothing wrong!

For hours he had replayed the savage series of events inside his head, examining each nuance of his own re-action to the terrorists, intent on sniffing out the small-est trace of cowardice or negligence. And he had come up empty. He hadn't done a damn thing wrong.

So why did he feel guilty for surviving? Why was it impossible for him to look at Julie Drake without the color rising in his cheeks? He had done everything within his power to protect her, suffered in her place, and he had sheltered her throughout the long, last hours of captivity. Whenever Julie met his eyes she smiled, and there was no suggestion of reproach, but still...

He was familiar with the so-called Stockholm syn-drome, the phenomenon where hostages began to sym-pathize, identify with, even love their captors...but the feelings that tormented Steve were something else entirely. He would happily have killed the Raven and his men if someone had provided him with weapons or the opportunity. And yet, despite the knowledge that he hadn't yielded, hadn't given them an inch, he still felt . . . weak.

Korning dismissed it. He couldn't afford self-pity at the moment. Understandably the passengers were growing restless. Their freedom was only moments away if the Raven kept his word. That was an "if" that Korning didn't care to bet his life on, but it was encouraging that they had been allowed to dress.

The government—American, Israeli—had decided it could live with these particular demands. This time the terrorists had won . . . or had they? Were negotiators waiting for them on the tarmac with a surprise in store? A flying squad of Black Berets, perhaps? A sniper team waiting for a chance to frame their cross hairs on the Raven's grinning Nixon face?

The flight attendant smiled and shook his head, dispelling the fantasy. They wouldn't try that kind of shit now, when everything was settled and the hijackers were preparing to release their prisoners. One sloppy shot, one miss, would give surviving gunners time to open fire, or jerk the pins on their grenades and turn the 747 into a titanic crematorium.

The Western powers wouldn't risk that kind of bad publicity, assuming they could even pull it off in Lebanon, where officers of the chaotic government were more inclined to sympathize with terrorists.

They ought to nuke the bastards, Korning thought, surprised by sudden violent anger that he hadn't known he harbored in himself. But then again, the past two days had been just loaded with surprises.

Two days ago he hadn't thought that he could kill a man, and now he pictured the Raven and lingered on the possibility with relish.

Two days ago he wouldn't have imagined he would risk his life for Julie Drake, but he had done so. Twice.

Two days ago he wouldn't have believed they had a chance, but when she faced him now he saw respect, and gratitude, and something else behind her eyes.

She couldn't see the guilt, the personal uncertainty he felt. If he could only make her see…but that would take time, and right now Korning had 350 passengers to console and reassure before they put Flight 741 behind them. When the job was done, perhaps, he and Julie could share their fears, their feelings, and he might find out that she felt a number of the same sensations he was privately experiencing now.

The prospect taunted Korning, and he couldn't finish with his other duties fast enough. The cabin seemed to close upon him now, and for the first time since the gunners hauled their weapons out, he felt a taste of claustrophobia.

It was another token that the terrorists were leaving with him. A small reminder of their close encounter.

He owed them something, Raven and the rest. If nothing else, a statement to the waiting media about their savagery, their disregard for human rights and human life.

He owed the Raven plenty, and he was anxious to begin repaying all those debts in full.

For Julie Drake, the uniform was better than a suit of armor. It restored a measure of her wounded pride, her dignity. But there was more to her recovery than simply putting on some clothes. She recognized something more each time she raised her eyes and found Steve Korning watching, studying her face with anguish written on his own.

She didn't know what to say, and so she welcomed all the countless tasks that went along with the evacuation of a grounded 747. Keeping busy drove the nervousness away, and it would give her time to think, rehearse her words before she bungled everything and made herself seem foolish in his eyes.

She had to thank him, certainly—but thanks alone were so inadequate for all that he had suffered. She longed to feel his arms around her as she had when they were huddling beneath the guns . . . but that would have to wait for another time, provided that she got the chance.

A passenger had tried to help her, too, and she would have to check the roster soon to learn his name and thank him properly—but something in her heart went out to Steven now.

If she was wrong about her feelings, there was nothing lost.

If she was right . . .

She felt the color rising in her cheeks again, and quickly turned her back to Steven, busying herself with chores. The gunners were relaxed for once, their scrutiny more casual than any other time since they had seized the plane.

Earlier, it would have been the perfect signal for a break. But now, with freedom in the bag, there seemed no point in trying to antagonize their captors.

The Raven could have kept them all aboard the 747 until dawn, but Julie thought the darkness might allow him an easier escape. The Lebanese would not attempt to hinder him, of course; her training classes with the airline had included briefings on the several governments that harbor and encourage terrorists while keeping up a civilized facade. Among them, Lebanon was known for its confusion, impotence and willingness to overlook the violent acts of certain Muslim terrorists.

But it was over now, or nearly so. A few more hours and they would be at liberty. Once home, she would demand a transfer to domestic flights. Surrendering the extra pay was nothing in comparison to living with the fear that Julie knew would never leave her now, if she continued working international.

It wasn't fair that she should have to live with fear, but life was seldom fair. The good died young, the evil seemed to live forever, and the average man or woman just kept trying to survive. No point in looking for a cosmic plan behind it all, she realized. It was a crapshoot, and if anybody came out even in the end, they ought to count it as a victory.

She glanced in Steven's direction, found him busy with the passengers and spent a moment studying his face in profile. She saw strength, integrity, a *caring*.

Slow down, she warned herself. The past two days had put her through a blender, physically and mentally. She wasn't ready yet to trust her own emotions when it came to the extremes. She needed time to think, to rearrange her life, but nothing said she had to do it all alone.

But first things first. And number one was getting off this plane as soon as possible. With singleness of purpose, Julie concentrated on her job, responding to the questions of excited passengers as best she could. She didn't have the answers they required, but that was nothing new. God knows, she didn't even have the answers for herself.

But she would find them, no matter where she had to look.

And maybe—just maybe—she could find someone to help her with her search.

THE AIRPORT TERMINAL WAS JAMMED with military personnel, police, assorted diplomats and network television crews. Mike Blanski raised a hand to screen his battered face from cameras aimed in his direction, veering away from others who were obviously looking for a chance to share their story with the world.

An aging man and wife in matching pastel leisure suits were holding forth for NBC, and CBS had fastened on a bronze Adonis who regaled them with his memories of standing up to the Raven and his henchmen. For Blanski, who remembered this Adonis as a whiner, one who cringed whenever one of their abductors passed too close, it was a pitiful display.

Blanski shook his head and was about to move away when he collided with a pair of roving journalists and found a microphone thrust in his face.

"You were among the passengers on 741?"

It was a stupid question, and he answered it reluctantly. "I was."

The men were staring at his face. "And you received those injuries from terrorists?"

"No, actually, I always look this way."

There was a slight hesitation followed by startled laughter as they realized that he was toying with them.

"Ah, but you retain your sense of humor."

"When I can."

"You met the Raven?"

Blanski nodded, and the thin, sardonic smile vanished from his face.

"And what was your impression of him?"

"He's a lunatic. A germ. He ought to be exterminated like the vermin that he is."

The vehemence of his reaction seemed to shock his two-man audience. It took a moment for them to compose themselves.

"I understand your feelings, Mr...uh..." When Blanski failed to take his cue, the man was forced to push ahead. "I understand your feelings," he repeated, "but you must agree that the philosophy behind the Raven's actions here today—"

"Is total bullshit," Blanski finished for him, almost snarling. "Maggots like the Raven kill for money, sometimes for the pleasure of it. He's a mercenary hit man who accommodates fanatics for a price. He makes their ugly dreams come true."

"But certainly, the Shiite cause—"

"Has not moved forward one iota based upon what happened here today. The Raven has his cash in hand. He's gone. Do you see any evidence of an improvement for the Shiite people? Are they better off in any way?"

"Release of certain prisoners in Israel has been guaranteed."

"Oh, sure. Assuming that they are released, by someone who's inclined to honor an extorted promise made to savages, precisely who is getting out of jail?"

"Political detainees?"

Doubt had found its way into the newsman's voice.

"I'd call them terrorists, but *you* decide. You've got the list of names. Go check it out. Find out how many lives each one of those political detainees has destroyed through mindless acts of terrorism. Get the story straight for once, and tell it *all*, or do the world a favor and go find yourself another line of work."

"See here—"

"I see just fine. I'm looking at a pseudoliberal armchair revolutionary, full of crap and misplaced high ideals. You sit behind a desk and crank out reams about the 'people's struggle,' 'liberation armies' and the rest of it. You've come closer to the firing line tonight than either one of you has been before, and you're excited by the smell. But take another whiff before you burst out into purple prose. That's *death* you smell out there. It's permanent, it's real, and there's enough to go around without encouraging sadistic assholes like the Raven to commit some new atrocity."

The interviewer took a moment to recover from this outburst, and his tone was softer, almost chastened, when he spoke again.

"Well, at the very least, we can agree to being thankful that this incident is over."

"Is it?"

"Why... of course."

"What makes you think so?"

"Ransom has been paid, the hostages have been released...."

"It's not enough," he told them simply, stepping in between them, brushing past.

"What do you mean?"

Mack Bolan turned to face the newsmen, staring through them, and his eyes were cold, the color of a winter's morning off Cape Cod. And when he spoke, his voice was like an echo from the grave.

"It's not enough."

Chapter Eleven

Early lunchtime traffic had begun to snarl the New York streets, but for the most part Bolan escaped it, as he turned off Forsyth onto Hester, piloting his rental deep into the lower Bowery. Here the heavy traffic was pedestrian and most of it was stationary, huddled figures staking out doorways, alley mouths and stoops, examining the stranger with suspicious, rheumy eyes.

A former haven for immigrants, the Bowery had enjoyed a certain vogue among theatrical producers of the nineteenth century, but the prosperity had been short-lived. The cellar dives and rampant crime had strangled any fledgling aspirations of success, and for a century the neighborhood had simply been skid row.

The winos, addicts and assorted predators who made their living from the homeless derelicts had staked their claim from Fourth Street on the north to Chatham Square. Anyone foolish enough to walk those streets alone, by day or dark, was risking his life. Bolan felt no apprehension as he found a space at curbside, killed the rental's engine, left it locked.

The Executioner had business here, and any predator who interfered would live just long enough to rue the day.

The Makarovs, RGD grenades and the Kalashnikov had been no problem. They were standard issue for assorted terrorists from Northern Ireland to Japan, and all points in between. The KGB was generous with arms, cash, and factories in several of the ComBloc nations were working overtime to arm a horde of Third World dissidents. No matter where the weapons had been forged, Mack Bolan knew the source.

The Ingrams were a different story altogether. They were made in the United States, exported on occasion, but the majority remained at home among the several thousand law-enforcement agencies from coast to coast. The military had its share, of course, and semiautomatic versions, legally available to anyone, could be converted easily enough to automatic mode.

There had been no conversion of the weapons used on Bolan's flight from Frankfurt to New York. One piece was left behind for reasons still unclear, but Bolan marked it off to carelessness. The sear mechanism had been intact, according to an FBI report leaked to Bolan by way of Leo Turrin in Washington, D.C. The bureau made its registration number, too, and verified that it was one of several automatic weapons stolen from the New York waterfront last spring.

It was a quantum leap from dockside in New York to airborne over Germany, and Bolan didn't have a shred of evidence to help him trace the weapon's transatlantic progress. But he had a fair idea of where to start.

A pair of sullen black youths stood watching Bolan from a shadowed doorway. When he was directly opposite, the soldier paused and turned to face them squarely, giving them the opportunity to make their move. A moment passed in lethal silence, then the older of them nudged his sidekick and they faded back, ingested by the ancient brownstone. He put them out of mind at once, intent upon his mission now.

Bolan's target was another brownstone halfway down the block. On the third floor he would confront the man whom he had traveled seven thousand miles to see.

He had called ahead for an appointment, but he wasn't taking any chances. The dealer might have smelled a setup, taken on some extra help for the occasion, and the Executioner did not intend to let himself be taken by surprise.

Inside the doorway of the brownstone, Bolan paused to double-check the special quick-draw rig beneath his arm. The sleek Beretta 93-R was secure and instantly accessible at need. Satisfied, the soldier moved past a pair of doors that hadn't locked in years, ignoring the decrepit elevator and proceeding toward the stairs.

The staircase doubled back upon itself repeatedly inside the narrow, musty stairwell. Bolan recognized the danger, if they had an ambush waiting for him upstairs, if the dealer had a hideout team prepared to close the exit at his back. There wouldn't be much way for them to miss him on the stairs, but he would take some of the bastards with him, if it came to that.

He put the morbid thoughts away and concentrated on the task at hand. He had arranged to meet the dealer as a customer, but what he sought was information, and he didn't plan to lay out any cash. The dealer had a last-ditch chance to clear himself, and Bolan would provide him with the simplest of choices.

Life or death.

The gunrunner's name was Tommy Noonan, and his normal stock-in-trade was paramilitary weapons. Having paid his dues—and done his time, on more than one occasion—Noonan properly eschewed the junkies and the greenhorn stickup men who sought a cheap revolver or a sawed-off shotgun for a bang-up one-night stand. His clients now included mafiosi, bigots black and white, well-heeled political fanatics . . . and the Raven. If the information passed to Bolan was correct, it would be Tommy Noonan who supplied the Ingrams used aboard Flight 741.

Bolan reached the third floor and hesitated on the landing, marking the single sentry posed at the far end of the corridor. It was too warm inside for any kind of coat, and Bolan recognized its purpose as concealment of some heavy hardware.

He would have to watch the outside gunner as he left. . . . It would be risky, but the whole damned operation was a gamble, and the Executioner had nothing left to do but raise.

He rapped the designated signal on a freshly painted door approximately halfway down the corridor. The standard, flimsy wooden door had been replaced—at Noonan's own expense, no doubt—with a substantial one constructed out of steel. It would require a ram and some determined SWAT team personnel to get inside the dealer's shop if Noonan chose to make them wait outside.

A moment passed, and Bolan was about to knock again when someone threw the bolt inside and opened up a crack just wide enough to accommodate one eye. It studied Bolan briefly, and a disembodied voice demanded, "You the guy?"

"Mike Breslin."

"Got some paper?"

Bolan passed the phony license through to greasy fingertips. It disappeared, the door was tightly shut—and just as quickly opened wide, permitting him to enter. Noonan's doorman was a slender Hispanic in a greasy lab coat, open to reveal the Smith & Wesson Magnum tucked inside his belt.

"Dis way."

He led the Executioner around a plasterboard partition, erected, from appearances, to screen the inner room from outside scrutiny. When they had made the circuit, Bolan understood the need for privacy.

The two-room flat could not really be called a warehouse, but it made a handy showroom for the dealer's wares. And Tommy Noonan dealt in quality. His stock on hand included handguns, automatic rifles, shotguns, submachine guns, with a scattering of heavy iron among the small arms. Bolan spied an MM-1 projectile launcher and an Armbrust throwaway bazooka in among the Colts and Armalites and foreign brand-name weaponry, before he was distracted by a figure on the far side of the crowded room.

His host was just emerging from the tiny bathroom, toweling off his hands. "This goddamn Cosmoline," he growled. "I never get it out from underneath my fingernails."

"I know the feeling," Bolan told him.

"Do you now?" Suspicion in the dealer's voice, beneath a touch of brogue. "You're Breslin?"

"Right."

"You don't look Irish."

Bolan didn't smile, but Noonan spent a moment waiting for it, finally giving up and punching Bolan on the shoulder playfully.

"A joke, okay? Hey, come on in and take a look around the inventory. Must be something here our friends in Belfast would appreciate."

The Executioner was posing as a runner for the IRA, and Noonan hadn't blanched at doing business with the

Irish terrorists. If anything, the thought of stirring up
some extra blood and thunder in old Ireland seemed to
make his day.

"Try this one."

He chose a CAR-15 and passed it over with a flourish. Bolan liked the weapon's feel, familiar from the
Asian hellgrounds and some later missions stateside—
and he knew at once that it was empty.

Certainly.

No self-respecting dealer was about to hand a loaded
weapon over to a stranger. Not if he intended to survive.

"You like it?"

"Yes, I do."

Bolan was already gauging distance, angles, proba-
bilities.

"I *knew* you'd like it," Tommy Noonan said, and he
was stepping closer, reaching out to rest a hand on Bolan's shoulder.

The Executioner jammed the carbine's muzzle into
Noonan's solar plexus, hard enough to take his breath
away. The dealer doubled over, retching, dropping to
his hands and knees at Bolan's feet.

The soldier was already moving, wheeling on the
Hispanic as his secondary target recognized the danger
and clawed for his Smith & Wesson in a practiced, fluid
motion. And he would have made it against a lesser
man, but Bolan had anger and determination, speed
and dexterity, on his side.

He whipped the carbine up and over, drove its butt
against the Hispanic's nose, and was rewarded with a
muffled *crack* and double sets of crimson sprinkling the
lab coat. Bolan's target folded instantly, unconscious,

and Bolan plucked the Magnum from its place inside his jeans.

Behind him, Tommy Noonan was recovering slowly, already back to kneeling now.

"I dunno what the fuck you're tryin' to prove," he gasped. "That piece ain't loaded, anyway."

"You're right." He dropped the carbine back among its mates and bent to press the Magnum's muzzle square between the dealer's eyes. "But this one is."

"Some kinda ripoff, right? Okay, you see a piece you like, go on an' take it, on the house."

It didn't work that way, of course, and Bolan knew that any customer emerging from the showroom with a sample in his hand would be cut down by Noonan's lookout in the corridor. He crouched in front of Noonan, wedged the Smith & Wesson underneath his captive's chin and held it there.

"I don't want any of your iron," he growled. "I'm looking for information."

Noonan glowered at him. "Try the yellow pages, sport."

Bolan cocked the Magnum. "Wrong answer," he told the dealer. "One more chance, before I decorate the ceiling with your brains."

"I ain't no stool."

"I'm not the heat. That makes us even."

"Yeah?" The cunning had returned to Noonan's eyes. "So what's the beef?"

"I need to trace some merchandise."

"Oh, sure. I thought you said no heat."

"It's private," Bolan answered. "And that's all you need to know."

"I give up any of my steady customers, I'm dead."

"You're dead already, sport. I'm offering some extra time."

"Well, since you put it that way..." Noonan hesitated. "How about you let me up?"

"I like it this way," Bolan told him. "Makes a shorter drop in case I think you're shitting me."

It registered, and Noonan paled. "Okay. Tell me what you wanna know."

"MAC-10s," Bolan answered.

"Hey, no sweat. I got some beauties at the warehouse."

"Moved any of them lately?"

"Yeah. How many pieces are we talking?"

"Four, at least. There may be more."

"What happened to 'em?"

"They were used aboard a 747, out of Frankfurt."

"Wow, no shit? I heard about that gig." Beneath the cunning and fear, there was an undeniable excitement in the dealer's eyes. It pleased him to be linked in any way with a notorious event.

"I want the buyer's name."

"Hey, what's a name? You gonna tell me yours is really Breslin?"

Bolan slipped the Magnum out from underneath his chin to let it rest against Noonan's temple.

"I guess there's no way you can help me then."

"Not so fast. I didn't say I couldn't help you, man."

"I'm listening."

"The buyer was Canadian. He used the name Vachon. He paid me extra for delivery."

"To where?"

"A warehouse in Toronto."

"I assume you can remember the address."

"It's comin' to me, man. Le's see, it's on the water-front, I think."

Another moment was sufficient for him to recall the number of the pier, the warehouse logo—Viking International—and a description of the man who called himself Vachon.

"That's all I've got, man. Honestly."

His voice was pleading, but the eyes were something else again. They had a crafty gleam, and he was looking over Bolan's shoulder now.

And Bolan heard the telltale scuffle, cursed himself for being so caught up in questioning the dealer that he hadn't double-checked the Hispanic. There was time to glance a blow off Tommy Noonan's temple, time to spin and raise the Magnum, barely time to fire before his adversary sprang.

The weapon bucked and roared, a hollow point impacting on the slender human target just below his breastbone, lifting him completely off his feet. The guy was dead before he fell, rebounding off a table loaded down with submachine guns, sliding to the floor.

Without a moment's hesitation, Bolan shot the dealer at point-blank range. Noonan would be on the phone to tip his customer before the Executioner could book a northbound flight from Kennedy, and he couldn't well afford to have his interest in the stolen Ingrams mouthed around. It was imperative that the arms dealer be silenced.

This left the outside gunner, doubtless acting in response to the explosive gunfire. Bolan straightened and waited for him, the captured Smith & Wesson braced before him in a double-handed target stance.

The door swung inward slowly, confirming that the sentry had a key in case of such emergencies. The guy was being careful, but there are times when careful has its drawbacks, too.

Mack Bolan drew a bead on the partition, slammed a round directly through the flimsy plasterboard, the hollowpoint exploding through a fist-size hole, raining dust.

Again, twelve inches to the left, and if he couldn't hope to nail the gunner blind, it was enough to keep him on the move.

The guy erupted from his shaky cover with a silenced Uzi, seeking target acquisition. Bolan never let him find it, ripping off the Smith & Wesson's final round at twenty feet, explosive impact taking off the gunner's face and spinning him around. His dying reflex milked the Uzi, and a short parabellum burp chopped abstract patterns in the wall.

Bolan dropped the Smith & Wesson, confident that checkered grips and target trigger wouldn't hold his fingerprints. He spent a moment wiping down the CAR-15, intent on leaving nothing of himself behind on this one, certain that police would blame a deal gone sour, once they got a look at Noonan's stash.

The subterfuge would provide him with the breathing room he needed for the operation's second phase. That second phase would take him to Toronto and a meeting with the buyer—who was almost certainly a middleman. Vachon was not the Raven, Bolan would have bet his life on that, but he might have some inkling where the Raven could be found.

And that would launch phase three.

Destruction of the parasitic savage who, with impunity, had killed two men in front of Bolan. Elimination of a cannibal who had been preying on the decent folk for too damned long.

The answers would be waiting for him in Toronto, and the Executioner was anxious to begin.

To even up the score.

He owed it to the passengers aboard Flight 741.

Chapter Twelve

The scorpion detected movement nearby and pivoted, its eight legs rippling in reverse like treads on some diminutive but lethal half-track. Pincers spread, the whip tail arched above its back, sting glistening with venom, it was ready to receive another victim. Vibration in the sandy soil, a blur of movement overhead, too distant for tiny eyes to readily identify. The hunter hesitated, reaching upward with its claws, astounded by the size of its potential prey.

Carl Lyons brought his boot heel down and twisted once, for emphasis.

"I hate those goddamn things," he muttered.

In the darkness Campos smiled. "The scorpion is a predator, like you," he answered, speaking in a whisper.

Lyons grunted. "How about yourself?"

"And me. Of course."

"I don't buy that," the Ironman growled.

"The truth is not for sale. It simply *is*. The scorpion, she feeds on spiders, ticks, *las cucarachas*—any vermin. Is it not the same with you? With us?"

"You've been out in the sun too long."

"Perhaps."

The sun was not a problem now. Six hours had elapsed since it flamed out behind the tall Sierra Madre, dropping darkness like a velvet curtain on Durango's dusty streets. The darkened alleyway between two shops provided Lyons and his backup with a perfect vantage point for staking out their adversary in the night.

The target was an auto-body shop, long closed according to the business hours posted in its window. But a light still burned inside, and over ninety minutes Lyons had observed six men arriving for the sit-down, bearing heavy satchels or arriving empty-handed, some with furtive glances up and down the street, still others with the quiet confidence of power in their stride.

The last man in looked familiar, profile captured by an errant moonbeam and as quickly lost in shadow. There was something...but the Able Team warrior couldn't pin it down. Besides, it was almost time to move.

He risked a glance along the street in each direction, studying the shadows for suspicious shapes or furtive movement. Finally satisfied, he aimed a pencil flashlight at the roof directly opposite and pressed the button twice. An answer flickered back at him, assuring Lyons that Ornelas held the high ground and was ready to assist them when they made their play.

Lyons spent a moment double-checking the Konzak—his customized version of the big Atchisson assault shotgun. Awesome even on the drawing board, the weapon had been modified by armorer Andrzej Konzaki, late of Stony Man Farm. With Andrzej's death in the line of duty, Lyons had surrendered to a momentary flash of sentiment, rechristening the shotgun in a comrade's memory. But that was the extent of sentiment and softness where the Ironman's weapon was concerned.

Equipped to load a drum of twenty 12-gauge rounds, the Konzak was designed to operate in semiautomatic 3-round bursts, or fully automatic mode. On auto, it could empty out that drum in just four seconds, putting some 240 buckshot pellets in the air, each equivalent to a .33-caliber bullet, at a cyclic rate of 3,600 rounds per minute. Lyons had dubbed the piece his "crowd killer."

"You ready?"

Campos nodded, white teeth flashing in the semidarkness. He was balancing a satin-finish, stainless autoloading pistol in his hand.

"No prisoners?"

"Their choice," the blond American replied. "They wanna dance, we brought the band."

At least six men were gathered in the body shop, and Lyons wanted all of them. Alive, if possible; if not...well, he could play it any way the cards were dealt.

He had been working on the solo mission for the better part of two weeks, his Able Team comrades called away on other business. A string of Drug Enforcement Agency informants had been murdered—butchered, really—and the boys in Wonderland were starting to experience some heat. Their own man on the scene, one Manuel Arroyo, had allowed himself to be identified somehow, and he was number seven in the chain of grisly homicides. And the word had come down from Justice, channeled via Hal Brognola's office.

Those responsible would have to pay.

The Able Team warrior's backup men were one-time *federales*, still pursuing predators in Mexico but with a different source of income, different contacts, different channels for receiving their assignments. They had welcomed Lyons grudgingly, a gringo come to reinvent the wheel and teach them how to do their jobs. But slowly a mutual respect had grown between them.

There had been three of them, at first. Ornelas, Campos and a smiling would-be ladies' man named Estevez. He wasn't smiling when Lyons saw him last. In fact, he didn't have a face. The fragmentation bomb wired underneath the dashboard of his vintage Mustang saw to that.

"Let's move," Lyons growled.

A final glance along the street revealed no snipers in the shadows, and he broke from cover, running in a crouch, the Konzak ready to answer any challenge from the enemy. Behind him, Campos kept up easily, his navy peasant shirt and Levi's blending with the velvet night. They sheltered up against the north wall of the body shop, alert to any signal that would indicate they had been seen. Another moment, counting down the heartbeats, waiting while Ornelas had a chance to leap from one roof to another, carrying an Uzi submachine gun strapped across his chest. He should be in place now, crouched beside the skylight, covering the action in the lighted room below.

"They'll break in the direction of the alley," Lyons said unnecessarily.

The *federale* had anticipated him.

"You take the rear," he whispered, reaching out to tap the shotgun's elevated muzzle with an index finger. "This should stop the rabbits, if they try to run."

The Ironman checked his Rolex. "Give me two."

"You have it."

Lyons pounded back along the alley and found the loading dock behind the body shop. He tried the back door. Locked. He pressed his face against the gritty window set into the panel. Filtered light from the far end of a narrow corridor reflected off stained linoleum and ancient, fading paint. He settled back to wait.

One minute.

Lyons drew a breath and held it, listened to the pulse as it began to hammer in his ears. A grim anticipation was already churning in his stomach, and he recognized the old excitement mounting, knew that it could kill him if he let it take control.

The Ironman was a warrior in his heart and in his soul. He thrived on combat, action—not for killing's sake, although the life-and-death encounters were a part of it. He fought, and put himself in danger's way, because the action made him feel alive, and that was all that you could ask for out of life. The other motivations—nailing down the savages and getting even for a good man's death, eliminating a substantial portion of the narco pipeline feeding poison to the north—were merely icing on the cake.

And Lyons was prepared to cut himself a slice.

Right now.

A flying boot heel snapped the lock and he was suddenly inside, already pacing off the corridor, his shotgun up and probing out ahead of him. He heard a distant crash and a shouted warning—Campos crashing in the front—before a thunderclap of gunfire overrode the other sounds and set his eardrums ringing in the narrow hallway.

Lyons recognized the *federale's* .45, another answering, and furniture was toppling, a hoarse voice cursing as a medley of handguns joined the tune. Two long strides along the corridor, and now Ornelas brought his Uzi into play, the skylight shattering with a sound like all the windows in the world collapsing simultaneously.

A strangled scream, the gunfire hit a thunderous crescendo, and as suddenly it died away. Two silhouettes exploded into view, and as he hit a combat crouch, Lyons glimpsed revolvers in their hands, already rising.

The custom Atchisson was set for 3-round bursts, and Lyons stroked the trigger once, dispatching thirty-six projectiles at a range of twenty feet. The buckshot did not have time to spread beyond a foot or so before it riddled flesh and fabric, blowing rag-doll men away and pinning them against the greasy, blood-streaked wall.

He passed them as they slithered to the floor, intent on finding out what had happened in the shop. He hesitated for a moment, then cleared the final doorway in a rush. The shotgun in his hands swept up and out, and he was prepared for anything except what met his eyes.

A single man was standing in the middle of the room, an automatic pistol in his hand, and in the fractured second left before he made the choice to live or die, Carl Lyons saw the rest of it.

A body crumpled near the doorway, leaking from a single bullet hole between the shoulder blades.

Two others were huddled underneath a bullet-riddled conference table, pistols clutched in lifeless hands.

Ornelas lay stretched out on the table, broken by his tumble through the skylight, rugged face a mask of blood where glass and bullets had obliterated classic features.

By the door Campos was still breathing, but with only microseconds left, his punctured lungs already filling up with blood. One hand was clutched to his chest; the other held his .45, the slide locked open on a firing chamber that was empty, like his eyes.

The sole survivor turned to face his adversary, pistol tracking in a classic dueling stance. The familiar eyes were boring into Lyons, almost mesmerizing him before adrenaline and combat instinct broke the lethal spell.

He stroked a 3-round burst out of the Konzak, watched the straw man ripple, spin, disintegrate. He took it all, stone dead before he hit the concrete floor.

Lyons crouched beside the ventilated body, turned it over, spent a moment studying the waxen face. A stray had drilled his jaw, but there was plenty left for Lyons to identify.

And he *had* seen that face before. Somewhere.

The Ironman racked his brain, aware that he was running out of time. The firefight would attract police, and he was not inclined to wait around and answer any questions at the moment. Not with two dead *federales* in the game.

But before he split, he had to jog his memory. Complete the link.

The face was Hispanic, possibly a Caribbean type, and he had seen it. But where? On television? On a Wanted poster?

And suddenly he had it. He *knew* that face, goddamn it. There was no mistake.

The man was "The Raven," sought by Interpol and the police of half a dozen nations on assorted terrorism charges spanning several years. The photos that Lyons called to mind were fuzzy, mostly distance shots and hazy profiles, but the Ironman had devoted time enough to learning certain faces and names that he was confident of his ID.

But he would still need proof. Without a doubt his statement would not be believed somewhere down the line. The Raven had been reported dead too many times for anyone to buy another death without some evidence.

He slipped the boot knife from its sheath and weighed it in his hand, selecting the serrated edge. He clipped the Raven's index and middle fingers off at the second knuckle, then wrapped them in a handkerchief and stowed them in a pocket of his tunic. Prints would finally identify the bastard, and an army of determined agents from a dozen nations could at last devote themselves to stalking other cannibals.

Provided that the prints proved out.

No further time to argue with himself. The locals would be on their way by now, and Lyons heard the doomsday numbers running in his head. He would have liked to take Campos and Ornelas with him, but it was beyond his present capability. Durango's finest would take care of all the paperwork, notify the next of kin. At the moment Lyons ranked survival as his top priority, and that included breaking clean, without his own name getting tangled up in what had happened here tonight.

But there was more.

For openers, he had to figure out precisely what a terrorist like the Raven had in common with a crop of middle-rank Durango pushers. Something didn't fit, and it was nagging at him now, compelling him to seek the answers, dig until he knew the truth.

For Campos and Ornelas, sure.

But also for the Ironman.

"There, I've got him."

Yakov Katzenelenbogen took a step back from the window, making room for his companion to observe their target as he crossed the narrow street and disappeared inside the hotel opposite.

"You're sure?"

"There's no mistake."

"All right," replied David McCarter. "We wait."

Their corner room was situated on the second floor of the distinctive Alpenrose, a village inn selected for its commanding view of Obermarkt, the main commercial artery of Mittenwald. Directly opposite, across the one-way street now teeming with pedestrians, the object of their scrutiny was the larger Post Hotel, and those who hid themselves inside.

The village was an alpine classic, strategically straddling a crucial pass in the Karwendel range. It drew the crowds year-round, located as it was within an easy hike of Austria, an hour's drive due south of Munich. Formerly a center of the violin-maker's art, the town still clung to its medieval flavor, buildings decorated with exotic frescoes, furnished with antiques.

The two Phoenix Force members had little time to savor all the sights of Mittenwald. Once contact had been made, survival and their mission would demand

110 percent of their attention. Lives were hanging in the balance, certainly. . . and still, the body had its needs.

The French Israeli edged around McCarter, checked the minibar for snacks, found none and closed it with his steel prosthetic hand.

"I'm hungry," he declared.

His partner thought about it for a moment. "La Toscana?"

"Now you're talking."

Glancing back across the street in the direction of the Post Hotel, McCarter frowned.

"I guess we've got the time," he said.

"They won't be going anywhere," Katz seconded. "They're here to do a job, and that's tomorrow. We've got all night."

They double-checked the L-shaped room and locked it up, McCarter taking time to pluck a hair from Katz's head, ignoring the Israeli's growl and wedging it between the door and jamb, above the lock.

"James Bond?"

"I taught the bugger everything he knows."

Downstairs, they joined the press of Sunday tourists jostling along the sidewalks, passing jewelry shops, confectioners, a bakery and boutiques, the sporting shops with windows full of climbing gear and switch-blade knives.

The bank.

Closed on Sunday, it would be reopening next morning, the employees unaware that they were targeted for terror.

In the Post Hotel, a tiny group of men and women were preparing for a rather sizable withdrawal from the bank of Mittenwald, unhindered by the fact that none of them were currently depositors. Their banking methods were unorthodox and often bloody. In the past twelve months they had already "liberated" cash from seven German banks—and they had murdered fifteen people in the process.

Of the five who had been publicly identified, three men and one woman had a record of connections with assorted Baader-Meinhof cells in Munich, Frankfurt, Düsseldorf. The rest, another three or four at most, would likely show the same affiliations once they had been caged or stretched out on a slab to be identified. They called themselves the Wolf Pack, but Washington and Bonn were laying money on a strong, continuing connection with the Baader-Meinhof Gang and, through it, the KGB.

They needed stopping now, before they spilled more blood and wasted any other lives. Their own were forfeit, and the Phoenix warriors were prepared to take them any way at all, with personal survival as the top priority.

It could get hectic, Katz knew, and as they passed the bank he wished the other members of the team had been available to help them wrap it up. But they were busy staking out a syndicate of Corsicans, whose high-grade heroin had started turning up in children's veins around New York, Chicago and points west. The other Phoenix warriors' lives were on the line and they were in for the duration. The Wolf Pack was reserved for Katzenelenbogen and McCarter.

They deliberately had shunned involvement with the local law, preferring anonymity and the powerful advantage of surprise, so they had no reason to suspect a leak in Mittenwald. A single misplaced word, they knew, could blow the operation now, and they had mutually agreed to pass the risk.

No side streets interrupted Obermarkt in central Mittenwald, but La Toscana was roughly two blocks from their lodgings at the Alpenrose. They cut into a cobbled alleyway and caught the narrow, dimly lighted stairs, following their noses and a waft of heavenly aromas to the second floor.

A smiling waiter showed them to their window seats. Outside, the daily drizzle had started, but it failed to scatter hearty tourists.

Inside the eatery, McCarter ordered pizza, and the stocky Israeli opted for an order of giant prawns that La Toscana grilled to sizzling perfection. Strangely absent from the guidebooks, it was easily the finest restaurant in Mittenwald—perhaps in southern Germany—and Katz was almost sorry that their tour of duty would be winding down tomorrow.

Almost.

But he was not a tourist in Mittenwald. He hadn't been dispatched to browse through shops or hike the sixty miles of mountain paths that ringed the village. He was on a lethal mission, in and out, with savage violence almost guaranteed. The moment he forgot his business there, began to think like any other traveler, he was as good as dead.

The waiter brought their meal, and Katz was halfway through his prawns when movement in the doorway caught his eye. The early-evening crowd was light so far, and his attention was immediately captured by the couple who had just arrived.

He recognized them both.

The woman had bleached her hair, but Katz would have known her anywhere. Her name was Eva Zelner, and since dropping out of college in her junior year, she had become a driving force within the Wolf Pack. Katz hadn't seen her yet in Mittenwald, but he had known she would be there before the action broke…and so she was.

It was the lady's slim companion, though, who almost made the French Israeli drop his fork. Katz did a double-take, then realized he was staring, bent to choose another prawn. He nudged McCarter's foot beneath the table, nodding casually in the direction of the new arrivals as they were escorted to their seats.

McCarter's startled look told Katz all he had to know. He hadn't been mistaken. But what precisely did it mean?

While they had never met, the woman's escort was an old, familiar enemy. His grainy likeness, always slightly out of focus, had been taunting Katz from assorted television screens and posters now for years. He had believed that they would never meet—but now, no more than twenty feet away, he was confronted by the Raven.

It was mad, of course—the world's most wanted terrorist, about to take a quiet meal at La Toscana. Based upon the latest rumors he should probably have been in Libya or Algeria, recuperating from the show at Beirut airport. Prior to his surprise appearance on Flight 741, he had been variously placed in Moscow or East Germany, in Cuba, Nicaragua and a quiet grave outside San Salvador. Katz had preferred the latter, but the recent hijack had removed all doubts about the Raven's durability.

And here he was.

Dark hair and eyes of flint, the face that could have passed for Hispanic, Indian or even Palestinian—but there was no mistake. Katz would have known him anywhere.

"This changes things," McCarter told him softly, smiling for the benefit of any casual observers, keeping busy with his pizza as he spoke.

"It changes nothing," Katz replied. "We have a job to do."

"If he's involved, there must be more at stake. He wouldn't risk another outing just for cash. He's not had time to spend a fraction of the hijack ransom."

Katz thought about it, knew the Englishman was right, but he was adamant.

"We go ahead. What's one gun, more or less?"

"He doesn't travel light," the former SAS commando quietly reminded him. "Let's just suppose he's traveling with friends."

"I'd love to meet them," Katz replied.

McCarter thought about it briefly, and he grinned.

"Me too."

THE SHOPS OF MITTENWALD are closed by 6:00 P.M., with only scattered theaters and restaurants remaining to entice the local residents and tourists. Sundown drives the visitors away and brings the locals out, their young collecting at the ice cream parlor or the grill a short block farther on, some revving motorbikes to get attention from the girls, while others try to deal from silent strength, adopting cocky poses at the curb. Once paired and fed, they may adjourn to find a cinema or beer hall, to while away the evening hours.

Sequestered at the Alpenrose, the Phoenix warriors waited while darkness slowly swept the streets. Where milling hundreds had congested Obermarkt by daylight, scarcely half a dozen souls were visible by ten o'clock. Across the narrow street, the Post Hotel was brightly lit inside, the dining room and tavern serving to capacity.

Katz and McCarter figured they could afford to wait another hour. It would provide their targets time to finish dining, scouting out the streets, preparing for tomorrow. When they had regrouped inside the suite that Katz had laid out thirty marks to finally identify, they would be sitting ducks.

Except that now there was a vulture among them.

A Raven.

His presence bothered Katz, but tight surveillance had revealed that he was traveling alone. But from the way he had looked at Eva Zelner as they dined in La Toscana, sitting close beside her at the table, reaching down to stroke her thigh when he believed that they were unobserved, the terrorist would not be bedding down alone tonight.

But Katz was not concerned about the bastard's love life. If everything ran true, they would be tucking in the Raven personally—and permanently.

Their meager luggage was already packed and stowed inside the rented BMW, primed and ready in the Alpenrose garage. The single flight bag left would be sufficient for a pair of Ingram MAC-10 submachine guns, extra magazines and half a dozen frag grenades the Phoenix warriors hoped they wouldn't have to use inside the Post Hotel.

But now the Raven's presence had upset the whole equation. They were dealing with an unknown quantity, and still prohibited from making drastic alterations to the plan. Each added hostile gun increased the odds against success, but there was no alternative. They would be forced to go ahead on schedule.

Katz killed some time double-checking the Ingrams, while his companion watched the street and Post Hotel, alert to any sign that members of the Wolf Pack might be leaving prematurely. Beneath them on the street, pedestrians had all but disappeared.

A raucous dinner party exited the Post Hotel, dispersing to their cars with laughter and catcalls. McCarter chuckled, shook his head, eyes fastened on the doorway opposite until they were gone.

"It's time," he said. Katz noticed that he hadn't checked his watch.

"All right."

He stowed the Ingrams, making certain they were cocked and loaded, with the safeties on. There was no room inside the bag for silencers. Once they had let their adversaries see the guns, there would be no more time for stealth in any case.

Downstairs, the two men passed the night clerk, and she gave them her workaday smile, which vanished as they crossed the street.

The lobby of the Post Hotel was sparsely furnished, basic in its architecture, with the ornate decorations saved for restaurant and tavern walls. Another night clerk eyed them briefly, seemed about to ask if he could help, and then thought better of it when they brushed on past his cubbyhole. They continued past the tavern and the restaurant toward the stairs.

The target suite was three flights up and to the rear. The corridors were kept in semidarkness, ceiling fixtures weak and far apart as if the ancient wiring could not easily accommodate more wattage. That was fine with Katz; it would reduce the possibility of accidental witnesses describing them to the authorities when constables arrived. Assuming, of course, that he and

McCarter were not stretched out among the other casualties.

He shrugged the morbid thought away and halted in the middle of the corridor, still twenty feet from target. There was light beneath the door, soft music audible from just inside.

Katz knelt to open up the zipper bag, dispensing hardware, ammunition, grenades. McCarter filled his pockets, slipped the safety off his Ingram, and the French Israeli followed suit. They left the flight bag and stalked across the final twenty feet in perfect step, and Katzenelenbogen hit the door latch with a vicious kick that snapped the mechanism, slammed the door right back against the inside wall.

Their entry was explosive, and it took the members of the Wolf Pack by surprise. Katz saw young faces weathered by a life in hiding, by the magnitude of crimes committed, others still in store. There were two women and seven men collected in a ring around the coffee table, on which a service station map of Mittenwald had been spread out to help them plot their getaway.

Eva Zelner was the first to move, recoiling back along the sofa, stretching for a pistol that protruded from her handbag, slung across a straight-backed chair. Katz tracked her with his Ingram, squeezing off, and watched the clinging tank top ripple, spouting crimson geysers as she died.

The suite erupted into chaos, members of the Wolf Pack scrambling for weapons or exits, reaching neither as the Phoenix warriors swept them with a lethal cross fire. Katz had time to register that none of them appeared to be the Raven, then his combat instincts took control and he was fighting for his life.

Two members of the Pack, both male, were breaking for the bedroom, one already digging out a pistol from his waistband when McCarter caught them with a knee-high burst. The former SAS commando was reloading, crouched behind an armchair, when the second woman found her weapon and the range. Two bullets burrowed into the stuffing of the chair mere inches from McCarter's face, before the big Israeli stitched her up and down, forever silencing the anger in her eyes.

His own clip empty now, Katz discarded it, already snapping in a fresh one when the last surviving Wolf Pack member tried for freedom. He surged up from behind the couch and dodged toward the bedroom sanctuary, sprinting for his life. Twin Ingrams hammered out the final punctuation to his run, and he was wallowing along the floor in blood and fluid before he knew that he was dead.

Katz did a rapid scan of leaking bodies around the room, and verified that none of them had been the Raven. There were two alternatives: the bastard was in hiding somewhere in the suite, or they had missed him in the intervening hours before their strike.

A sound of furtive movement came from the bedroom, followed by the crash of breaking glass. The warriors moved instinctively, hesitating only slightly at the darkened doorway, finally going through it high and low, their weapons searching for another target in the murk.

Too late.

Katz reached the window, swept the drapes away and craned outside, but in vain. The bedroom window, unused to opening upon the fire escape, had resisted the Raven, and he had finally smashed it out—perhaps had dived directly through the pane. A flitting shadow in the alleyway below dropped from the wrought-iron fire escape and was gone before Katz had a chance to aim and fire.

"We missed him."

"Bloody hell."

And there was no more time to count the loss. Not here, not now. Already frightened voices could be heard along the hallway from the buildings opposite, responding to the gunfire in the night. Already someone would be dialing the police.

No time at all.

But Katz would think about it later. And he would wonder what in hell the Raven had to do with killer kids still wet behind the ears. He might still have a chance to answer that one.

It meant that much.

For the moment, it meant everything.

"But are you sure?"

"Of course, I'm sure." Carl Lyons shifted in his seat, his blue eyes never leaving Hal Brognola's face. "You think I made this up?"

"Hell no," the man from Justice replied, "but you can see what kind of spot it puts us in."

"We're not in any spot at all," the former LAPD sergeant snapped. He jabbed a finger down the conference table, toward McCarter and the burly French Israeli. "I dropped my man; theirs got away. If there was a mistake, they made it."

David McCarter faced him squarely, spoke a single syllable.

"Balls."

Beside him, Yakov Katzenelenbogen pushed a sheet of paper toward the center of the table. Lyons recognized it instantly, a likeness generated by an artist and Ident-i-Kit.

Brognola took the sketch and placed it next to one prepared by Lyons earlier. The two were not identical but they were close enough. The differences could be written off to memory—a few more age lines around the eyes; a bit more hair; a slightly wider nose—but both could certainly depict one man.

The Raven.

He passed the sketches on to Lyons, but he waved them off. "I've seen it, and it doesn't prove a thing."

McCarter's voice was stiff. "We weren't hallucinating, Carl. We both observed the subject at close range. There's no mistake."

"A look-alike. Coincidence."

"That's bloody nonsense."

"I brought evidence, goddammit! All you've got is some guy sitting in a restaurant."

Brognola cleared his throat. "Unfortunately, Carl, the prints don't prove a thing. In fact, we couldn't lift a print."

"Say *what*? I had those fingers bagged and tagged, right down the line. Don't tell me that they couldn't lift the prints."

"No prints to lift," Brognola answered softly. "They were clean."

"What do you mean, clean? What kind of crap is this?"

"The prints had been surgically removed."

"So what? Go down another layer and try the corium, for Christ's sake. What's the matter with your people in the lab? You can't just wipe out fingerprints."

"Whoever did this took the time to do it right. Deep grafting, reconstructive surgery...the whole nine yards."

"Okay, so there's your evidence! Who else is gonna take that kind of time and trouble to erase his mark? It has to be the Raven."

"No. In fact, it isn't."

"What?"

"We have a jacket on the Raven two feet thick. You know that, Carl. Wherever he's been sighted in the past five years, however tenuous. Whenever he gets mentioned in connection with an incident, no matter if we know he wasn't there. We file it all, and most of it is bullshit, granted—but we know a lot about the man himself. His childhood, education, psychiatric profiles...name it. We could write a test about the bastard that his mother couldn't pass."

"So what's the point?"

"When he was six years old—six years and seven months to be precise—the Raven had an accident. He broke the first and second fingers of his right hand... here."

Brognola raised his own right hand and used the index finger of his left to indicate a point between the first and second joints.

"Well, shit." And Lyons knew the punch line now. "The fingers that I clipped—"

"Were never broken," Hal agreed, dejection in his voice. "Whoever you took out—"

"Was not the Raven," Lyons growled. "Goddammit!"

"A look-alike," McCarter goaded him. "Coincidence, old son."

"I wouldn't go that far," Brognola said.

The Able Team warrior shot a glance across the table. Katz and McCarter looked at each other, frowning, then turned their eyes back toward the man from Wonderland.

"Afraid you've lost me there," McCarter said.

"We think your buddy in Durango *was* the Raven—or, to be precise, *a* Raven."

"What the hell?"

"I know enough to trust my senses," Katzenelenbogen said. "We recognized the Raven and his playmates in Mittenwald. I know his face, and there was no mistake.''

''We don't believe there was,'' the big fed said.

''Well, bloody hell.''

''A double?'' Lyons asked.

Brognola spread his hands. ''Why not? It worked for Hitler, Churchill, Castro—and we still hear rumors on a certain president. It wouldn't be the first time that a famous face decided to diversify.''

''And I took out the ringer in Durango?''

''If we're right, it looks that way.''

''Well, shit.''

''Don't sweat it. If you hadn't dropped him, half our people would be chasing shadows now.''

The French Israeli agent couldn't quite suppress a smile. ''So Mittenwald was number one.''

Brognola shrugged. ''Assuming there are only two.''

Katz stiffened. ''What are you suggesting, Hal?''

Brognola spent a moment looking at the unlit cigar in his hand, rolling it between his thumb and index finger.

''We've been curious about the little shit's mobility, you know that, Katz. A double-header in Beirut on Monday, bombs in Paris on a Wednesday, Nicaragua by the weekend. Granted, he could cover it by air, but we've been watching for the bastard like he has the fucking plague. There was a lapse while he was out of sight and semi-out of mind—but since Flight 741, I'll bet my pension that he's grounded somewhere in the Middle East, afraid to show his face.''

''He showed it in Durango yesterday,'' Lyons said.

''That wasn't any hologram we saw in Mittenwald,'' McCarter seconded.

"Which proves my point. Mobility has always been his strength, his trademark. Take away his combat stretch, and he's a sitting duck."

Katz scowled. "You think we saw a double, too?"

"A triple, maybe. Who's to say? We tipped GSG-9, and they had people down in Mittenwald by lunchtime. Found the guy's room, in fact. He called himself Kurt Mueller on the register."

"And?"

"And nothing, gentlemen. The room was clean. No traces of saliva, semen, nothing. And no fingerprints."

"Okay. He wiped it down."

"Or else he had no prints to leave," Lyons offered.

"I'll grant you that we're speculating, Carl, but at the moment this is all we've got."

"Not quite." The former LAPD sergeant's eyes were flashing now. "We know those bastards in Durango had a tight connection stateside, handling their distribution."

"Gerry Axelrod." Brognola nodded curtly.

"'Kay. So yank the DEA men off his case and let me have a crack. I'll shake the scumbag till he rattles when he walks."

"We're way ahead of you on that. He's in Toronto. Caught the red-eye from Atlanta late last night."

"Assessment?"

"Justice doesn't think he's running. There's a possibility he knows about Durango, but we're betting that he's on another deal."

"I'll check it out."

Brognola swiveled in his chair to face the men of Phoenix Force. "What's happening at Steyr?"

Katz frowned. "We're getting close. Your information was correct about the leak. They're losing pistols, submachine guns, but no one wants to talk about it."

"That's confirmed," Brognola said. "Their SMGs are turning up in Baader-Meinhof hands, among the Red Brigades...we've even got a rumble on a shipment to the IRA. Your business from the Wolf Pack had a couple in their closet stash."

McCarter grinned. "They never got that far."

"We need to get a man inside," Brognola said.

"I'm working on it," Katz replied. "I've got a friend in personnel."

"Yeah? What's she look like?" Lyons cracked.

And he could almost swear the French Israeli blushed, beneath his weathered tan.

"She has the necessary assets."

Hal Brognola didn't join the laughter.

"I'd be happier if we could bring the others in," he said at last.

"Don't worry, Hal. A simple in-and-out."

"It's never just a simple in-and-out. You watch yourself."

"I always do."

"The man's a flamin' egomaniac," McCarter offered, smiling.

Brognola laughed this time, but he appeared distracted all the same.

"I want this Raven," he declared, when they were silent once again. "And if there's more than one, I want them all."

"Why now?" Carl Lyons asked. "I mean, the special effort. He's been running free for what—eight years?"

"It's more like nine. And that's about nine years too long."

"This Beirut business hit you hard."

Brognola shook his head. "Not really. Not the way you mean it, anyway. The bastard's done a lot worse things before."

He thought about the OPEC snatch, the Paris bombings, other skyjacks and assassinations where the Raven had been positively linked to more than fifty deaths. Except it wasn't positively anymore. And still, the carnage wasn't all of it.

"I've got a roster of the passengers on 741," he said. "They've been debriefed in Frankfurt by the CIA and processed stateside. All except for one."

"Let's have the other shoe," Carl Lyons said, suspicion in his voice.

"We've got a missing passenger," Brognola told them. "He was flying coach, and there are verified reports that he was beaten by the terrorists. It seems one of the gunners tried to rape a stewardess, and Mr. Blanski intervened."

Carl Lyons caught it first. "Did you say Blanski?"

"First name Michael."

"Jesus Christ."

Now Katzenelenbogen saw the link. "How can this be?"

Brognola shrugged again. "We never thought about it, really, but he has to travel somehow...just like everybody else."

"His port of embarkation?"

"Munich. And we've checked. A pair of Baader-Meinhof heavies bit the big one there two days before his flight was hijacked."

"Hell, we were right next door."

McCarter hadn't made the name, and he was getting angry at the double-talk.

"Will someone kindly tell me what the hell is going on?"

"It's Bolan," Katz informed his partner. "He was on Flight 741."

"My God."

"You called it."

"He'll be looking for the Raven."

"We believe so," Hal responded to the room at large.

"He'll find the bastard, too."

"But will he? And assuming that he does, which Raven will he find? How many Ravens will he find?"

"How many of the bastards are there?" Lyons asked.

"If I'm right about our Raven from the airline being grounded, then we're looking at a minimum of three."

"And if there's three—"

"There might be four."

"Or five."

"Goddamnit, there could be five hundred."

"No." Brognola shook his head. "Beyond a half a dozen, give or take, you're looking at diminishing returns. I don't believe we've got an army on our hands."

"Well, that's a great relief, at any rate," McCarter said sarcastically.

"Mack will take the bastard," Lyons said, with less conviction than he would have liked.

"I hope so."

"What, you think he can't?"

"I think he might be walking into something that he doesn't understand," Brognola answered from the heart. "He's looking for *the* Raven, not a flock."

"So, maybe we can even up the odds," the Ironman said.

"It's not our job," Hal Brognola returned.

"The hell you say."

"You've got your orders, Carl. Stick to them."

"Sure, no sweat. But let's suppose I get a chance to do some Raven hunting while I'm at it. Hell, I couldn't let a chance like that slip by."

"Agreed. But make damn sure your mission isn't compromised."

"Who, me?"

Brognola shook his head in weary resignation, knowing that he wasn't really in control. Not now. The leash had somehow slipped at mention of the Executioner, but Hal was not dismayed. The Able warrior and the men of Phoenix Force would do their jobs. They always did.

He only hoped this job would not be their last.

He had not always been the Raven. During childhood he was simply Julio—or Ilich to his father, who preferred the middle name with all its revolutionary overtones—and he had played as children will, around the family's neighborhood in a Caracas suburb.

There was little in those days to set the boy apart from other kids, although in retrospect his classmates would lay claim to recollections of a brutal nature, evidence of violence hidden somewhere just behind the smiling, boyish face. They would remember incidents, however trivial or ancient, that when taken altogether seemed to sketch the portrait of a rather different little boy.

There were schoolyard fights that Julio invariably lost but never backed away from. Teachers had to break up the scuffles because the younger, smaller boy would keep on coming at his enemy, regardless of the beating he had taken, heedless of his injuries.

The string of petty thefts at school, around the neighborhood, in which he was suspected—but never proved guilty—of cooperating with a local street gang, acting as their finger man.

The kittens, doused in kerosene, that streaked like comets through the streets at dusk, while Julio would laugh and laugh.

It was impossible at this late date, to sort out truth from fiction, fact from fantasy in these childhood reminiscences. And did it really matter, after all?

Julio Ilich Ramirez was born in 1949, a year before Korea threatened reenactment of the recent global war. His father was a well-to-do physician in Caracas; his mother served her husband as his nurse until she started bearing sons, of whom Julio was the first. Despite his wealth, inherited and earned, Esteban Ramirez was an armchair revolutionary and a closet communist. With a passion for Russian history, his one regret in life was being born a Venezuelan.

Fate had robbed him of his chance to march with Lenin and the Bolsheviks, to face the Cossack charge and rout the brutal Hun at Stalingrad. Afflicted with the curse of affluence, he could do little more than worship from afar and teach his sons a proper reverence for Soviet ideals. As the children arrived at two-year intervals, he named them Ilich, Vladimir and Lenin—each in honor of the hero who would rest forever in Moscow's Red Square.

Perhaps because he was the oldest and the first to hear his father's message in those days before it had grown trite, young Julio would prove to be the only revolutionary son his parents ever raised. And even here, his ardor would be tempered by a certain pragmatism, colored by a darker ''something else'' that lay thinly veiled beneath the surface of his soul. It was entirely possible that by his teens, Julio had already weighed the usefulness of communist philosophy, the chic expediency of branding aberrant behavior as a revolutionary act.

Julio was a fair but undistinguished student in his native schools, and during 1966 his father had decided that the boy would benefit from a proximity to European culture. He was flown to London in the spring, and spent the next three years in various academies, collecting mediocre grades and earning quite a reputation as a ladies' man. He seemed perfectly at home among the mods and rockers, more in tune with Lennon and McCartney than with Lenin and Marx, cultivating a taste for blondes and low-slung sports cars.

But Julio did not ignore the call of revolution absolutely. In addition to the Beatles and the Stones, the flower generation and a trend toward chemical escape from everyday affairs, the late sixties were renowned for youthful protest. Civil rights. The war in Vietnam. Free speech on campus and "police brutality." The rights of women, homosexuals, transsexuals, asexuals. The downfall of imperialism—invariably translated as U.S. imperialism by the strident voices of the New Left.

Ramirez dabbled in the London revolutionary scene, uncertain of himself at first, but gaining confidence as time went by. If angry blacks rejected his assistance in their demonstrations, there were enough angry whites to go around.

Julio was pleased to find that revolutionary women shared their favors freely among the soldiers of the cause. The combination of his Hispanic heritage and Marxist name assured Ramirez of a willing partner any time the activists convened to hatch their plots.

A sexual experience with Julio not only met minority requirements, but exposed his partner to a certain thrilling risk, as well. Increasingly, the rumors spread that Ilich liked to punch his girls around—and still they came, attracted by the danger that was missing from their flaccid demonstrations in the streets.

Julio and his cronies of "the revolution" spent their idle hours picketing embassies or military bases, chanting simple-minded slogans while police stood by impassively, the bobbies stifling a yawn or two when TV cameras were diverted toward the crowd. As idle weeks turned into lazy months, the crowd began to disappear, and with it went the cameras. The revolution was in desperate need of something to draw attention from the media, and during 1968 Ramirez hit upon the perfect scheme.

Abortive bids for independence by the Czechs had lately brought about a Soviet invasion to crush the strident voices and restore a puppet government at gunpoint. Julio suggested to his comrades that it might be "interesting"—and worth some airtime on the BBC— to stage a protest at the local Russian embassy. If nothing else, the move would set their tiny group apart from all the others that were battling for headline space. Aside from aging Jews, no other group had picketed the Soviets for many years.

On May Day, Julio led his tiny troop of activists to face the Russian bear. Their ranks were supplemented by assorted Zionists, religionists, a scattering of old White Russian exiles come to thumb their noses at the grandsons of the Bolsheviks. The Metropolitan police were almost friendly for a change, surprised and pleased to see the Soviets receiving some of what they were notorious for dishing out.

That is, until the incident.

It had begun with chanting, the obligatory signs and clapping hands, the human chain obstructing sidewalks, spilling over into traffic lanes while officers endeavored to restrain the demonstrators. Embassy officials kept their blinds drawn, counting on the grim-faced guards outside to keep them safe from any harm…but the Soviet diplomats could not contain their surprise. A demonstration aimed at Mother Russia was incredible.

But it was happening, and Julio was in his glory, heading up a protest demonstration for the first—and *only*—time. He postured for the cameras and shared his words of wisdom with assorted housewives who had taken breaks from domestic chores to watch the telly for a while. And he might have pulled it off without a hitch, except for trouble from the Zionists.

The Jews had many grievances with the Soviets, and they had come prepared to raise some hell. Julio spotted the Semitic types in army-surplus coats, producing little jars of ink and paint from bulging pockets, and he realized that he was on the verge of losing it. Control. The public eye. Attention. Another man might easily have shrugged it off, but surrender of the spotlight to another rankled Julio.

In a flash, he shouldered through the crowd, snatched paint grenades away from an astonished Zionist and hurled them toward the embassy. The paint was crimson—for the blood of Czechs and Jews—and TV cameras captured Ilich beaming as the bloody streamers etched their random pattern on the embassy's facade.

He was arrested, and the word was relayed to his school. He was sent down, amused as much as wounded by the euphemism for expulsion.

In London, Julio found another school—though not without some difficulty—and resumed his studies. In order of importance, he set out to study women, wine and the philosophy of revolution. He rarely attended scheduled classes, opting instead to immerse himself in Castro, Che Guevara, Trotsky, Chairman Mao. He came to see that certain people—the Czechs, for instance—needed guidance from a stronger, more intelligent authority until they had the strength to rule themselves.

And when he next stopped by the Russian embassy, he went with hat in hand, a letter of abject apology appended to his application for a visa that would let him study in the motherland of revolution.

He was finally accepted in 1969 at Moscow's Patrice Lumumba University. The KGB was well aware of Julio's potential now, their psychological evaluations filed away for future reference. His studies were a motley bag of literature, philosophy and Russian "history," but he was being groomed for bigger, better things. Negotiations had commenced on his arrival in the Russian capital, and he was eager—even anxious—to oblige the KGB. They offered him adventure of a sort, potential profit, international publicity in time—and Julio could not refuse.

In April 1970 an incident was engineered, resulting in his ouster from Patrice Lumumba University. Allegedly, he had seduced the daughters of distinguished citizens—including some professors at the university—and there was reason to suspect his revolutionary zeal. Upon his disappearance from the campus, classmates naturally assumed that he was bound for Caracas, but their guess was off by several thousand miles. In fact, Julio Ramirez had been cleared through KGB for immediate enrollment at a different sort of school in Jordan, where instructors from the PLO were busy cranking out a graduating class of future terrorists.

And Julio was a natural. He loved the weapons and explosives, the instructions in surveillance, the work with codes and ciphers. Overweight upon arrival, Julio had slimmed down quickly in the desert heat, existing on the Spartan diet of the *fedayeen* and doing daily calisthenics, running obstacles and slithering beneath barbed wire with live rounds snapping overhead. He loved it all, and after graduation he anticipated striking hard and often at the bulwarks of the West... but it was not to be. Not yet.

A terrorist of quality must have a cover, and the Soviets had plans for Julio Ramirez that did not include a string of futile, suicidal firefights. In the fall of 1970 he surfaced once again in London, making contact with his friends from school and offering his services as tutor in Spanish. The position, unofficial as it was, provided Ilich with a documented source of income and a measure of respectability—although the latter would be tarnished by his exploits in the bedroom. Julio accepted only female "students," switching off between a list of nubile youngsters who appreciated his panache, and several older women who could well afford his services. Regardless of their age, Ramirez spoke their language fluently. In fact, his playboy reputation pleased the KGB no end. It was a facet of his cover—primo Western decadence—that Moscow hadn't thought to improvise.

The best part of a year was passed in idleness, while Ilich made himself at home in London. He spent the summer months of 1971 in Lebanon, brushing up his skills and learning new ones at a PLO facility outside Beirut, and in the wake of Black September, when the government waged brief, abortive war against the foreign terrorists, he surfaced with the underground in France.

For two years he served Amal Haddad, the PLO's top gun in Europe, running errands, taking messages, occasionally standing guard at secret conclaves where the fate of Israel was discussed in grim apocalyptic terms. Still young at twenty-four, he was not trusted yet to pull the trigger on a major score, but Julio was slowly rising through the ranks, ingratiating himself with all the right people, waiting for the day when he would finally reach the firing line.

His opportunity arrived at Easter, 1973, when crack Israeli gunmen—shooters for a hit team dubbed the Wrath of God—at last surprised Haddad at his apartment. He had settled in behind the wheel of his Mercedes when a taxi pinned him at the curb, a second screeching up behind him, cutting off retreat. Converging fire from half a dozen Uzi submachine guns guaranteed that Julio Ramirez would be elevated to the leadership of Amal's European cadre.

There had been other contenders, but Julio could be persuasive when he tried. A shooting, blamed on the Israelis, had removed his chief competitor; the next, and last, had fallen victim to an ugly accident at home.

With Ilich at the helm, the underground became at once more active and more profitable. Certainly, revenge for the assassination of Haddad took top priority, but if another group desired assistance on French soil—the Baader-Meinhofs, for example, or the Japanese Red Army—they could count on Julio for full cooperation—at a price. His moment had arrived, and he would make the most of it before it slipped away. If KGB observers were surprised, they took no steps to rein him in. A terrorist was valuable anywhere.

Ramirez started making headlines in the fall of 1973—anonymously at first, unrecognized by the authorities, and later as "The Raven," product of a journalist's imagination. Julio didn't mind the name—it was immensely preferable to "The Jackal," one of his competitors—and he began to use it in communications with the media. They ate it up, reporting every threat and hanging on his every word, assuring that his infamy preceded him across the continent. Their stories made him more effective than he ever could have hoped to be without their help. He was reported here and there and everywhere. The Western powers quailed, or so he thought, at mention of his name. And no one knew for certain, anymore, precisely which assassinations he had engineered along the way.

The Sûreté had linked him positively to the murder of a Jewish businessman—retaliation for Haddad—and to the blasts that killed or wounded thirteen persons in a Parisian sidewalk café. When jealousy erupted in the ranks, a rash defector fingered Ilich for the DST—the *Direction de la Surveillance du Territoire*—and agents of the French security service had almost cornered him in a flat on Rue Toullier.

Almost.

He had surprised them on the stairway, blasting with an Uzi while their guns were still in holsters, riddling a pair of DST investigators, taking time to finish off the former comrade who was serving as their Judas goat and guide. From that point on, it had been underground or nothing, and his name had surfaced in connection with a string of incidents around the world. No single agency—including the KGB—could say with any certainty that Ilich had participated—or had not—in any given crime.

He had been linked with the assassination of a Spanish military officer, and with the bombing murder of a British nobleman, allegedly conducted on commission from the IRA. The Red Brigades had used his services in certain bold abductions, and the Baader-Meinhof gang had almost certainly employed him to eliminate a series of informers in the ranks. The Tupemaros knew him well enough to call upon him for assistance with a string of bombings, and he had been seen in the company of ranking spokesmen for the PLO.

In short, the Raven had been anywhere and everywhere, involved in anything and everything . . . until he vanished from the scene, abruptly, inexplicably, in 1983. There had been later sightings here and there around the world in intervening months—the Raven had been positively placed in Cuba, Vietnam, the Philipines, and a look-alike had been arrested in Mexico City—but none of them panned out. He was mysteriously and completely gone.

The rumors multiplied and fed upon themselves. The Raven was retired and living like a king in Libya . . . or was it Lebanon? He had been terminated by Khaddafi on a whim, or tagged by the Israelis in a border strike, his body spirited away by *fedayeen*. He had been surgically remodeled, head to toe, and was relaxing on the Riviera or in Rio, in Miami or Las Vegas.

But no one knew for sure.

Until he surfaced on Flight 741.

Until he was eliminated by Carl Lyons in Durango.

Until the men of Phoenix Force surprised him at a meet in Mittenwald.

And no one man could cover that much ground, that quickly. No man could resurrect himself in Germany the morning after he was killed in Mexico.

Which meant it wasn't just *the* Raven anymore. Perhaps it never had been. But if there was *more* than one . . .

Then everything they said about the bastard could be true, and more. He *could* be everywhere at once, and there was precious little anyone could do to stop him.

Until they tracked the several Ravens down and killed them all.

Mack Bolan was already on the scent, but there was no way he could possibly anticipate the danger, weigh the odds against him. If he scored a single kill, he would be lulled by false security, made vulnerable to reprisal from the rest.

The Executioner was on his own.

Again.

As always.

Chapter Sixteen

By night, Toronto's waterfront looked much like any other in the world. The freighters ranged along her docks, the great warehouses jammed with produce, textiles and machinery, might have been lifted from New York or San Francisco, Liverpool or Tokyo. The major difference was olfactory, since Lake Ontario did not possess the salty aroma of the open sea; instead, it smelled like fish and diesel oil.

Mack Bolan took the exit from the Gardiner Expressway toward the water, searching for the warehouse owned by Viking International. A phone-booth pit stop had confirmed the address given him by Tommy Noonan, and a street map brought him to the water's edge with only one false start. He left the rental's headlights on and kept his speed up, scanning left and right as ranks of carbon-copy holding barns slid past on either side. He had the pier, all right. It shouldn't cost him too much time to find...

And up ahead the logo caught his headlights, shimmered briefly, slipping past to starboard, fading in the rearview mirror. Viking International. Still rolling, he killed the lights, already looking for a place to stash the rental while he made his probe. Some fifty yards along, he pulled into the shadow of an empty warehouse, parked against the loading dock—beneath a sign that read For Lease—and killed the engine.

There should be no watchman on an empty, but he wasn't taking any chances. He could not afford to lose the car or the gear inside it out of carelessness. A moment's searching in the darkness turned up a bottle, and Bolan weighed it in his hand, considering his options and his targets, finally letting it fly. His missile hit the wall, rebounded with a hollow clink and shattered on the loading dock.

He waited, counting down the numbers, giving anyone inside a chance to register the sound. Five minutes, and he gave it up. The empty barn was silent as a tomb.

He spent another moment rigging up for combat, buckling the web belt, shrugging on the harness, daubing the cosmetic camouflage across his forehead, underneath his eyes, along his cheeks and nose. The sleek Beretta 93-R nestled underneath his arm in custom leather, and the silver AutoMag, Big Thunder, rode his hip on military webbing. Canvas pouches circling his waist held extra magazines for both, and pockets in the midnight skinsuit carried other gear; stilettos and garrotes, a pencil flash and lock-pick set.

The soldier was prepared for war... and hoped he wouldn't have to fire a shot. The probe would be a soft one if he had his choice, a stealthy in-and-out with none the wiser when he left. A simple look around—except that simple sometimes turned to life and death without a heartbeat's warning. A trick alarm, a roving watchman, anything at all could blow his plans sky-high and leave him out there on the firing line. A savvy soldier always girded up for war... and thanked the universe if it turned out that his preparations were unnecessary.

He glanced both ways and crossed the narrow black-top in a sprint, his form a gliding shadow in the moon-light. Forty yards flat-out, and he was huddled in against the loading dock at Viking International, the Beretta in his fist, alert for any sign of danger from within the warehouse.

Silence.

Bolan holstered the 93-R and scrambled topside, crouching on the dock and running down the numbers in his mind once more, aware of every night sound in his own immediate vicinity.

He bypassed giant roller doors, his full attention centered on an entrance marked Employees Only. It was locked, but after scanning for a moment with the pencil flash, he satisfied himself that it was not connected to a burglar alarm. Vachon was confident or careless.

Bolan crouched before the lock with tension wrench and diamond pick in hand. The wrench was nothing more than slender, tempered steel; the pick so named because its tip was diamond-shaped. With agile fingers, Bolan slipped the wrench inside the lock and twisted to the right, creating tension on the plug—a small cylinder that turns with the key to operate a lock. Probing with the pick, he felt for the tumblers, five pins of different lengths, housed in hollow shafts inside the cylinder. If he could raise them all together, as a key's serrated edge would do, he would defeat the lock. The tension wrench was meant to turn the plug a thousandth of an inch, and thereby keep the tumblers from falling back in place once he had lifted each in turn.

Three minutes. Four. The lock was not a simple one, but neither was it burglarproof. He had it now, the door already swinging open into semidarkness, with a night-light shining from the far end of a narrow corridor. He waited for the sound of a surprise alarm, ready for a confrontation, but ringing silence mocked him. Bolan slipped inside, allowed the door to close and lock itself behind him while he felt along the jamb for wiring, anything to indicate a silent burglar alarm.

Nothing.

If Vachon had dogs, they would be homing on him now like hungry guided missiles—trained, perhaps, to strike without a warning bark. Bolan waited for another moment, finally satisfied that he was alone at Viking International.

He cleared the forty feet of corridor, emerging into the warehouse proper at the other end, confronting ranks of wooden crates and cardboard boxes piled from floor to ceiling, stretching out one hundred feet and more in the direction of the lake. Confronted with the wilderness of crates, he realized that he had no idea of where to start, or even what he might be looking for.

An office. There would be one somewhere on the premises, no doubt, with files and ledgers—a directory, perhaps, of those in charge at Viking International. A pointer to the individual he still knew only as Vachon.

He scanned the room, picking out employee rest rooms—his and hers—without discovering an office. It would be closer to the water, certainly, for the convenience of loading crews and captains dropping cargo on the pier. He chose an aisle at random, navigating by the single row of dim fluorescents overhead, and moved between the stacks of crates.

No time for opening the crates and cartons, searching aimlessly for weapons now. An army could have spent the weekend digging here, and still have missed an arsenal.

He had run out of aisle, confronting giant roller doors identical to those that faced the street behind him. To his left, a pair of forklifts sat like dozing dinosaurs, their rusty tusks directed toward the giant roller doors and Lake Ontario. The office was an eight-foot cubicle of glass and plywood, planted in a corner by the lakeside doors, a single naked light bulb burning there, illuminating desk and chairs, a telephone and IBM Selectric, filing cabinets.

He heard the sound of distant voices, footsteps ringing on the concrete floor behind him, and he realized that he was out of time. Above him the fluorescents sputtered briefly, winking into life and bringing instant daylight to the warehouse floor.

It was do-or-die, and Bolan knew that he could never hope to win a game of hide-and-seek inside the warehouse. Not if he remained at ground level, anyway.

The nearest crates were labeled Farm Machinery and built of sturdy wood, arranged in something of a pyramid with smaller crates on top. He scrambled to the nearest forklift's driver's seat and leaped up to find a handhold on the packing crates. He reached the apex and levered over, flattening himself along the topmost crate and peering down to watch the nearest aisle.

He discerned three figures clopping toward him between the walls of cartons, one gesticulating, speaking rapidly. Unless the soldier missed his guess, the guide would be Vachon. The other two consisted of a man and woman, keeping pace and listening attentively to every word.

Despite the awkward angle, Bolan recognized them both.

He knew the man, from photographs as Gerold Axelrod, American, a mouthpiece for the new survivalist-cum-neofascist underground. Except that many of them were above ground now, recruiting followers among the homeless and the unemployed, harassing immigrants and ethnic groups, assassinating journalists and sniping law-enforcement officers in the performance of their duties.

It was all familiar, sure. And fifty years before, in war-torn Germany, it had been much the same. Inflation, unemployment, racial bigotry—the diverse symptoms merging, giving shaky credence to the Nazi movement, elevating a pathetic madman to the status of a god.

It couldn't happen here, and yet . . .

Within a span of eighteen months, the FBI and local agencies had fingered neo-Nazi activists in robberies, assassinations, arson, transportation of explosives, shoot-outs with police in several states. The raving right had training camps where "patriots" could learn guerrilla warfare tactics—for a price—and they were beaming mock-religious diatribes to several million homes by radio and television.

A segment of America was listening, remembering the message with its easy answers to a host of complicated problems. Lost your farm? It was the Christless Jewish bankers in New York, Miami, Tel Aviv. Health failing? Blame the federal government for poisoning your water and your food. Unemployed? Why, look no further than the niggers, gooks and spics who took the white man's jobs away . . . or were they just intent on eating up your taxes through the welfare rolls?

Among the latest crop of neofascists, Georgia's Gerold Axelrod was something of a figurehead. He had escaped indictment in the several crimes committed by his followers, and would deny that he led *anybody* into *anything*, but he was guilty, sure. Of peddling hate in homes and schools and churches coast-to-coast. Of arming idiots who didn't have the sense to understand the modern world, and setting them against their neighbors in a kind of grass-roots holy war. Within the law, his manicured hands were clean so far, but Bolan saw them dripping with the blood of innocents.

The Executioner was not surprised to find a neo-Nazi in the company of someone like Vachon. Illegal weapons dealers were uniquely apolitical, concerned exclusively with cash. If Vachon had peddled weapons to the Raven yesterday, he would not shrink from dealing with the Raven's enemies today. His weapons were a mere commodity, like soybeans or cotton, except that soybeans had never slaughtered anybody on a 747, dammit.

So, Axelrod was no surprise, and if it came down to an opportunity for Bolan to remove him, there would be no hesitation on the soldier's part.

It was the woman who surprised Mack Bolan, her appearance setting off a tremor in the warrior's memory, the moment that he recognized her face.

Toby Ranger.

God*damn* it.

There could be a thousand different reasons for the lady fed tagging after Axelrod—or was she with Vachon? No matter. Either angle—arms or private armies—fit the bill for her role with SOG.

Toby had been working on the Mafia when Bolan first met her, so many lifetimes ago in Vegas, and he hadn't heard of Sensitive Operations yet. His old friend Hal Brognola was an adversary in those days, and duty-bound to drop the Executioner in his tracks. Toby and her Ranger Girls were on the federal payroll, keeping tabs on Mob infiltration of show business while burning up the charts as one of the hottest female song-and-dance acts in the country.

The sight of Toby took him back, however briefly, to the times and turmoil they had shared in Vegas, in Detroit, Hawaii and New York. There were no Ranger Girls today, of course. Georgette Chebleu had died in Michigan, a screaming turkey mutilated by the syndicate's "physicians." The others—Toby, Smiley Dublin, Sally Palmer—went their separate ways, though all remained in federal service, working undercover on the Mob, on terrorists, wherever cannibals convened to dine upon the innocent.

He pushed the memories away and concentrated on the individuals below him now, observing Toby as she kept pace with the men, attentive to Vachon and everything he said but watching Axelrod with dark, proprietary eyes. Without a word she reached out, slipped her hand inside the bend of Axelrod's arm and moved in closer to him.

It told the warrior everything he had to know. Her presence here was no more than mere coincidence, perhaps, and unrelated to his quest. If he could tag the dealer privately, it need not interfere with her assignment.

"The volume is no problem now," Vachon was saying, punctuating every sentence with his hand. "I have my sources on the inside, at the factory."

"All right," the Georgian drawled. "And when can I expect delivery?"

They reached the tiny office, and Vachon was fumbling with his keys. They passed inside, their voices muffled now by distance and the intervening glass. The dealer opened a filing cabinet, withdrew a thin manila folder, spread the contents on his desk for Axelrod's inspection. Toby watched them from the sidelines and several moments passed before they started nodding in agreement. Finally they sealed the deal by shaking hands. Their business done, they locked the office and hastily retraced their steps.

"I guarantee you will be satisfied," Vachon was telling Axelrod.

"Well, you've never disappointed me before," the Dixie führer said. "I'm counting on you, Paul."

A first name. Bolan's grin was hard and hungry, etched into his face. With any luck he could pursue the dealer to his lair with what he had right now, but there might be a simpler way.

He waited for the footsteps and the voices to recede before he scrambled down, alighting on the forklift nearest to the aisle. As he touched down, the bright fluorescents were extinguished overhead, the single row of night-lights glowing dim and ghostly in the corrugated metal barn.

He listened for the closing of the door, a whispered *click*, before he made his move. If he could clear the warehouse, reach his rental car before Vachon and his companions disappeared, it would be simple to pursue the death merchant to his base of operations. Along the way there would be time to think of Toby Ranger and her role in the unfolding drama. Was she working on the arms connection? Simply keeping tabs on Axelrod? Or was there something deeper? The soldier didn't plan to blow her cover, knowing it could mean her life, but hoped he'd have a chance to speak with Toby.

He had to relocate her first, and that meant tracking down Vachon. The dealer, after all, had been his reason for arriving in Toronto in the first place. Other business could afford to wait.

Mack Bolan had a score to settle with the Raven, and with the vultures who had made his terrorism possible. If Paul Vachon was one of those, his days were numbered.

But Bolan needed something more substantial than the dying words of Tommy Noonan. He needed evidence, and he would find it waiting for him at the home of Paul Vachon—or there would be no evidence to find.

If he hadn't lost his edge already, he was going home with Paul Vachon.

In search of evidence.

In search of targets.

Chapter Seventeen

It was a relatively easy tail. Paul Vachon was a believer in conspicuous consumption, and a blind man could have tracked his silver Mercedes without much difficulty. The hour had reduced Toronto's traffic to a scattering of cars along the routes they chose, and Bolan's hardest task was hanging back, cutting off his lights from time to time on lonely stretches when there were no other vehicles in sight.

The Gardiner Expressway took them east until they caught the Don Valley Parkway northbound. The luxury German import was fat and shiny underneath the streetlights, and impossible to lose. Bolan took the opportunity to scan Toronto's skyline, running slow and mellow in the limo's wake. And he was with them when they caught the off ramp onto the Macdonald-Cartier Freeway, running into Scarborough, angling eastward in the final leg of the pursuit.

Vachon's estate was situated just off Ellesmere Road, by the greenery of Morningside Park. The walls were roughly six feet high and built of stone, but they had not been topped with concertina wire as far as Bolan could tell. He drove by the wrought-iron gates, and saw his quarry's taillights winking insolently on the curving drive.

Flight 741

The penetration was imperative—and fraught with danger, for himself as well as Toby. She was not expecting visitors, and he could not predict her gut reaction if they came together by surprise, with Axelrod or Paul Vachon at hand.

He found a stand of trees where he could stash the rental. Pulling in, he killed the lights and engine and prepared for EVA.

No simple probe this time. His drive by had revealed the grounds lit up like daylight, with the manor house a beehive of activity. The warrior knew he could approach by stealth, but he was almost certain to encounter sentries here, and that would lead to killing long before he reached his destination. He would need another angle of approach to pull it off, and Bolan had a plan in mind.

He stood beside the car in darkness, shed the harness with its military webbing, stowed it in the trunk. Next off, the rigging for his black, selective-fire Beretta and its extra magazines. He peeled the blacksuit off and stood there in his Jockeys, night wind playing on his body, while he scrubbed the camouflage cosmetics from his face with tissues and a jar of cream.

That done, he dressed himself again in crisp white shirt and tie, a charcoal business suit and loafers. They would take a beating on the wall, but he could minimize the damage with a bit of care, and darkness was his friend. If anybody looked *too* closely, there was still the sleek Beretta nestled inside the jacket of his suit.

He locked the trunk and double-checked the rental's doors, then hiked the hundred yards back to Vachon's perimeter. The six-foot wall was bare on top, and Bolan found no sign of sensors, cameras, no security devices whatsoever. That was careless, but if Bolan's target felt secure inside his walls without the other gadgetry, so much the better. Sentries, with perhaps a dog or two, would be the only obstacles before him now.

The wall was easy. It had been constructed more for looks than any real security. He wondered if the weapons trade in Canada was really so pacific, or if Paul Vachon was merely a peculiar, sloppy aberration. Either way, the soldier thanked his lucky stars once he was safe inside the stone perimeter.

He met the sentry moments later, pacing off his circuit with a walkie-talkie dangling from one wrist, a Steyr automatic rifle—one of the futuristic AUGs tucked underneath his other arm. At sight of Bolan in his suit and tie, the picket did a double-take and swung the rifle up. His fingers wrapped around the walkie-talkie, lifting it in the direction of his face. His voice betrayed surprise, and something very much like fear.

"Who are you?" he demanded.

A touch of French around the vowels. That made the kid Vachon's, and Bolan offered up his best Southern U.S. accent in return.

"Jus' take it easy, boy. I'm in with Gerry Axelrod. Security, ya know?"

"I wasn't told," the kid replied, defensive now.

"No reason why you shoulda been." A plastic smile. "Hell, I ain't checkin' up on you. Jus' thought I'd take myself a little look-see round the place, if tha's all right."

The sentry's eyes were narrowed with suspicion, and he held the AUG rock steady, with the muzzle square on Bolan's chest. He couldn't hope to drop the kid without a heavy-duty risk, and even if he killed him clean, there was a chance the sentry's dying reflex would be adequate to chop him down.

"I wasn't told," the picket said again.

And it was time to push his luck a little.

"Well, shit fire, why doan you buzz the house and get it squared away?" The tension in his voice came out as Bolan had intended, sounding like impatience. "Tell you somethin', I'm not used to the *quee-zeen* y'all are dishin' up around this place. It goes right through me, if you get my drif', an' I doan have a lotta time to stan' around an' chat right now."

The sentry thought about it for a moment, finally smiled and dropped the muzzle of his AUG.

"Good luck," he said.

"I'll need it, way I feel right now." He brushed on past the guard, moving toward the house.

He left the sentry, moving briskly now as if he owned the place. Role camouflage and Paul Vachon's own carelessness had seen him through this time, and Bolan felt secure that he could handle any further challenge. When he passed the second sentry, he only had to wave and nod distractedly to put the man at ease. Long hours and unfamiliarity with new arrivals did the rest.

Bolan hesitated to approach the house, aware that once inside, his options would be strictly limited. A fumble on the inside and he would be as good as dead. And yet he had not come this far and risked this much to walk around the house, a stranger on the outside looking in.

A sudden burst of laughter from the rear, and Bolan thought he recognized the voice of Paul Vachon.

He ambled in the direction of the sound, half circling the manor house before he came upon a wide veranda, fitted out with hot tub, redwood dining tables and a deep-pit barbecue. Vachon knew how to entertain in style, and he was holding forth for Gerry Axelrod as Bolan cleared the corner of the house. Across from Axelrod the lady fed looked bored behind a practiced smile.

She spotted Bolan instantly, and he could feel the short hairs rising on his neck as she leaned forward, whispering to Axelrod. The would-be führer nodded silently, still listening to Paul Vachon as Toby rose, excused herself and moved with agile, dancer's strides across the patio.

Mack Bolan tracked her toward the sliding doors that he surmised would open onto a dining room or kitchen, lost her as she passed inside. She had made him and decided to retreat from the line of fire. Bolan cursed beneath his breath. He was running out of time, and ran the risk of being challenged at any moment.

Too late.

A screen door banged behind him, and he was already turning, loosening the buttons on his jacket, reaching for the Beretta and a bullshit story simultaneously when he recognized the husky voice.

"What are you doing here?"

The lady was as beautiful as he remembered, but she was not amused.

"I've got some business with Vachon," he told her simply, skipping over the preliminaries by a sort of mutual consent.

"First come, first served," she told him flatly.

"Different orders," Bolan countered. "I can't see why yours and mine should intersect."

"I've heard that song before."

Was there a trace of bitterness beneath the shock and natural resentment of intrusion on her own preserve? "I guess you ought to know the tune by now."

"No sale. I've been with Axelrod for seven months. That's way too long and way too much for me to flick it in for Captain Midnight."

He risked a smile. "What happened to that smiling face—"

"You used to know and love?" she finished for him. And the tone was definitely bitter. "Don't make me laugh."

He saw the color rising in her cheeks and recognized the cutting edge behind her words. There was a great deal more on Toby's mind than jealousy concerning jurisdiction, but he didn't have the time to psychoanalyze.

"I don't have time for cat and mouse," he told her flatly, wiping off the smile. "I need to pick the dealer's brain."

"My mission has priority," she snapped. "We're dealing with a pack of home-grown terrorists, in case you haven't heard."

"No conflict there. I tag Vachon, your mark goes begging for his hardware."

"And he finds it somewhere else, next week, next month. No good. This deal is in the works, and I will not stand by and see it blown."

"So, step aside."

"I'm warning you...."

Her voice and all the pent-up anger trailed away at once, as if someone had pulled the plug and let it all run down. When Toby spoke again, her voice was softer, barely pitched above a whisper.

"Please. I need some time."

"How much?"

"They're handing off at noon tomorrow...if nothing queers the deal."

Eleven hours, give or take. And it could be a heart-beat or a lifetime, depending on your point of view.

"All right."

The lady looked suspicious, frowning now, as if she half expected him to wink and call out, "April fool!"

"You promise?"

"If I have to."

"Well...you'd better not let anybody find you here. They play for keeps."

"I didn't know you cared."

Her anger flared at once, as if his voice had tripped a personal ignition switch. "God *damn* you." And the voice was teary now. "God *damn* you all to hell!"

She spun away and disappeared inside the house, the screen door banging shut behind her. Bolan watched her go, uncertain what was eating at the lady. But he could hear the numbers running in his head, and knew that he had used his time—and then some.

It was time to go, before he overstayed his welcome and became a permanent addition to the scenery.

Reluctantly, he put the house behind him, knowing he would have to do it all a second time when Toby and her mark were safely off the premises. At least he knew the general layout of the house and grounds. Next time around, without the Georgia delegation to distract him, he would have a chance to speak with Paul Vachon at length. A lifetime for the dealer, unless he had the information Bolan needed for his Raven hunt.

Bolan retraced his path across the grounds, in the direction of the wall. He reached his point of entry, was about to scramble topside when a whispered, continental voice reached out to trace an icy finger down his spine.

"I thought you might be back."

He knew the voice and recognized the sentry long before he turned around to face him, concentrating on the AUG he held in both hands now. Less chance of missing, with his free hand wrapped around the folding pistol grip in front. The recoil, moderated by design, would not be adequate to throw the piece off target at point-blank range.

"Take the holster off."

Bolan shrugged the leather harness off his shoulders and worked his left arm free, allowing it to dangle momentarily from the right. His captor was right-handed, too; a left-hand sweep would drag the AUG across his body, keeping him within the range of fire for just the extra heartbeat that the kid would need to loose a fatal burst. But on the other hand...

The other hand was moving swiftly, unexpectedly, before the plan was fully formed in Bolan's mind. He made no move to draw the pistol from its holster, knowing he could never hope to beat the kid's reaction time. Instead, he whipped the shoulder rig around in front of him, a kind of flail that caught the muzzle of his opposition's rifle, slamming it away for just a second.

And then he sprang, a reflex that propelled him forward, even as he let the harness go and saw it wrap around the barrel of the AUG, its extra weight retarding the reaction of his enemy. His left hand found the gunner's wrist and yanked it forward, countering the sentry's own reflexive trigger pull, and he was twisting, bearing down as they collided, levering the rifle from his adversary's grasp.

A knee exploded in the sentry's groin, and he was folding, going down with Bolan's weight on top of him, before he had a chance to shout a warning toward the house. A muscled forearm found his larynx, crushed it as they both made impact with the earth, and Bolan lay atop the kid until his final tremors faded.

The Executioner straightened, found the shoulder harness, slipped it on. The corpse would have to travel with him, of course. He simply had no choice. A missing sentry might be AWOL, but a stiff would tell Vachon that he was being stalked, and Bolan couldn't give that much away. Not yet.

For Toby's sake.

And for his own.

In death, the sentry seemed to weigh a ton, although he was a slender youth in fact. He sagged against the Executioner as Bolan eased him up across the wall and pushed him over into darkness on the other side. He tossed the AUG across, took one more look around for any telltale signs of struggle and was gone.

The rental's trunk would hold his trophy for a while, until he found someplace to dump it safely. He didn't want the body found until he had his little chat with Paul Vachon.

A single trip would do it, with the sentry draped across his shoulder in a fireman's carry, shirttails wrapped around his face in case his bloody spittle leaked to ruin Bolan's suit. The AUG was weightless by comparison.

The trunk would hold them nicely. For now. And while he looked for someplace to discard his kill, the Executioner would puzzle over Toby Ranger's hostile attitude, her angry words. The lady fed was keeping something to herself, and it was eating at her. If there was time and opportunity, he meant to find out what that something was.

If not, well, the mission took priority. And he had come in search of information from Vachon, not soothing words from one of Hal Brognola's SOGs.

The Raven hunt was numbers one through ten on Bolan's list right now, and he was in no mood to juggle the priorities.

Not yet.

And not without a damned good reason.

Chapter Eighteen

Toby Ranger turned on the shower, adjusted it for heat and shed her robe to step beneath the stinging spray. She stood with her face upturned, eyes closed, and let the water pummel her, anticipating the relief from pent-up tension she had felt since meeting Bolan on the lawn outside.

Toby slowly turned beneath the shower head to let the steaming spray beat against her shoulders and her spine. Her eyes were open now but out of focus, staring through the shower's mist and seeing Bolan's face in front of her, as if the man had never left.

Goddamn him, anyhow!

He had no right to show up here and jeopardize the mission that she had pursued for eight long months. There were no mafiosi here for him to hunt, but Toby felt a worm of dread insinuate itself into her brain, reminding her that Bolan might appear most anywhere, at anytime. His targets were not limited to capos and their button men. It could be Axelrod—or someone else.

Either way, Bolan's presence in Toronto spelled disaster for her mission.

Unless he let her play her hand without unnecessary interference.

Fat chance.

The man was hell on wheels, and when he focused on a target, no mere words could put him off the track. She knew the Executioner that well, and Toby cherished no illusions that their little heart-to-heart outside had changed his mind. If his mark was inside Vachon's estate, the soldier would be back, and *he* would choose the time.

Her tension was returning, muscles knotting in her shoulders, and Toby willed herself to relax. He had the same effect on her each time they met, mingled feelings of concern and irritation welling up inside until she felt that she was going to explode.

She worried about the soldier, sure. They had been through too damn much together for her to write him off. Whatever the official line from Washington, she knew that he was not a renegade in the accepted sense. The Executioner was still selecting targets with a surgeon's skill, and he had yet to overstep the line by tagging any innocents. His lonely, private war was from the heart, and Toby recognized that fact, but there was more to waging war than simply running like a maverick.

The man displayed a perfect genius for intruding on established operations, blowing them sky-high and walking off with all the marbles in his pocket.

His very presence in the vicinity would be enough to generate the kind of shock waves that could blow her mission, and yet she found herself concerned about his survival in the hellgrounds.

It was a long time since Vegas, but she could still remember her initial meeting with the Executioner, the rare smile he flashed when the spirit moved. More rarely now, she could imagine, since the debacle at Stony Man Farm, the death of April Rose....

Toby experienced a sudden stab of jealousy, and turned to face the shower head again in shame. Perhaps the stinging spray would dissipate the tears that sprang unbidden to her eyes.

They were irrational, these feelings toward a woman who was dead and gone. And yet she felt a measure of the soldier's grief, the pain sparking recognition of the emotions they would never fully share.

It had been close before, but time and circumstance had constantly prevented her from cleaving to the soldier, fighting at his side on any more than an occasional excursion. They had shared the intimacy of a clench or two on distant killing grounds, but in her heart she knew that the encounters meant a great deal more to her than to the man whose very life was balanced on the razor's edge of death.

The guy was married to his war before they ever met, and in the last analysis, she wondered just how much there had been left to share with April Rose...with anyone.

She wondered and she wept, the tears infuriating Toby when she could not turn them off. He had no right to make her feel this way.

Goddamn it!

If he jeopardized her in with Axelrod...

It had been easy making the acquaintance of the top survivalist-cum-neo-Nazi in America. Brognola had arranged the introduction through a minor plant in one of Axelrod's splinter groups, a back-door introduction to a barbecue at his estate outside Stone Mountain, Georgia.

It was Klan country, but the bigots didn't run toward sheets so much these days. They had acquired a taste for business suits and camouflage fatigues, a thin patina of respectability to mask the madness in their eyes. They didn't drool so much in public anymore— and most had given up on burning crosses as a waste of precious gasoline—but underneath the practiced smiles their message was the same.

Pure hatred.

And they did not confine their vitriol to blacks or Jews or other ethnic groups. The United States government was now the enemy to bands of superpatriots across the country, scheming in their desert bunkers or their mountain hideaways, their madness loosely but inevitably linked by the manipulative genius of a single man.

Gerold Axelrod.

She knew the rags-to-riches story of the Georgia farm boy who had risen to become the symbol of American survivalists, and likewise knew what lay beneath the surface. The man was like a Chinese puzzle box, with racial hatred tucked away beneath the polished outer surface, brooding revolutionary fervor hidden under that, and at the core, a deep, abiding greed.

Survivalism, bigotry and all the rest of it were paying propositions to the likes of Axelrod. He had found a sellable commodity in paranoia, and he was milking it for every dime available. From powdered eggs and sleeping bags to anti-Jewish pamphlets, he had rapidly become the redneck's Sears, Roebuck, filling every bigot's secret needs, provided that the bigot had some ready cash. Along the way he had become a millionaire, and powdered eggs accounted for a fraction of his recent income.

It had been the automatic weapons and explosives that aroused concern in Washington. The Ingrams that were used to strafe a television station in Seattle, the plastique that wrecked a synagogue in Newport News, the arsenal recovered from the rubble of a suicidal racist's hideout in Wyoming—all and more had been connected to the right-wing underground that Axelrod had organized and on which he served as chairman of the board. There had been nothing to link him personally with the violent incidents, which recently included robberies, assassinations, firefights with police and FBI, but that was where Brognola's SOG came in.

And Toby Ranger.

Her mission was to get the goods on Axelrod. Her method: live-in secretary, with an eye and ear for everything that happened underneath his roof.

The job seemed distasteful, but once she made herself available to Axelrod and recognized that he would want her more for window dressing than for any other kind of satisfaction, Toby knew that she could pull it off. There had been worse assignments, and she had sacrificed a great deal more on other missions ordered out of Washington.

But Gerry Axelrod was gay.

It was the deepest, darkest secret of his life, known only to a handful of his close associates—and now, to Toby Ranger. He laid it on the line when he suggested that she come to live with him, assuring Toby that her "honor" would remain intact. He was desperately in need of a woman to preserve the image of his rugged manhood for the faithful in the rank and file.

If he had been dispensing heroin or running whores, his sexual proclivities would scarcely matter, but a man who made his living selling God and apple pie was something else again. The taint of homosexuality could ruin him, perhaps endanger his existence once the crazies had some time to think about it, but with a flashy woman on his arm....

In Georgia, there were separate beds in separate bedrooms, and when circumstance forced them into closer quarters, he veered away from any private contact once the bedroom door was closed. At home, she had pretended not to notice the arrival and departure of his pretty boys, recruited from Atlanta's cornucopia of flesh, and in their travels he had been a model of attentiveness. For Toby's part, she was preoccupied with noting the details of business deals, his contacts in the neofascist underground. His private passions might become a lever, but for the moment they were insignificant.

Of course, Mack Bolan wouldn't know that Axelrod was gay. He would have seen them, shadowed them, and he would think the worst.

And did it matter what the soldier thought? Of course.

That was the problem.

Toby *cared* what Bolan thought. And while she knew that he would not condemn her—that his soul was burdened with enough guilt and pain for half a dozen men—still, she wished that she could set him straight.

Because she loved him.

She stood beneath the stinging spray and thought of Sally Palmer, Smiley Dublin. They had kept in touch since Vegas, since the firestorm in New York, on through the birth pangs and upheavals of the Phoenix project. Both had worked with Bolan on their own, and they had shared the censored details in sporadic conversations, keeping her apprised of Bolan's progress, his survival in the shooting gallery. But they had not shared everything, and Toby felt the pang of jealousy again, pursued at once by self-disgust.

There was no place for petty rivalry when lives were riding on the line, and Toby had concealed her personal emotions from the others who depended on her. She regarded Bolan as a friend, a professional competitor of sorts, but the truth—which sometimes surfaced in the middle of her lonely nights—was something else again. And seeing him outside tonight had brought those hidden feelings flooding back, the onslaught threatening to wash her common sense away.

She hoped that he would back off, permit her to complete her work in peace—and knew that she was bucking heavy odds. The soldier would not have surfaced at Vachon's unless he was in hot pursuit, preparing for a strike. And if it was Axelrod, why here?

Since Bolan's separation from the Phoenix project, there had been no solid way of keeping tabs on his activity except through chance encounters on the firing line. She knew about his brush with "justice" down in Texas, had devoured daily headlines and considered flying south to stand beside him, but Hal Brognola had been adamant in opposition.

The thought of calling Hal Brognola now had already crossed her mind, and Toby had rejected it. There would be time if Bolan showed himself again, and she was still uncertain of precisely how Brognola would react.

It would be a relatively simple matter to report the soldier's presence in Toronto. Not tonight, from Paul Vachon's, where anybody might be listening on the extension—but tomorrow, the next day. . . .

No.

Tomorrow they were finalizing business with the Frenchman, and the next day they would be in Georgia, safe at Axelrod's retreat.

Toby turned off the shower and pulled a towel off the rack. Instead of helping clear her thoughts, the heat had only fogged her mind. Fatigue weighed heavy on her now, and Axelrod would be up late, discussing terms with Paul Vachon. She would be sleeping soundly when he came to bed, if she turned in right now.

If her private thoughts would let her sleep.

If Bolan did not visit her in dark and bloody dreams.

She dreaded seeing him again—yet longed for it, the longing sharp and painful, like a bitter wound.

And Toby knew she owed him everything.

She always had.

She always would.

Chapter Nineteen

Gerold Axelrod felt vulnerable without his guns. He had become accustomed to the weight beneath his arm, the counterweight wrapped snug against his ankle. Not that there was any danger here, of course. But facing Paul Vachon across a low-slung coffee table, feeling naked, he was sorry he had left the pistols in his room.

The guns were twin Detonics .45s with squat, abbreviated grips, the only kind of side arm Axelrod could handle comfortably with his tiny hands. From his childhood he had been humiliated by the miniature appendages connected to his muscular and absolutely normal arms, the chubby fingers like Vienna sausages, which made him look deformed. On second glance, the fingers were in proportion to tiny thumbs and pink, unblemished palms; they were an infant's hands, untouched by puberty or manhood, simultaneously linked and separated from the rest of Axelrod by slender, girlish wrists.

His vanity would not permit him to conceal the tiny hands in gloves, but Axelrod confined them to his pockets when he walked and kept them tucked beneath the tabletop at conferences or during meals. The smiling photographs adorning pamphlets, posters, paperbacks, invariably captured head and shoulders only. Only at the semiannual conventions of the Brother-

hood was he compelled to show his hand—both literally and figuratively—on the firing line. So far, the
squat Detonics .45s had seen him through in style.

And they had seen him through some private scrapes,
as well, although the media had never been apprised of
his successful midnight marksmanship on those occasions. Dead-and-buried secrets could be lethal to his
image—to his very freedom—if they should be revealed. The feds and local law-enforcement agencies
were hungry for a chance to lock his ass away, to poke
around inside his books and slip his growing empire
underneath the microscope for closer scrutiny.

His empire.

He liked the sound of that, the concept of a vast domain that stretched from . . . well . . . from sea to shining sea. The Brotherhood and its affiliates were
everywhere these days—among the farmers and the
auto workers, taking membership away from the established Klans and Nazi parties, even in the prisons. It
was inspirational, the way a simple message could take
root and grow.

Transactions with Vachon and others like him didn't
bother Axelrod. The underworld was all a state of
mind, in any case. As he was wont to tell the faithful at
their convocations, Christ's disciples were the original
underground, driven into catacombs and sewers by the
Roman legions and damned as outlaws. A patriotic
Christian today could look for persecution if he lived
the Word explicitly, and if survival should force him
into contact with the modern Philistines . . . well, now,
the Lord was understanding, don't you know?

They ate up that bullshit in Birmingham and Ma-
con, in Topeka, Kansas City, even way the hell out west
in Bakersfield. It was a word whose time had come, and

Axelrod was pleased to be the messenger—especially since it paid so very well.

But words alone would never pay the rent. It was the word made *flesh*—or molded into tempered steel—that paid his overhead. The members of his Brotherhood and its affiliated outfits needed guns the way a diabetic needs his insulin. They lived on firearms and explosives, drawing strength from mere possession of the paramilitary toys. And they were using them for more than parlor decorations lately. That talk-show host in Colorado Springs, for instance. Freaking bastard never knew what hit him when he reached for the ignition key of his Caddy, but Axelrod knew well enough.

The list was long and repetitious. Automatic rifles for a tri-K faction down in Jacksonville; too bad about the traffic cop who tried to stop them with the weapons in their car. Grenades to Omaha, and who could guess that those abortion clinics would be hit so hard? LAW rockets in New Jersey, perfect lock-picks for an armored payroll truck. Plain, old-fashioned TNT for San Francisco, where the gay-rights boys were getting *last rites* now.

The brief, unconscious grimace never made it through his practiced smile. If anybody in the rank and file suspected . . . well . . . there would be hell to pay. He would be forced to cut and run before they found him, change his name perhaps. These frigging zealots didn't lose the scent the way a mercenary might; they would pursue him to the corners of the earth and waste his ass if they suspected for a moment they had been betrayed.

But they would never know, of course. It was the beauty of his scheme. It was one reason for keeping everybody satisfied with new and better arms.

If only he could find some new and better hands...

"I beg your pardon?"

He had not been listening, and now Vachon was looking at him with a puzzled little frown.

"I said you will be pleased with the supplies."

"I hope so," Axelrod replied. "I've heard good things about the product out of Steyr."

"Simplicity and craftsmanship. You'll get your money's worth, and more."

"You really have a contact in the factory?"

The French Canadian's smile was enigmatic. "I have tried...to get rid of the middleman."

"No leaks?"

"My sources are secure. And if they should be burned, there will be other sources, other manufacturers."

"I like a man who plans ahead," Axelrod said.

In fact, he liked Vachon. His dark complexion was almost flawless save for one small scar above an eye. It made him look piratical, and certainly exciting. Axelrod began to mentally undress the dealer, careful to preserve the bland expression on his face. He wondered if Vachon might swing both ways, decided not to risk the deal—or future deals—by pushing it too far.

Toronto was a business trip. There would be time enough for pleasure when he was safely home again.

Vachon was smiling broadly now, but not at Axelrod. Instead, he looked beyond the Georgian, toward the parlor's open entryway. Startled, Axelrod was swiveling to face the doorway when a slender, dark-skinned man materialized beside him, moving silently across the deep shag carpeting.

Vachon was on his feet, a hand outstretched. "How good of you to join us."

"Not at all."

The new arrival's voice was soft and liquid, vaguely Hispanic. His smile was cruel, and there was glacial ice behind his eyes.

The Georgian didn't rise, did not extend his hand until the new arrival thrust his out, that steely grip enveloping and crushing Axelrod's diminutive fist. A grimace was the best that he could do by way of pleasantries.

"Allow me," Paul Vachon was saying, every bit the gracious host. "Monsieur Gerold Axelrod, from the United States. Señor Ramirez, from...ah..."

"Caracas."

"Yes, of course."

Ramirez.

So, the face was familiar, after all.

The Georgian nodded. "I'm familiar with your work."

"And I with yours."

So much for editorials that speculated on the bastard's death. He was in perfect health, as far as Axelrod could see. If anything, he looked a few years younger than the fuzzy pictures carried periodically by *Time* and *Newsweek* with their articles on terrorism.

He turned to face Vachon. "I didn't realize that we were having company."

The Canadian spread his hands. "Señor Ramirez is an old and valued friend. He has an interest in our business here."

"What interest?" Axelrod inquired.

"An involvement in procuring the merchandise."

"I see."

Ramirez settled on the sofa near Vachon, leaned forward with his elbows on his knees. "The man at Steyr works for me."

"So much for phasing out the middleman."

Vachon looked hurt. "We have a partnership of sorts."

"I wasn't told." Axelrod's face was serious.

"We tell you now."

"And if I take my business elsewhere?"

"There is nowhere else to go," Ramirez told him, speaking softly, settling back into the couch. "Not for the quantity and quality we offer you."

"The price has been agreed to."

"Certainly. I have no wish to alter your arrangement with Vachon."

The bastard's smile was crafty, self-assured, and Gerry wondered if there might be a hint of madness lurking there. He wondered if he ought to make some patriotic noises, jerk the asshole's chain about the flight from Munich, but he let it go.

Instead, he said, "You're very hot right now."

The Raven's smile remained in place. "It's hot in Europe. No one knows me here."

The Georgian glanced at Paul Vachon. "No one?"

Ramirez shrugged. "No one whom I cannot trust implicitly."

"All right."

He should have walked, or had his head examined if he made the choice to hang around, but Axelrod was in too deep to let it go. A half a million dollars riding on the line, and he would triple that on retail when he moved the weapons stateside. Still, he didn't like surprises, and he wondered how secure Toronto was for someone like the Raven.

Politics had always bored him to the point of tears. He could tolerate the bullshit just so long as contributions were arriving from the hinterlands, but Axelrod cared nothing for left or right, the red or black of modern terrorism. Green had always been his color, as in cash, and he was not averse to dealing with the Raven now because of anything the bastard might have done.

What worried Axelrod was the risk of being caught.

Vachon had seemed secure, professional, a man who knew his trade. The general consensus on Ramirez now was something else again. The man was a fanatic—possibly psychotic—and completely unpredictable in combat. That alone was cause enough for apprehension on the eve of a transaction like the one he had arranged with Paul Vachon.

Still, there were the profits....

"I assume that you are ready to indemnify me in the case of any...unexpected interference?"

"Certainly."

The Raven didn't even glance at Vachon before he spoke, and Axelrod was pleased to see a sudden touch of pallor on the Canadian's face.

"Of course," Vachon echoed, sounding vaguely ill.

"Then we're in business."

"Excellent."

They stood and shook hands all around, the Georgian faking joviality he didn't feel, his small right hand retreating to his pocket when they were finished with the ritual. He kept the plastic smile in place as he excused himself, remarking on the curse of jet lag. He felt their eyes upon him as he left the parlor, thankful that they could not watch him climb the stairs and hurry down the hallway toward his room, where Toby would be waiting for him now.

The woman was window dressing, but he drew a certain comfort from her presence and the knowledge that she helped to keep his secret safely locked away. He recognized that she was beautiful—the Georgian might be gay, but he was far from blind—and knew that his disciples in the Brotherhood were envious. The girl had been a lucky find, more durable and less demanding than the others who had gone before.

In time she would be bound to tire of the charade. And he was ready for it when it came. No leaks were tolerated in the Brotherhood, and when the role of mannequin got old, she would be dealt with like the others.

A little midnight marksmanship, a final ride into the marshlands, and the latest in a line of sultry decoys would be gone, forgotten. There were always others waiting for the opportunity to grace a rich man's arm. But Axelrod refused to think about it anymore tonight. Right now he had other problems on his mind. A lover might have eased the tension, briefly, but reality would still be waiting for him on the other side of ecstasy, and it was better that he face the problem cold.

The Raven was a wild card, introduced by Paul Vachon without a word of warning once the game was under way. The Georgian was within his rights to call the whole thing off, but having once rejected that alternative for private motives, he could only try to insulate himself, protect his flanks and cut his losses if the deal went sour overnight.

Ramirez might be safe around Toronto, as he claimed, but his involvement in the recent skyjack had reopened ancient wounds, and agents from a half a dozen governments would certainly be searching for him. He might be held for trial or shot on sight, depending on who found him first—but either way, discovery right now would spell disaster for the Georgian. Even if he wasn't prosecuted, the publicity would scuttle everything that Axelrod had worked for over seven years. Considering the quality of membership attracted to the Brotherhood, he would be very lucky if the headlines only got him jailed, instead of killed.

And neither of the grim alternatives appealed to Axelrod.

But he was stuck with Paul Vachon, with Julio Ramirez, with their weapons lifted from the Steyr plant. He had $500,000 on the line, with stateside buyers guaranteed, and he could not afford to go home empty-handed. Not if he expected the assorted rednecks to keep coming back for more.

It was a frigging shame, but there was nothing he could do about it now. He was committed to the deal, and he would see it through despite the risks.

Next time around, though, he would look for a different supplier. He would not trust Vachon a second time.

The Georgian didn't like surprises, and no living man had ever managed to surprise him twice. As for the dead, Vachon would have a chance to meet them, if the deal went sour in the morning. And Ramirez, too.

He chuckled at the thought of the publicity he would achieve by killing Julio Ramirez. He would be an overnight sensation, hero of the Western world.

Chapter Twenty

The cemetery was an old one, rarely used from all appearances, its mausoleums and headstones larger, more ornate than those predominating in the latter-day facilities.

Mack Bolan crouched, waiting in the shadow of a tomb. His thoughts were morbid, filled with death. It was a perfect killing ground, this cemetery. Anyone who bought it here would not have far to go.

He was running out of patience, chafing at the quarter-hour delay since he had followed Paul Vachon and company from the estate in Scarborough, cutting off at Kingston Road and trailing at a distance till they reached the cemetery proper, watching through the twelve-foot wrought-iron gates as the Mercedes disappeared from sight. His rental Ford was parked one hundred yards behind him, tucked away behind a marble crypt.

The sleek Mercedes sat another hundred yards downrange, half-hidden by a row of overhanging trees that lined the cemetery's winding access road. The Executioner could see enough from where he sat, however; he had seen Vachon with Axelrod and Toby Ranger, flanked by burly hardmen, bulges prominent beneath their jackets. Number six was still inside the car, chain-smoking in the driver's seat and darting nervous glances at the headstones all around.

The outside flankers would be Axelrod's security, but Bolan read the driver as Vachon's. He wondered if the nervousness was something personal, or if the guy was privy to a double-cross in progress, finally deciding that it didn't matter either way. He had determined not to move no matter what went down, unless it threatened Toby's life somehow. Vachon could wait another day or two, until his business with the Georgian was concluded and the lady fed was safely out of range.

The cemetery was a drop. Whatever deal the neo-Nazi had with Vachon, they were about to consummate it here, and Bolan had no abiding interest in the merchandise. His business with the Canadian would be carried out in privacy and darkness—later on tonight, perhaps—and he was seeking information, not a load of contraband.

His target was the Raven.

A kind of private demon, leering back at Bolan from his nightmares, laughing hollowly behind the rubber Nixon face. He knew what lay beneath the mask, had studied all the old composites and the fuzzy photos, and he was looking forward to the moment when that face was inches from his own, his fingers wrapped around the windpipe, watching eyes and swelling tongue protrude in death.

Soon.

The Executioner could wait as long as necessary, but a hot impatience wriggled in his bowels. He recognized the symptoms, knew that they could get him killed if he allowed impatience to control his mind.

Bolan slipped a hand beneath his raincoat, double-checked the sleek Beretta and the silver AutoMag. He knew the weapons were accessible within a heartbeat, but the contact made the waiting bearable once more. The sky was crystal overhead, the raincoat had been his concession to the possibility of mourners visiting their loved ones, but he was alone with Paul Vachon and company. Approaching twenty minutes now, without a sign of any other human being.

As if in answer to his silent thoughts, an engine coughed to life on Bolan's right. It idled for a moment, revving echoes through the morning silence, finally dropping into gear and rumbling closer, passing slowly through the ranks of headstones, still invisible.

The merchandise was coming, and Bolan knew that it was time to get a closer look. Vachon and Axelrod were standing in the middle of the narrow blacktop road, expectant, with the Georgian's burly gunners on either side. Beside the car, he caught a glimpse of Toby Ranger, staring raptly in the direction of the engine sound. Behind the wheel the driver was alert, his latest cigarette forgotten, dangling from his lower lip.

And it was time to move, before their concentration broke and someone cast an accidental glance in his direction.

Before it all ran out, perhaps forever, and he found a final resting place among the long-forgotten dead.

THE PICKUP POINT had been Vachon's idea, and while he questioned the elaborate security precautions, Axelrod could see the dealer's point. If he was under any kind of regular surveillance, it would be insanity to store the weapons in his home, and if Vachon was as clean as he maintained, why take the chance in any case? A neutral drop was standard in the business, but there had been something in his choice of transfer points that set the Georgian's teeth on edge.

He hadn't been afraid of spooks and bogeymen since he was eight years old. You couldn't make sufficient noise to wake the dead, not if you opened up with every AUG and submachine gun he was buying from Vachon.

But it was the concrete fact of death, the chiseled stone reminders all around them, that had shaken Axelrod. The man from Georgia seldom dwelt upon his own mortality, convinced that when death found him there was nothing he could do about it. His obstinate refusal to take death seriously had extended into business. There was no one in the world he cared enough about to name as heir, and so he had no will. The greedy jackals who surrounded him would have to fight it out for every penny when he went, and it would serve the bastards right.

He heard the engine before the six-ton rig lumbered into view. They must have been waiting in the cemetery since the crack of dawn, and Axelrod was irritated at the thought that he had wasted twenty minutes waiting for the load when it had been there all the time. At least Vachon was conscious of security precautions, though a tail would certainly have shown itself by now.

Axelrod would have liked to put the weapons on a plane and fly them home, but he could not afford to gamble with the customs men. If anything went wrong, his ass was on the line, and he had no desire to spend the next few years inside some federal country club for losers. If the paperwork was clean, as Paul Vachon had promised, Jimmy Duggan would be stateside in an hour or two, and he could take his sweet time driving south.

Vachon was smiling at him now, self-satisfied. He gestured toward the truck as it approached and said, "The merchandise."

"I'd like to see a sample," Axelrod replied.

"Of course."

The smile remained in place, but Axelrod imagined that he saw a spark of irritation behind the Canadian's eyes. And that was fine. He hadn't flown to Canada and driven to the middle of a graveyard just to trade his money for the weapons sight unseen. He would examine three or four at random, maybe ask to fire some practice rounds.

No, he wouldn't bother with a test fire. Paul Vachon was known for moving quality, and if he'd ever stiffed a customer, no memory of such an incident survived. The Georgian could have simply laid his money on the line, but there was principle involved. You never showed a dealer too much confidence—and that was doubly true of foreigners. If you appeared complacent, careless, they inevitably tried to screw you in the end.

He smiled at that, a mental image of Vachon in leather coming to his mind, and quickly pushed the thought away as he concentrated on the truck. It lumbered to a halt some twenty feet from the Mercedes. The driver scrambled down, his shotgun rider cautiously remaining in the cab. The muzzle of an Uzi submachine gun nosed above the dashboard for a moment, then retreated out of sight.

And in that moment he recognized the shotgun rider, placed him from the night before and from the countless fuzzy stills on network television.

It might have been a burn, of course, but Axelrod was not concerned about that now. He knew that if Vachon had meant to kill him, he could easily have done it at the house. Unconsciously, the Georgian let himself relax. Another hour, and he would be sitting down with Toby at Lester Pearson International Airport, relaxing with a drink and waiting for the homeward flight.

Another hour.

Reaching back inside the limo, Axelrod retrieved the fat valise and handed it to Toby, swallowing a smile as Paul Vachon cast hungry eyes upon the bag. The Canadian obviously still had things to learn about the value of a poker face. His greed was like a neon sign across his forehead.

"The merchandise?"

"Of course."

The driver of the van preceded them, released a paddock that secured the load and rolled the tailgate upward. Inside, the wooden crates were neatly stacked and labeled as machine parts.

The driver scrambled up among the crates, a pry bar suddenly appearing in his hand. He chose a crate apparently at random, was about to pry its lid up when the Georgian shook his head.

"The next one back," he said.

Vachon looked irritated, but finally shrugged and nodded to the driver. Leaning back across the crates in front, the driver popped one in the second rank and laid the lid aside. He lifted out a submachine gun, snapped a magazine in place and passed it down to his employer.

"The Steyr-Daimler-Puch MPi 69," Vachon said, almost lovingly. "Chambered for 9 mm parabellum. An improvement on the Uzi, with blowback operation on an advanced primer system. The wraparound bolt provides increased muzzle velocity and accuracy. A cyclic rate of 550 rounds per minute, and the weapon can be disassembled in a maximum of fifteeen seconds.''

Axelrod hefted the weapon, getting its feel, extracting the magazine, working the bolt. He had a sudden urge to fire the little SMG, to waste a magazine redecorating ranks of ancient headstones, but he let it pass.

''All right.'' He handed the SMG back to Vachon. ''The rifles now.''

STRETCHED OUT AMONG THE DEAD, Carl Lyons watched the deal go down from fifty feet away, a stubby riot shotgun tucked beneath one arm. He had been lying motionless between the tombstones for something like two hours now, since following the van and gunners to their boneyard rendezvous. It had been less risky than pursuing Axelrod and Paul Vachon directly from the Canadian's walled estate, and the results had been identical. He had been waiting when the silver-gray Mercedes showed, and he was watching as the occupants unloaded, fanning out around the limousine.

Vachon.

The target, Gerry Axelrod.

Two gunners standing by, a third behind the wheel.

And Toby Ranger.

The Able Team warrior felt his stomach turning over slowly as he recognized the lady from a distance. It had been a while, but there could be no mistake.

And that changed everything.

He had been braced to tackle Axelrod and company right here, to bag the Georgian and persuade him to discuss his contacts in Durango, his relationship with someone like the Raven, but with Toby in the cross fire, it would have to wait. Despite the churning eagerness inside, the urge to see it done, he would not jeopardize the lady fed or see her mission blown.

Goddammit!

He would have to follow Axelrod back home, attempt to infiltrate his hardsite there. It galled him when he thought of all the wasted time, but there appeared to be no alternative.

The buyer was examining a submachine gun, drawing back the bolt, dry firing, finally returning it to Paul Vachon. The Canadian passed it to his gunner in the truck, and waited while the flunky handed down a futuristic-looking rifle. Lyons recognized the Steyr AUG, and whistled softly to himself.

The neo-Nazi underground was stepping up in class from all their usual army-surplus hardware. They were going modern, and that spelled trouble for their countless enemies. They were girding up for Armageddon now, and once the weapons were in hand, the bastards would be itching for a chance to try them out on human targets.

Except that Axelrod would never take delivery of this load in Georgia. Lyons was determined that the arms would not go through. Axelrod was bought and paid for, living out his days on borrowed time, and if he had connections with the Raven, if the contact in Durango had been anything beyond a fluke...

The Able warrior's smile was grim, devoid of warmth. A killing smile. And he was looking forward to the moment when he faced this member of the "master race." A moment that might change the neo-fascist's life forever, or bring it to a close.

His target was examining the rifle now, inserting a plastic magazine into the butt-stock receptacle behind the pistol grip and peering through the Steyr quick-

reflex sight. He swept the muzzle in an arc across the
ranks of tombstones, and for half a heartbeat Lyons
thought he might be visible between the markers, but
the moment passed and Axelrod returned the rifle to
Vachon. It disappeared inside the truck once more, the
tailgate was secured, the Georgian and the Canadian
backtracked toward the Merc, where Toby waited with
a fat valise in hand.

The engine sound was jarring in the cemetery stillness, bringing Lyons's face around in the direction of
the noise. A V-8, rapidly approaching from the same
direction as the van, perhaps one hundred yards away
and still concealed behind a line of trees that bordered
on the curving drive. He slid the shotgun forward, eased
the safety off, already sighting down the stubby barrel
and prepared for anything before the Jeep growled into
view.

Prepared for anything except the Raven, riding
shotgun in the Jeep and looking very much alive.

The bastard had an AK-47 tucked beneath one arm,
and he was smiling broadly at the evident effect that his
appearance had on Gerry Axelrod. Vachon was shooting cautious glances at the Georgian, clearly worried
that they might have blown the deal, and Axelrod was
snapping questions at him, getting shrugs and noncommittal gestures in return.

The Ironman couldn't catch their words, but it was
clear enough that Axelrod was being asked to pay the
Raven, rather than Vachon. The Georgian argued for a
moment, finally took the fat valise from Toby, passed
it to the terrorist and backed away. The Raven took a
peek inside, seemed satisfied and nodded to his driver.

They were turning now, preparing to depart, and
Lyons realized that he might very well be kissing off his

only chance to bag the bastard. Toby's mission, all the rest of it was secondary now. The Raven's presence transcended all priorities.

He had one chance, and Lyons knew that he would have to make it count. The Jeep was just below him, still accelerating, as he raised the scattergun and fired.

Chapter Twenty-One

The Executioner was up and moving, angling to intercept the Jeep, when thunder suddenly erupted from the headstones opposite and the tableau disintegrated into milling chaos. Breaking stride, he saw the Jeep begin to swerve, the Raven rising from his seat, the AK-47 tracking off to starboard as the right front tire exploded. The wheelman tried to save it, turning with the skid, and then a second thunderclap reached out to drill the grill and blow the hood back in his face.

The Raven scrambled clear before the Jeep had come to rest, his autorifle stuttering a burst in the direction of the headstones as he scuttled toward the truck. Around the Mercedes, Axelrod and company had gone to ground, the gunners hauling weapons out from under their jackets, searching for a target that was still invisible.

They hadn't noticed Bolan yet—and wouldn't, if he took to cover now, allowed the action to proceed and find its own conclusion. He could let the cannibals devour one another, watching safely from a ringside seat. It would be easy.

Except for Toby... and the Raven.

The lady was in danger, and Bolan would not permit the Raven to escape if there was any way on earth to bring him down. He had no way of knowing who had sprung the trap and did not particularly care. The Raven's unexpected personal appearance was a shock, but grim experience had taught the Executioner to seize on any opportunity that might arise.

Vachon no longer mattered. Axelrod was less than nothing in his mind. The single target of his hatred crouched before him now, concealed from hostile fire behind the van but totally exposed from Bolan's line of sight. The soldier eased his AutoMag out of its holster with a steady hand.

Across the narrow drive another shotgun blast erupted, the pellets rattling off Vachon's Mercedes. A gunner scrambled from the truck, his Uzi stuttering across the hood before he hit a crouch behind the fender, edging forward to achieve a better line of fire. Wild, sporadic rounds were coming from behind the limo now, chipping marble from the tombstones opposite. From where he stood, the soldier caught a glimpse of Axelrod with a pistol in his hand, hunched down behind the limousine with Toby at his side.

A sudden hint of movement behind a sculpted angel, and he caught a fleeting glimpse of the attacker. Blond hair, and the glint of sun from aviator's glasses as he raised his shotgun, worked the action, fired, retreating instantly before the hostile guns could find their range. One of Vachon's torpedoes stumbled, clutching at his midriff, toppling forward on his face.

One down, and seven left to go... but only one of them held any real significance for Bolan now. The twisted brain behind a brutal hijack and his own humiliation crouched before the soldier, less than thirty yards away. The range was virtually point-blank for Bolan's AutoMag. He couldn't miss.

A handgun opened up across the drive—a Magnum by its sound—and Bolan idly wondered if the shooter over there was calling in reserves. No matter. Bolan had his target now, was tightening his finger on the trigger when the big Mercedes roared to life and started rolling, gathering momentum and abandoning the figures crouched behind it.

Bolan glimpsed the driver, riding low behind the wheel, a look of desperation plastered on his face when he was forced to risk a glance above the dash. Vachon and company had scrambled clear, the Canadian beating on the driver's window and shouting at him, jerking furiously at the door latch.

A booming Magnum round reached out to claim the second gunner, spinning him around and dumping him facedown on the grass. Before Bolan could react the Raven was in motion, scrambling toward the cab of the abandoned truck, already disappearing through the open door.

The AutoMag exploded in Bolan's fist, the heavy round evaporating windshield glass downrange, its passage spraying shiny pebbles out across the hood. The Raven spun to face him, obviously taken by surprise but running on his instincts now, the AK-47 answering with deadly, searching fire. The soldier hit a slide and came to rest behind a gravestone, angry hornets swarming overhead and clattering against the stone, mere inches from his face.

But his easy, one-time-only shot was gone, and the warrior knew he would be lucky now to make it out of there alive.

GERRRY AXELROD COULD NOT BELIEVE it when the goddamn limo started moving, carrying his cover out of range and damn near dumping him beneath the fat rear tires. He rolled away and came up cursing, scrambling for safety as the car began to gather speed. Vachon was pounding on the driver's window, bellowing in French for him to stop the frigging car before they all got killed, and then another Magnum round came sizzling in from somewhere on the slope directly opposite, and hardman number two was nothing but a memory.

Reflexively, the Georgian aimed his squat Detonics at the tombstones, squeezing off a round that didn't make him feel the least bit better. They were sitting ducks down here, and now the chicken-shit chauffeur was taking off with half their transportation, leaving them with nothing but the truck.

It struck him then, and Axelrod was conscious of precisely what he had to do. No time for second thoughts, no time for *anything* except a dead-end run for cover at the van.

He had given up on wondering who the gunner was. There had been too damn many shocks already—first, the Raven popping up from nowhere, making off with the valise of cash, and then the hidden gunner, damn near popping him before he had a chance to clear the scene.

The Raven was alive, as far as Axelrod could tell. His driver hadn't been so lucky—he was stretched out in the middle of the narrow blacktop, leaking from half a dozen holes—but from appearances, the Raven had emerged unscathed.

Vachon had thrown himself across the limo's windshield, heedless of the gunfire all around him now, obscuring the driver's view and forcing him to creep along by jerks and starts. Incoming rounds were whining off the armored body, etching cobweb patterns on the

safety glass, and still the tank kept inching forward, like
an armadillo suddenly deprived of sight.

A shotgun blast sent pellets swarming overhead, and
Axelrod bugged out, aware of Toby scrambling for
cover on his left, intent on finding sanctuary among the
headstones there. The bitch was on her own; he had no
time for anything except survival now, and even that
was hanging by a thread.

Ahead of him, he saw the Raven make his move, already at the truck and climbing to the cab. Great minds,
he thought, and he was almost there when someone
opened up in front of him, a frigging cannon roaring in
his face and taking out the windshield of the truck.

He flattened on the shoulder of the pavement,
watched the bullet-scarred Mercedes lurching out of
sight behind the van. And he was watching as the bullet took Vachon, its impact punching him away and
backward off the windshield, frantic fingers scrabbling
at the glass for purchase. The French Canadian caught
a windshield wiper, bent it backward with his sagging
weight . . . and it was just enough to keep his bulk from
rolling clear. As Axelrod lay watching, Paul Vachon slid
beneath the limousine. One tire passed over both his
legs, the femurs snapping with a sound of muffled
gunshots, lost within the echo of a strangled scream.

The Merc shot forward, suddenly accelerating, but
the driver lost it as a gunner suddenly descended from
the tailgate of the van and blundered straight into the
limo's path. The impact rolled him up across the hood,
and Axelrod could see the driver's hands fly up as if to
intercept a blow before the big car started drifting,
gathering momentum on a collision course with the
abandoned Jeep. The armored nose of the Mercedes
almost cut the Jeep in two, and then the gas tank blew,

an oily ball of fire devouring the limousine and bringing it to a halt.

He didn't wait around to watch the driver scramble for his life, his suit in flames. The Raven was already cranking on the van's ignition, struggling to put the juggernaut in motion, and it was the only hope that Axelrod retained of getting out alive.

The Georgian lumbered to his feet and sprinted toward the truck, aware of fleeting movement on his left. A man in black was rising up to risk a shot, and what the hell was that, a *cannon* in his fist? The squat Detonics roared, his target dropped from sight instinctively, and Axelrod was at the truck, with no time left to think about the enemy.

He scrambled for the cab—and came up short, the muzzle of an AK-47 in his face. The Raven recognized him, hesitated for a heartbeat, finally let the rifle drop.

"Come on!" he shouted, wrestling the gearshift into first, already standing on the gas to put the van in motion.

And he flooded it. The engine shuddered and died.

The Raven slammed one fist against the dashboard, cursing bitterly in Spanish as he twisted the ignition key, and Gerry Axelrod was wondering when his life would start to pass before his eyes.

"Let off the gas!"

"Shut up!"

Still pumping at the van's accelerator, cursing as the engine cranked and groaned, the Raven turned to Axelrod... and smiled. A chill raced up the Georgian's spine, the short hairs lifting on his neck as he realized that he was riding with a lunatic.

The bastard was insane. He was enjoying all of it, as if the massacre had been arranged for the purpose of entertainment.

And everyone was wrong, the Georgian knew with sudden clarity. Your life did not begin to flash before your eyes when you were on the verge of death. Instead, your future ran before you, like a newsreel in fast forward, tantalizing you and tearing at your guts with all the things that might have been.

The spokesman for American survivalists hunched down inside the cab and stolidly prepared himself to die.

CARL LYONS FED ANOTHER ROUND into the shotgun's magazine and worked the slide. Crawling on his belly near the headstones, he was searching for a target, aware that he was running out of time. If nothing else, the smoke from burning vehicles would soon attract attention, bringing firemen and police around his ears.

He scanned the narrow battlefield, intent on finding out precisely who had joined the battle. He hadn't seen the gunner yet, but he could scarcely miss the gunshots, echoing among the headstones like the rumbling of artillery.

A Magnum, definitely, but...

The half-formed thought was teasing him when Lyons caught a glimpse of movement among the headstones opposite. A flash of color, and he recognized the lady fed, evacuating while she had the chance. She cleared a statue of the Virgin, was proceeding toward another monument when someone tackled her and rode her to the ground.

Goddammit! Lyons couldn't see a thing now for the drifting smoke and intervening obstacles. He risked a closer look, and someone down below released a burst of automatic fire, the parabellum rounds defacing family headstones on his left and right.

The guy was too damn good, and Lyons had determined to eliminate the threat...when, suddenly, he heard an engine turning over, revving, slipping into gear. A glance, and he was startled as the truck began to move, a grinning figure hunched behind the wheel and keeping low, providing him with little in the way of target.

Out of nowhere, Gerry Axelrod was pounding toward the truck, his ruined jacket flapping out behind him, and Lyons was about to drop the bastard when he saw a figure rising, wraithlike, from behind a tombstone just in front of the survivalist. He didn't need a second glance to recognize the black-clad figure or the silver hog-leg in his hand.

Mack Bolan.

The goddamn guy was sighting on the truck, intent on picking off the Raven, when Axelrod cut loose a double punch and drove him under cover. Lyons fired instinctively, his buckshot chewing pavement at the Georgian's heels, and Axelrod was out of sight, already in the cab before he had a chance to pump and fire again. He fired another round, etched jagged snowflake patterns on the driver's door—and ducked for cover as the Raven let him have another pinpoint burst of automatic fire.

The shithead must have nerves of steel, or else he must be running purely on survival instinct. Lyons heard the engine revving up again, was rising on his knees to risk another shot...and then it stalled. He felt a savage smile distort his face, aware that he could have them now with Bolan's help.

Rising out of smoke and shadow, a surviving gunner broke in the direction of the truck, his Uzi tracking on the hillside, milking short, staccato bursts toward Lyons's nest. The guy was firing blind but coming close enough to force the Able warrior down, and Lyons pumped an angry round in his direction, knowing it would miss his target by a mile.

And he was watching as the bastard reached the truck, got one foot on the running board, one hand upon the windowsill. He meant to join the party, tag along to safety if they ever got the van in motion. The guy was shouting something, still inaudible from Lyons's vantage point, when Axelrod reached over, pressed his automatic up against the gunner's cheek and fired.

As if on cue the engine caught, and Lyons was convinced that he could hear a twist of high-pitched laughter drifting upward from the open window of the van. The Raven poked his AK-47 through the driver's window, firing off a burst, but Lyons held his ground, the twelve-gauge roaring as he worked the slide with lightning speed. When it was empty he discarded it and ripped the four-inch Python from its armpit holster, banging off six rounds at the retreating cab.

Across the narrow drive, Mack Bolan's AutoMag was bellowing in concert with his Colt, the heavy rounds impacting squarely on the target, savaging the Raven's flanks as he accelerated out of there. The truck began to shudder as he took it through the gears, and crates were spilling off the open tailgate, shattering on impact, spewing AUGs and submachine guns in the street. Another moment and the bullet-punctured dinosaur had vanished, lost behind a screen of trees that lined the curving drive.

The Ironman cursed beneath his breath. He'd blown it, let the bastards get away, and there was nothing left to show for all the carnage but a scattering of two-bit gunners, dead or dying from their wounds. Worse yet, he'd blown it with Mack Bolan looking on.

Carl Lyons shook his head, returned the Python to its harness, stooping to retrieve the shotgun. Grimly, knowing he had failed, he started down to face the Executioner.

"Long time."

Mack Bolan nodded, shook Lyons's hand.

"Too long," he said.

"Well, if we're done with class reunions here..."

The lady's voice was peevish, and she made no effort to conceal her irritation as she joined them, hobbling down the hillside, shoes in hand.

"I didn't have the Raven figured for a personal appearance," Bolan said, ignoring her.

"You saw him, then?" There was a trace of doubt in Lyons's voice, as if he half suspected he had been hallucinating.

"Everybody saw him." Toby's voice was mocking, almost bitter. "He was sitting right up there as plain as day."

"I blew it," Lyons said, disgusted with himself.

"Then so did I," the Executioner replied. "I had him cold before he hit the cab."

"Goddamn it!" Lyons shook his scattergun in the direction of the vanished truck. "We were that close."

"Spilt milk," the lady fed observed. "We'll be that close to jail if we don't get our tails in gear."

"We've got a minute," Bolan told her, trying to project a confidence he didn't feel. "I want to check on something first."

He moved among the corpses, pausing here and there to turn a body over, checking for a pulse or peeling back an eyelid, seeking signs of life, but all in vain. He was about to call it off when he reached Paul Vachon, the Canadian lying on his back with shattered legs, his shirt and jacket saturated with the scarlet seepage of a chest wound.

And the guy was still alive.

Against all odds, his eyelids fluttered, rolling back on glassy orbs. The Executioner knelt down beside him, slipped a hand beneath the dealer's head to help him breathe. The eyes were unseeing, and Vachon believed that he was being comforted by Gerry Axelrod.

"It's not my fault," he gasped.

"I know that," Bolan told him.

"Did you . . . save the shipment?"

"No. We lost it, Paul."

Vachon stiffened, trembling. *"Merde."* He fought for breath a moment, finally found it. "Steyr. I have people there, inside. You tell them that I send you."

And he knew that he was dying.

"The Raven, Paulie. What's his action?"

"Partner. His connection . . . Steyr."

Strength and life ran out together, and the guy was suddenly flaccid in the soldier's hands. As Bolan rose he heard the distant sirens drawing closer, running all the numbers down to doomsday zero in his mind.

"You ready now?"

The lady's voice betrayed anxiety in place of anger and Bolan nodded, striking off along his backtrack toward the hidden rental car.

"I've got some wheels back there," Carl Lyons told him, nodding vaguely toward the cemetery's southern quadrant.

"We can drop you off," Bolan told him, pushing on among the headstones, putting death behind him for the moment.

"We?" The lady fed was close behind him, walking in his tracks, avoiding contact with the graves. "You got a hamster in your pocket there, or what?"

The soldier let it go, his mind already occupied with other problems. They had blown it, and there was nothing left to do but try and save the pieces now. Whatever happened next, the three of them were in it together. Wherever it might lead them, they could not afford to let it go.

The Executioner could not afford to let it go.

He had too much invested in the chase to simply watch his quarry slip away. He had no option but to forge ahead, regardless of the cost.

And if it cost his life, it would be worth it, to feel the Raven's throat within his grasp, to see the spark of life snuffed out behind those gloating eyes.

Chapter Twenty-Two

"All right, what have we got?"

Mack Bolan settled back into a straight-backed wooden chair and lit a cigarette, his eyes on Lyons and the lady fed. Around them, cheap motel decor reminded him of something from a grade-C movie set.

Lyons glanced at Toby, finally shrugged resignedly.

"Okay. Three days ago I popped a drug connection in Durango. It was a snafu from the beginning, and we lost two friendlies going in. One of the hostiles was the Raven."

Bolan felt the short hairs rising on his neck. "You've seen him then? Before today?"

The Lyons grin surprised him. "Seen him? Hell, I killed the bastard."

Toby frowned. "You're rambling, Carl."

"I wish I was," he told them both. "There's no mistake. I dropped the guy, stone cold. Eyeballed him closer than I am to you right now. I took a couple of fingers with me for the technos back in Wonderland, you dig it?"

Toby grimaced. "And?"

"No prints. An expert surgical removal."

"So you can't be positive," Toby Ranger said.

"Like hell. Did anybody have a problem recognizing him today?"

The lady wasn't buying it. "But if we saw him, then—"

"He's either risen from the grave, or else—"

"He was a ringer," Bolan said.

"Affirmative." The Ironman's eyes were sparkling with the excitement of the hunt. "Brognola thinks we may be dealing with a team."

"What makes him think so?" Toby asked.

"Another Raven showed himself in Germany the same time I was popping mine in Mexico."

"Says who?"

"McCarter. Yakov."

"Did they tag him?"

"Nope. Clean miss, from what I understand."

"How could they let him get away?"

"How could *we* let him get away?"

Mack Bolan cleared his throat. "Let's start at the beginning," he suggested. "Each of us is here on different missions, but they obviously interlock. I think it would be helpful if we pooled our information."

Toby's brow was furrowed with suspicion. "You go first."

"That's fair. I came up looking for Vachon. His name was given to me by a contact in New York. According to my source, he moved the weapons for an operation that the Raven ran down recently."

"Flight 741."

Lyons's voice was soft but clearly audible across the room. His eyes met Bolan's, and the Executioner was suddenly aware of something there, inside, that had not surfaced heretofore.

"That's right."

He kept the answer simple, fighting down the sudden flood of images. The crowded cabin of a 747, reek-ing after so many hours of close confinement. Naked bodies pressed together in the narrow seats. A slender figure, masked for Halloween and brandishing an ax.

"Brognola knows," the Able warrior said.

The simple statement startled Bolan, sent a crackling electric current racing up his spine.

"How long?"

"He didn't say. I got the feeling it had been a while."

The lady fed was glancing back and forth between them now, confused, her irritation growing by the moment. "Hey, what is all this? Would you two like to be alone, or what? I thought that we were coming clean."

Her fiery tone provoked a smile from Bolan, which appeared to irritate her all the more.

"I was on Flight 741," he told her.

Toby's mouth was open, working silently, and Bolan thought it was the first time he had ever seen her at a loss for words. It didn't suit her. "But...I mean..."

"It's over."

"Is it?" Lyons asked.

The soldier thought about it, finally shook his head. "No way."

"So you were Raven hunting."

"Tracing his connection," Bolan answered. "When I spotted Gerry Axelrod and company, I put the probe on hold for the duration. I was looking forward to a conversation with Vachon when all his guests went home."

The lady fed was staring at her hands, a flush of color rising in her cheeks. "My turn," she said. "I've been with Axelrod a while...inside the Brotherhood. It wasn't what it looked like. Hey, I mean he doesn't like the ladies, 'kay?"

Carl Lyons chuckled to himself. "You're serious? The ranking redneck in America is gay? How did he plan to raise another master race come doomsday?"

Toby blushed again. "We never talked about it. I was there for show, a household decoration. When it came to business, he was something else."

The Able warrior waved an open hand, limp-wristed, simpering. "I'm sure."

"All right, Carl. Are we playing games, or what?"

"Go on." The Executioner was not amused.

The lady cleared her throat and started over.

"Axelrod's been moving weapons to the right-wing underground the past two years or so. We know it, but we haven't had a thing to hang indictments on. The SOG's been looking at him lately, after all the coverage his Brotherhood's been getting in the media. We'd like to take him down a peg or two before the stakes get any higher."

"Is there anybody on it with you?" Bolan asked.

She shook her head. "I'm it...reporting back through channels, natch. The brass thought Axelrod might get suspicious if he saw too many unfamiliar faces all at once."

"The bureau must have people in his family."

The lady shrugged. "I guess. It's need-to-know so far. Whatever, they've been getting feedback after the event. Hal wanted some preventive medicine before the fever spreads."

"I guess it's spreading anyway."

"In spades." The lady sounded tense again. "You know the score. These bastards feed on misery. A father out of work. A family looking at eviction somewhere down the road. It's nice to have a scapegoat and some easy answers. Blame the Jews, the Democrats, the PTA.''

And Bolan knew the story, sure. It was the classic line employed with fine impartiality by zealots of the left and right, recruiting cannon fodder for their private wars by playing on the weakness of their fellow man. Appeal to greed or bigotry or sheer naïveté, but make the sale at any cost. And once you had your sucker on the line, committed to a course of action he would never even contemplate in saner times, you wrapped him up in guilt, indebtedness, intimidation—anything it took to keep him loyal and close at hand. It was a classic, sure, and it was rarely known to fail.

''Vachon,'' he prompted her.

''Okay. The Canadian was an arms connection—one of Gerry's favorites, I think. He had some kind of in with European sources, something hot. I never got the details, but I gathered that the Brotherhood was sitting on a mother lode of automatic weapons. I mean, mass-production time.''

The Executioner recalled Vachon's last words, the whispered name of Steyr. A town in Austria...and more. A multinational concern that had been turning out the latest word in light, efficient automatic arms the past few years.

An in at Steyr would be the mother lode, indeed. Mack Bolan didn't even want to think about those sleek, sophisticated weapons in the hands of Gerry Axelrod and his affiliated brothers of the blood. He didn't want to think about it, and then again, he had no choice.

He turned to Lyons. ''Fill me in about Durango.''

''Sure.'' The Able warrior took a moment to collect his thoughts. ''We had a rumble out of DEA that ma-

jor moves were in the works to tap a brand-new source
of heroin. Unlimited supply, improved delivery, the
works. The agency had lost two men by the time I got
the tag. Our rumbles were that the delivery was being
made to Axelrod.''

"Say *what*?''

The lady fed was clearly startled, craning forward in
her chair as if to spring at Lyons, wrench the story from
his throat before he had a chance to speak. The Ironman frowned.

''You didn't know that he was into chemicals?''

''Aside from the explosive kind, I didn't have a clue.''

''Well, there's your need-to-know.''

"God*damn* it!''

Bolan kept his eyes on Lyons. ''Go ahead.''

''Where was I? Oh, Durango, right. Well, anyway, I
made connections with some local eyes, we made the
pop…and in the middle of it all, we find a Raven on the
menu.''

Bolan's mind was racing, feeling out the different
possibilities, the implications of this new intelligence.
He didn't like the rapid, dizzy changes of direction, not
at all.

''You mentioned Germany.''

Lyons nodded. ''This is straight from Katz and
McCarter. They were sitting on some Baader-Meinhof
types around the time that I was in Durango. Someplace south of Munich, I forget the name. Whatever,
when they sprang the trap they found a Raven in it with
the other bastards. Bastard got away, but Katz was sure
he made the face.''

''And that was—what?—how long ago?''

''Four days.''

''So Mr. Germany had time to catch a plane.''

"I guess. Hell, yeah. So what?"

The Executioner stubbed out his cigarette. "I'd like to know how many men we're dealing with."

"It couldn't hurt."

"You got an eyeball on our man today?" Bolan asked.

"Damn straight. That's why I opened up. I didn't want the bastard shagging out before I had a chance to scorch his tail."

"How did he stack against the Raven in Durango?"

Lyons thought about it for a moment. "Close," he said at last. "I mean, I made him right away...but it was at a distance, right? If I could get a look up close..."

"The bottom line."

"Okay. Let's say they'd pass for twins...but not identical. You follow?"

Bolan followed, sure—and he was far from happy with the ultimate direction that his mind was traveling.

"Would someone kindly tell me what the hell is going on?"

"A ringer," Bolan answered simply. "Could be more than one. There isn't just *a* Raven anymore."

She took it in, a hint of color fading from her cheeks as she ran through the gruesome possibilities.

"But why?"

"You know the why," he told her. "Optimum mobility and maximum exposure. Ask your average citizen to name a terrorist, and nine times out of ten he'll name the Raven. Julio Ramirez. He's a legend in his field. The perfect bogeyman."

"He's indestructible," Lyons added, with a hint of wonder in his voice. "It means there's no way we can tag the guy, not really. Hell, the real Ramirez may be dead already... if there ever was a real Ramirez."

"Jesus," Toby muttered, "this is something else."

"In spades," the Executioner replied. "A custom-tailored monster for the media. They eat him up and keep on coming back for more."

Both Lyons and the lady noted bitterness in Bolan's voice. They let it go.

"There could be half a dozen Ravens," Toby said, incredulous. "There could be twenty, or—"

"There could be hundreds," Lyons finished for her. "Moscow could be mass-producing them by now. It makes the goddamn guy immortal."

"No. Not yet." The grim resolve in Bolan's tone demanded full attention. "He's been too sporadic up to now; let's call it too disorganized. I'd say it's possible the ringers are a relatively new idea."

"Which means that we could head the bastards off, provided we knew where to start."

Bolan smiled at Lyons's new enthusiasm.

"Well, we've got a start," he told them, "thanks to Paul Vachon."

"How's that?"

"The Raven was accepting payment on the deal with Axelrod. I'd say that indicates direct involvement with supply."

"Yeah, so what?" Lyons said.

"So, we already know his source."

"The Steyr plant?"

"Uh-huh," Bolan replied, smiling thinly, the expression totally devoid of warmth.

"Now wait a second," Toby cautioned, glancing anxiously from one determined warrior to the other.

Lyons grinned. "I understand Bavaria is nice this time of year."

The Executioner was way ahead of him already, scanning through the moves that would be necessary, calculating risks before he put the wheels in motion. Finally, he knew it made no difference in the end. No matter what the cost, no matter what the dangers, he was totally committed to the chase. He would pursue the Raven now because he *had* to, right. He simply had no other choice.

The bastard had humiliated Bolan, made him play the silent, helpless witness to atrocity. At any other time, in any other circumstances, Bolan would have seen him dead before the drama had progressed beyond the first, abortive stages.

Except that there had been no other circumstance. Bolan had been dealt a losing hand by fate, the universe, whatever. He had played the only cards he had, and now he was compelled to seek a rematch, with the odds presumably more equal the second time around.

Presumably.

But he had never counted on a second Raven, or a third, a *fourth*. How many were there, waiting for him, circling the globe like plague birds, seeking helpless prey? Was there a chance that he could ever bag them all? That he could even hope to find the Raven who had led the raid against Flight 741?

The bastard might be dead already, Bolan knew. Carl Lyons might have tagged him in Durango, making all of this a wasted exercise.

It didn't matter, Bolan realized, if he should ever find *his* Raven. By definition, they were all his enemies, and he was pledged to take them out by any means at his disposal. It was not a personal vendetta, after all; the soldier knew that hate could only fuel a righteous flame so long. Beyond that point some other fuel was needed.

Dedication.

And heart.

In Pittsfield, when his family lay in ruins at his feet, the Executioner had pledged undying enmity against the Mafia . . . but hatred had not carried him through more than two-score winning battles with the syndicate. In time, his loss had been absorbed, preempted by the pain and suffering of victims everywhere, his fight becoming every man's, his sacrifice a universal offering to gods unknown. His war did not revolve around a single incident, a single act of barbarism. He was waging war against the cannibals, for life, and he would still have been compelled to hunt the Ravens, even if he had been unaware of the atrocities aboard Flight 741.

But Bolan was aware, and he would not forget while life remained. His hate was not the driving force behind his war, by any means, but it would help to keep him warm, to steel his nerves and guide his hand when it was time to strike.

And hatred had its uses. It could be very therapeutic, in its way.

He smiled again, and there was warmth behind the Executioner's expression now, a hidden fire.

Chapter Twenty-Three

The plan had been simplicity itself... and it had come about by accident. The individuals who played a relatively minor role in its conception were catapulted to the status of superior tacticians in the secret war against the West.

Their contribution was regarded as significant and they were rewarded with prestige, a kind of covert fame that was the best they could hope for in the circumstances. None of those were as startlingly successful, as "inspired" as the original... but then, they were not provided with another Julio Ramirez.

No one seriously thought the Venezuelan was special. He showed a certain recklessness in college, cutting classes, disregarding the instructions of the party when it suited him, applying too much energy to the pursuit of women and a swinging bourgeois life-style. Some within the party apparatus were prepared to write him off, convinced that further schooling in the arts of war would be a waste of time, but they were overruled—by chance, coincidence, what-have-you. Being communists, they could not call it fate, although a few would happily have credited—or blamed—the gods in days to come.

Ramirez did not seem to be a natural for covert training. The pretentious middle name, Ilich failed to move the officers of the KGB. They saw through such transparent stratagems at once, and they were not deceived. The young man's record was average, at best, but his Hispanic heritage might count for something, after all.

The training camps were swamped with Palestinians, a scattering of Germans, Irish, Japanese—but in the Western Hemisphere, despite the Cuban revolution, terrorism lagged far behind the times. Conservative regimes held sway from Mexico to Argentina; Sandinistas, Tupemaros, Salvador Allende and the rest were still unknown outside their limited preserves. The memory of Che Guevara, cherished by assorted unwashed radicals in the United States, was scorned within his native land.

Ramirez, and perhaps a dozen others like him, were accepted as apprentice terrorists to meet a quota, chosen on the basis of their Hispanic names and olive skins to meet a need at Dzerzhinsky Square. Ideally, they were to be the vanguard of a revolutionary movement in the West. If nothing else, their actions might inflate the withered ranks of Hispanic revolutionaries toward the day when South America would rise in arms against her neighbor to the north.

In training, Julio Ramirez revealed a certain unexpected skill with weapons and explosives, taking to the theater of violence avidly, but he was still no more impressive than the average *fedayeen*. His background, staunchly upper middle class, was a solid strike against him in the camps, and many of the terrorists in training bitterly resented him from the beginning. Still, his progress was adequate, and he was posted to a fighting cell in Paris with the expectation that his Latin charm would serve the movement in peripheral capacities. He

was a sort of flesh-and-blood recruiting poster in those
early days, but circumstances swiftly got the better of
intended strategies.

The Israeli Wrath of God chose Easter 1973 to execute Amal Haddad in Paris, and the sudden vacancy in
leadership kindled a new ambition in the Venezuelan's
mind. And if the KGB was not precisely overjoyed by
Julio's emergence at the forefront of an armed commando squad, it deigned to make the best of an uncomfortable situation.

Julio Ramirez was a wild card from the outset,
choosing targets on his own, ignoring the "sugges-
tions" of his KGB control more often than he followed
orders. Still, where terrorism was concerned, there
could be no such thing as bad publicity; each bombing,
each shooting on the street, discredited the Western
governments and left them looking completely ineffec-
tual. It was touch and go in 1973 after the shoot-out in
Rue Toullier, but the confrontation with security police was a blessing in disguise.

It was only then, with two policemen and a paid in-
formant dead, that members of the media singled out
Ramirez for special treatment in the headlines. He had
been a nameless "suspect" in the past, but he was guilty
now, and any killer of policemen merited a special
scorn. He was "the Raven" now—a scavenger of car-
rion—in headline stories and on television. Julio was
angered briefly by the nickname, but in time he came to
see how it might work to his advantage.

And for once the KGB reached a similar conclusion
on its own.

Ramirez was a terrorist, no worse nor better than a
thousand others huddled in their warrens throughout
the Middle East, in Europe, Southeast Asia. But the

Raven . . . now there was an idea. In time it could become a legend if cultivated properly. The media fastened on a single terrorist and were prepared to make him something more: a superterrorist, perhaps.

In spite of the publicity, Ramirez almost blew it on his own. Not content to lose himself until the heat from Rue Toullier dissipated, he began to read the headline stories, to listen to his own publicity, to *believe* what was being said about him in the media. And by believing, he saved the day.

Sporadic missions marked his year in hiding. A border raid against the tough Israelis, bagging several women and a luckless child before the terrorists were driven back to sanctuaries in the east; a bank job in Berlin, with two guards murdered in a brief, one-sided fusillade; a skyjack, ending with the death of six Israeli passengers and demolition of the plane while newsreel cameras rolled. There were other strikes and other deaths, but it was OPEC that made the difference in the end.

In 1975, the Organization of Petroleum Exporting Countries maintained its general headquarters in Vienna, Austria. Already putting pressure on the West, inspiring temporary shortages of energy to boost the flagging price of oil, OPEC did not surrender totally to interests in the Middle East. The union of petroleum exporting nations was already moving toward a sort of jury-rigged omnipotence, a recognized invincibility. Composed primarily of Third World countries, OPEC was beset by strife and civil war around the globe, but terrorists had left the oil-producing states alone.

Until Ramirez.

In OPEC Julio saw a target ripe for the picking, fat with petrodollars, weak from years of being catered to by larger, stronger nations. The plan was bold, and it made the Raven more than just another terrorist. With one inspired, demented stroke, Ramirez made himself a star.

That Sunday in December, OPEC ministers were bogged down in debate on oil price differentials. An undertone of bitterness had colored the proceedings, bringing the discussions to a standstill. The media were generally aware of trouble in the ranks, and enterprising journalists descended on Vienna, each alert for any opportunity to scoop the competition.

There was nothing special, then, about the three young men and one young woman who displayed their press credentials for the guard on duty, whisking through the relatively lax security on Sunday morning. Camera cases passed unscrutinized, the pistols, hand grenades and automatic weapons safe inside. When Julio Ramirez gave the signal to attack, his "journalists" were armed and ready for the kill.

Three guards were slaughtered in the first exchange, another on the very threshold of the OPEC conference room. Surprise was absolute; no terrorist was even wounded as the armed quartet secured their hostages—some seventy in all—and broadcast terms for safe release. Twelve million dollars was the asking price, together with safe passage to Algeria by jet.

A fourteen-hour siege by members of the Austrian Einsatzkommando unnerved Ramirez to the point that he was forced to set a grim example for the world…and he did so via television, live, in screaming color for the leaders of the West to see.

The Raven selected representatives of Libya, Gabon and Venezuela, herding them downstairs at gunpoint through the double doors that faced the street. When he was satisfied that camera teams were ready to immortalize his deed, Ramirez fired a single burst that dropped all three captives. The Libyan and Venezuelan delegates were dead on impact with the sidewalk; paralyzed for life, the spokesman for Gabon would live to tell his story—and perpetuate the Raven's reputation for ferocity.

The double murder forced Vienna's hand...and set the strategists back in Moscow to thinking. Clearly, Julio Ramirez was a man of some initiative and daring, marked for bigger things provided that he did not risk his life too often, too unwisely. If his energy could only be controlled and channeled into special areas...

The answer was Project Raven, and the rest was history. Instead of disappearing after OPEC, suddenly the Raven had been everywhere at once, in touch with rabid groups of terrorists in Europe, South America, the Middle East. His sheer audacity ensured attention from the media; the almost casual violence of his raids assured that he would top the "wanted" lists of every Western nation while he lived. It seemed impossible that any single man, no matter what his underground connections, could attack with such rapidity at widely separated points, inflicting heavy casualties in quasi-suicidal actions, fading back into the woodwork instantly, without a trace.

It seemed impossible...because it *was* impossible.

Recruitment of the ringers was not a problem. There were numerous candidates from the outset, and if Moscow suffered any difficulties, they arose from struggling to narrow down the field of possibilities. Five "Ravens" were selected in the end, selected less for their resemblance to Ramirez—though physique, complexion and the like were closely scrutinized—than for their basic aptitude. Each member of the Raven team was finally selected after psychological reports and testing in the field confirmed his ability to kill—with energy, with relish, with enthusiasm. Anyone could learn the fine points of ballistics, demolitions and the rest, but killer instinct was a quality that could not be acquired.

The first selected was a Cuban mercenary named Raul Escobar. A child of Castro's revolution, he grew to manhood on the fabled exploits of Fidel and Che Guevara, chafing at restrictions placed upon him by his family, society, the party that declared the revolution in Havana had already reached its goal. With no worlds left to conquer, no wars left to fight, Raul turned to crime and served a stint in Castro's prisons, reemerging as a bitter, streetwise gunman, hungry for excitement in a world that promised only tedium. His innate talents were recognized belatedly by agents of the DGI, and he was recruited for the training camps in Jordan.

Brief, sporadic action with the Tupemaros preceded his recruitment into Project Raven, and Raul proved himself the perfect stand-in for Ramirez, moving arms and drugs and friendly fugitives from Mexico to Nicaragua, striking at Americans whenever opportunities arose. His sudden death in Mexico, cut down by unknown gunmen in Durango, surprised and worried planners in Dzerzhinsky Square.

The second Raven clone was Carlos Castresana, yet another Cuban, chosen on the strength of Escobar's success. A radical by inclination, he was employed with Castro's DGI, dispensing lethal punishment to actual or suspected traitors, stalking Western agents in Havana and environs, leading brief, ferocious sorties aimed at disaffected peasants in the countryside. A man whose ego dominated everything except his taste for bloodshed, Castresana resisted plastic surgery at first…until he grasped the full potential of his opportunity. For Carlos Castresana, Project Raven was a hunting license and the world was his preserve. He took to random murder as an alcoholic takes to liquor; there was no looking back and no regrets.

The Soviets were slow to realize that Hispanic blood was nonessential for their ringers, but they finally got the message and selected Janos Ludovescu as their third in line. The slim Bulgarian could pass for Hispanic if he tried, and surgery would help, but his instinctive thirst for blood was the real deciding factor. Known and feared as an assassin in his native land, suspected of involvement in the torture slayings of assorted prostitutes as recreation on the side, he became embarrassing to a regime not generally known for sensitivity to human rights. He was marked to die by members of his party, men who realized that they could not control him any longer, and the order was cut when Project Raven granted him a brand-new lease on life.

The KGB was slightly more successful in controlling Ludovescu, but control was not the problem, after all. By definition, Project Raven was designed to foster chaos in the West, and Janos Ludovescu was a perfect doomsday tool in that pursuit.

The Palestinian—Mahmoud Karmin Khaldi—was Raven number four, selected on the basis of his work with Black September and the PLO. Reputedly an architect behind the Munich massacre of 1972, he was marked for execution by the Mossad, a standing "hit on sight" directive issued out of Tel Aviv. In Project Raven, he grasped a second chance to strike against the Zionists and their protectors in the West, to carry out his destiny as handed down by Allah in his youthful dreams. It mattered not that he surrendered name, identity, the links to family and friends in Palestine. His life was in the movement now, his soul committed in the struggle to eradicate the state of Israel. Nothing else bore any true significance, and he would die in that pursuit without regret, with pride.

For Luis Calderone, the Nicaraguan, Project Raven was a shot at fame and fortune once removed. He did not mind the built-in anonymity; if truth be told, he viewed as heaven-sent the opportunity to hide behind the mask of Julio Ramirez, dealing drugs and revolution from Miami to Colombia.

The KGB did not object in principle to numbered Swiss accounts, so long as monetary profits kept the fifth and final Raven on his toes, in fighting trim. If Calderone attempted to defect or simply disappear, the planners in Dzerzhinsky Square would take delight in teaching him that even Zurich could be reached, the most secure of bank accounts eliminated with the stroke of a computer key.

Except for Escobar, the Raven clones—recruited over twelve short months—had proved durable in combat and elusive when pursued by agents of the West. It helped, of course, that none of them resembled Julio Ramirez *too* exactly...just as it was helpful that no close-up photographs of Julio himself remained. The blurry telephoto shots from OPEC, hopelessly outdated yearbook photographs from London and Caracas—none would do the Raven justice now. The several different artist's renderings were even worse, compiled from memories of witnesses who had been praying for their lives and studying the automatic weapon in his hands instead of concentrating on his face.

The Project Raven clones—complete with matching dental work, devoid of fingerprints—would stand inspection well enough in life or death, and through the safety guaranteed by numbers, Julio Ramirez became immortal. Even when the man himself was gone to dust, his legend—and his living likeness—would continue fighting for the cause that had become his life.

Confusion.

Orchestrated chaos.

Mayhem in the streets.

The Raven's message was a simple one: destruction for destruction's sake. And if a transient cause could be co-opted for the moment, used to justify the moment's carnage...why, so much the better. Let the IRA or Red Brigades, the Baader-Meinhof gang or M-19 receive the "credit" for his crimes. The benefits—in pain and suffering, in the embarrassment of Western governments—would still accrue to Moscow in the end.

The plan had been simplicity itself...and it had worked with the precision of a fine machine. But Project Raven had a blind side, too.

Dzerzhinsky Square had never counted on the Executioner.

Chapter Twenty-Four

Mack Bolan's flight approached the airport at Salzburg, Austria, through a drizzling alpine rain, the clouds and leaden skies obscuring his view until they leveled off for touchdown. Toby Ranger, in the window seat, was calling off strategic points of interest as they passed below, but Bolan kept his eyes averted from the oval pane of Plexiglas, his thoughts turned inward.

Flying transatlantic, touching down at Frankfurt and again at Munich, had recalled a host of memories that Bolan would have gladly done without. The Raven's grinning Nixon face had never truly left his mind since he had seen the terrorist aboard Flight 741, but now—confined within the aircraft, the Bavarian Alps rising up to meet him like so many dragon's teeth—the images came flooding back with crystal clarity. He felt the fabric of the seat against his naked back and buttocks, saw the gout of blood as ax bit flesh and bone, remembered rolling in the aisle as boot heels drummed against his ribs and spine.

His palms were clammy and he wiped them unobtrusively against his slacks. The images receded slowly, ancient anger and a sense of outrage rising in their place, dispelling nausea and setting Bolan's teeth on edge. It was a different flight, a different time...but he was glad the memories were fresh enough to make him sweat. If they had paled, grown dim, he might have lost the grim resolve that drove him on.

Bolan had a score to settle with the Raven. For himself, and for the other hostages of 741. For every victim on the bastard's sheet. And there was only one way Bolan knew to even up that kind of score.

In blood.

The jet touched down and Bolan waited, restless, as they taxied toward the terminal. Beside him Toby seemed relaxed, but he could sense an underlying tension almost equal to his own. The lady fed was way out on a limb this time, ignoring her instructions, flying in the face of established procedures. In the wake of the Toronto blow-out, she had ducked the chance to call Brognola, making Lyons promise that he wouldn't pass the word of her departure from the States until they reached their destination, safe beyond recall. She was determined to pursue Gerry Axelrod, and Bolan wondered if the job was getting to her.

Before the thought had taken on cohesive form, he put it out of mind. The lady was a slick professional, no question there, with all of the detachment that the term implied—but she had heart, as well. She felt for all the victims, bled along with them . . . and Bolan wondered if she might not have invested too much of herself this time.

He had initially resisted her demand to join the game, convinced that he could do the job alone, or with the help that Katzenelenbogen and McCarter might provide. The lady's part of it was over from the moment that her mark had climbed aboard the Raven's van and left her scrambling for cover in an old Toronto cemetery. There was nothing more she could do for Bolan's war.

But she had finally convinced him that the war could not be his alone. With Axelrod at large, with "Ravens" multiplying all around them, his conception of the struggle was no longer valid. The pursuit of sweet revenge had turned to something else entirely—something that demanded a sophistication and coordination of response.

And Toby knew the Georgian. She knew him inside out and upside down. At length, reluctantly, the Executioner had been convinced that she would be an asset when he was required to deal with Axelrod.

The seat belt warning lights switched off and Bolan left his seat, allowing Toby to precede him down the narrow aisle. A short, brisk dash through pelting rain, and they were safe inside the terminal, already scanning for the one familiar face they were expecting. Toby spied him first; the tall man's face was handsome, broken by a smile, his hand outstretched.

"Striker," he said, as Bolan took the offered hand and shook it warmly.

"Good to see you, David," Bolan told McCarter, and he meant it.

Phoenix Force's man in Salzburg waited with them at the luggage carousel, amusing them with jokes and making small talk, touching on the weather, politics, security around the airport.

Bolan didn't need to be reminded of the latter. There were fewer guards in evidence than they had seen in Munich, but there was tension all the same. As Bolan casually scanned the terminal, he marked no less than seven men in uniform with pistols on their belts and automatic weapons slung beneath their arms. The recent rash of skyjacks, bombings and the like had everyone on edge, from London to the Balkans, and he was relieved that he had come unarmed.

McCarter would supply him with the necessary hardware for the job he had in mind. For now, the AutoMag, Beretta and the rest of it were safely stateside, ready for retrieval if and when he made it home. Whatever happened afterward, he would at least clear terminal security without the risk of an arrest for smuggling arms.

It took another twenty minutes for the luggage to appear. McCarter waited while they checked through customs, had their passports scrutinized and stamped. The clerk on duty didn't waste a second glance on "Mitchell Bowman," seeming more preoccupied with "Bowman's" traveling companion. Toby gave the guy a smile that made his day, and they were through in moments, following McCarter toward the lot where he had parked his rental car.

"We're meeting Katz in Steyr," he informed them when he had the car in motion, "at the Hotel Ibis."

"What's the local action?" Bolan asked.

"You're right about the leak," McCarter said, "although you'll have the devil's time persuading anyone to say so openly. They're losing arms in quantities, and nothing seems to stem the flow."

"Security?"

"They've been through half a dozen chiefs this year. No matter who they sack, the problem stays the same."

"I didn't think Vachon would have that kind of weight."

"He didn't. This is major movement, not your standard pistol-in-the-lunchpail pilferage."

"Contacts?"

"Katz is working on the Earth Party now, putting out some feelers for a buy. As soon as someone takes the bait, we move."

They were traversing Salzburg eastbound, following the flow of traffic through the heart of town. On their left, romantic Old Town huddled on the Salzach River's bank, between the rippling water and the Monchsberg—narrow, twisting streets, arcaded courtyards and tall, narrow houses harking back to the age of Mozart. On the right bank were the newer districts of the town, with the Kapuzinerberg and its conspicuous Capuchin friary rising above them to the east. Despite the rain, a throng of tourists filled the narrow sidewalks.

Toby turned from the romantic scenery, looking wistful. "Any sign of Axelrod?" she asked.

McCarter shook his head. "Not yet. We've been expecting him since Ironman passed the word, but if he's here he hasn't shown himself."

"Where can he be?" The lady sounded angry, worried, all at once. "He wouldn't run back home without the goods. I know that much."

"He'll surface," Bolan told her, less concerned with Axelrod than with his own primary target of the moment. "What about the Raven?"

"Not a sign. We're working on the theory that there may be multiples, but even so..."

"I'd say it's pretty well confirmed."

"Okay. We still can't move until the bastards show themselves. They could be anywhere and everywhere by now."

Mack Bolan understood the problem, but he was hoping that the cumulative weight of recent incidents might be enough to draw the several Ravens home— wherever home might be. He had no reason to believe it would be Steyr; the town and weapons factory were just another stop along the way, a new potential source of information to assist him in his quest. The Raven's lair might just as easily be somewhere in East Germany, in Cuba or the Middle East, for all he knew.

They cleared the city limits, rolling east through Salzburg province, bounded on the north by the Upper Bavarian plain and the hilly Alpine foreland. They followed the Salzach valley through terrain that varied widely as they passed; the mountains of the Dachstein massif dominated overall, with dark, forbidding forests. At other points the highway opened out and traveled arrow straight for some kilometers, before the hillsides finally closed around them once again. It should have been no more than sixty miles to Steyr, but the winding mountain roads would add another twenty miles before they reached their destination.

"I understand it hit the fan in Canada," McCarter said.

"You got that right."

There was a trace of bitterness in Toby's tone, and Bolan wondered if the lady would be able to divest herself of anger, act with cool deliberation when the time was right. Before the doubt was fully formed, he put it out of mind. The lady was a trained professional, damn right, and he had seen her work firsthand. She had the strength required for this—or any other—job.

"You saw the Raven in Toronto?"

"We saw *a* Raven," Bolan answered.

"Bloody hell. I wish we had some decent photographs." The Phoenix warrior's eyes were narrowed as he watched the road. "How many do you think there are?"

The Executioner had thought of little else since the encounter in Toronto, torturing himself with thoughts of nailing down a score of Ravens, never positive that he had tagged the one responsible for capturing Flight 741.

"It wouldn't take an army," he replied at length. "No more than eight or ten, perhaps as few as half a dozen. Any more than that, they'd run the risk of duplicating efforts, laying trails that might disrupt the whole damned operation."

"Do you think there ever *was* a Julio Ramirez?"

Bolan shrugged. "Why not? The idea had to come from somewhere, and the background on this bird is pretty firm."

"You've seen his file?"

"At Stony Man."

The reference, with its memories of death, betrayal and revenge, brought momentary silence to the three of them, each concentrating on his private thoughts. McCarter broke the ice again when they had driven on for several miles without a word.

"This smells like KGB."

"They'll have a piece of it," the Executioner agreed, "no matter where the plan originated. Anything this size could only work to Moscow's benefit."

Behind them, Toby had been worrying at something else, and now she spoke her doubts aloud. "We know the Raven—one of them—was supplying Axelrod with guns through Paul Vachon. If Lyons is correct, another Raven's been providing him with drugs from Mexico. But dammit, all this time...I'd swear he never knew the Raven, never met him face-to-face."

"Entirely possible," McCarter said. "The bloke's devious enough to work through cutouts, after all. To tell the truth, I can't imagine why he surfaced for a simple buy-out in Toronto. Risky business, that—and all for what?''

"Nobody ever said the guy was stable," Bolan offered.

"True enough. And if the guy is really *several* guys, with different temperaments..."

"Stability goes out the window," Bolan finished for him, smiling to himself. "They just might have a cowboy on their hands."

The prospect cheered him, giving rise to hopes of possible dissension in the hostile ranks, a clash of personalities that might prevent the several Raven clones from working smoothly as a team in an emergency. One down, in Mexico; at least two others burned, unless the Ravens seen in Germany and Canada turned out to be identical. In either case, the savages had lost their image of invincibility. They could be seen—and, more importantly, they could be killed.

It was the kind of edge an Executioner could work with.

The highway took them out of Salzburg province into Upper Austria, a region drained by the Danube and its several tributaries. The area is notable for heavy industry, including steelworks, manufacture of commercial vehicles—and the thriving weapons plant at Steyr. They were close enough to smell their quarry now, and Bolan rode in silence for the last few miles.

Positioned at the junction of the Steyr and the Enns rivers, the town of Steyr is an old, established focal point of the Austrian iron and steel industry. Drawing much of its iron ore from the Erzberg at Eisenerz, the old town—squatting on a tongue of land between the two rivers—still preserves a certain medieval quality. At a glance, it would not be suspected as the home of Austria's most famous small-arms manufacturer.

As McCarter homed on the Hotel Ibis, they motored down the Stadtplatz, surrounded on all sides by old, arcaded homes and shops, some dating from the fifteenth century. Except for traffic on the streets, the modern wares displayed in windows of the shops, they might have been transported back in time, across the centuries into the Middle Ages. Bolan scanned the quaint facades of buildings as they passed, and he hoped they would not have to make the town a shooting gallery before they finished there.

It was the nature of his work that he must wage it in the streets, among the gentle folk who were, at bottom line, the very spoils of war. He did not know a soul in Steyr except for Katz; no man would know that Bolan passed among them here unless his war spilled over into fire and blood. When he was gone, the city would continue on about its business, healing wounds and finally forgetting what had brought him here.

But Bolan could not forget. The image of Flight 741 was with him now and always—just as images from Pittsfield filled his dreams. The soldier had forgotten nothing from the outset of his private war. He was forgetting nothing now.

It was his task to gather memories of pain and suffering, to nurse them, keep them fresh against the day when opportunities were granted to avenge those wrongs, to strike against the cannibals and drag them screaming from their burrows. No matter if the savages were mafiosi, mercenary terrorists or "pacifists" with automatic weapons in their hands. Whatever mask they hid behind, the Executioner was pledged to hunt them down.

It was his destiny, the only way of life that he had ever known.

For Steyr, right now, it was the only game in town.

Chapter Twenty-Five

Julio Ramirez lit a slim cigar and blew a wispy smoke ring toward the vaulted ceiling of his study. Swiveling his padded chair in the direction of the picture windows, he once more admired the sweeping panorama of the Alps, the craggy, snowcapped Matterhorn slightly to his left. That view had cost him upward of a million dollars . . . and how many human lives?

He did not dwell upon the subject. The thought of death did not unnerve him, but he hated letting mundane thoughts intrude upon the majesty of nature. After years of living, working, fighting in the cities of the world, Ramirez had a fine appreciation for the wilderness, those portions of the globe unscarred—or nearly so—by man.

The Matterhorn, for instance. Mastered by a handful of intrepid climbers, it remained majestic. Still dangerous, it had the cold capacity to kill and maim without remorse. At one time or another he had lived in jungles and in deserts, but Ramirez loved the mountains best. They humbled man, and having done so, let him reach beyond himself in search of something greater, something infinite. Their challenge summoned forth the best in man and weeded out the worst.

Like war.

A veteran of countless wars and mountains, Julio Ramirez spent another moment staring at the Matterhorn, wishing he was up there among the crisp, eternal snows, decked out in climbing gear and reaching for the summit of the world. A climbing party had been scheduled for the afternoon, but weather was preventing their departure. Maybe, if they got away tomorrow, he would watch them through his telescope...and dream.

The wound prevented him from climbing now, of course. Unconsciously he ran one hand along his thigh and traced the outline of the ancient scar. It wound around his kneecap like a pale tattoo, the outline of a surgeon's stitches barely visible when he had gone too long without the sun. Sometimes in winter he recalled a vestige of the pain, flashed back to memories of other climates, other wars. The flashbacks never lasted long, but they invariably left him bathed in perspiration, trembling like a frightened child.

It had been pure coincidence, of course; the damned Israelis never knew that he was in the bunker, never had an inkling of how close their strike had come to snuffing out his life. They had been after other targets—Palestinians in general, and Black September in particular—that afternoon. Their spies had not observed him, he was sure of that, but the result had been the same.

Unbidden, memories returned. The baking desert sun, and temperatures inside the bunker higher than they were outside. You paid a price for your security in Lebanon, and he had learned that lesson well. A younger man, impetuous, courageous at the cost of wisdom, he had lingered with the *fedayeen* beyond his deadline, basking in their adoration once the job was done. He should have been moving toward another rendezvous with revolution, but his stubborn independence led him to ignore the cryptograms, remain among the ragtag soldiers who were carrying his gospel to the world.

A shriek of Phantoms, diving from the sun, no quarter asked or given to the antlike figures on the ground, their cannons belching high-explosive death in rapid-fire. He saw them coming, saved himself by breaking for the open, going wide while most of the guerrillas headed for the bunker, seeking safety underground. He saved himself—almost—by opting instantly, instinctively, for the unusual, unexpected course of action.

Pain, as real in daydreams now as it had been in life, the shrapnel slicing through his flesh, and he was airborne on a gust of smoky thunder, falling endlessly until he woke beneath white linen in a Beirut hospital room. The doctors had no firm idea of who he was, but they had been advised by Arafat and others to see that he received the very best of care.

And they had saved his leg. No matter that it stiffened on him now below a certain temperature, that he limped at any pace beyond a stroll. The wound had put him out of action permanently, and for days he had believed that it would render him expendable, ensure his swift elimination once the word leaked back to Moscow. Later, he had realized the folly of his fears. The Russians needed him, would pay to keep him happy and cooperative while they continued their secret war.

He was a star, albeit more notorious than famous with his public. As the Raven, he had taught the West to live in fear, to taste the bitter gall of paranoia every time a diplomat or wealthy businessman set foot outside embassies or foreign offices. He was *the* terrorist of any given year, most wanted by the bourgeois nations, most pursued by strategists of Third World countries on the rise. In time, he would have served them all, and named his price.

But there had been no time these past three years. He was sidelined by his wound, unceremoniously relegated to the bench while others carried on in his behalf. They used his name, his face, his style . . . but none of them would ever really *be* the Raven.

Julio Ramirez felt no conscious bitterness at having been cut off before he reached his prime. Khaddafi and the Soviets had been most generous; they might have simply murdered him, instead of purchasing a villa, granting him a very healthy pension and allowing him to serve as strategist and elder statesman for the Raven force.

He had been fortunate, and yet he missed the action, the smell of cordite, blood and fear, intoxicating, stimulating the adrenal glands. He missed the rush of combat, the excitement of pursuit, the hounds behind him, running close and baying at his heels. He missed the power, the adventure of it all. The mantle had been passed to others but they wore it in his name, and while it lasted, Julio Ramirez could at least derive vicarious release by following their exploits, charting raids and second-guessing their mistakes.

Mistakes had never been a problem . . . until recently. Of late the game had taken unexpected turns, and now he sat before his favorite view, cigar in hand, and wondered what the hell was happening.

No problem with the skyjacks. The plans had gone like clockwork, with America predictably capitulating, giving in to his demands while making noises like the victor. Propaganda notwithstanding, everyone on earth had seen the giant humbled, forced to bow and scrape before his tiny band of warriors. Everyone on earth had seen, and understood.

The drugs were a problem from the start, and he recognized the fact that there would be some difficulties. Ramirez had no scruples when it came to dealing drugs—indeed, he had few scruples when it came to *anything*—but he realized that Western nations would respond to the narcotics traffic with missionary zeal.

The West never came to terms with drugs, would never understand the Eastern mind in that regard, and so Ramirez prepared himself for opposition. It was worth the risk—especially since his sponsors would be picking up the tab and guaranteeing his supply—but looking back, he realized that everything had soured when they entered the narcotics trade.

Durango was the first disaster. Escobar had blown it, pushed his luck too far against an unknown enemy, and he was snuffed out. Fine. Given the dynamics of their trade, a death had been inevitable somewhere down the line. Five agents in the field, competing for the most bizarre and dangerous assignments, could not hope to live forever. But Ramirez had enjoyed the company of Escobar, his sense of humor. As the first recruit for Project Raven, he had shared a special closeness with his namesake, viewing Julio Ramirez as a mentor, almost as the brother he had never known.

Durango had been painful, whereas Mittenwald was merely startling. It had been close for Ludovescu, but he escaped—unlike the others. Ramirez had no inkling what happened, nothing but the bare mechanics of the raid, the chaos that it inspired in Baader-Meinhof ranks. Two years of close cooperation were jeopardized, and there were some within the German group who blamed the Raven, stopping short of any blatant accusations, hinting broadly that his inefficiency—or worse—had doomed their friends to death.

He could not begin to fathom what happened in Toronto, with Khaldi's weapons transfer. There was no opportunity to talk about it on the telephone, but he would be receiving personal reports within a day or two. He knew, already, that an ambush was waiting when they went for the exchange, and that was disturbing in itself. Security was clearly failing, and it was but little consolation that his ringers escaped unharmed in two of three encounters.

A back-check on security had shown Ramirez that official agencies, per se, were not involved. The hostile bodies in Durango had been *former* DEA, but if they had enduring ties with federal agencies, those ties were not apparent to his inside sources. As for Mittenwald and Canada, he had no clue regarding who blew his scores, or why. The German operation was not official; the Soviets had ears inside GSG-9, and would have known if antiterrorist commandos were responsible. As for Toronto, the encounter there was being handled as a clash of criminals, reported in the press as something of an eight-days' wonder, unexplained beyond the reference to weapons found abandoned at the scene.

He would be hearing from the Russian, damn it; there would be no way around him now. If there had been no casualties, perhaps . . . but what the hell, it did no good to worry over the inevitable. Soon—tomorrow, or the next day—there would be a call, informing him that Comrade Rylov was in town and looking forward to the pleasure of his company.

He had dealt with Soviets before and would no doubt be forced to deal with them again. They were his bread and butter, masters of the project that supported him in luxury and ease. He owed them that . . . and still, it rankled him, being at their beck and call.

The Russians were in debt to him, and it was time they realized as much. Without his name, his image, Project Raven would have floundered from the start.

He was ready for the meeting, almost looking forward to it now, although he knew that Rylov would be angry, asking questions that Ramirez could not hope to answer. Panic was a gut reaction with the Russians, an instinctive veering off the target any time they hit a snag. It was the reason they were dying in Afghanistan, outfought by ragtag peasants in the bush. For all their might, their revolutionary rhetoric, they lacked the fighting spirit of the *fedayeen*, the Irish, the Japanese. Given half a choice, Ramirez would have cut the Soviets loose . . . but he could not afford to kill the golden goose. Not yet.

It would be necessary to appease his contact, make the Russian think that Julio had the situation well in hand. No small task in itself, considering his own confusion at the moment, but with any luck at all he should be able to confuse the issue, keep the money flowing in from Moscow while he tried to nail the problem down.

There was a problem, and Julio Ramirez knew that it would only worsen if he took no countermeasures. First, however, he would need a definition of the trouble, something that would lead him toward determination of the enemy's identity. If it had *only* been Durango and the drug connection, *only* Mittenwald or Canada, he would have opted for coincidence, the natural result of doing business with the underworld. A triple strike, however, staged in widely different target zones by enemies unknown, was something else entirely.

Three strikes within a single week, in Mexico, in Europe and in Canada, spoke clearly of concerted hostile moves against his team. By whom? The possibilities were endless: the Americans, Israelis, French, Italians, Spanish, Greeks, a handful of assorted other nations theoretically too small to mount effective actions on their own but rich enough to hire it done. The drugs might be another angle; he knew that certain syndicates—most notably the tough Colombians—were anxious to eliminate competitors.

The Raven shook his head and took another draw on his cigar. The drugs were out, he thought. No syndicate possessed the sheer sophistication necessary to pursue his men around the world, to seek them out and strike when they were in the midst of highly sensitive exchanges. Escobar, perhaps...but the Colombians had no enforcement arm in Canada or Germany, no interest in the dealings of Vachon or Baader-Meinhof functionaries. Clearly, there was something else....

His mind would not accept the possibility that Escobar, Khaldi and Ludovescu had all been burned by sheer coincidence. The odds against it happening were too high. Reduce those odds, perhaps, because his men—*himself*—had been on every Western "wanted" list for years; the odds against three identical encounters happening by chance, and several thousand miles apart, were astronomical.

An acid feeling in his stomach made the Raven pause. He focused on the Matterhorn, its craggy silhouette permitting him to put away the images of covers being blown, disguises penetrated, operations going up in smoke. His men were tough professionals, hand-picked, recipients of all the finest training.

But human beings made mistakes, of course, and anything was possible in theory.

A sudden, dark suspicion surfaced in his mind. There was no leak within his team, he knew that much with certainty...but what about the Soviets? With all the scandals and defections recently, who knew precisely what was happening in the clandestine services? You only read about the failures of the CIA or MI 5; the Russians dropped their failures in a hole, or put them on a cattle car directed toward the Gulag. It was entirely possible, he thought, that someone in Dzerzhinsky Square, or elsewhere, might have blown the lid on Project Raven.

Another grim suspicion nagged at him. Suppose the Russians had no leak, what then? Suppose that someone in authority had made the cool, deliberate choice to scuttle Project Raven? Might the rash of incidents result from conscious, orchestrated leaks—or from the intervention of the KGB itself?

A chill had worked its way along the Raven's spine, the short hairs on his neck bristling against his collar. If the Soviets were trying to dispose of him, his ringers, it would only make good sense to let the Western powers do their dirty work. A whispered word, directions to the drop, and CIA, Mossad, GSG-9—whatever—would be thrilled to take the ball from there, and damned few questions asked. The Russians would preserve deniability and thereby save face with other factions of the underground.

He didn't see the mountains now, although his eyes were open, staring at the panorama set beyond his window. He was looking inward, searching out the shadowed corners of his life, intent on finding any clue that might reveal duplicity by Rylov or the KGB.

He was at a loss to understand why anyone in Moscow should decide to yank the rug from underneath his feet. He had been loyal since he was first recruited out of college in the Sixties. There had been the usual indiscretions, certainly, but only in the early days, while he was rising to the status of celebrity among his fellow terrorists. The KGB had seemed to understand, had even tacitly encouraged him to play the renegade, assert himself in choosing targets in the public eye. It would be damn unfair of them to look back now and turn their hand against him.

But when had fairness entered into his profession? When had justice risen from the status of a revolutionary watchword to achieve reality?

He knew that Rylov might be planning to eliminate him even now. He would be ready when the Russian called, tomorrow or the next day at the latest—ready with some questions of his own, and with some answers for any queries that the KGB man had in mind.

He would be ready with some swift, decisive action of his own in case his dark suspicions proved correct. If Rylov and his crew intended to discard the Raven, they had better think again. Ramirez might be lame, but he was not an invalid, by any means. The tiny troop at his disposal would be capable of wreaking bloody vengeance before they all went down in flames.

He concentrated on the fine cigar, and on the Matterhorn, remote and cold beyond the windowpane. When this was over, he would need to get away, to find some solitude and rest.

When it was over.

Soon.

Chapter Twenty-Six

The rattler's high-pitched warning buzz froze Lyons in his tracks, one combat-booted foot raised in preparation for his next step through the kudzu thicket. Rapidly, he scanned the ground around his feet, index finger tensing on the trigger of his automatic shotgun, praying that he wouldn't have to use the weapon now, when he had come so close. The blast could be his death knell, sounding clearly through the piny forest, bringing down security before he had an opportunity to disengage.

He saw the reptile, a five-foot-long timber rattler, its flattened, heart-shaped head barely visible beneath the drooping ferns a yard in front of his position.

Lyons slowly pulled back his upraised foot before his leg began to tremble uncontrollably. The reptile watched him with lidless eyes, its warning rattle like a swarm of angry hornets, grating on his nerves. He took another backward step, another, and the serpent's tongue flicked out to test the air, a flickered blur of motion at its snout. Another step, and he was moving sideways now, aware that while the snake might soon lose sight of him, it would be sensitive to his projected body heat within a wider radius. He needed distance—but without completely losing his direction in the trees.

A little tremor gripped him, sparked by primal memory, and Lyons shrugged it off. The serpents that he really had to watch for were ahead of him, inside the compound, and they would be walking upright. A rattlesnake or two would be the least of Lyons's worries if they found him now, decked out for doomsday, closing on their sensitive perimeter.

Five miles behind him, the Atlanta skyline was a monument to modern architecture, progress and technology. He could retrace his steps, retrieve the rental car and find himself on crowded city streets within five minutes. Out here, the homes were few and far between—more often aging mobile jobs or weathered shanties. There were still outdoor privies tucked away behind the cabins here—or, rather, you might spot them from the highway. Here among the trees, you found no sign of human life at all.

He had been hiking for the best part of an hour, since he dropped the rental car, deliberately pausing every dozen yards or so, alert for any trace of sentries, dogs or technological security. He could have traveled faster, but for the moment Lyons was content to take his time.

Another fifty yards, and he could see the compound now. The base maintained by Gerry Axelrod for training of his would-be Aryans reminded Lyons of Vietnam. It had the same barbed-wire perimeter, the barracks and command post up on stilts to guard against the snakes....

Unconsciously, he glanced around him, probing at the kudzu with the muzzle of his shotgun, alert for any hint of slender, gliding forms. The silent shadows mocked him, and he bellied down among the ferns to scan the compound from a distance, searching for a handy point of entry.

It was getting on toward dusk, as he had planned, long shadows deepening among the trees, reducing visibility for any sentries on the night shift. Lyons counted off a dozen figures moving in the compound, all decked out in camouflage fatigues, but they did not appear to follow any military regimen. One sentry on the gate, his cigarette a winking beacon in the semidarkness, and no evidence of any guards along the wire. They were *playing* soldier here, and that made all the difference in the world.

The Able warrior had prepared himself for doomsday, unaware of what he might encounter when he reached the compound. Camouflaged from head to toe, rigged out in military harness, he was ready to confront the enemy on any level they required. The Colt Python .357 Magnum was secure beneath one arm, an autoloading .45 in military leather on his hip. His head weapon was the lethal Konzak shotgun.

Lyons worked his way along the perimeter, remaining under cover in the omnipresent kudzu. A wiry vine of Asian origin, the creeping pest had been transplanted accidentally, and it had proved indestructible in Georgia's warm climate. Now the tangled vines made perfect cover for Lyons, rendering him invisible as he pursued a means of access to the target zone.

He found a stretch of wire behind the makeshift barracks, safe from scrutiny by the guard on duty at the gate. If he timed it properly, his entry to the compound should be unobserved.

Bellied in against the fence, he took a pair of insulated cutters from his belt and snipped the wire. He spent another moment listening for any sound of movement, then wriggled through, securing the flap behind him with a pair of twist ties, safe from any casual inspection.

If Axelrod had been on hand, there might have been a walking sentry on the fence. But the ruling honcho of the Brotherhood was nowhere to be found—perhaps still running from the shitstorm in Toronto.

He crossed a narrow stretch of open ground, found shelter in the shadow of the command hut. There was no light inside, and Lyons risked a glance around the corner. Voices from the mess hall told him that the troops were occupied; on station at the gate, the solitary lookout kept his back turned toward the compound, staring at the darkened woods outside.

It would be now or never, and the Ironman made his move, the pry-bar in his hand and ready as he reached the door of the CP hut, found it locked. He wedged the jimmy in against the jamb and twisted the bar. A loud metallic snap and he was in, the jimmy tucked inside a pocket now, the pencil flash in hand.

The CP hut was unremarkable, equipped with CB radio and telephones, an Army-surplus desk and filing cabinets, gun racks on the wall with riot shotguns, semiautomatic rifles, carbines. Strictly legal on its face, but Lyons would have bet his life that there was other hardware on the grounds. He knew of Axelrod's proclivity for automatic arms, the reputation of the Brotherhood for preaching Armageddon...and preparing for it on the side.

He crossed the room to stand before the filing cabinets, scanning with the pencil flash. Unable to decipher coded labels, Lyons chose a drawer at random, rifled through the bank of thick manila folders. He picked out business correspondence, bills of lading—food, supplies of every sort—and carbon-copy requisition forms. Another drawer was stuffed with maps, a third with files on personnel that he did not have time to scrutinize in any great detail. He started on the second cabinet and scored immediately, lifting out a bulky folder labeled Euro-Earth.

He spread the folder on the desk and riffled through its contents, reading by the narrow flashlight beam, his hackles rising by the moment. Lengthy correspondence, much of it in code, revealed what Hal Brognola had suspected: a working link between the Brotherhood and the pacifist Earth Party, based in Germany and France.

It made a crazy kind of sense, despite the widely differing philosophies involved. The Brotherhood was frankly neofascist, from its thunderbolt insignia—inherited from the Gestapo, via factions of the Klan—to public declarations that minorities and communists were undermining Aryan America. The Earthers were socialists who sought a unilateral disarmament of Western powers, bending over backward in their zeal to toe the Moscow line. The factions should have been inherent enemies, and yet . . .

There had been indications recently of deep dissension in the Earth Party ranks, suspicions that the group might be connected with the fighting spearhead of the Baader-Meinhof gang and Red Brigades. Their enemies—the bankers, Zionists, established government—were not so very different from the targets of the Brotherhood. If Axelrod had managed to establish common ground in terms of cash for military hardware, lifted from the source at Steyr . . .

Footsteps sounded on the wooden stoop outside, and Lyons stiffened, knowing instantly that he was out of time. There was no hiding place inside the hut, no open window granting access to the night. Lyons braced himself and killed the pencil flash, the final numbers toppling in his mind.

The door swung inward, granting him a glimpse of someone cast in silhouette before his fingers found the light switch. A startled Aryan was blinking at him, studying the muzzle of the Konzak and seeing sudden death behind the intruder's eyes. One hand was drifting toward the holstered hardware on his hip.

"Don't try it," Lyons cautioned, almost whispering.

The bastard tried it anyway, a warning shout erupting from his throat before he reached the holster, wrestling with the flap. The Konzak erupted with a single blast, dead on from fifteen feet away, the impact slamming him beyond the door frame.

Already men were shouting from the mess hall, rallying to meet the enemy. Lyons took the time to drop a thermite bomb behind him, cleared the open doorway as its fuse ran down, and he was sprinting for the fence and safety when the night caught fire.

The CP hut was instantly engulfed, the white-hot coals of thermite burrowing through walls and roof and floor, igniting anything they touched. A squad of startled soldiers grouped outside the mess hall, staring at the bonfire, stunned, and Lyons hesitated long enough to let them meet the Konzak firsthand. He tracked the piece from left to right and back again, its recoil trembling along his arms, and watched the straw men come apart downrange.

Two gunners stumbled, sprawled with the initial blast, the others scattering for cover now, too late. A third was breaking for the mess hall when his legs were cut from under him; he fell across the line of fire and took a second blast, already dead before he hit the ground. Two more were wounded, thrashing on the ground and rolling in their blood as Lyons turned away and left them to it.

Sporadic small-arms fire erupted at his back, but they were firing blindly now, still unsure of what was happening. The CP hut was burning brightly, casting shadows everywhere, obscuring the battlefield with drifting smoke. Ideally, he should have saved the suspect files, but there had been no opportunity and he had seen enough to satisfy himself in any case. The Brotherhood was dealing with its own acknowledged enemies, and any premature exposure of the fact could only damage Axelrod.

Thirty feet still to the wire, and suddenly a silent figure came at Lyons from the smoke. The sentry was confused, disoriented, and he struck at Lyons with his rifle butt instead of firing. The Ironman sidestepped, grunting as the stock impacted on his shoulder, throwing him off balance. As the sentry tried to follow up his advantage, Lyons whipped the Konzak around, its muzzle cracking hard against the guard's jaw. He stumbled, going down on one knee, and Lyons shot him in the face at point-blank range, the sentry's skull evaporating into crimson mist.

The shotgun blast had given his pursuers a direction, and they were already closing on him now. He ripped a frag grenade off his harness, pulled the pin and lobbed it through the smoke in the direction of their milling voices. The night was torn asunder and the shouts were suddenly transformed to cries of pain. A second looping overhand—more thermite now, to feed the failing flames—and he was sprinting for the fence as sizzling hellfire rained down on the forest compound.

Lyons reached his exit gate and ripped the makeshift ties away, already wriggling through as aimless, scattered small-arms fire erupted from the clearing. Behind him, hell on earth was rapidly devouring the barracks and the mess hall, thermite coals igniting secondary fires among the trees and undergrowth. Considering the recent rains, it would be easy to control—but Axelrod would have some questions waiting for him when he returned from his secluded hideaway.

Assuming that he *did* return, of course.

It was entirely possible that he would keep on running, to his Swiss accounts and on from there to parts unknown. The bastard made a living at survival, after all; he could survive the momentary setbacks caused by the destruction of his Georgia base and the publicity that followed after. There were other camps around the country, Lyons knew, and other hideaways where members of the Brotherhood could lick their wounds in relative security. The group was still young, as native-born extremist movements went, but it had not been wasting any time. Arrangements could be made with other neo-Nazi factions, with the Klans if necessary, to conceal the would-be führer of America.

But Axelrod could not conceal himself forever. In time, he would be forced to surface—by his ego, if by nothing else. The man simply could not abide obscurity. He would pursue the limelight to his own destruction, given half a chance…and Lyons meant to give him every chance available.

He would be waiting when Axelrod revealed himself again, prepared to ring the curtain down and bring his redneck road show to a close.

If Bolan didn't find the bastard first.

But Lyons worried all the same. His little show tonight had proved nothing, in the long run. Axelrod was vulnerable, but they had already known as much. In spite of setbacks he remained a smooth and dangerous competitor, perhaps with other tricks in store. If he was working with the Raven now—or was it Ravens—then the danger would be magnified.

The Able warrior snagged his jacket on some kudzu, cursed and wrenched it free. The game was far from over yet, he realized, and anyone could take the jackpot with enough determination, guts and will to win. He knew from grim experience that abstract justice didn't count for anything when lives were on the line and it was down to jungle rules.

Survival of the fittest was the game, and they were *all* professional survivors.

Bolan.

Axelrod.

The Raven and his clones.

Carl Lyons.

Toby Ranger.

Katz and Dave McCarter, working undercover, who knows where.

The mixture was explosive, and it was possible that none of them might walk away this time. For damn sure, it would be impossible for everyone to come out on the other side alive. The competition simply didn't work that way.

There were no consolation prizes in the jungle. You were either good enough, or you were dead. There was no middle ground.

Tonight, Carl Lyons had survived, against the odds. But there was still tomorrow, waiting for him, hungry, anxious to be fed. Alone with darkness, Lyons wondered who was on the menu for the bloody day to come.

Chapter Twenty-Seven

David McCarter lit another Players cigarette, held out the pack to Bolan, tucked it back inside a pocket when the Executioner declined. They had been waiting for the best part of an hour, and the Phoenix warrior had already been through half a pack. His nonstop smoking was the only clue that he felt less than totally at ease.

"I think we're blown."

"We're fine," Katz told him evenly.

Their rental car was parked beside the central lake of Steyr's Schlosspark, with the sixteenth-century castle clearly visible to the northeast, dominating the junction of the Rivers Enns and Steyr. They were on the high ground, with the lights of river craft remotely visible from where they sat, but Bolan's eyes and mind were concentrating on the narrow roadway that approached their vantage point from either side.

"They're late," he said, unnecessarily.

"They'll be here," Katz replied.

"You're sure they bought your line?" McCarter asked.

Katz sighed, his breath a frosty plume that hung before his face a moment, finally lost.

"They set a time," he told the Englishman. "They picked the drop. You know as much as I do."

"Bloody hell."

Katz frowned. "They had some kind of party get-together scheduled," he reminded his companion. "Something's held them up, that's all. They'll be here."

Bolan wondered. He was having second thoughts about the drop, remembering Toronto as they waited in the darkness, huddled in their sheepskin jackets, weapons clasped beneath their coats to keep the metal warm and working smoothly.

In the place of Bolan's normal side arm, he was carrying an H&K 9 mm VP-70. The heavy pistol lacked his own Beretta's option of selective fire, but it was double-action, with a magazine capacity of nineteen rounds. He wore the lethal hardware in a clip-on holster fastened to his belt, butt foremost, for a cross-hand draw that would provide him with a fraction of a second's edge in case the meet went sour.

McCarter and the burly Israeli both wore Uzi submachine guns underneath their jackets, rigged in leather harnesses for easy access on a moment's notice. Neither Bolan's piece nor theirs were fitted out with silencers; if anything went down, the sleepy town of Steyr would know about it in a hurry.

It had been almost providential, Katzenelenbogen's smooth connection with a secretary at the Steyr weapons plant. The lady knew a guy who knew a guy... and after several days, the ex-Mossad commando was in touch with individuals who didn't mind diverting shipments, if the price was right. He had already paid his money, promising a great deal more if all went well, but his connections in the plant refused to deal directly with a stranger. They relied on intermediaries, for security, and thus Katz had become involved with politics.

Ostensibly, the Earth Party was composed of pacifists, repulsed by war in all its forms. They led parades against the Bomb, surrounded military installations with their chanting pickets and monopolized the media whenever possible. With faces painted, skull-like, they were fond of blocking traffic outside embassies and legislatures, grabbing headlines for their doomsday message. It was an echo of the sixties, but with an evil eighties twist that banished any brief nostalgic memories of flower children instantly.

Mack Bolan knew about the Earthers' leftist leanings, their proclivity for targeting the Western nations, carefully avoiding any deviation from the Moscow line. They were concerned about American or British nukes, and never mind the Soviets, East Germany, Bulgaria. The pickets chanted anti-NATO slogans, but they managed to ignore the Warsaw Pact entirely. Outraged by the rumors boiling out of Nicaragua, they had no time left to worry over wholesale slaughter in Afghanistan.

The Executioner was not dismayed by the phenomenon. Two decades earlier, he had observed a different generation, equally committed, that condemned the war in Vietnam... or, rather, that condemned *a portion* of the war. United States involvement was the "crime" that rallied countless thousands, braving jail and beatings to express their anguish over nightly bulletins of slaughter on the network news. They never saw, and never raised their voices to protest, the *other* crimes, committed in the name of people's liberation by the Vietcong, the Soviets and the Chinese. The Executioner had grown accustomed to all sorts of bleeding hearts, and recognized that most of them were totally sincere—however sadly misinformed.

But here in Steyr he was facing something else.

According to the evidence produced by Katz, the
Earthers—or their leadership, at any rate—were not the
sixties-style idealists they appeared to be on camera.
Their covert links with brutal terrorists—the Baader-
Meinhof crew, the Red Brigades and ETA—were amply documented. There had been covert meetings, pay-
offs, sanctuaries opened up to killers on the lam…and
lately, there had been a steady flow of arms from party
sources to the arsenals of half a dozen trigger-happy
private armies on the Continent. There had been insuf-
ficient evidence for prosecution up to now, but Bolan
wasn't interested in convictions. He was looking for the
answer to a deadly riddle, and the clues began in Steyr,
with a weapons leak and functionaries of the party who
were said to deal in stolen arms.

"You might have set the meet indoors," McCarter
groused.

"You need the air," Katz told him gruffly.

"I've got your air right here."

He was about to light another Players when a pair of
headlights made the turn off Blumauergasse, headed
south into the park. The former SAS man flicked his
cigarette away and snapped his lighter shut, already
opening the buttons on his heavy jacket. Beside him,
Katz and Bolan were alert and occupied with preparations of their own.

The headlights were approaching slowly. At one
hundred yards, the high beams blazed for half a second, and again the signal eerily reflected on Mack Bolan's face. Katz leaned in through the driver's window
of their rental, flashed the lights in answer twice, before rejoining Bolan and McCarter on the firing line.

Bolan didn't know precisely what to look for, but he
imagined something in the nature of the van that had

contained the shipment in Toronto. Now, instead, a sleek sedan was rolling toward them through the darkness, lights extinguished as it coasted into range.

"Small load," he said to no one in particular.

"It's a foot in the door," Katz replied. "If we're lucky, it's all we'll need."

"If we're lucky," McCarter said gruffly, "we won't need a hearse when we're finished."

Close up, Mack Bolan saw that the sedan was a Mercedes, and he was impressed. From all appearances, the business of promoting peace paid very well indeed. He watched as doors sprang open on both sides, the dome light momentarily illuminating faces.

And a moment was all it took.

He recognized the left-side passenger from tabloid photographs and glossies in the file at Stony Man. Beside him, he could feel the Phoenix warriors tense with recognition of their own. McCarter muttered something indistinct beneath his breath.

The Raven had surprised them once again, appearing where he had been least expected. And Bolan felt the gooseflesh rising on his arms, his stomach twisting into knots the way it had so recently in the Toronto cemetery. The way it had aboard Flight 741. He sensed a certain hesitation now in Katz's attitude and wondered if he recognized the face from Mittenwald. Assuming that their theory was correct, that there was not a single Raven in the field, this might or might not be the man they had encountered earlier. Despite the darkness, Bolan was convinced that he had not seen this man before.

The Raven in Toronto had been someone else entirely. Bolan would have bet his life on it. In fact, he realized, he had already done exactly that.

But if the Raven clone in front of him had not been in Toronto, which one had been aboard Flight 741?

"You're late," Katz told the new arrivals, speaking now in flawless German, keeping any trace of tension from his voice.

Bolan only followed bits and pieces of the conversation after that. He gathered that the Earthers had been unavoidably delayed, that they were anxious to conclude their business now. But he was concentrating on the Raven, fighting down an urge to draw and fire that had been growing in him since he recognized the face.

There were four men in the sedan, and Bolan was convinced that he could take them, with Katz and McCarter backing up his play... but it was not that simple. They had come in search of information, and a corpse could not participate in dialogue. Far better, Bolan thought, to follow Katz's script and see precisely where the dark charade might lead.

He noticed that the Raven stood apart from his companions, keeping silent while the Earthers haggled over terms with Katz. They were being cautious, glancing frequently about them at the lurking shadows. There was something furtive, overanxious in their manner, and he wondered if it might not be his own imagination. Cut off from communication with McCarter, suddenly convinced that any spoken word of English might prove fatal, Bolan felt a brooding sense of dread. He couldn't put a finger on the source of his anxiety, but there was something....

Katz was concluding his negotiations, shaking hands in consummation of the deal. He nodded to McCarter, and the former SAS commando faded back, opening a back door of the rental, reaching for the satchel stowed inside. The Earthers were exchanging pallid smiles, their leader glancing at the Raven, and Bolan half imagined that he saw a signal pass between them, carried in a furtive glance.

The Raven smiled, an artificial grimace, and muttered something to his comrades. Bolan felt his stomach churn with bitter disappointment as he failed to recognize the voice. An Hispanic accent, clearly, which would fit the profile on Ramirez—but it was not the voice that had issued from a latex Nixon mask aboard Flight 741.

The clone was drifting back along the length of the Mercedes, ambling in the direction of the trunk. He fished a key out of his pocket, turned the lock, became invisible behind the rising lid. The Earthers' spokesman was explaining something now to Katz, stepping back a pace and talking with his hands. The last remaining trace of color had evaporated from his cheeks.

And Bolan smelled the trap before it closed around him, knew that they were being set up for the kill. He found the H&K 9 mm, ripped it free and was already scanning for a target as the first alarm bells sounded in his brain.

"Look out!" he shouted, knowing it was far too late to salvage the charade. "They set us up!"

Behind the Mercedes, sudden hulking movement as the trunk disgorged a pair of gunners. The Raven suddenly emerged from cover on the left, his flankers on the right, and all of them were armed with deadly Steyr-Daimler-Puch 9 mm submachine guns, muzzles up and spitting flame.

McCarter and the big Israeli went to ground instinctively, their jackets flapping as they clawed for Uzi stutter guns. The initial burst of fire from the Mercedes missed them cleanly, shattering the rental's windshield. The Earthers tried to scatter, obviously stunned to find themselves between the hostile guns. Before they had a chance, their leader caught a parabellum round between the shoulder blades and stumbled into Bolan, throwing off the soldier's aim.

He cursed and thrust the standing corpse aside, already squeezing off a double tap in the direction of the Raven's hiding place. He was rewarded by the sound of breaking glass, and then converging streams of fire were searching for him, forcing him to scramble for the cover of his own sedan. McCarter ripped a burst beneath the chassis of the sleek Mercedes, ankle-high, eliciting a bleat of startled pain.

The two surviving Earthers made a sudden break for safety in the darkness, but a shadow figure lurched erect downrange and dropped them both with a precision burst of automatic fire. The gunner hesitated, perhaps admiring his achievement, and a round from Bolan's autoloader took him in the temple.

One down, one wounded, and the steady hostile fire showed little sign of fading. Belly down beside the rental, Bolan listened to the Uzis dueling their invisible assailants, trading short, staccato bursts at virtual point-blank range. Both cars were taking hits, and neither one would pass the casual inspection of a traffic officer when this was over. Startled by the thought, Mack Bolan realized that there was no assurance that either vehicle would ever leave the Schlosspark.

And time was running out.

Katz and McCarter must have felt the rising tension, too, for both simultaneously redoubled their assault upon the sleek Mercedes, raking fore and aft with automatic fire. Another bleat of pain and there was only one piece answering them now.

He *felt* the Raven's move before it came, and he was braced to take the bastard down, his autoloader gripped in both hands, elbows locked. The soldier was prepared for anything—except a sudden move by Katz bringing the Israeli right into his line of fire. No time to shout a warning, as the target of a lifetime sprang erect behind the Mercedes, moving swiftly, tracking with the weapon in his hands.

Katz saw the quarry, triggered off a hasty burst, and then the Raven's rounds were sizzling in on target, flinging him aside, his bulk rebounding from the rental's fender, sprawling gracelessly across the tarmac. Bolan's blinding rage erupted through the muzzle of his VP-70, and he had squeezed off half a dozen rounds in rapid-fire before the Raven stumbled, fell.

He kept the Raven covered as he moved toward Katzenelenbogen, feeling for him, half afraid to see the old, familiar damage done by parabellum slugs. He rolled the big Israeli over on his side . . . and Katzenelenbogen kept on going, groaning, sitting up to look around him in the darkness.

"That was close," he muttered, probing underneath his jacket cautiously.

McCarter stood above his comrade, trembling.

"You bloody sod," he blurted, "you wore a vest!"

Katz grinned, still taking inventory of his battered ribs.

"I can't afford so many chances at my age."

"God *damn* you!"

Bolan left them to their wrangling, moving toward the Raven in a combat crouch. The guy was dead as hell, he knew it in his heart, but he would not take any risks with this one. Crouched beside his enemy, he felt for vital signs, found none. A single round had drilled the Raven's throat; the other five were clustered in a fist-size ring around his heart.

And he had not been wearing body armor.

The Phoenix warriors stood behind Bolan, listening to sirens drawing closer in the darkness.

"Time to go," McCarter said.

The soldier hesitated. "Do you recognize him?"

"What? From Mittenwald?" McCarter glanced at Katzenelenbogen, shook his head. "It's close, but no cigar."

"And you?"

"I never saw his face," the Executioner replied. "His voice was . . . different."

"So, it's a scratch."

"Not yet."

He rifled through the dead man's pockets, seeking anything that might reveal the secrets of his life, his alter egos still at large and moving toward some other rendezvous with carnage, possibly a world away. He found the billfold filled with spurious ID, and let it fall beside the corpse. Another pocket gave up ammunition magazines, a lightweight automatic pistol worn beneath one arm.

And airline tickets.

"He had a flight booked to Geneva in the morning," Bolan said. A glance inside the folder told him everything he had to know. "And hotel reservations in Zermatt."

"So what?"

McCarter sounded skeptical, and more than slightly nervous as the sirens closed around them.

"So, it's more than we came in with," Bolan told him, rising, turning from the dead.

Katzenelenbogen smiled and said, "He likes the mountains."

Bolan's eyes were hungry in the darkness.

"So do I."

Chapter Twenty-Eight

The winding mountain drive between Geneva and Täsch consumed two hours. Toby was enraptured by the soaring Alps, the forests that resembled something from a childhood fairy tale. Bolan concentrated on the highway, with its countless switchbacks, tunnels, hairpin turns. The rented Saab seemed built for alpine driving, taking curves and grades in stride.

He kept an eye on the rearview mirror, spotting Katz and McCarter in their separate cars from time to time, alert for any other sign that they were being tailed. The soldier feared he might be growing paranoid, but he had seen too much and come too far to let his guard down now. The Raven—or his clones—had been a step ahead of them at every turn so far, and he could not afford to let the trend continue if he planned to come out on the other side of it alive, if they were ever to dismantle the conspiracy.

It had been McCarter's plan to make the final drive in separate cars, and Bolan had agreed at once. If something happened now, if they were ambushed on the road, it would require an army of the enemy to tag them all. Whatever happened now, short of a multicar disaster on the highway, two or three of them were bound to make it through alive, at least as far as Täsch.

The Executioner reviewed his knowledge of the target zone. No autos were allowed past Täsch; the transport in Zermatt itself would be by foot, horse cart or electric-powered cab. Perched at the head of the Nikolaital Valley, at something more than five thousand feet in elevation, Zermatt boasted a population of three thousand souls. They might be easily outnumbered, ten or twelve to one, in tourist season, which extended more or less year-round. Zermatt was one of Switzerland's great international resorts, the winter sports capital of Valais. In spring and summer, awe-inspiring scenery, the atmosphere and lavish shops made up for any slump in skiing.

"Lovely, isn't it?"

The lady's voice distracted Bolan from his driving, from his private thoughts of battle, but he summoned up a smile.

"It is."

"I'd like to settle in here somewhere and forget about the rest of it. Just let it go."

"You would?"

He wondered whether this was true, if Toby might be burning out. It happened, Bolan knew; a lifetime in the trenches took its toll, and some would pay more heavily than others. A woman, youngish, healthy, might begin to wonder what she had been fighting for—what cause had managed to consume her private life.

It took a moment for the lady fed to answer him. Her eyes were on the mountains, seeking something that was still invisible from where she sat. When she turned back to face the Executioner, her eyes were misty, faraway.

"I might," she told him earnestly, and then she cracked a winning smile. "But who the hell would have me?"

Bolan read the hurt behind the smile and spoke to Toby's eyes. "That wouldn't be a problem."

"No?"

"I'd bet my life."

"You do that every day."

"It's all I have."

The smile had vanished, and she half turned toward the window, showing off the classic profile. "That's the problem."

"Oh?"

"That's all you have," she echoed him. "That's all *I* have. And that's a shame."

"Not necessarily."

"You bet it is."

He read the bitterness in Toby's voice, knew better than to try and smother her in platitudes.

"We all make choices, Toby. This was mine, and once I made it, it was understood that there could be no turning back. There's no retirement plan, no pension, no retreat. But that's *my* choice," he told her earnestly, "not yours. You have an out."

"It doesn't feel that way."

"Might be because you don't *want* out," he said.

"What makes you so damned smart?"

He grinned. "I eat right, get a lot of rest...."

"Enough, already. How much longer?"

Bolan checked his digital. "Another twenty minutes, give or take."

"Let's give. I wouldn't mind a few more minutes of this scenery."

And she was back. The soldier read it in her tone, her eyes. She was adept at dealing with her doubts as they arose, dismissing them before they could subvert her personal commitment to the struggle. And the lady's personal commitment was as deep as Bolan's own, he knew that much.

The twenty minutes stretched to thirty-five, and it was almost noon before they finished the ascent to Täsch along a narrow, two-lane ribbon climbing to the clouds. Their destination was a parking lot outside the station of a narrow-gauge electric railway, which would carry them the final three miles. While Toby bought the round-trip tickets, Bolan piled their luggage on a rolling cart and stowed it in the separate baggage car. The parking lot and station platform were alive with tourists, but they found a window seat up front and settled in for the ascent.

The Phoenix warriors would be following them on a different train. Trains ran back and forth every twenty minutes, transporting tourists by the thousands in a single afternoon. Most came back down again by dark, but hundreds lingered on in the hotels, to taste the nightlife, sample the cuisine of gourmet restaurants and laze along the narrow streets of ancient homes. The mountain village was a paradise for tourists and, perhaps, a sanctuary for the fugitive elite. Tonight it would become a hunting ground for Executioner Mack Bolan.

Just beyond the station, they were cast in darkness as the train slid through a tunnel, rattling and swaying slightly on its tracks. Once through, the town below them was invisible, the forest close at hand on either side, a primal vista that surprised them both and spoke to Toby in particular.

"It's like another world," she said.

The soldier at her side said nothing, smiling at her almost sadly. He reflected that there was no other world; the one at hand was all they had, and when the final showdown came—tonight, tomorrow—he could only hope that Toby would be thinking of the job. Nostalgia, wistful longing for a simpler time and place were fine, in moderation, but a working warrior could not well afford an overdose of sentiment. Distractions got you killed in combat, and they were here to stalk a predator with countless kills behind him. He was slick, professional . . . and he was not alone.

If Toby's mind was in the clouds, she would be little use to Bolan in a crisis situation, but he let her dream for now, content to see her happy for a change.

The train was climbing steeply, the pull of gravity forcing Bolan back into the cushions of his seat. When they were topside, they would be on foot, but they would compensate by spending extra energy in the pursuit of Julio Ramirez and his clones. If there were any Ravens to be found within the shadow of the Matterhorn, he meant to root them out and see them dead before he caught the next train back to Täsch.

It had occurred to Bolan that the ''Raven'' tagged in Steyr might have been anticipating a vacation, traveling to Switzerland for pleasure or on private business of his own . . . but it had been the only lead, and he felt compelled to play it out.

It had occurred to Bolan, also, that he might not leave Zermatt alive. If he was right in his suspicion that the Ravens might be gathering, there was a chance that he would find himself outnumbered by the enemy. The odds did not intimidate him—he had dealt with them before, and he was still around—but any time he faced the savages there was a chance that he would not be walking out the other side.

He had been cognizant of all the risks from the beginning, and his only worry now was that his friends—

the lady, Katz, McCarter—might go down in flames beside him if his plans went sour.

The train was at the station, groaning to a halt, the doors unfolding to release a stream of tourists on the platform. Bolan waited to retrieve their baggage, flagged the driver of an electric minibus and pointed him in the direction of the Grand Hotel Zermatterhof. Five minutes later, after weaving in and out through eddies of pedestrians, he dropped them at the entrance to a lavish hostelry. Beside the sloping drive, a giant sculpted frog presided over gushing fountains, and the liveried captain hurried down to help them with their bags. The concierge was waiting to receive them, anxious to confirm the reservation of a dead man, now in Bolan's name.

Beyond the lobby, two flights up, they found the suite already open, bellman standing at attention by their luggage. Bolan tipped him, saw him out and locked the door behind him. Toby had already found the French doors, and she was through them now, exploring what appeared to be a giant patio beyond. In fact, their room, and all the other suites adjoining, faced upon the roof of the restaurant and lobby just below, providing guests with space to ramble and a striking profile of the Matterhorn. They stood together, side by side, and overlooked the teeming street below, the tourists small and bustling in their haste. Another moment, and the lady slipped her arm through his, surprising Bolan with the sudden sadness in her voice.

"It's beautiful," she said. "So beautiful."

A stab of sharp regret pierced Bolan's chest—regret that he had let her come along, regret that he had ever heard the Raven's name or seen him face-to-latex-face aboard Flight 741. In other circumstances Toby might have joined him here in the pursuit of love and life, instead of fire and death.

Bolan stopped himself abruptly, shaking off the mood. There *were* no other circumstances. If not for Bolan's private war, he never would have known the lady fed at all. They never would have met, would not have loved, could not have hoped to share the Alpine vista arm-in-arm. A cruel twist of fate, perhaps . . . but it was all they had, and it would have to do.

She sensed his mood and disengaged herself, stepped back a pace to give him room.

"What now?" she asked.

"We wait."

Until the Phoenix warriors were in place. Until they found a way to trace the Raven through the crush of tourists on the street below. There was a possibility, he realized, that someone would attempt to reach him in his room. It had been on his mind when he decided to maintain the Raven's reservations. If there was no contact, he would have to find another way, another means of reaching out to find his quarry and bring him down.

"It won't be easy," Toby told him.

"No."

"The others might not even be here."

Bolan shrugged. "It's all I've got."

"I know, but what next?"

He hadn't needed her to voice the question. *What next?* What if it all fell through and left him empty-handed, looking like a fool? What then?

"I try again."

She faced him, turning from the mountains, looking him directly in the eye. "How much of this is personal?"

He wasn't sure, and told her so.

"I was afraid of that," she said. "The Ahab syndrome."

"What?"

"The Ahab syndrome," she repeated. "*Moby Dick*, you know?"

"You've lost me, Toby."

"Captain Ahab spent his life pursuing Moby Dick because the whale had publicly embarrassed him by chewing off his leg."

"That's some embarrassment."

"I'm serious. It killed him in the end. It dragged him *down*."

"We're miles from water, Toby."

"I'm serious."

"I know you are."

"Goddammit." Toby stared in the direction of the mountains for a moment, sudden moisture gleaming in her eyes. "How long?"

"What's that?"

"How *long*?" she asked again, exasperation in her voice. "Until the others make it in?"

"An hour, maybe two."

"All right."

She turned away, already moving toward their suite. The soldier trailed her with his eyes until she reached the open door, but made no move to follow. Standing in the doorway, Toby glanced across her shoulder at him, frowning. Nervous fingers were already working on the buttons of her blouse.

"Get in here, soldier," she demanded. "Time's a'wasting."

And Bolan realized that he might have so very little time to spare.

Somewhere below in the streets, or in the hotel suites and plush chalets clinging to the mountainsides, his quarry was already waiting for him. He could feel it in his vitals. Their time was coming, and there was no way on earth to tell which one of them—if either—would survive the confrontation when it came.

Their time was coming, but it was not yet.

Tonight, right now, was Toby's time, and Bolan owed it to her. He owed it to himself, as well. In unity of the body, they could reaffirm a unity of the soul, their momentary passion an expression of some deeper understanding, deeper love, which circumstance and fleeting time would not permit to blossom in their present world.

It was the only world they had, the only world that they were ever likely to possess, and Bolan had no real regrets about the course his life had taken. He would leave the bitch-and-moan department to professionals, the whiners who bemoaned their lot in life no matter what that lot might be. As for the Executioner, he had gone into war with both eyes open, and had known precisely what the hellgrounds held in store.

But there were still some sweet surprises on the way.

Like Toby Ranger.

Like stolen hours, waiting for the reinforcements to arrive.

He ambled back in the direction of the suite, already shrugging off a measure of the apprehension that had dogged him since they landed in Geneva.

And for once, he hoped the cavalry would take its own sweet time.

Chapter Twenty-Nine

The Russian was a gray man, craggy features chiseled out of living stone. Gray hair was swept back from his forehead, lacquered down against his skull. Gray eyes stared out, unblinking, from beneath gray brows. His heavy topcoat, like the suit and tie beneath, was gray. An ancient scar descended from the corner of his left eye to the angle of his jaw, fish-belly white against the parchment coloration of his skin. He bore the mark of Moscow's winters on his face, the brand of Moscow machinations on his soul.

Ramirez had been waiting for the Russian, hoping that he might not come and knowing that his hopes were all in vain. The Russian traveled seldom, clinging whenever possible to his sanctuary in Dzerzhinsky Square, but circumstances had compelled him to consult the Raven personally.

Throughout the years of their acquaintance, Julio Ramirez had mistrusted Viktor Rylov, working with him through necessity and covering himself against the possibility of double-cross. The Russian would not hesitate to sell him out, he knew, if something better came along. If Project Raven ceased to yield results, then Rylov and his KGB friends would find a way to terminate the exercise, along with everyone involved. Ramirez and his doubles were expendable. Extermination by his allies was a concept that Ramirez had examined with a fair degree of objectivity on more than one occasion. Until recently, however, he had not been forced to take the idea seriously.

That had changed, of course, when Escobar was ambushed in Durango. Up till then, they had escaped without a major casualty—aside from Julio himself—and sudden death in Mexico reminded KGB that even Ravens had a finite life span. Other near-miss incidents in Canada and Germany had brought things to a head, and so he was expecting Rylov when the Russian turned up uninvited at his door.

An invitation would have been superfluous, of course, since Moscow paid his rent and various expenses. There had been no funds from Libya for two years now; Khaddafi had apparently found other protégés, leaving Julio Ramirez to depend upon the KGB's largesse.

Their money was the least of it, however. In his gut, Ramirez knew the Soviets would never be content to simply cut him off without a ruble to his name. Alive, embittered by the turnaround, he might be dangerous to Moscow's public image. Worse, he might be dangerous to Rylov and the others physically, a seasoned terrorist with men at his disposal, time to kill and nothing left to lose.

If they intended to discard him now, to scuttle Project Raven, they could not afford to let him live. Ramirez knew that much...and knew that Viktor Rylov would not try to do the job himself. A proven killer in his younger days, the man from KGB had learned to insulate himself from violence, carefully avoiding contact with the wet work that he ordered from his office in Dzerzhinsky Square. He might be guilty of a hundred or a thousand murders in a given year, but Rylov's manicured hands had not been bloodied in a decade.

He would try to gain the Raven's confidence. He would speak of friendship, unity of purpose and the sanctity of revolution. Careful to avoid explicit criticism, he would note that problems had arisen with the project. Moscow was concerned, of course. Perhaps the Raven might consider premature retirement? At full pension, of course, with all the benefits to which a hero of the people is entitled.

Except that Julio knew better. He could see beyond the lies. The KGB had no retirement plan for terrorists, and least of all for those whose mere existence might prove critically embarrassing to Moscow. There would always be a place for Julio Ramirez, certainly: a shallow, unmarked grave.

Settling into his easy chair, the Matterhorn invisible behind drawn curtains now, Ramirez pushed the morbid thoughts away. He had to hear the Russian out before he jumped to any rash conclusions. It would be disastrous to mistake his motives, act in haste and bring the wrath of KGB upon himself unnecessarily. There was a chance that Moscow might desire to save the Project from extinction. Anything was possible, and he could ill afford to close out his options before they were revealed.

"I trust your journey was a pleasant one?"

He spoke in Russian out of courtesy to Rylov and to indicate that they were equals here. In fact, although the Russian had a global army at his beck and call, he was extremely vulnerable at the moment, and he knew it.

"Satisfactory."

"What brings you to Zermatt?" Ramirez inquired.

"I think you know."

They faced each other silently across the room, the Russian seated with his back against the wall, away from door and windows, fearful of assassins even with the curtains closed against the dusk. The years in Moscow had conditioned him to living in a bunker, constantly surrounded by security devices, bodyguards, the apparatus of the state. He might be wise, Ramirez thought, to fear for his survival here. A human life was fragile, almost brittle to the touch, and easily snuffed out.

When Julio did not respond at once, the Russian cleared his throat.

"There have been incidents," he said at last.

"Ah, yes."

"Your sponsors are concerned."

"Unnecessarily. The risks were calculated in advance."

The Russian's scowl was carved in stone. "You chalk the recent contacts off to mere coincidence?"

"Of course," Ramirez lied. "The drug trade is notoriously violent. I have been opposed to Escobar's involvement from the start. In Germany, the Baader-Meinhof factions have been turning on each other, wasting time and energy on power politics within the ranks. There have been other shooting incidents. As for Vachon . . . who knows? Competitors, perhaps—or one of his subordinates, intent on going into business for himself. Such altercations take place every day."

"But four within a week . . ."

"I beg your pardon, comrade? Four?"

The Russian feigned surprise, and something in his face informed Ramirez that he had been waiting for this opportunity to drop his bomb.

"Forgive me," Rylov said with mock sincerity. "but I assumed you knew."

"Knew *what*?"

Ramirez heard the sudden anger in his voice and cursed himself for letting Rylov peek beyond the cool exterior. And he was doubly wounded now, his ignorance and violent temper simultaneously revealed before his enemy.

The Russian hesitated, savoring the moment and his triumph, gloating silently behind his mask of stone. When next he spoke, his tone was low-key, overfilled with false concern.

"It grieves me to surprise you with such tidings...."

Julio Ramirez fought a sudden urge to spring across the room and throttle Rylov, squeeze the sluggish message from his throat. He waited, cold eyes boring into Rylov's own like needles probing for the brain.

"Last night, there was an incident in Steyr. You know the city?"

"Yes."

"I have it on authority that one of those eliminated was your Mr. Castresana."

"Ah."

The sound was noncommittal, neutral, or at least he hoped that it would sound that way to Rylov. Something cold and terrible clutched at his gut.

"Forgive me. I assumed you would have been informed."

But there was no contrition in the Russian's voice. If anything, there was a note of exultation. It was seldom that he had a chance to take Ramirez by surprise, and Rylov clearly meant to make the most of his advantage.

"We were briefly out of touch," Ramirez said, embarrassed by the sudden impulse to explain himself. "I knew of his transaction with the Austrians, of course . . . but there has been no word of any incident."

"The local gendarmes are investigating," Rylov told him. "They have not released the names or any details to the media."

"I see."

"There was, I understand, some link between the Steyr operation and your problem in Toronto."

So. *Your* problem. Rylov had already washed his hands of the predicament. Ramirez would be called upon to stand or fall alone, without assistance from the KGB. Ironically, the casual dismissal failed to shake him. If the Russians cut him loose, if they permitted him to solve the problem on his own, he still might have a chance. For now, his task would be to pacify the gray man from Dzerzhinsky Square.

"Link?" Julio's thoughts were not with Rylov, but he knew the Russian had a point to make.

"Precisely."

Julio Ramirez shrugged. "My late connection in Toronto handled some material from Steyr. He handled many things. I see no evidence of any link between the incidents."

"Your sponsors disagree."

Ramirez frowned. "If they have any information that I may have overlooked . . ."

"They are concerned about security."

"As I am."

"Certainly." The Russian risked a tight-lipped smile. "Preventive measures must be taken."

"Measures *have* been taken, comrade."

It was true...to an extent. His agents—the three survivors—would be gathering within a half day's time to sort out the problem. Motivated by survival instincts, each of them was anxious to eliminate the enemy who had appeared from nowhere, targeting their operations on three continents.

"Comrade?"

Rylov had been speaking, and the Raven was embarrassed once again, compelled to ask the Russian to repeat himself.

"Your contacts," Rylov said again. "Are they secure?"

"They are."

But were they? Clearly, there were breaches in security on every side. Vachon had been exposed, the Steyr operation, the connection in Durango. Somewhere there had been a leak. It might have been Vachon himself, or one of the assorted other casualties. Ramirez refused to entertain the thought that one of his selected doubles had turned traitor.

He thought of the American, this Axelrod, and the coincidental way in which his various transactions coincided with the Raven's own disasters. The Durango shipment had been slated for delivery to Axelrod, as had the weapons in Toronto. The Canadian consignment had its origins at Steyr. Mittenwald aside, the several incidents might well be linked, and they revolved around Gerry Axelrod.

Ramirez spent a moment pondering the possibilities, ignoring Rylov, perfectly content to let the Russian fidget in his chair. It seemed preposterous that Axelrod himself might be the leak. He had already squandered something like a million dollars, drugs and weapons thrown together, and his various investors would be

clamoring for refunds or his head if merchandise was
not forthcoming. Still, Ramirez was familiar with the
devious techniques of law-enforcement agencies, their
profligate expenditure of time and cash in the pursuit of
an arrest. It was remotely possibly that Axelrod might
be some sort of undercover operative, spending federal
dollars to entrap the Raven.

As soon as he conceived the notion, Julio Ramirez
dismissed it. He had investigated Axelrod, his bigot
Brotherhood, his tenuous connection with the underworld. There had been nothing to suggest the Georgian
was a mole, but strict security had been maintained, in
any case. The drug deal in Durango had remained entirely separate from Axelrod's transaction with Vachon
in Canada. At no time prior to the disastrous encounter in Toronto had the Georgian been aware of dealing,
even indirectly, with the Raven. Ramirez would have bet
his life that Axelrod was in the dark concerning the
identity of his connection with the factory at Steyr.

Toronto, though, had altered everything. Not only
had Khaldi revealed himself, but there had been an
ambush, forcing Ramirez to flee the scene with Axelrod in tow.

Ramirez had decided to continue dealing with the
brash American. The choice had not been easy, but
Ramirez finally gambled on his own ability to judge a
man on sight, to gauge the darkness of his soul. They
would continue doing business, and if the Georgian
proved to be a hindrance, he would be instantly eliminated.

In retrospect, Ramirez wondered if his choice had
been a wise one. Might it not have been more prudent
to eliminate the risk, however slight, and then establish
links with Axelrod's subordinates? The Georgian was

now privy to a portion of the Raven's own involvement in the Steyr transaction, but he would remain expendable.

It was possible, Ramirez knew, that Axelrod himself had been the target in Toronto, even in Durango. Any one of several syndicates or agencies might have him in their sights, prepared to muscle in on profits or to lock him up and throw away the key. It mattered little to Ramirez whether Axelrod should live or die, but now his curse had been transmitted like a lethal plague bacillus to the Raven's own preserve. If criminals or law-enforcement officers were stalking Axelrod, they had already crossed the Raven's path three times—at least— and they had cost him two of his most valued operatives. Mahmoud himself had narrowly escaped the ambush in Toronto, and Ramirez wondered if it might not prove unfortunate that he had rescued Axelrod.

The Raven knew that they would have to wait and see.

"There are precautions to be taken."

Rylov's voice surprised Ramirez. He had almost managed to forget the presence of his uninvited visitor.

"Of course."

"If you require assistance . . ."

"Thank you, comrade, no. I have my own resources."

Rylov frowned and shifted in his chair. "I am *instructed* to assist you in your preparations."

Now Ramirez knew that the Russian was under orders. It made him smaller, somehow—and at once more dangerous. He would perform upon command, and if the orders from Dzerzhinsky Square included the elimination of one Julio Ramirez, he would carry out those orders with the grim precision of a murderous machine.

Unless the Raven took preventive measures to neutralize the Russian, make him disappear without a trace.

It would not do to strike out prematurely, Ramirez realized. The Soviets were still his sponsors; he could hope for no one else at this point in his life. Alone, without their backing, Project Raven would be doomed to wither on the vine. If they should move against him . . . well . . . the veteran terrorist did not delude himself that he could stand alone against the bear.

He must preserve the link with Moscow, but Ramirez wondered if it would be necessary to preserve the link with Rylov simultaneously. By his very presence, Rylov was exposed to danger, charged with overseeing the security arrangements for an operation under siege. So many things could happen to advisors on the field of battle.

Ramirez smiled, a death's-head grimace that communicated nothing to his guest. The Russian watched him stoically, but now Ramirez thought he could read a trace of fear behind the washed-out eyes. It satisfied him for the moment, simply knowing that the man from the KGB was not invulnerable, after all. Like Axelrod, the Russian clearly was expendable. The only question left was how and when to spend his life most wisely in pursuit of ultimate success. A wasted pawn could never be regained, and Julio Ramirez had already lost too many pieces in a game that he was just beginning to understand.

The game was called survival of the fittest, and he knew the rules by heart. Whoever stood between the Raven and success—between the Raven and survival—would instantly be sacrificed.

Chapter Thirty

Toby Ranger came awake slowly, uncertain what had roused her from a dream of Bolan. In the dream she saw him tall and naked in the drifting smoke of some nameless battlefield. Around him, piled in drifts that reached his knees, the skulls and bones of vanquished enemies stretched out for miles in all directions. As she watched, he started slogging forward through the acres of remains, high-stepping through the dunes and gullies of corruption. She looked away in search of some horizon, and glancing back, discovered he had disappeared.

She reached for Bolan now, beneath the sheets...and found him gone. Alarm bells started clamoring inside her head, and Toby sat bolt upright in the bed, sheets pooling at her waist. No sound from the direction of the bathroom, and the tall French doors were closed, their drapery tightly drawn. She fumbled for the bedside lamp, and discovered Bolan's note on the nightstand. Blinking in the sudden light, she slid across to read the message.

Gone to meet with K. and M. Back soon.

He had not signed the note, of course; there was no need. She recognized his slanting script, and knew that he had taken pains to let her sleep, dressing in the bathroom. There was a key beneath the note, one of the two they had received on checking in.

She knew that Katzenelenbogen and McCarter had secured reservations at the Schweizerhof, within an easy walk, but she decided not to follow Bolan there. Her case had vanished in Toronto, after Axelrod had disappeared. She had no business here, should certainly have caught the next flight back to Washington instead of trailing Bolan on a transatlantic jaunt to nowhere. Stretched across the king-size bed, she wondered what Brognola would have waiting for her when she landed stateside. With any luck at all, she thought, he might be mad enough to fire her from the program, free her to find a normal life.

Normality had countless definitions, sure, and hers did not include the picket-fence approach to life suburban style. From adolescence, she had looked for something more: adventure and accomplishment, a sense of doing something, which had finally arrived with her enlistment in the federal service. No, Brognola would not dump her, Toby knew; the big, gruff fed was like a second father to her, and his little brood of operatives had been whittled down enough already.

Her mind flashed back to Bolan. She had no active part in his Swiss campaign, no solid contribution to the cause. Her handle had been Axelrod, and he was gone, without a trace. His trail had disappeared at Steyr, and with it Toby's reason for remaining on the case. Zermatt had been a luxury, and Bolan didn't need her now. She might as well go out and see the town while light remained.

She dressed in skirt and sweater, slipping on a jacket as an afterthought, aware that nights were cold above five thousand feet no matter what the season. There were year-round glaciers within a thirty-minute train ride, and the wind descending from surrounding alps could slice through normal clothing like a knife through butter.

She picked up her room key from the nightstand, locked the door and was off. The concierge glanced up and flashed a brilliant smile before the giant doors swung shut behind her. Breathing deeply, instantly invigorated by the mountain air, she moved along the sloping driveway toward the street.

Zermatt's main artery of commerce is a single narrow street that runs between the railway station and the market square. Along its length, the visitor is treated to a startling and charming contrast of stately hotels, elegant shops and traditional Swiss alpine homes. Despite the time—close to eight—it was scarcely dusk. Full dark would not arrive for some two hours yet, and tourists jammed the sidewalks, anxious for another look around the quaint resort before they settled into hotel suites or caught the last train down the mountainside to Täsch.

Toby crossed the street not far from her hotel and bought herself some pastry at a small café. Around her, tourists from a score of countries jostled one another, veering back and forth across the narrow street. Toby moved among them, feeling every inch the tourist as she nibbled on her pastry, window-shopping like a schoolgirl. Fleetingly, she wished that Bolan could have joined her, but his visit to Zermatt was strictly business, and she put the notion out of mind before it had a chance to spoil her mood.

Midway between the railway station and the Grand Hotel Zermatterhof, she found a jewelry shop that offered pendants of the Matterhorn for sale, in gold or silver. Toby did a quick conversion, francs to dollars, and was startled to discover that she could afford one. Rummaging inside her bag to double-check the cash on hand, she glanced up at the jeweler's window once again—and froze.

A figure, tall and lean, reflected in the glass. She felt the breath catch in her throat, continued breathing only with an effort. It was almost certainly a trick of lighting, a distortion of the glass. She half turned, risked a glance across her shoulder and confirmed the worst.

It was Gerry Axelrod.

She spun away from him to face the jeweler's window once again. Inside the shop, a handsome young clerk was smiling at her. He moved closer to the window, smelling an impending sale. Behind the glass, he waited for her eyes to rise, bowed stiffly from the waist in continental fashion once their glances met and swept a silent hand across the glittering display of pendants. Toby kept her eye on the reflection in the window, realizing that the clerk must think her fascinated with his smile, his charm. A touch of intimacy crept into his manner, and he winked at Toby. He was turning from the window now, proceeding toward the door.

Behind her, Axelrod was moving out in the direction of the market square. She turned to follow, narrowly averting a collison with the smiling clerk as he emerged to speak with her. Toby stepped around him, leaving him to ponder on the fickleness of females at his leisure. Axelrod was more than a block ahead of her, still visible because he stood a head above the crush of tourists, but it would be possible to lose him, Toby knew, and she could not afford to fail a second time.

There was no need to wonder what he might be doing in Zermatt. He had escaped from the Toronto ambush with the Raven, and he had not collected on his shipment out of Steyr. Toby had no way of ascertaining whether he had gone direct to Austria, or whether he had been in Steyr when Bolan and the men of Phoenix staged their little fireworks exhibition in the Schlosspark. If the bastard had been able to secure his weapons, he would not be in Zermatt right now, and Toby thanked her lucky stars that he had crossed her path again. Brognola would not have to worry now. The mission was on track.

She took the opposite sidewalk, pacing Axelrod, determining that he appeared to be alone, unhurried. Toby watched him stop for coffee and an English newspaper, dawdling along with his attention split between the headlines and the scenery. Toby thought of stopping briefly to acquire some shades, perhaps a hat to alter her appearance, and as quickly put the notion out of mind. The average disguise did more to call attention than diffuse it, and the lady fed was well aware that she possessed the best disguise of all: a milling crowd.

Around the market square, she trailed her quarry past the old communal council house, the Marmot fountain and the handsome church of St. Maurice. They crossed the burbling Visp on a narrow footbridge with a cemetery close at hand, presenting monuments to climbers who had failed and fallen on the Matterhorn.

And Toby realized, too late, that they were climbing now, the crowds of tourists thinning out around them. Axelrod had lured her away from cover, up a narrow side street lined with tall and narrow homes. In every window planters were alive with flowers, brilliant colors dazzling the eye. But here, among the houses that reminded her of something from a fairy tale, the dusk was deepening, its shadows driving earnest shoppers back downslope. It would be dark here, she realized, before dusk reached the terrace of the Grand Hotel Zermatterhoff.

She would be alone with Gerry Axelrod before much longer, stripped of her disguise, exposed before him if he chose to turn and glance in her direction. Toby wondered if her footsteps might alert him to the fact that he was being followed, causing him to bolt or turn upon her in a homicidal rage. He would be armed, she knew that much from personal experience. The man could not exist without the twin Detonics .45s, which fit his tiny hands the way no other firearm ever could. At first, his quirk had brought a smile to Toby's face. It amused her, until she joined him on the firing range one day and watched him as he made the autoloading pistols do their work. The guns were an extension of himself, and Toby knew that if he saw her, Axelrod could drop her anywhere within the weapon's effective range.

Impulsively, she almost turned back then and there. It was enough to know the bastard was in town. She could report to Bolan, warn him in advance and let him deal with Axelrod. It made no sense to trail him up and down the narrow, winding streets, unarmed, devoid of backup. She thought about it seriously for a second and a half before she pushed the thought away and concentrated on her quarry. Axelrod was her assignment, and it was all that mattered.

There were no tourists now, besides herself and Axelrod. She did a rapid head count, coming up with half a dozen locals homeward bound. Ahead of her, the Georgian never broke his stride or glanced across his shoulder. He was totally at ease, secure…and Toby had him where she wanted him.

Within the next two blocks, they lost five locals, men and women peeling off toward homes that lined the street or had been tucked away in alleys opening on either side. The sixth, a teenage girl dressed up to look like Heidi, suddenly turned to retrace her steps down-slope. She flashed a shy, embarrassed smile at Toby as she passed, and Toby felt her own smile like a grimace, etched into her face.

She was alone with Axelrod.

Except that he was gone.

It must have happened in the twinkling of an eye. Within the time that it had taken to return a young girl's fleeting smile, her quarry had evaporated. Axelrod had simply disappeared.

She hesitated, tasting fear. If he had seen her, she was finished. He could lie in wait for her in any one of several dozen shadowed doorways. If he had not observed her tailing him, the disappearance was coincidence.

Whichever, Toby knew that she would not turn back. There would be ample time for warning Bolan and the others *after* she had run her prey to ground. From that point on, she would be perfectly content to let the Executioner take over... but she had to do the groundwork first.

With labored strides, the lady fed resumed her climb. The altitude was yet another strike against her, robbing lungs of vital oxygen and making Toby almost giddy as she climbed. Another block or two, and she would pack it in. The general area might be enough for Bolan— certainly enough, at any rate, for him to send the men of Phoenix Force against their hidden enemy.

An alley opened on her left, abrupt and unexpected. If the street was steep, the alleyway struck Toby as an exercise in mountaineering, winding up between the

ancient houses with their blooming window boxes.
There were a hundred hiding places in the alley, and
Toby knew that she should pass it by, return to safety in
the crowds below.

No good.

She turned into the alley, climbing stiffly, peering into
darkened doorways, excavated spaces under homes, the
runways that extended back between chalet-style structures into deeper darkness, choked with grass and stacks
of firewood. She had covered half the distance, was
about to call it quits, when she was frozen into sudden
immobility by a sound behind her.

A footstep, scraping on the rocky soil.

A voice, familiar to her in the way that funeral
marches are familiar.

"Toby."

Only that, and she was horrified to recognize her
name.

The lady turned, and recognized the silhouette as she
had recognized the voice. An errant glint of sunlight
caught the Detonics autoloader in his fist.

"You followed me."

She had no choice now but to bluff it out.

"I saw you on the street," she told him, summoning
her most alluring smile, defeated by the darkness. "I
called to you, but with the crowds and all . . ."

"Zermatt?"

"I get around," she said, and knew how lame it
sounded once the words had crossed her lips. "Small
world."

"Too small."

He gestured with the pistol, and she flinched, already braced for the explosion that would finish her.
But it never came. Instead, she heard scuffling foot-

steps on her flank, too close for any solid counteraction as they closed the distance. She swiveled, swung her bag, aware that it was futile. She could hear the whisper of the sap in flight before it struck her skull a solid blow behind the ear, and utter darkness folded her inside its shroud.

Chapter Thirty-One

Julio Ramirez settled back into his chair and scanned the solemn faces ranged around the conference table. Ludovescu sat on his right, heavy features molded in a scowl that had become the Bulgar's permanent expression. Next in line was the Nicaraguan, Calderone, waiting patiently with both hands on the tabletop. Mahmoud Khaldi, to his left, still had a bandage plastered to his cheek as a memento of the ambush in Toronto. Staring at his clones, Ramirez was disoriented for an instant—startled, as he always was, to see himself reflected in the mirror of their flesh. Two chairs stood empty at the far end of the table, looming monuments to failure and disgrace.

"You know why I have called you here."

He spoke in English, since it was the only language common to them all. Before the meeting had convened, Ramirez had already activated jammers in the conference room and elsewhere, their chaotic signals capable of neutralizing any listening devices that the unknown enemy might have secreted in his home. He knew the possibilities were slight, but in the wake of four disrupted operations, Julio did not possess the same assurance he had cherished a week before.

So much could happen in the span of seven days. How many lives could be terminated in that time? How many dreams destroyed? From grim experience, the Raven knew that such disasters had no limitations. *Any*thing could happen, *any*time, to *any*one, and this time it was happening to him.

Their purpose now was to determine the identity of any enemy who might attempt to scuttle Project Raven. Since the possibilities were almost limitless, they would be forced to search for clues that could betray the opposition. Only when they had arrived at names and numbers could they hope to take effective countermeasures.

"Should we not wait for Castresana?"

Khaldi's voice was soft, deceptive in its timbre, cultured from the years at university. Ramirez thought that it was not a killer's voice, but rather like a surgeon's, bent on soothing his intended victim while the scalpels were prepared, offstage. The eyes were killer's eyes, however, and Ramirez focused on them with his own, ignored the gentle voice.

"Castresana is not coming. He was killed last night, in Steyr."

A muffled curse from Calderone punctuated the startled silence. Narrowed eyes turned toward the empty chairs, as if in search of reassurance that there had been some colossal error. Finding no peace of mind, they swiveled back to look upon Ramirez.

"We are under siege," he told them flatly. "Four attacks in seven days, with casualties in every case. Our brothers have been martyred in the cause, and we shall join them soon, unless . . ."

He left it hanging, each man free to draw his own conclusions. They glanced at one another nervously, as if the stain of guilt might be apparent at a glance, in search of traitors from within. Ramirez had expected this, although he did not personally feel that any one of them would sell the others out.

Ramirez turned on Ludovescu.

"Tell me what went wrong in Mittenwald," he ordered brusquely, brooking no denial or evasion of the issue.

Ludovescu shrugged. "The deal was set," he said. "Simple cash-for-weapons transfer. Nothing that we haven't done a hundred times before. The customers were hot, of course, but still . . ."

"They were observed," Ramirez said. It didn't come out sounding like a question.

Ludovescu nodded slowly. "Possible. They had their stupid faces plastered over every bank and cashier's office in West Germany. Of course, it's possible."

"GSG-9?"

The Bulgar thought about it, finally shook his head.

"The strike force was too small," he said. "I saw two men, and two men only. Even if I missed a couple more, it doesn't fit the pattern for GSG-9. They like to saturate a target zone with uniforms and gas the place. You know their style."

"Then who?"

"Ah, well . . ."

"The CIA?" suggested Calderone.

Ramirez almost laughed aloud, but Calderone was plainly serious. His Hispanic background had conditioned him to look for indications of the Company wherever trouble reared its head. Despite the changing times, the senate hearings and exposures in the media, the mind-set never changed. Politically, he would be living in the 1960s till the day he died.

"They wouldn't act alone this way on friendly soil," Ramirez said. "Too much publicity, all bad. It doesn't play."

"Mossad?"

It was the logical suggestion for a Palestinian, and Khaldi had delivered it straight-faced. Ramirez tried to best his answer likewise.

"In Beirut, perhaps. But Germany?" He shook his head in an emphatic negative. "There are too many targets in the Middle East. When the Israelis go abroad to hunt, they look for Nazis in their wheelchairs." Pausing to appreciate their laughter, he continued in a moment. "No, I think our enemy is someone new to us this time."

While that sank in, Ramirez stared at Khaldi, waiting for the Arab to glance up and meet his gaze. Their eyes met, locked and held.

"What happened in Toronto?" he demanded.

A shrug. "Vachon's security was weak, and we were taken by surprise."

"By whom?"

"Competitors, I think . . . but who can say?"

"And the authorities?"

Mahmoud considered it briefly, finally shook his head.

"Police announce themselves before they open fire. The Western governments are totally predictable in their concern for 'human rights.'"

Ramirez grimaced, swept the table with his eyes.

"Has it occurred to no one that these incidents might be related? Do you pass it off as mere coincidence that we have lost two brothers in the space of seven days? Is no one interested in survival? In revenge?"

His voice had risen to a shout, and they were staring at him curiously, waiting for Ramirez to compose himself. He took a moment, breathing deeply, staring at them each in turn until they dropped their eyes or glanced away.

Among the three survivors, only Calderone appeared to feel no guilt, no loss of confidence. He faced Ramirez squarely, finally cleared his throat to speak.

"There is a common thread among these... incidents." He hesitated, for effect, before proceeding. "Escobar and Castresana both were doing business with a Westerner, this Axelrod. Is it not possible that *he* has been the target all along?"

Ramirez had already touched upon a similar suspicion in his mind, uneasy with the implications. Now he trotted out his doubts, in hopes that they might be dispelled, some workable hypothesis extracted from the jumble of conflicting evidence.

"He was not present—was not even in the country—when our brother fell at Steyr."

The Nicaraguan frowned, considered the anomaly and finally dismissed it out of hand. "No matter. His *supply* was there. We may assume our enemies extracted information from Vachon or one of his associates. When Axelrod escaped them in Toronto with the money, they assumed that he would try to make the purchase at its source."

"And Carlos?"

"Ah. Whatever happened, we may never know the details, *si*? Assume that someone—Carlos, one of his connections—learned of strangers asking after weapons. Asking after Axelrod. A trap is set for the intruders, but it backfires. Carlos is a victim of his own devices."

Calderone's hypothesis was logical, it covered all the sketchy evidence available . . . and still, it left the Raven with a sickly feeling that the drama had another act in store. Their enemies would not be satisfied with Steyr, not if they were after Axelrod. And not if they had stumbled onto Project Raven, certainly. If Escobar and Castresana had been killed by members of the same conspiracy, if they were recognized for what they were . . .

The Raven stopped himself before the whirlpool of imagination could devour him. It was entirely possible, he realized, that he was on the verge of losing everything that he had worked and fought for all these years. A single leak was dangerous, potentially disastrous, and today they seemed to be awash with leaks on every side. Despite the Nicaraguan's crafty calculations, they could not assume their enemies were interested in Axelrod alone. Not any longer, with two members of their company already slain, two others narrowly escaped from traps in Canada and Germany. Coincidence could not explain the seeming chain reaction of disasters that had overtaken them this week. If anything, the incident at Steyr was final proof of a conspiracy, concerted action by determined enemies.

"Security must be improved," Ramirez said at last. "Until we have the situation well in hand, we undertake no further operations, move no merchandise."

Mahmoud looked worried. "There are certain dealings with the PLO. . . ."

"Postpone them. The survival of our operation takes priority," Ramirez snapped. "Are we agreed?"

There were reluctant nods around the table. These were men of action, and it went against their grain to hide themselves away while enemies were on their track.

No strangers to the underground, they still preferred to face the dangers of their chosen life-style squarely, guns in hand, and forcibly eradicate whatever threats might challenge their ability to move about the globe at will, pursuing profit and the cause of people's revolution.

"Where is Axelrod tonight?"

The question came from Ludovescu, and Ramirez had been waiting for it, braced for their reactions.

"Here. Zermatt."

The Nicarguan and the Bulgar glanced at each other, turning back to glare at Julio Ramirez, pinning him with angry eyes. Mahmoud sat quietly, expressing no surprise. Indeed, he had transported Axelrod to Switzerland, on orders from Ramirez, following the firefight in Toronto. His was not to question why, and he would hold his peace until Ramirez pacified the other members of the team.

"You bring this plague among us?" Calderone demanded. "Why?"

Ramirez smiled, exuding confidence. "We needed bait, and the American will serve our purpose. If anyone is hunting him, they will be forced to seek him here."

"Precisely," Ludovescu blurted. "And while they are hunting him, perhaps they blunder onto us."

"Indeed."

"Es loco." Calderone made no attempt to hide his disenchantment with the Raven's plan. "Two dead already, and we bring the opposition here? By invitation? It is suicide!"

"¡Silencio!"

The Raven's voice cut through the Nicaraguan's protests like a knife through cheese, and left him with his mouth agape, the source of angry words choked off inside his throat.

"Have you so little confidence in one another? In yourselves?" His eyes were scornful as they skipped from face to face. "What better way to finally identify our enemies and root them out? What better means of sealing all our leaks at once?"

"But Axelrod—"

"Is bait, and nothing more," Ramirez said. "If he should be devoured by the shark, or simply thrown away when we are finished with him, who will mourn? He is an outlaw in America, a public nuisance. He will not be missed. Once we have finished with his enemies, *our* enemies, he is expendable."

They waited for him to continue, hanging on his every word, and they would turn upon him like a wolf pack if he seemed about to lose control. Ramirez let them think about it for a moment, finally played his ace.

"I had a visitor this morning, from Dzerzhinsky Square."

The silence had become a living thing. It crouched before them on the table, daring any man to violate its sanctity. When several moments had elapsed, Mahmoud leaned forward almost deferentially and asked, "What troubles the KGB?"

Ramirez spread his hands.

"What troubles all of us? What brings us here tonight?" His smile was narrow, mirthless. "They believe that Project Raven has outlived its usefulness. The time has come, they say, to scrap our operation and begin afresh, with other faces, other soldiers of the cause."

He was exaggerating, putting words in Rylov's mouth, but it did not require a psychic to predict their future if the string of ugly incidents continued unabated. They were standing on the eve of private Armageddon, staring down into the pit, and he did not intend to take that last step voluntarily.

"What shall we do?"

The question came from Ludovescu, the Bulgarian, who had been raised to manhood in the shadow of the Soviets. He knew firsthand of their duplicity, their infinite capacity for sacrifice—provided that the sacrifice was limited to rank-and-file subordinates.

"We must defend ourselves," Ramirez said, "against our enemies on every side. Our project must continue. Will continue."

"But the Soviets—"

"Are easily impressed," Ramirez finished for him. "They reward success and chastise failure. When we demonstrate that we have dealt with the elusive opposition, KGB will reconsider their decision...but we must resolve the matter swiftly, to our total satisfaction. And if Moscow's representative should have an accident, meanwhile..."

"He should have been more careful," Ludovescu quipped, provoking laughter from the others.

Calderone recovered first. "How soon can we arrange this accident?" he asked.

Ramirez raised a cautionary hand. "We must attend to our priorities," he said. "Our other enemies demand attention first, then Axelrod. Unless we deal from strength, the KGB will crush us underfoot."

"We do not crush so easily," Mahmoud declared.

He had them now, and Julio Ramirez managed to suppress his smile with a concerted effort.

"First things first," he said. "All things will come to us in time."

But time was running out, he knew. With Rylov in their midst, already searching for excuses to dismantle Project Raven, their future might be measured in a span of hours now. If they could not neutralize the threat from faceless enemies, the Russian would be able to proceed against them with impunity. Before they could eliminate the man from Moscow, they would have to deal with others still unknown, protect their flanks and form a hard, united front against their overcautious sponsors.

Rylov was the problem now. Of those who had originated Project Raven, he alone survived, and as a founding father, his opinion carried weight in Moscow. If he had decided that the project should be scuttled—and he *had*, or shortly would, that much was clear—the heavy hand of KGB would move at his command. Once he had been eliminated, his successors might be more amenable to reason. Even if they finally voted in the negative, it might be possible for Project Raven to continue on an independent, unaffiliated basis.

After Rylov was eliminated.

After they had dealt with all their enemies in turn.

The prospect did not frighten Julio Ramirez. He had spent a lifetime waging war of one sort or another—on civilians, on the Western military powers, on the bourgeoisie. He had already set a record for longevity among his fellow terrorists; no one but Arafat had struggled longer in the cause, and lately the exalted leader of the PLO was sounding more like a negotiator than a soldier of the people, sniveling before the television cameras and apologizing to the world for the activities of bolder men. It made Ramirez sick to see his onetime idol shaking hands with Jesse Jackson, standing up in the United Nations and condemning "senseless violence" in the name of the assembled *fedayeen*.

There was no senseless violence, in the Raven's view. Some violent acts were fruitful, some were not—but history was written in the blood of martyrs, soldiers of the cause. No single act of mayhem was entirely wasted if it served a larger purpose, driving home the grim determination of the people's army to be heard. If acts of savagery provoked reaction, why, so much the better. Let the bourgeois enemy expose himself for what he was: a bloated leech that drained the common people of their strength. And if there must be friendly casualties, then let the chosen meet their fates with heads held high.

There was a profit to be made in revolution, and Ramirez had been lucky in acquiring sponsors who could recognize his talent, use it to their own advantage. He had grown with their ambitions, cultivating some objectives of his own, and he was not about to watch his world disintegrate around him now. If Rylov, Axelrod or any of their other, faceless enemies were anxious to destroy him, they would find the Raven ready, willing and extremely able to resist. There were no silent martyrs in Zermatt.

The Raven was prepared for war. In fact, he was anticipating it with an excitement that he had not felt in years.

Chapter Thirty-Two

Night finally fell on Zermatt. As Bolan made his way back from the Schweizerhof to the Grand Hotel Zermatterhof, the streets were still alive with tourists, bound for supper or for one more stroll around the town before returning to their rooms. The air was brisk, but Bolan did not feel the chill. His eyes were on the faces jostling past him or turned toward lighted windows of the shops that were now closed. The Executioner was hoping for one glimpse of the Raven.

Although he was scrutinizing features that surrounded him, Bolan's thoughts were back in the Zermatterhof, on Toby. He had tried to call her from the Schweizerhof before the conference with Katz and McCarter broke, but she hadn't answered in the room or restaurant. He wasn't worried yet—there were a thousand things for her to do around Zermatt—but something dark and dangerous was stirring at the back of Bolan's mind.

A thousand things to do, he told himself again. And just as many things to see. The town was famous for its shops, its scenery, its ambience. Why should he have expected her to wait around the suite when she could take the opportunity to sample Switzerland firsthand?

Their afternoon together had been a slice of heaven, extracted from the living hell of warfare everlasting. He had recognized a softness in the lady that belied her strength, and Bolan wondered—as he had on other evenings after other close encounters—whether Toby had the inner steel required to see her through the killing fields. She had been down this road before, and often, but no two campaigns were ever quite the same. Each sortie came complete with perils of its own, and they could catch a warrior unawares if he or she was not prepared.

He reached the driveway of the Grand Hotel Zermatterhof, already moving faster as he left the flow of pedestrians behind. The restaurant was crowded, warm lights glowing through the picture windows, casting deeper shadows on the night outside. He would return if necessary, to interrogate the maître d', but for the moment Bolan's mind was focused on the suite he shared with Toby, and the hope that he would find her there.

Bolan checked his watch before he hit the stairs, confirming that a minimum of twenty minutes had elapsed since he tried to call her. She might have easily returned, completely unaware that he tried to reach her. Everything could be explained . . . and still, the nagging apprehension dogged him.

He took the staircase three steps at a time, already opening the buttons of his jacket for easy access to the VP-70 that rode his hip in clip-on leather. It would be unlike the Raven to prepare a welcoming committee— he would prefer a hit-and-run attack to any stationary ambush—but the Executioner could not afford to gamble on the odds. He was on unfamiliar soil, with unknown numbers of the enemy arrayed against him, and the first misstep could be his last.

The corridor outside his suite was empty. Bolan reached the door, one hand inside his jacket now, his fingers wrapped around the autoloader's grip, his free hand reaching out to test the knob. Still locked, but that meant nothing. Any prowler worth his salt would lock the door when he was finished; any hit team dry behind the ears would do the same, to keep from spooking their intended target. Standing off to one side of the door, he found his key and turned the lock, already braced to dodge and run if hostile weapons opened up inside. He wondered if the walls were thick enough to stop the first barrage, decided that it didn't matter in the long run. Counting down the doomsday numbers in his mind, he gave the door a shove and followed through to hit a combat crouch, the VP-70 extended, searching for a target.

The suite was empty, mocking him with stony silence.

Bolan rose and closed the door behind him, moving swiftly toward the darkened bathroom. Once again he braced himself, prepared for anything as his fingers found the light switch, flicked it on—and once again, the emptiness made mockery of his precautions.

Holstering his pistol, Bolan checked the tall French doors and found them locked. A quick scan of the shadowed terrace revealed nothing to arouse suspicion. He was moving toward the telephone to call the Schweizerhof when he discovered Toby's message on the vanity. It had apparently been tucked into a corner of the standing mirror, but had fallen from its place and thus been overlooked. Bolan tore into the envelope, withdrew a piece of hotel stationery, recognizing Toby's script at once.

Gone shopping. Back by seven. T.

Bolan checked his watch again, confirmed that it was after nine. The lady should have been there waiting for him, and her absence set alarm bells jangling in Bolan's mind. Retreating to the bed, he sat down heavily, attempting to examine every explanation for her delay.

There was a possibility that she had been compelled to write the note, surprised by someone in the room or on the terrace. It seemed unlikely. No sign of struggle in the suite, but maids had plainly come and gone. The bed was made, fresh towels in place, and any minor evidence of conflict might have been eradicated. Bolan made a mental note to check the desk before he left and see if the concierge remembered Toby leaving, whether she had been alone or in the company of strangers.

It would be more logical, he reasoned, to accept her note for what it was. She had gone shopping, plain and simple . . . but had not returned. Whatever interrupted her had happened after she was on the street. Again he racked his brain in search of answers. She might have met someone and lost track of time. Before he could dismiss the notion as preposterous, another was already jostling for position in his mind.

Toby *might* have seen someone she knew—or someone whom she recognized, at any rate. If not a friend, perhaps an enemy. Perhaps the Raven.

A sudden chill was worming up the soldier's spine. If Toby had spotted their quarry, he was certain that she would be forced to choose between a phone call to the Schweizerhof and keeping him in sight. No choice at all, to Bolan's mind. She would have followed him, made certain that she tracked him to his lair, and in the process she would risk discovery and capture.

The chill was wrapped around the base of Bolan's skull. He had to check the restaurant, and after that, a quick call to the Schweizerhof. But he was wasting time, and the soldier knew that Toby wasn't downstairs having dinner. She had not touched base with Katzenelenbogen or McCarter. She was simply gone.

A surge of grisly memories left Bolan feeling ill, his stomach rolling as unbidden images of others who had fallen in his cause paraded for review. So many wasted lives on Bolan's tab, so much beloved blood upon his hands. He wondered if another mutilated soul, the sacrifice of one more friend might push his mind beyond its limit.

He hesitated in the doorway, made the empty suite a promise from the heart. If Toby had been taken he would spend his life to retrieve her from the enemy. And failing that, he would devote his life—whatever might remain of it—to wreaking savage vengeance on the animals responsible for her demise. No matter how experienced or how professional, the terrorist could always learn a thing or two about the boundless depths of terror. Long accustomed to dispensing pain, he could experience the agonies of hell on earth before the Executioner permitted him to die.

Bolan left the lights on, just in case, and closed the door behind him, moving swifty toward a rendezvous with retribution in Zermatt.

"WHAT'S THE TIME?"

"Two minutes later than the last time you asked."

"God*damn* it!"

Gerry Axelrod was pacing back and forth across the narrow room, his small hands clasped behind him, features etched into an angry scowl. He had been waiting for an hour and a half, and there was still no indication when their host might condescend to speak with Axelrod in person. His associates had spirited the woman off, presumably to some interrogation chamber in another part of the chalet, and left the Georgian with an order to remain available.

"Relax."

His blond companion, seated on the couch, was watching Axelrod with pale-blue eyes that harbored just a hint of dark amusement. His apparent nonchalance did nothing to restore the usual confidence that had been slipping steadily away from Axelrod. The frigging Raven had them both on hold, and Billy seemed to think that it was all some kind of joke.

"What's funny?" Axelrod demanded.

"Nothing."

But the smirk was back on Billy's face, and for an instant Axelrod was sorry he had brought the bodyguard along.

"You think it's funny?"

"No."

"You're goddamn right, it's not. It's fucking rude, that's what it is!"

"You're dealing with a terrorist, for God's sake, not Ann Landers," Billy gibed. "You can't expect the man to stand on ceremony."

"Listen, Billy—"

"Yes?"

He hesitated, still unable to resist those eyes.

"Goddamn it!"

Axelrod resumed his pacing, cursing softly beneath his breath. He cursed the Raven, and the woman who had plainly meant to do him harm. He cursed the blond Adonis who was mocking him with the expression on his face, a look that told him Billy had been disappointed by his master's irritation, by his failure to adjust. Above all else, he cursed himself, for trusting Toby in the first place and for attempting to do business with a terrorist whose face was plastered over Wanted posters all around the world.

He hadn't known, of course; not at the start. Vachon had been a regular supplier for the Brotherhood. They had done business two dozen times before the roof fell in. But it had been a shock to meet the Raven at Vachon's, a greater shock to see him at the cemetery drop. The greatest shock of all had come when unknown enemies had opened fire and ruined everything that he had worked for over two long months. It was too bad about Vachon, but he had recognized the risks from the beginning. Axelrod would miss him, miss his prices most of all, but there were other sources.

Provided he was still in business.

The news from home was grim, and Axelrod was thinking seriously of abandoning his operations stateside. Billy had arrived with word of the attack upon their compound at Stone Mountain, the investigations underway by state and federal authorities. Indictments were distinctly possible; a prison term was not beyond the realm of possibility, by any means.

His anger at the bodyguard was a reaction to the bearer of bad news. The Georgian recognized that much, but he could not control the hot resentment that erupted every time he glanced at Billy. Subconsciously, Axelrod wondered if the blonde was cutting loose, if he had found somebody else already. One more slick betrayal, in the wake of Toby's treason. Axelrod was sickened by the subterfuge of those around him.

He was sounding paranoid and knew it, but his fantasies were based on solid fact. The woman had betrayed him. Why else would she have surfaced in

Zermatt when he had left her scrambling for cover in
Toronto's oldest boneyard? Logic would have placed
her in the States, if not awaiting word from Axelrod,
then searching out another sugar daddy. Axelrod was
certain she could not afford a trip to Switzerland...unless, perhaps, a wealthy uncle had been
picking up the tab. A wealthy uncle by the name of
Sam.

He would have questioned her himself, extracting
answers to the questions that were haunting him, but
Julio Ramirez had insisted that they wait. The Raven
felt no sense of urgency, no pressing need to punish
Toby for her duplicity. If anything, the terrorist had
seemed annoyed with Axelrod for acting on his own initiative and taking Toby hostage. He would oversee the
questioning when time allowed, and not before.

At present, though, the Raven was beyond his reach
and likely to remain so. Gradually, his anger coalesced
around the bodyguard and sometime lover, who was
leafing through a magazine and actively ignoring him.

The younger man had been in his employ for eighteen months, since Axelrod noticed him among the
Klan's security detachment at a rally in the Carolinas.
He made an offer Billy French could not refuse: a wage
precisely triple his anemic earnings from the Klan, the
perks that came along with graduation to the big time
and the warmth of Axelrod's reflected glory as they
toured the redneck circuit. Within a month they were
lovers, and the blonde from Carolina revealed some
hidden skills that made him worth his weight in gold to
Gerry Axelrod. Till now.

His attitude had shifted since Toronto, growing
cocky, almost insubordinate at times. Axelrod felt a
certain chill from Billy French, and he was counting

down the hours now, until his bodyguard cum paramour decided it was safer elsewhere—anywhere away from Gerry Axelrod.

The bastard wasn't getting off that easy, though. Not after all the gifts and advances on his salary, the risks that Axelrod had run by courting him so openly. It had been Axelrod's relationship with Billy French that forced him to employ a female shadow, and to that extent, the blonde was every bit as guilty of betraying Axelrod as Toby was herself.

"Goddammit, what's the time?"

The blue eyes pinned him where he stood. "You've got a watch."

The child-size hands were trembling, and he jammed them in his pockets, taking two long strides toward Billy French.

"I'm asking you a simple question."

Billy dropped the magazine, stood up. He was as tall as Axelrod, some five years younger, and could easily have decked him. The Georgian braced himself, but there was worse in store than any right cross to the jaw.

"I don't have time for this."

He read the meaning, understood exactly what the blonde was telling him and felt compelled to push it anyway. "You've frigging well got time for anything I ask you, dammit!"

"No."

Just that, and Billy left it hanging.

"What?" Axelrod was incredulous.

"I'm going out."

"The hell you are!"

"Good night."

Axelrod turned his back, unable to accept the curt dismissal by a paid subordinate. He felt the angry color rushing to his cheeks, and longed to strike at someone, anyone, before the shrieking in his skull drowned out the voice of sanity.

It was the woman's fault, and she would pay. As soon as Julio Ramirez realized the implications of her presence in Zermatt. When the interrogation started, Gerry Axelrod was shooting for a ringside seat, and he would prime the Raven with some questions of his own. And if the bitch was hesitant to answer, well, he knew some tricks that even high-priced terrorists might be surprised to learn.

Chapter Thirty-Three

David McCarter stood with his hands thrust deep into his pockets, scanning the sidewalks that were slowly clearing of pedestrians. The night life of Zermatt was gradually retreating, going undercover in the pubs and restaurants, in hotel suites and private homes.

The Phoenix warrior's breath was visible in front of him, a frosty plume illuminated by the nearest streetlight. It was getting colder by the hour, and the few determined sightseers who remained abroad were bundled up against the alpine chill. McCarter, for his part, was looking for another pub or restaurant to scrutinize for suspects, anything to get him off the street and safe indoors.

They had been galvanized by Bolan's call, alerted to the fact of Toby's disappearance and the likelihood that she had stumbled into danger. Bolan had his money riding on the Raven, but there were other possibilities as well. McCarter ran a mental checklist, ticking off the hostiles who had been connected with the Raven's web of terror in the past few days. There were assorted factions of the Baader-Meinhof gang, for starters, always spoiling for a firefight on the slightest provocation...or with none at all. From stateside, there was Gerry Axelrod and his fascist Brotherhood, already linked to Julio Ramirez through the dual connections of

narcotics and illicit arms. Most recently, the Raven had
revealed connections with the "pacifist" Earth Party,
and who knew what machinations would be finally revealed from that relationship?

A world of possibles, and McCarter wasn't taking
any chances as he homed in on another pub. He would
be looking for the Raven, or his likeness, but he would
be watching other faces, too. A score of mug shots and
assorted candid photographs had been received from
Interpol, and from Brognola's team in Wonderland.
The faces were tucked away inside the Phoenix warrior's mind and ready for a swift recall at need. So far,
there had been no need. Three pubs, four restaurants,
and he was empty-handed, running out of targets on the
darkened street.

One last tavern, and he would have to rendezvous
with Katz and grudgingly admit defeat. The former SAS
commando hated the idea of facing Bolan and confess-
ing failure, but he had no alternative. It didn't mean
their quarry had escaped, but merely that the bastard
had already gone to ground. If Toby had been taken
prisoner, it stood to reason that the Raven would be
busy, picking through her brain in search of answers.

It made McCarter slightly ill to think of Toby in the
Raven's clutches. Even though he didn't know the lady
well, had never worked with her before, he dreaded
picking up the pieces when the Raven finished with her.
He had recognized the look on Bolan's face, could
sympathize with what the Executioner was going
through. How many would it be? How many friends
and allies martyred in a hopeless cause?

Too many.

He should be used to it by now, but a warrior *never*
grew accustomed to the emptiness that came with sud-

den death in battle. If they couldn't reach her, he could
only hope that Toby's death would be precisely that: a
sudden one. And even as he formed the thought,
McCarter knew it was a hollow hope. The Raven—if he
had her—would be after information, and the lady
would be pro enough to fight him all the way. A
professional could make the questioning go on for days,
if necessary, wringing answers and confessions from a
tortured soul when every other vestige of humanity had
passed away.

McCarter hoped that they could spare her that. If
not, there would be no restraining Bolan in his rage, no
sanctuary for the Raven or his minions in Zermatt.

No sanctuary in the world.

The last saloon was packed with tourists dressed in
stylish sweaters and expensive ski clothes. Smoke and
strident music greeted him as padded doors swung shut
behind him. It took a moment for McCarter's eyes to
finally accommodate the atmosphere, and in the
meantime he imagined Bolan, Yakov, making independent rounds and finding nothing. Four hours wasted,
and another yet to go before they met outside the Grand
Hotel Zermatterhof to pool their information. If there
was still no sign of Toby, of the Raven, they would have
to try another means of jarring loose the quarry from
his lair.

The lady had been missing now for almost six hours.
It could be a lifetime in the hands of a professional interrogator. Logically, McCarter knew they should
abandon hope, content themselves with tracking down
her murderers and wreaking vengeance on the bastards, but experience had taught the Englishman that a
cautious warrior never celebrated victory or mourned
defeat before the final shot was fired. And so, despite

the evidence, the nagging premonition that was nibbling around his gut, the Phoenix warrior determined to continue with his search.

He had completed a circuitous examination of the crowded dance floor, was about to pack it in, when suddenly he found their handle sitting at the bar. The profile was inconclusive, but a closer look cinched it for him, calling up the mental mug shot for review. Final recognition hit him like a gust of alpine air inside the overheated pub, as he produced a name and put it with the face.

The blond Adonis seated at the bar and working on a stein of beer was Billy French.

According to the cables out of Wonderland, he was a bodyguard and "confidant" of Gerry Axelrod. McCarter knew from Billy's file that he had been involved around the fringe of racial terrorism long before he caught the fancy of America's premier survivalist. A onetime member of the Klan and hanger-on of half a dozen neo-Nazi splinter groups before he joined the Brotherhood, the guy had been a college sophomore when the master race philosophy provided him with focus and a means of dealing with his sexual proclivities. He had been servicing the would-be führer now for better than a year—as had a dozen other handsome soldiers of the cause—while Toby Ranger had permitted Axelrod to keep his macho image more or less intact.

The Englishman knew that Billy's presence in the bar meant Axelrod was somewhere close at hand. Another scan confirmed that French's paramour was not in the pub. But it was unthinkable that Billy French would visit Switzerland without his master somewhere in the shadows. And if Axelrod was in Zermatt...

The pieces fell in place so easily that he was startled by the puzzle's sheer simplicity. If Toby had encountered Axelrod, her instinct would have been to follow him back to a hotel or to a meeting with the Raven. Her acquaintance with the head survivalist and members of his entourage would make it doubly risky. And if she had been snared by Axelrod, he would regard her as a traitor.

McCarter hung back from the bar, attempting to suppress the sense of urgency that had been building up inside him since he spotted Billy French. The blonde was flanked by women who were giving him the eye, but he ignored them, concentrating on his drink and on his own reflection in a mirror behind the bar. They got the message, and the sleek brunette on Billy's left departed first. McCarter spied another solitary drinker homing on the stool, but the Phoenix warrior edged him out by seconds, settling beside his quarry with an exaggerated sigh.

"You mind?"

French scarcely glanced in his direction. "Suit yourself."

"Thanks awfully."

The barkeep took his order, hesitated as McCarter raised a cautionary finger, nodding toward the young man seated on his right.

"You want another?"

Billy took a longer look this time, and nodded, knocking back the dregs before the barkeep claimed his empty glass.

"You're English."

"Very good. American?"

French nodded silently.

"On holiday?" McCarter pressed on.

"A business trip."

"Well, you know what they say. All work . . ."

"It's not *all* work."

"That so?"

"Tonight, for instance. Strictly relaxation. Yourself?"

McCarter shrugged. "You might say I'm recuperating."

"Illness?"

"No, dear, I'm healthy as a horse." He hesitated, trying for a wounded tone and coming close enough to pass. "It's just the wretched loneliness, you follow?"

Billy nodded, urging on McCarter with his silence.

"Well, this friend and I . . . some weeks ago, we reached a parting of the ways."

"The two of you were close."

It came out sounding like a statement rather than a question, and McCarter didn't bother with an answer. "By the sound of it, you've been there."

Billy grunted noncommittally and drained his beer. McCarter took a gamble, laid his hand on French's thigh. If Billy warned him off, he would be forced to find another angle of attack. It might be possible to take him when he finally left the pub, but there would be the risk of a disturbance in the street, police, potential loss of any chance to get at Axelrod.

McCarter would have had a better chance with reinforcements on his side, but Katz and Bolan would be prowling on their own till two o'clock, and after that they would be waiting for him at the fountain out in front of the Zermatterhof. He had no means of making contact with them now, and later would most certainly be too damn late to do him any good.

But French's hand had come to rest atop Mc-Carter's, fingers intertwining with his own. It made the Phoenix warrior's skin crawl, and still he forced himself to smile, a Cheshire grin of pure contentment.

"Someplace we can go?"

"I'm at the Nicoletta," Billy told him. "Nothing fancy, but we shouldn't be disturbed."

McCarter arched an eyebrow, frowning. "Oh? Do I detect a certain lack of confidence?"

"I've got a roomie," French responded, studying his face for a reaction, hastening to add, "but he'll be tied up tonight with business."

"Well, if you're certain, then."

"No sweat."

McCarter forced a grin, and hoped that it would pass for lechery with some assistance from the subdued lighting in the pub.

"Don't be so sure, my boy."

"All right."

He paid the tab and followed Billy across the dance floor, up a narrow flight of steps and out into the night. The alpine chill assaulted him immediately, worming in around his collar, up his sleeves. Beside him, dressed to kill in silk and leather, Billy French appeared impervious to cold. His rolling strut was reminiscent of a John Travolta film, and McCarter wondered what had happened to the goose step he had spent so many hours practicing. The brown shirts wouldn't recognize their brother now... or would they?

Billy led him back along the main street, past the silent shops and up a sloping alley to the Nicoletta. The concierge on duty paid them only passing notice, marking Billy French as one of those in residence, dismissing his companion as a visitor.

His quarry's room was on the second floor, by European reckoning—which placed it three flights up, above the lobby. No one moved about the halls, and he was thankful for the lack of witnesses as Billy found his key, unlocked the door and led the way inside. It was a smallish bedroom, with a private bath that opened off the narrow entryway. McCarter strained his ears for any trace of sound from rooms on either side, heard nothing from the other guests.

Slipping off his leather jacket, Billy French watched him, anticipation clearly written on his face. His eyes skipped past McCarter, briefly settled on the dead bolt just behind him.

"Be a love and lock us in, eh?"

"My pleasure."

As he shot the bolt, McCarter's hand was already snaking inside his jacket, making contact with the Browning automatic slung beneath his arm. His fist was wrapped around it when he turned to face the blonde— and found his mark with slacks already pooled around his ankles, thumbs hooked in the waistband of his shorts.

"That's far enough."

"Hey, what the hell—"

"I've got some questions for you, Billy. Play it straight—no pun intended—and you walk away with everything intact."

The blonde was glaring at him. "How'd you know my name?"

"I know a lot of things about you, Billy. I know *all* about your thing with Gerry Axelrod."

"That right?"

"Indeed. It isn't you I'm interested in, you know. I'm looking for your boyfriend."

"Why?" And there was sudden cunning, fleeting hope behind the pale-blue eyes.

"My business. If you've got an address for me, we can cut this short."

"What are you, man? Some kinda cop?"

"You're getting warm. Now how about that address, eh?"

"Go fuck yourself."

McCarter decided to cut it short, anyway. He closed the gap between them swiftly, counting on the other's state of deshabille to hamper any sudden movements. Billy tried to duck him as he swung the Browning sharply, but the guy was hobbled by his trousers. The weapon's muzzle clipped his jaw, the impact dumping him full-length across the bed.

"Let's try that one more time."

The Phoenix warrior caught a flash of warning in his quarry's eyes, and he was ready—*almost* ready—when the captive made his move. He was agile, McCarter had to give him that. In one swift motion, he kicked free of the tangled slacks and vaulted backward, rolling off the bed before McCarter could restrain him. It would be an easy kill, but any warning shot would rouse the house against him in an instant. Stripped of any plausible alternative, he sprang across the bed, its mattress serving as a kind of trampoline, and tackled Billy French, the impact dropping both men on the carpet.

Billy tried to wriggle out from under him, all fists and knees and elbows now, forgetting any trace of systematic self-defense. He didn't scream or speak as McCarter grappled with him, clubbing with the automatic, opening his scalp in several places. Dazed, the blond American gave one last heave that almost shook his captor, slashing with an elbow at McCarter's ribs. The bodyguard struggled to his knees, lost balance, pivoted to face McCarter as the Browning's muzzle caught his nose and flattened it against one cheek.

The impact banged his head against the dresser, and the fight went out of Billy French at once. McCarter crouched in front of him and wedged the Browning automatic underneath his chin.

"I'm running out of patience, lad," he snarled. "Once more... or you can kiss it all goodbye."

"All right, f'Chrissakes!"

Billy's voice was pained, a nasal whine, but every word was clearly audible.

He told McCarter everything before he died.

Chapter Thirty-Four

Toby Ranger kept her eyes closed, praying that the nausea, the pain, would fade away. She wished the throbbing in her skull would ease before she had to face the glaring lights. Before she made a move, the lady started taking inventory, tensing arms and legs that were immobilized by bonds but still intact. The smell of canvas and the rasp of fabric on her cheek informed her she was lying on a cot. Her wrists were bound behind her—nylon climbing rope, if she was not mistaken—and her ankles had been likewise hobbled to prevent her standing up.

Her memory was coming back in bits and pieces, giving her another look at Gerry Axelrod, the looming shape behind her, the sap slicing into impact with her skull. Angry with herself at being caught so easily, she wondered how the bastard had detected her. Had she become that clumsy on a tail, that he could pick her out amid a crowd?

She strained against her bonds experimentally, and found them secure. Worse, the rope around her ankles was secured to the cot as well, preventing her from sitting upright or from rising off the narrow bed.

Reluctantly, she opened first one eye and then the other, wincing at the pain that artificial light ignited in her brain. When Toby tried to turn her head, she felt the crusty tug of drying blood against her hair, and knew the sap had split her scalp. Somehow, knowing that the bastards had drawn blood increased her anger and determination to escape.

The room was small, no more than eight by ten. A cell, devoid of windows, with a single door directly opposite the cot. The single light bulb set into the ceiling overhead would still be beyond her reach if she was allowed to stand.

She started taking stock of her surroundings. It was not a hotel room, she knew that much . . . which meant that Gerry Axelrod had access to a private home. His own? She had no memory of any property in Switzerland, had even heard him speak disparagingly of the foreign bank accounts that other businessmen employed to keep their liquid assets from the prying eyes of federal tax accountants. Someone else's then. But whose?

It hit her with a certainty that took her breath away and very nearly banished hope. The Raven—the *impostor*—killed at Steyr had been coming to Zermatt. With sudden clarity, she knew he had been coming to consult his mentor, his control. He had been scheduled for a sit-down with his master, and that told Toby everything she had to know.

She was a captive in the Raven's house, and not the home of an impersonator this time, but the one and only unimproved original. He was alive, despite the countless rumors and reports. She knew it as surely as she knew she was living on borrowed time.

The Raven would have questions for her, but in the long run it would matter little whether Toby answered them or not. The man could not afford to let her live, reveal his secret to the world.

But would he be any more secure once she had been eliminated? Bolan would have found her note by now, would realize that she was overdue. He might be scouring the streets already, but to what result? How could he hope to find her here, when Toby didn't know herself where she was? There might be records, deeds to real estate, but offices would still be closed, civilian access limited by the infernal Swiss desire for confidentiality. Assuming that the deed existed, that it could be found, why should the Raven use his name or any alias of record?

It was hopeless, dammit.

How many hours had elapsed since she was captured in the alley? Toby felt her watch in place, but with her hands secured behind her, there was no way she could check the time. An hour, certainly; most likely more. It could, she realized, as easily have been a day, a week. But no, the Raven would be anxious to interrogate her, while it all was fresh. Logic told her that it wasn't morning yet. The bastard would not let another day begin without some answers to the puzzle Axelrod had carried home.

She wondered how much information they might have already. There were no credentials in her bag, no straight ID. They might have taken fingerprints, but Toby realized that she was stretching it. The Raven would not have facilities for complicated screening. He would have to feed his curiosity by playing twenty questions, and she knew instinctively that she would not have long to wait before the game began.

Unbidden, images of martyred friends came fresh to Toby's mind. She saw Georgette Chebleu—or what the turkey-makers had preserved for their amusement—lying on a Mafia "operating table" in Detroit. There had been others, but there had been none worse, and Toby wondered how long she could hold before she cracked.

You couldn't beat professional interrogators, Toby knew that much. She would break, and her knowledge of the Executioner, of SOG and other agents in the field, would all be compromised. How much of it would help the Raven, and how much would find its way to his control at KGB? No matter. Any breach, however slight, was unforgivable. And Toby was aware of only one reliable technique for cutting off the flow of information, right.

She had to find a way to kill herself before the Raven made her talk.

That much decided, she pondered possible techniques. She had no hollow teeth, no cyanide compressed as buttons or disguised as costume jewelry. There was—had been—a pistol in her purse, but it had disappeared, and Toby knew that she would not be seeing it again. It was impossible to hold your breath until you died; survival reflex made you breathe again as soon as you lost consciousness. If they had not secured her ankles, Toby might have leaped to reach the small electric socket in the ceiling, might have dashed her head against the walls or heavy wooden door...but she was fantasizing now. What she needed was reality, a workable solution to her plight.

She might provoke the Raven into killing her, provided that he did not send a surrogate to do his dirty work. A trained, dispassionate interrogator would not let himself be goaded into lethal violence prematurely, but a terrorist might lose control just long enough to see her through. She would attack his ego, ridicule his manhood and the Hispanic's inbred concept of machismo—anything to spark a homicidal rage. With determination and a total disregard for life it could be done.

Toby cursed herself for these defeatist thoughts. She had no disregard for life. Besides, there was Bolan, Katzenelenbogen and McCarter to be thought of, together with all the others whose survival would be jeopardized if she was broken here and now.

She heard footsteps outside the room. The door swung inward silently, revealing a solitary figure of a man. She recognized the face at once despite the fuzzy photographs on file, despite advancing age, and Toby felt a cautious surge of hope.

"Ramirez."

"Ah, you have me at a disadvantage."

"Don't I wish."

He closed the door behind himself and moved to stand beside the cot. No more than average height, he seemed to loom above her as she lay secured to the cot.

"We should begin with introductions, eh? Perhaps your name?"

Her silence was the only answer, and it hung between them like a veil of gossamer.

"I see." The Raven's smile was weary, almost sad. "I had hoped that we might speak as civilized adults, without resort to the unpleasantness of violence. Apparently, I was mistaken."

Toby mustered all her courage into something like a sneer. "I wouldn't want to cheat you out of any kicks."

The terrorist was momentarily confused. "I beg your pardon?"

"Well, I mean, it's got to be a treat. You must not have a chance to torture women every day."

He stiffened and took a backward step, away from her. She noticed for the first time that he limped.

"You have misjudged me. I derive no pleasure from inflicting pain."

"Oh, really? My mistake. I guess you just must do it for the money, then."

His eyes were boring into her, and Toby felt her grim resolve begin to slip away. At once she wondered if she had the strength to see it through.

"I will not trouble you again," the Raven said, surprising her, and Toby felt her hopes collapse. "There will of course be others. Very soon. Perhaps you will be more communicative then."

He was already at the door, and Toby saw her last chance slipping through her fingers.

"You bastard! Can't you even take care of the dirty work yourself? You're scum!"

The door clicked shut behind him, locking automatically, and Toby felt like weeping as she heard his footsteps fade away. When he returned—when *they* returned—the rough interrogation would begin in earnest, and her final hope of cheating fate had slipped away beyond recall.

There will of course be others. Very soon.

She couldn't stem the tears, the sobs that racked her frame. She was alone, condemned to live through hell on earth, and no one in the world had any clue to where she was, precisely what had happened. She was finished, and her greatest fear was that the Raven's turkey doctors would be proficient at their butcher's trade, that she would be condemned to live until they satisfied themselves that she was holding nothing back.

The lady cherished life, and dreaded it. She prayed for death—and, failing that, for madness. Pinned beneath the cold, unblinking light, she waited for the darkness that was coming, struggled to convince herself that it could not be far away.

"I'VE GOT THE BASTARD."

Dave McCarter's smile was brilliant in the darkness, fired with personal enthusiasm for the swift approach of combat. He was looking forward to their contact with the enemy, but Bolan had no time for guessing games.

"Ramirez?"

"Correct. Throw in a couple of his clones...and Gerry bleeding Axelrod."

"Goddammit!"

Bolan saw it all before the Phoenix warrior had a chance to spell it out in detail. Toby would have spotted Axelrod while she was shopping, would have tailed him instead of running for a telephone and risking disengagement. Somehow, Axelrod or one of his compatriots had tumbled to the tail, and they had taken her.

McCarter's hasty narrative confirmed as much. The Georgian's playmate, Billy French, had spilled his guts before McCarter spilled his blood. They had taken Toby to the Raven's hideaway, and Billy had revealed the address in a vain attempt to save himself.

"How long?"

"He made it close to seven-thirty."

"Damn! We'll have to case the house," he said.

"Wait, there's more," McCarter said.

"Like what?"

The Briton's smile was broadening. "The bugger's got a Russian tucked away up there. Billy reckoned he was KGB."

"Ramirez's control?"

"I'd say."

"How many guns in residence?"

"Billy wasn't sure. There's Axelrod, Ramirez and at least a couple of his clones, some housemen. Anywhere from six on upward to a dozen."

Shaky odds and weak intelligence, but it was all they had, and Bolan knew that they would get no closer look before they crashed the Raven's hideaway. Some reconnaissance might offer them an opportunity for verifying numbers, a chance to check the layout prior to barging in and firing blind, but for the most part, Dave McCarter had supplied them with the information they would have to move on, if they moved at all.

And there was never any doubt in Bolan's mind. They had to move, as Toby's life depended on it. He was closer now than he had been at any time since disembarking from the 747 in Beirut, and if he let the opportunity slip past, it might not come again.

"If we can pen them up inside, we've got a chance," Bolan said.

The gruff Israeli shifted nervously and scuffed his boots against the cobblestones. "And if they bolt—"

"We might not ever run them down," McCarter finished for him, glumly.

"Okay. We do it right the first time, then. No one comes out of there alive."

Bolan realized the implications of his words. If Toby was alive, he would do his best to bring her out intact. But for the moment, Bolan forced himself to face the worst.

"Let's check it out."

McCarter led them through a twisting labyrinth of narrow streets, with Katzenelenbogen at his side and Bolan bringing up the rear. Away from streetlights and the night-lights of the shops, oppressive darkness settled around them, cloaking Bolan's spirit like a pall of fear. He was afraid to look inside the Raven's lair, to find what might be left of Toby—and to find what might be still remaining of himself. He had a debt to settle here—*two* debts, in fact—and Bolan wondered if he had the wherewithal to stand his ground and make it stick. The several Ravens had humiliated him in Lebanon, in Canada, had taken Toby Ranger hostage in Switzerland. So far, the opposition team was running far ahead, and Bolan was no longer sure if he possessed the drive, the stamina, to overtake his enemies.

It was an unfamiliar feeling, this uncertainty, and Bolan realized that he must beat it now. A warrior burdened with uncertainty and doubt was beaten long before he took the field. Self-pity followed after, yet another signpost on the road to suicide.

The Executioner would need his faculties this night, unburdened by the excess baggage of emotion. Any motivation he required would amply be provided by his rage, the righteous fury of a warrior fighting for a cause—and for his loved ones, right.

Knowing that the odds were long against him—even longer against the lady—Bolan still could not turn back. He owed the Raven hell on earth, and more. He was prepared to pay that debt tonight, and with his own life's blood, if necessary.

But there would be blood enough to go around, before they finished in Zermatt. The blood of Ravens and survivalists, of Russians far from home. Maybe the blood of Phoenix warriors, and a lady who had opted for the hellgrounds over hearth and home.

And, possibly, the blood of one bold Executioner.

Committed to the struggle, Bolan's road lay straight ahead, directly through the fire, and there was simply no way he could turn aside while life remained. His duty called him to confront the savages, and he was ready for the battle to be joined.

Tonight.

Chapter Thirty-Five

The cold settled into Bolan's joints and stiffened them until he felt more like a living statue than a man. His feet were numb, but he could not afford to shift position, run the risk of letting sentries spot him now. He had been waiting for the best part of an hour, letting Katz and McCarter find their own positions, chafing at the unavoidable delay. Alone, he might have stormed the Raven's hideaway at once, without the necessary preparation.

Soon, he counseled himself. Whatever had befallen Toby Ranger, he would know the worst of it within another hour.

The Phoenix men should be in place by now, he thought, and double-checked his watch. Another minute, and he cursed beneath his breath, the cold gnawing at his bones. He flexed his hands inside the leather driving gloves, intent on keeping fingers nimble for the task ahead. If anything should fail, it must not be the hands. Not yet, until their job was finally done.

Beneath the greatcoat, Bolan was in blacksuit, with the VP-70 in clip-on leather at his waist, positioned for a cross-hand draw. The pockets of his skinsuit had been weighted down with extra magazines for both the pistol and the larger weapon Bolan clutched against his chest.

The submachine gun was an H&K MP-5 SD-3, a favorite among West German military personnel and law-enforcement officers. Chambered in 9 mm parabellum, it came equipped with a modular muffler-type silencer. More accurate than most submachine guns because it fired from a closed bolt, employing a hammer notch, the MP-5 possessed a cyclic rate of some 800 rounds per minute.

At the moment, the initial magazine and Bolan's spares were loaded up with Glaser safety slugs, essentially designed to maximize ballistic stopping power while eliminating any risk of ricochet or wounded passersby. The slugs consisted of a birdshot charge, suspended in liquid Teflon, which would literally detonate in human flesh. The bullets would not penetrate a wall or pierce a human body, but their impact on a living target was horrendous. If the wound was not immediately fatal due to hemorrhage or tissue damage, there was still another deadly twist in store, as the internal residue of Teflon worked its way by slow degrees along the venous system, homing on the heart, to foul its valves and bring about a massive cardiac arrest.

The soldier checked his watch again and cursed the time. He would allow them thirty seconds more to take position, as agreed, before he made his move. Already, he could sense the gray dawn creeping up behind the mountains at his back. He needed darkness to begin his work, and it was fading fast.

There was a reason, Bolan knew, for timing military raids to coincide with dawn. It was a matter of biology, a simple fact of life that Homo sapiens responded to the coming sunrise with a metabolic charge that dulled the nerves and slowed instinctive reflex action. In military terms, you struck at dawn because the sentries were most likely to be sluggish, dozing at their posts, the night behind them and its dangers out of mind. It was the perfect hour to surprise an enemy and kill him in his bed.

Except that Julio Ramirez and his household had not been to bed this night. There had been lights on in the sumptuous chalet since Bolan and the Phoenix warriors started checking out the grounds. Whatever might have cost the Raven sleep, his would-be Executioner could only hope that it would have him dragging now, his normal swift reactions dulled by time and false security.

The thirty seconds had elapsed, and Bolan straightened slowly, giving stiffened joints a chance to crack and yield without producing muscle cramps. He stepped across a knee-high rustic fence, designed for decoration rather than security, and closed in on the west side of the Raven's roost. As Bolan moved, he eased the safety off the MP-5 and set the fire-selector switch to automatic mode.

Beyond his line of sight the others would be closing now, their weapons primed and ready. Three against as many as a dozen, with their only edge supplied by the advantage of surprise.

The Executioner meant to take as many of the bastards with him as he could, before they cut him down.

The Executioner was going in for blood, and at the moment, it mattered little to him if the blood should be his own.

"Shall we begin?"

Still groggy from the sleep that had surprised her, she had mistaken her interrogator for Ramirez. They resembled each other, Toby thought, but when her mind had cleared, she realized the physical resemblance was no better than approximate.

The new man had the Raven's hair, his dark complexion, stature...but there was a subtle difference that she could not define precisely. Something in his attitude, his mannerisms, even in his voice. There was a *cruelty* apparent in the younger man that Julio Ramirez had, perhaps, concealed from her. This one was cold and dark inside, impervious to flattery or insult.

"Shall we begin?" he asked again, and Toby's flesh began to crawl.

There was no room to maneuver on the cot. Bolted to the floor, it could not be upset or overturned. Her ankles were hobbled to the frame and her hands secured behind her back, so she could do little more than cringe against the cold, unyielding wall as he approached, setting down a leather doctor's bag between his feet.

"I am required to ask you certain questions," he informed her. "If you respond, all will be well. If you refuse...I am instructed to encourage you with every means at my disposal."

Toby had no doubt that he possessed considerable means, but she said nothing, feeling vulnerable as he loomed above her prostrate form.

"We must begin," he said, and smiled, reminding Toby of a hungry reptile. "Who is your employer?"

"I'm free-lance, self-employed."

"As what?"

"As a companion," she retorted. "Hey, why don't you save yourself some time and ask your buddy, Axelrod?"

"In time." The lizard smile was back. "With whom are you employed?"

"I told you—"

She expected him to strike, and flinched at his approach. But he surprised her. Fingers tangled in the neckline of her blouse, dug deeper, snared her bra as well and ripped the fabric down, denuding her. He finished swiftly, stripping tattered sleeves and cuffs, discarding shreds of fabric on the floor.

The air was cold against her flesh, and Toby tried to hide herself as best she could by burrowing into the fabric of the cot, but it was hopeless. Her interrogator seized a handful of her hair and wrenched her around, her shoulders flattened out against the canvas. She cursed at him and spit directly in his face, but he responded calmly, reaching out to seize a nipple, twisting savagely until her spine arched, her lungs on fire from screaming.

"We must really try to be more civilized," he told her when the echo of her cries had died away. "You are employed by whom?"

She did not answer this time, concentrating on the pain to come.

"Ah, well."

His hands were busy digging through the doctor's bag, producing soft metallic clinks as different instruments were jostled, pushed aside. When her interrogator straightened up again, he held an extension cord and what appeared to be the stylus for a wood-burning set.

She watched him as he found a socket in the wall, plugged in the cord and reeled it back in the direction of the cot.

"The simple means are best, I think. Don't you agree?"

She couldn't force herself to answer him. It felt as if a mouse had crawled inside her throat and died there, choking off all sound.

He tested the device against a callus in his palm and winced, the grimace instantly supplanted by a beatific smile. He knelt beside the cot, and Toby watched the stylus, wide-eyed, as he brought it nearer...finally pressed its tip against the canvas fabric of the cot. She smelled the fabric scorching, saw a tiny curl of smoke escape from underneath the branding iron.

"Ah, now...as you were saying?"

Toby mustered all her strength to keep a tremor from her voice. "Go straight to hell."

"Of course."

Stylus poised, she could feel the heat against her skin, the fingers spider-walking now across one breast as he decided on a point of contact, and she braced herself, determined not to scream until the pain became unbearable. With any luck, she might hold out for several minutes, might lose consciousness before she could begin to spill her guts.

Somewhere a sudden burst of gunfire cut the cemetery silence of the house. A voice started braying orders, barking sharp commands in Spanish and in German. Other weapons joined the free-for-all, and Toby cracked her eyelids, found her dark inquisitor distracted by the new commotion. He was frozen for a moment, listening, and then he rose to stand behind the cot.

"I will return for you," he said—and dropped the stylus on her naked stomach.

Toby gasped and twisted frantically to shake it off, her flesh already blistered from the fleeting contact. As she wriggled free, the stylus rolled between her body and the cot, pinned down beneath her as she thrashed from side to side. She caught the stylus with an elbow, burned herself again before it finally clattered to the floor.

Across the room, she heard the door close softly, locking automatically—and she was alone. The sound of gunfire meant salvation, she was sure, but she fought the optimism down, refusing to believe until she had some solid evidence.

The cavalry might save her, but then again, it just might get her killed.

At best, she had received a respite from interrogation, and for now, she thought, the respite would be miracle enough.

MCCARTER CLEARED THE SLIDING WINDOWS with a high-low burst of automatic fire and followed through, his Uzi stuttering in answer to the challenge of defending guns. He hit a flying shoulder roll and came up on his knees behind a sofa, clinging to the marginal security that it provided, popping up to hostile fire at one point or another, keeping on the move.

Their strike had been precision-timed, but they were bogging down already as the occupants of the chalet reacted swiftly and professionally, hosing automatic fire at windows, doors. There should have been no more than ten or twelve in residence—and he had dropped one coming in—but it was difficult to calculate from the converging fire that scattered stuffing from the sofa, whistling just above his head.

They wouldn't have much time, McCarter knew, before police responded to reports of gunfire. If his team meant to make a kill, they would have to do it soon, and no mistake.

McCarter fished inside the pocket of his overcoat and came out with an MU 50-G grenade. The plastic egg was filled with fifty grams of high explosive and another eighty grams of shrapnel. With a five-yard killing radius, it was the perfect tool for clearing out a roomful of the opposition in a hurry and McCarter was most definitely in a hurry now.

He risked a peek around the corner of the sofa, drawing fire, and marked the hostile guns for future reference. A pair of them were crouching on the staircase, firing between the banister supports, and number three was hunkered down beside a china cabinet, attempting to triangulate their fire. It would be risky, but they would kill him if he lingered where he was.

He yanked the MU 50's pin and let the grenade fly. Thunder rocked the parlor, bringing down a rain of plaster on his head.

McCarter bolted out of cover, tracking with the Uzi, seeking targets. On the stairs, his opposition was a tangled mass of arms and legs, their weapons silenced by a near-direct hit with MU 50-G. Across the room, their shaken backup was emerging from his hole, astounded by the damage and recovering too slowly to save himself. McCarter stitched him with the Uzi, bounced him off the china cabinet, shattered glassware raining down around him as he fell.

Sporadic gunfire erupted from the kitchen now, where Katz had engaged the enemy. McCarter thought of coming in behind them to help the Israeli mop it up, but decided that he didn't have the time to spare. He hit the staircase running, hurdling the risers and the twisted bodies, pausing long enough to recognize the shattered profile of a Raven clone. The bastard had a bandage plastered to his cheek, but no amount of bandaging could help him now.

McCarter fed the Uzi with a second magazine, then moved along the corridor, alert to any sound behind the several doors he passed en route. He kicked them each in turn, the submachine gun probing out ahead of him to meet the challenge when it came, and each new room yawned back at him, deserted. Below, the heavy metal thunder was continuing, and he was anxious to regroup with Katz and Bolan, join the melee while some fight remained in their opponents . . . but he had a job to do.

And on the fourth try, he found Toby Ranger.

She was naked to the waist, limbs bound with rope and tied in turn to a military cot that was bolted to the floor. McCarter noted angry welts across her stomach, ribs, and something churned inside him as he saw the stylus with its long extension cable lying on the floor beside her bed of pain. He crossed the room in four strides, knife out. He bent to slit her bonds when Toby snapped, "Look out!"

McCarter swiveled, his eyes resting on the figure of another Raven in the doorway. He was sighting down the barrel of an automatic pistol, and McCarter threw himself aside, at the same time holding down the Uzi's trigger as a single bullet slapped the wall above his head.

The blazing figure eight was dead on target, and he watched the Raven dance, an awkward little shuffle as the impact of a dozen parabellum rounds propelled him backward through the doorway and across the narrow corridor. His body slammed against the wall there, and the Raven clone was dead before he hit the floor. McCarter turned back to Toby, working at her bonds.

The rescue mission was accomplished, provided he could get her out alive while Katz and Bolan finished mopping up. Two Ravens down, at least one more to go, and he imagined sirens in the distance now, electric minivans converging on the slaughterhouse with riot squads inside.

"Come on, let's get you out of here."

He let the lady have his coat, and she retrieved the pseudo-Raven's fallen pistol as they passed his mutilated corpse. Together they started down in the direction of the killing ground.

JULIO RAMIREZ DOUBLE-CHECKED the Browning automatic, set it on the desk in front of him and started stuffing extra magazines into the pockets of his overcoat.

"What are you doing?" Rylov's voice was angry, strained, and it revealed a trace of fear that made Ramirez smile.

"I'm getting out," he answered.

"But the others—"

"Will maintain their posts," he snapped, "and hold the enemy in place until authorities arrive."

"I see."

There was a hint of condemnation in the Russian's tone, but it was tempered with relief at the idea of getting out. Around them, bursts of automatic fire were rattling the walls.

"Where shall we go?"

Julio had been waiting for the question with its presumption that they would be going *any*where together.

"*We* aren't going anywhere," he told the Russian pointedly, his fingers wrapped around the Browning autoloader, raising it to target acquisition, level with Rylov's chest.

"You must be mad," the Russian stuttered, wild panic in his eyes.

"Perhaps."

"The KGB will hunt you down."

"I wish them luck."

The Russian tried to twist away, groping for the little automatic holstered in his jacket, but he did not possess the necessary speed to pull it off. Ramirez shot him twice, the bullets ripping through his throat and chest at almost point-blank range, their impact hurling Rylov backward, draping him across the arms of a reclining chair. A final tremor gripped him, jiggling his feet as if he had been cut down in the middle of a dance.

Ramirez dragged a satchel out from underneath his desk, acutely conscious of the gunfire drawing closer now. He spent a moment at the wall safe, fingers working the combination. The final click was like a gunshot in his ears, then he eased the door open. The currency of varied nations and mixed denominations went into his bag, a portable defense fund that he had secured against a moment such as this.

The others would be forced to look out for themselves. He thought about the woman briefly, wondering what she had to do with all of this, then put her out of mind once and for all. His life was finished here, but there were other lives, with new identities, and he was ready for a change. As for the rest—his doubles, Gerry Axelrod—it mattered little to him if they lived or died. Ramirez would be busy looking out for number one.

A dull explosion rocked the corridor outside, and shrapnel pattered on the walls. Ramirez crossed his study, threw the French doors open, risked a backward glance in time to see the door burst inward, slamming back against the wall. A scowling warrior shouldered through, his submachine gun rising, tracking on Ramirez as the Raven raised his pistol, squeezing off in rapid-fire.

No way to tell if he had nailed his target. The Raven bolted through the garden, vaulting across the picket fence instead of veering toward the gate and wasting precious seconds. He was sprinting as he reached the narrow downhill alleyway that would eventually lead him to the street and waiting minicab. The vehicle was slow, but it would outdistance anyone on foot. It would provide him with all the edge he needed for his getaway.

The dawn reached out for him with golden fingers as he ran, retreating shadows always one long stride ahead of him. Ramirez wished that it was darker, that he had the safety of the night, but experience had taught him that the warrior cannot always choose his time or place.

The Raven's time was now. His place, well, that still remained to be decided, and the sound of running footsteps in the alleyway behind him told Ramirez he would have to make the choice while time and opportunity remained, before his enemies preempted the decision and destroyed him in the process.

And before he reached the minicab, he knew precisely where to lead the hounds, a place where he could isolate his enemy, destroy him piecemeal.

It was perfect.

It was Gornergrat.

BOLAN DITCHED the submachine gun's empty magazine and fed a new one into the receiver on the run. He hesitated at the tall French doors, alert to any indication of an ambush on the other side, and finally chanced it, diving through and landing prostrate on the flagstone patio. No target for the MP-5, and he was on his feet again before he came to rest, intuitively following his quarry downslope, toward the narrow alleyway in back.

Ramirez would have crossed the garden here, full-speed, frightened by the near miss in the study and intent on putting ground between them now. There might be other hiding places nearby, and Bolan knew that he would have to overtake his prey before the Raven lost him.

If he allowed Ramirez to escape, when they had come this close, his quarry would evaporate like mist before the sun. Once he had fled the Swiss resort, where could Bolan ever hope to find him? How could the outstanding blood debt ever be repaid?

It had to be today—or never.

He reached the alley, risked a glance around the corner, caught a glimpse of Julio Ramirez running with the sun against his back. Too far for sniping with the

MP-5, but he was still in sight, and that meant Bolan had a chance. He pounded downslope, letting gravity assist him in the chase. The momentum swept him past houses where the gentle people of Zermatt were waking to a bloody dawn, with gunfire ringing in the street. Past blooming window boxes, some with crimson flowers that reminded him of bloodstains spattered on the rustic walls. Past sleepy generations who had taken pride in their neutrality, and found it tested now through no fault of their own.

Downrange, Ramirez almost lost it on a corner, sliding on the dew-slick pavement, nearly going down on hands and knees before he finally recovered, disappeared from view. Still thirty yards to go, and Bolan heard a door slam, followed by the revving engine of a minibus. Spurred on by sudden dread, he tapped the energy reserves that lie in wait for desperate emergencies, ignoring caution now and sprinting furiously toward the open street.

A vehicle would mean that he was being left behind, the odds against him leaping astronomically.

He took the corner blind and skidded on the pavement where his prey had stumbled, going down on one knee painfully. His chest was heaving, lungs on fire, his throbbing pulse a bludgeon hammering the brain. As Bolan scrambled to his feet he spied the minibus, already fifty feet away and accelerating out of range. He chased it with a burst of automatic fire, rewarded by the slap of parabellum rounds on Plexiglas, and then the rig was meandering from curb to curb, Ramirez brandishing a fist with middle finger hoisted as he pulled away.

The Executioner began to chase him, long legs eating up the pavement, altitude and angle of descent conspiring now to undermine his footing, bring him down. He could not hope to catch the minibus, any more than he could let it go while life remained. The soldier knew that he would run until he dropped, until the men in uniform surrounded him and dropped him with a volley of their own.

From nowhere, looming up on Bolan's flank and bleating at him with its tinny horn, another minibus appeared. It swung around to pass, the driver grinning broadly, having fun with Bolan till he saw the automatic weapon in the sprinter's hand. The wheelman did a rapid double-take, and he was starting to accelerate when Bolan caught the running board. He thrust one arm through the driver's open window, latching on to the window post. He jammed the MP-5 against the driver's neck and barked at him to pull it over.

When they were snug against the curb, he dragged the driver clear and took his place behind the wheel, MP-5 wedged in beside him. Bolan gunned the minibus, its small electric engine winding through the gears until its whine achieved the volume of a dentist's drill. Ahead of him, the Raven's vehicle was nothing but a speck in motion, fleeing from the dawn. Wherever they were going, Bolan knew that they would be there soon. They would be running out of road and out of city in another quarter mile or less.

As he was running out of options, out of time.

If both survived the breakneck chase, there would be one more chance to pay his debt of blood. Whoever walked away would bear the mark of the survivor in a game where there could be no other laurels.

But survivors were not necessarily the same as winners, Bolan knew.

Beyond a certain point, there could be only losers, recognizable by the degree of damage they sustained while clinging to the tattered thread of dignity. Survivors were the ones who lost the least part of themselves. The ones who walked away.

Whatever happened, Bolan wasn't counting on a walk. He would be satisfied to take the Raven with him when he went, to know that every vicious tentacle was severed, left to wither in the dust.

Survival would be gravy on the side, a little something extra at the feast of death.

Still hungry, Bolan stood on the accelerator, both eyes fixed upon his prey.

Survival was a luxury he might not be able to afford.

Chapter Thirty-Six

Julio Ramirez swung his minivan against the curb outside the railway station in Zermatt and left the engine running as he vaulted clear. He dashed across the outer platform and hit the swinging doors without a backward glance. He had no doubt that his pursuer would acquire some means to trail him here; in fact, the Raven had been counting on it. It would not be enough, this time, to temporarily lose the tail. If he was to escape successfully and begin his life anew, the track must terminate at Gornergrat. No witnesses must be allowed to live, to point the way for other hunters to resume the chase.

And Gornergrat was perfect for his needs.

The isolation would provide him with an opportunity to do his work in peace, to play out the drama's final moments without an audience. The peaks and glaciers would protect his secret through eternity.

The railway station would not open for another ninety minutes, but Ramirez could not afford to wait. He needed transport *now*, and he was banking on the fact that some employees would be scheduled for the early shift, to get the terminal and trains ready for the day to come. He only needed one such early bird, but he would have to search one out, and time was slipping rapidly away.

He wasted several seconds on perusal of a timetable mounted on the wall. The run to Gornergrat took forty-three minutes, including three intermediate stops—at Riffelalp and Riffelberg, at Findelnbach. Elimination of the other stops would shave at least eight minutes off the run, provided he could find an engineer who knew his business and would push the train on the upgrade.

Footsteps ringing in the empty terminal, he went in search of someone who might fulfill his needs . . . and found him, emerging from a tiny office tucked away behind the empty cashier's cage. The man was middle-aged and dressed in a conductor's uniform. He frowned at the sight of Julio Ramirez, glancing at his watch to verify that it was not yet six o'clock.

Ramirez did not give the man a chance to speak.

"The train to Gornergrat," he said in textbook German, glancing past the older man in the direction of the platform.

The conductor shook his head and pointed to a large clock mounted on the wall beside the schedule of arrivals and departures.

"Tours begin at seven," he explained, as if interpreting the mysteries of nature for an idiot. "You're early, *mein Herr*."

"Do you know how to operate the train?"

It caught the older man off guard. He hesitated for a moment, finally puffed his chest out with Teutonic pride and smiled. "Of course."

"All right, let's go."

Confusion took the place of smug self-satisfaction. "*Vas?*"

Ramirez slipped the Browning automatic from his pocket, shoved it in the old man's face, the muzzle cold against his cheek.

"Right now," he grated. *"Raus!"*

The conductor led him across the platform to the waiting train. The power had already been turned on, facilitating tests and servicing in preparation for the hourly runs, but they were all alone as they approached the lead car with its glass-walled driver's booth. The old man found a key among the two score on his jangling belt ring, opened up the booth and slipped inside. Behind him, Julio Ramirez blocked the door from closing with his body, automatic trained upon his hostage as he scanned the platform for a sign of his pursuer.

Soon now. He could feel them close at hand.

The car began to tremble, inching forward, and Ramirez jammed his pistol tight against the old man's neck.

"Not yet," he snapped. "We're waiting for a passenger."

MACK BOLAN SPIED the Raven's minivan and swung his own vehicle hard to the left, bracing himself for impact with the curb. Momentum carried him across with only minor damage to the undercarriage, and he coasted to the entrance of the terminal. The MP-5 was in his hand as he dismounted, scanning for his quarry, watching for any sign of ambush.

It was an hour or more before the trains were scheduled to begin their morning runs, but Bolan found the entryway unlocked. He entered in a crouch, prepared to answer any hostile fire. The Raven might be able to ob-

tain an engineer at gunpoint, Bolan reasoned, but there
hadn't been sufficient time for the terrorist to get away.
Not yet. His prey was somewhere in the terminal, or on
the loading platform just outside, and Bolan meant to
run him down before he had the chance to comman-
deer a train for Täsch.

It never entered Bolan's mind that Ramirez would run
for higher ground, away from the security of town and
crowds—until the train began to move. A glance was all
it took to brief the Executioner on his mistake, and in a
flash he saw the Raven slipping through his fingers.

Unless he found a way to board the train.

A short dash through the exit, out along the platform, and the train was creaking forward. He caught a
glimpse of Julio Ramirez in the lead car with the engineer, cold eyes regarding Bolan through distorting glass.
The train was gathering momentum and his legs were
failing; there was no way he could catch the lead car
now. As Bolan faltered, broke his stride, a second car
slid past him, and a third.

It would be now or never, with the fourth car bearing down on him. He leaped and caught the steel rungs
of a ladder that was welded to the outer bulkhead midway down. His toes dragged on the concrete platform
for a moment, but the soldier's grip was solid and he
found a foothold on the ladder. Then the platform fell
away behind him, trees and shrubbery sprouting up in
place of man-made structures.

Bolan swung the muzzle of his MP-5 against the
window on his right, but it rebounded from the safety
glass. Again, and no result. His fingers were already
aching from the cold, the strain, when Bolan held the
submachine gun up against the window, turned his face

away and held the trigger down. The glass shattered on impact, and he swept the stubby weapon's silencer along the windowsill, removing jagged shards of glass. When it was clear, he hooked a leg across the sill and pulled himself inside, aware that any fumble now would drop him to the tracks and suck him underneath the grinding wheels.

He fed the MP-5 its last magazine, then paused to regain his bearings. He was in the last car on the train, with two more empties between Ramirez and himself. The cars were coupled to allow for access in between, but Bolan took his time about advancing through the train. The Raven had a hostage, and he would not hesitate to kill his captive if Bolan came too close. Their destination was unclear to Bolan, but he recognized the fact that Ramirez had been waiting for him, killing time until he had arrived.

The guy was looking for a showdown, but in a place and time of his selection, with the odds presumably arranged on his behalf. It was too late for Bolan to divert their course; he could do little more than stick around, hoping for a chance to drop Ramirez.

Behind them, in Zermatt, the men of Phoenix would be mopping up—or would have been mopped up themselves. He put them out of mind, aware that there was nothing he could do to help them now. A vision of Toby Ranger came to Bolan's mind, and he pushed it brutally away. If she was still alive, she would be safe with Katzenelenbogen and McCarter. If the cavalry had come too late, then Bolan held her vengeance in his hands.

He crossed between two cars, encroaching on the third, Ramirez visible in silhouette before him now. He could not risk a shot with the hostage standing rigid just behind his target. Any rounds he wasted now might well be missed when they reached their destination, and Bolan swallowed the frustration welling up inside.

He reached the front seat of the car and settled in, an empty car between the hunter and his prey. Ramirez was regarding him with curiosity and something else—a touch of fear, perhaps? The soldier forced a hungry smile and held his quarry's eyes until Ramirez finally glanced away. It was a hollow victory, but for the moment it was all he had.

They crossed the racing Findelnbach atop a trellis, and on the other side their tracks immediately disappeared inside a curving tunnel. Bolan waited for the darkness, primed to move as soon as visibility was slashed to zero, knuckles whitening as he clenched the MP-5 against his chest. Another moment and he would have his chance.

The darkness swallowed everything around him, and the Executioner was moving out before his eyes had time to properly adjust, acutely conscious of the fact that they might clear the tunnel's exit sooner than expected. He had no idea of its dimensions, but he could not count on an extended period of darkness. Moments, at the most.

He had traversed perhaps a quarter of the distance toward his destination when the soldier's ears alerted him to danger. Ahead, a heavy object had impacted on the floor, rolling toward him. The wobbling sounds informed him that the object was of baseball size, irregular or oval in design. Before a conscious thought had time to coalesce in Bolan's mind, he was already sprinting back along his track, ignoring flaring pain as he collided with the doorjamb in between cars two and three. Arms folded overhead to cushion any impact, Bolan launched himself into a headlong slide, intent on simultaneously gaining ground and getting down below the line of fire.

The hand grenade exploded midway down the second car, its shrapnel cracking windows, scarring wooden benches, whistling over Bolan's head as he lay prostrate in the aisle. With other windows broken now, the alpine chill was sucked along the funnel of the train's interior, raising gooseflesh on his back and arms.

And in that moment, Bolan blessed the cold. It cleared his head, his ringing ears, and swept the cordite stench of the explosion from his nostrils. Better still, it meant that he was still alive.

But he had underestimated Julio Ramirez, and it had very nearly cost the Executioner his life. It was a grave mistake, which he must not repeat if he intended to survive. If he intended to extract a lethal vengeance for Toby, for himself.

The Executioner could wait until they reached their destination.

Until the Raven made his move.

Until the quarry played into his hands.

EMERGING FROM THE UNTERALP TUNNEL, Julio Ramirez scanned the blasted second car in search of any evidence that he had wounded his opponent. The grenade had been an inspiration, timed to catch the hunter as he moved under cover of the darkness. It could not have failed entirely... but his rapid backward scan revealed no body lying in the aisle, no spattered trail of blood to mark the dying enemy's retreat. Instead, his eyes picked out a hulking figure seated in the third car, near the back and safely out of range for any more surprises from the driver's booth.

"Bastard!"

The conductor turned to eye him curiously, and Ramirez jabbed his Browning against the old man's spine, demanding greater speed. His eyes were on the grim pursuer as they swept through Riffelalp and Riffelberg in turn, three thousand feet above Zermatt and climbing now. The trees were thinning out, giving way to alpine snow and ice on either side, but Julio Ramirez had no interest in the panorama he was missing. He had seen the jagged Gabelhorns before, the Matterhorn ahead of them, but he was looking at a specter now, his full attention focused on the possibility that he would die today at Gornergrat.

The proximity of death had never fazed Ramirez till the close encounter with destruction that had landed him in traction so many years before. Personal mortality meant more these days, and if it was not true that a potential victim's life should flash before his eyes, at least the thought of death gave rise to lightning reassessment of potential for survival.

One man had pursued him from Zermatt. Considering his reputation, it was safe to say that others would have followed, had they been available. The solitary figure was his only adversary, then, a meager challenge for the Raven, who had skillfully eluded SWAT teams, even armies, in the past. If he could not defeat a single man, then he deserved to die.

But death was not on Julio's agenda for the morning. He wished to live, to feel the alpine wind against his

face and smell the evergreens as he began the long walk
down the valley to Zermatt.

But only when they were finished.

Ahead of them, the summit station and their man-
datory stopping point were fast approaching. He could
see the Gornergrat observatory, with its gift shop still
locked tight. The structure loomed above them like a
stark medieval fortress. The hostage engineer was
hauling backward on his throttle, slowing in the final
yards of their approach, continually glancing back as if
he half expected to receive a round between the shoulders for decelerating.

"Gornergrat," he almost whispered, dentures click-
ing in a mouth gone dry with fear.

The engine shuddered to a halt.

"Get out."

"Mein Herr?"

"Get out!" Ramirez snarled, the fingers of his free
hand wrapped around the uniform lapel, dragging the
conductor before the old man had a chance to follow
orders. Through the folding doors and down a narrow
set of steps, the frigid wind like knife blades, cutting
through his clothes.

"Up there!"

He shoved the old man out in front of him along the
winding path to the observatory, glancing constantly
behind in the direction of the train. His hostage stumbled, nearly fell before Ramirez slipped a hand beneath one arm, supporting him, remaining close beside
his human shield in case the hunter chose to open fire.

Another hundred yards and he was safe. The bastard
would be forced to root him out of rocks and crannies
that the Raven knew by heart. And he would die in the

attempt. It was a promise that Ramirez made to himself, and pledged to honor with his life.

HE LET THE RAVEN have a healthy lead before he disembarked. No point in goading him to shoot the hostage, not while any chance remained of saving something from the free-for-all. It was a meager substitute for Toby's life, but in the last analysis, it was the best he could do.

Ramirez had already disappeared along the winding staircase that encircled the observatory. Bolan cleared the loading platform, watching out for any ambush as he sprinted toward the shadow of the gothic structure, flattening himself against a wall of rugged, hand-hewn stone.

As he circled toward the staircase, a gunshot echoed overhead, immediately followed by another. Murderous rounds impacted on the stone a yard in front of Bolan, spraying jagged slivers out like shrapnel as he swung the MP-5 around and loosed a burst in blind response. He took the staircase in a rush, lungs burning from the lack of oxygen above nine thousand feet. Each loping stride drove daggers deep into his side, hot needles lancing through the muscles of his thighs.

The Raven surfaced out of nowhere, sighting down the Browning's slide and squeezing off another double punch. The soldier threw himself aside, colliding with a banister of solid stone, the submachine gun stuttering before he had a chance to aim. Spent cartridges were making music on the steps—and then the little stutter-gun went lifeless in his hands, its load exhausted at the crucial moment.

Bolan cast the MP-5 aside, dug for the automatic at his waist, prepared for lethal impact as the Raven cut him down...but now the stairs were clear. Bolan started climbing once again, more cautiously this time. The VP-70 nosed out ahead of him.

The wide observatory platform offered no cover, but he could not huddle on the staircase while the Raven made his getaway. Prepared to die, intent on squeezing off one last, true shot before he fell, the Executioner abandoned the protection of the stairs and ventured into the open killing field.

Some fifty feet away, the Raven stood against a railing with the train's conductor clutched in front of him, the Browning autoloader pressed against the old man's throat.

"No farther," he commanded, halting Bolan in his tracks.

"Why don't you give it up?"

The Raven smiled. "I might ask you the same."

Mack Bolan shook his head. "It's not my choice."

Ramirez nodded understanding. "So. You know my answer, then."

Bolan gestured with the VP-70. "You don't need him."

"Ah, but I do."

"The two of us. Alone. It's why you're here."

Ramirez appeared to think about that for a moment, breath like cigarette smoke in the air before his face. At length he whispered something to the engineer, the Browning slowly lowering as he released the older man and elbowed him away. It took a moment for the engineer to realize what was happening, and then he broke for cover, boot heels flapping on the pavement with a sound like faint applause.

"Your move."

The Raven mulled it over for another moment, shrugged . . . and brought the Browning autoloader up instinctively, the muzzle sweeping into target acquisition as his finger tightened on the trigger. Bolan got there first, the VP-70 extended in a double-handed grip and squeezing off in double action, half a dozen of the weapon's eighteen rounds on their way before his enemy could sight and fire.

The impact lifted the Raven off his feet and pitched him into flight, punching him backward in a somersault across the railing. Bolan made the rail in time to see his corpse rebound from jagged rocks below, a spinning rag-doll figure slithering across the dusky ice field of the Gornergletscher, slipping out of sight across the lip of a crevasse.

The soldier spent a moment longer on the precipice, inhaling deeply of the alpine air and savoring the taste of life itself. A moment, and he knew that it was time to go, before police began arriving on the next train from Zermatt. His debt was paid, and yet he felt no sense of satisfaction at the kill. It had already cost too much.

He thought of Toby, and insisted to himself that it was nothing more than altitude that burned his eyes.

It was a long walk down.

"So, this is R&R."

Bolan grinned at Toby, reached for the champagne and topped her glass off. "This is R&R."

"Not bad so far."

"So far?"

Her smile was enigmatic as she listened to the lilting music of the orchestra. "Let's dance."

He made a rueful face and shook his head. "I haven't got the moves."

Her laugh was tinkling crystal. "Well, we'll have to work on that."

"Looking forward to it," Bolan told her honestly.

The silence stretched between them, warm and not uncomfortable.

"Nice of Hal to let you have some time," he said at last.

"I didn't give him any choice."

"I see."

"Not yet," she answered, suddenly impatient. "Are we finished here?"

"We haven't eaten yet."

"I've lost my appetite."

The soldier frowned. "If you're not feeling well..."

"I think you'd better take me back upstairs."

"They've got a doctor here at the hotel."

"Forget about it, Captain Comedy. I've got an old home remedy in mind."

"If I can help in any way..." And he was smiling now.

"I thought you'd never ask." She took him by the hand and led him away from the bustle of the restaurant, retreating toward the elevators and the sanctuary of their suite.

"I think I'm going to enjoy this R&R," the lady said.

"Me, too," the soldier answered, and he meant it. From the heart.

MORE ACTION!
MORE SUSPENSE!
___ NEW LOOK! ___

THE EXECUTIONER

MACK BOLAN

Beginning in July, watch out for America's number-one hero, Mack Bolan, in more spectacular, more gut-wrenching missions.

The Executioner continues to live large in bigger, bolder stories that can only be told in 256 pages.

Get into the heart of the man and the heart of the action with the first big entry, **The Trial**.

In this gripping adventure, Bolan is captured and placed on trial for his life—accused by the government he had sworn to serve. And the prosecution is hunting for the soldier's head.

Gold Eagle Books is giving readers what they asked for. You've never read action-adventure like this before!

You don't know what
NONSTOP HIGH-VOLTAGE ACTION
is until you've read your
4 FREE GOLD EAGLE NOVELS